SPLIT
SECONDS

The Caspian Wine Suspense Thriller Series

Maggie Thom

QUADESSENCE PRESS

First Edition: Published 2017

Revised Edition: 2026

Published by: Quadessence Press

Editing: P. Terrell (P.I.S.C.E.S)

Cover Design: GMT Books

Images: DepositPhotos & Canva

ISBN: 978-0-9917272-7-8

Paperback

Read to Escape... Escape to Read...

To the stories that kept me turning the pages...

CHAPTER 1

"MOMMY."

"Mommy. Look."

Tyana knelt as her twin daughters hurled themselves at her. She hugged them tight, loving the feeling of their tiny arms wrapping around her. It reminded her of how right her decision had been. It may have been unconventional how they came into this world, but she wouldn't give them up for anything. Not even money. "What, Bugs?"

The two giggled. Their identical smiles and laughs made her forget that her time with them was going to come to an abrupt end... one day.

"Bee."

"Boo."

"Ti."

"Ta."

She laughed with them as they pointed to each other and did their name game. "Okay, Tijan and Tarin, how about we get cleaned up?"

"No, Mommy. Come."

"'ave to pee."

Tarin headed for the bathroom while Tijan grabbed her mom's arm and dragged her outside. Laughing, Tyana followed her bouncing daughter out the door, only to stop suddenly. Tijan let her go and ran the short distance across the brown lawn to the bottom of a big old tree with huge draping branches.

"Look! Look!"

But Tyana was frozen on the top step as she stared at the luxurious limo parked at the end of her driveway, like a king showing his minions, his wealth and power. She didn't even have to see who got out of the car to know who it was. To know this day was going to arrive. She'd done everything she could to prevent it. But it hadn't been enough.

She moved down the path, wanting to get between her daughter and the one person who could ruin both their lives.

"She's filthy. Her clothes look like you got them at the thrift store. They're badly stained with God knows what on them. She's got mud covering her hands and face. She's barefoot, for Christ's sake. What the hell have you been doing to her?" The man, who many would say had the clout and power of the US president, looked at her with disgust. "And I haven't forgotten what you did. Don't worry. You'll pay in ways you can't imagine. I do not appreciate being taken for a fool. And what is mine is mine."

Tyana pressed her hands to her cheeks as she came face to face with a man she had somehow managed to outwit and avoid for two-and-a-half years. The game had been about hiding where he would least expect it. This wild, in the middle of nowhere place, had been perfect and so far from what either of them had ever known, she had hoped it was beyond his scope of finding her.

Tyana so wanted to look over her shoulder but didn't. She prayed that her other daughter wouldn't rush out anytime soon. "Letting her live."

"Mommy. Come."

"What the hell were you thinking?"

"I had to. You'd never have let me see my babi—"

"Damn right I wouldn't have. She's mine; that's why I paid you." He pulled on one of the sleeves of his silk suit jacket to emphasize his wealth.

Her life had been about money and clothes, but she'd left that world far behind her. Or thought she had. Then she'd met him. A fate she'd thought had been better than what she'd been doing. He'd been her way to truly get away from the corruption of her family's wealth. Her family's greed and control. She'd been eighteen and determined to make it on her own. But she should have known money was money and those who gorge themselves on it are corrupt. She'd thought that running away from her up-bringing would have been easy, but it hadn't been. Making money had been hard. He'd come into her life when she was contemplating going back to her parents to become the cold shell of a woman they wanted her to be. But she hadn't needed to because he'd arrived. Only he hadn't been her answer to anything.

She'd gone from living a precarious, on-the-edge kind of life to living in downright hell. So she'd run.

The last few years had been so perfect and had shown her what she'd wanted. She'd finally been content, happy even. The girls hadn't known any of the life she'd pre-viously lived, and she never wanted them to know what she had done to survive. If she could go back and get a do-over, she'd change almost everything. Her daughter squealed, reminding her she'd change everything except her two precious gifts, no matter how stupid she'd been to bring them into the world. Not that she'd had them; it was how they had come about. But they'd taught her so much, and now she was in serious danger of losing them forever. The man who was going to ruin her life again didn't seem to know everything, though.

Going on a hunch, Tyana answered, "You bastard, you're so cold. She's only a baby. She needs her mother."

"You already managed to hide her for two damn years; I'm not letting you have her another second. Be grateful I haven't killed you yet."

Tyana turned away from the man in the three-piece suit, so out of place in this backwoods country. She'd hoped the rutted, densely treed area would have been enough to hide her and her girls forever. Her gaze landed on Tijan, who was staring with awe up into the branches.

She ran over to her child; fearful it might be the last time she ever saw her. Feigning interest as she couldn't share the fear that was clutching her in its vice-grip, she knelt down. Her gaze followed her daughter's tiny finger as it pointed up through the dense foliage. There, perched on a branch way above their heads, was the fuzzy baby owl they'd been watching all spring. This was the first time he'd been out of the nest, though, at least that they'd seen. His brother or sister had tried to fly too soon and had hit the one and only power line on the property. The girls had been heartbroken.

"Oh, he's beautiful," she whispered.

"No fly, Mommy. No fly."

"I agree sweetheart, we don't want him to fly yet."

"No die. No die."

"Dammit, that's enough. Get that disgusting kid ready to go."

Tijan jumped, her eyes round as she hid behind her mom, clutching her mom's legs with all her might. Tyana put her hands back to hold her daughter close while feeling the distance that was already creeping in. "You can't take her. Look how happy she is. Please don't."

"You signed her over when you took the $50,000 I paid you."

"I'll give it back. I didn't know... Please..." Now she wished she'd asked for ten times that amount. Not because she wanted the money but because maybe she could have used it to hide them better. A man with money, though, was almost impossible to keep away from, at least for long.

"Tee, run inside and get cleaned up, okay? I'll be in soon. Use soap."

She ran to the house but went way wide to avoid the man who was glaring at her.

Tyana shuddered. Even her daughter felt the evil in him. "Please, you can't, I'm begging you."

"Oh, save me the bullshit. I found you hustling for pennies. I gave you a life and a lot of cash. You were more than happy to live the good life. You're a whore. Do you really think I want you to raise my child? That's a laugh."

"But I was good enough to have her."

"Oh, don't worry, I had your background checked out. Funny thing, your family was searching for you. I got pulled in by mistake. Since I discovered you came from good stock, that was good enough for me. Besides, it's funny as hell that I got that stupid, rich ass's daughter pregnant. He doesn't have a clue I have his grandkid. At least not yet. That alone will sustain me into my old age. That and the fact that I'm sure his prestigious career might not survive his daughter being a call-girl."

"I wasn't a hooker."

"A high-paid whore, then."

She cringed. There was a fine line between what she'd been doing and what he was calling her. She'd been so bent on making her own way, her own money but had only gotten into college because of her family's name. But they wouldn't pay, and the college had still wanted payment. She hadn't had any money nor access to any, as her parents had cut her off. The only jobs that would hire her—someone with no known skills other than partying—were the menial labor jobs. Even though she'd rebelled against how she'd been raised, she'd always had a maid. But could not bring herself to do that kind of labor-intensive job, at least not for the measly few dollars they'd been willing to pay.The college had agreed to some leeway to pay later. After all, who'd want to piss off her multi-millionaire, influential parents? But the college had finally sent her a letter telling her to pay, or she was out. She had needed an education to be able to make good money. When she'd been approached to go on a date as a onetime thing for $1000, she hadn't passed it up. And hadn't been able to afford not to. She'd dumped her family, run from the overprotective, stale parents she felt didn't 'get' her into a life that had made her feel powerful. She'd controlled men. They'd begged for her time. She'd been the queen of it all.

Her fingers brushed over the ratty, holey jeans she wore and couldn't help but be grateful. They were far more comfortable than any Yves St. Laurent dress she'd been shoved into as a kid or as a paid escort. And the life she'd had with her daughters was what she'd really been looking for, not something money could buy. That almost made her laugh because that was exactly how and why they'd been brought into the world. If she'd thought her parents would have helped her, she would have gone to them, but they'd written her off a long time ago. Rightfully so, with what she'd done. And the truth was that they would never have let her keep her children. She'd brought enough scandal into their lives, and they hadn't even known most of it.

"Look, just let me come back with you. I'll take care of the—her. Please."

"You're a prostitute."

"You just said you knew my family. That I'm from 'good stock.'"

"You are but once a whore, always a whore. I paid you to have my child, so that makes you one. Get out of my way and get that kid ready. Now. My patience has run out, and if you don't do it, I'll send my driver in to get her."

Tyana looked at the 300-pound, six-foot-five behemoth that looked like one solid wall of muscle. She didn't want him anywhere near her children, especially since he only knew about one of them.

"Please. Don't do this."

"Three... two—"

"Alright. Just give me a few minutes with her, okay?" She didn't wait for him to respond but ran past him, fighting back the sobs that were tearing at her throat and chest. The wooden screen door slammed behind her, something she'd have given the girls heck for, but now it meant nothing. Grabbing her portable phone as she raced through to the bathroom to find her girls, she quickly dialed a number.

"I need your help. He's here," she gasped, pressing her hand to her chest as it felt like it was collapsing in on itself.

"I'm five minutes away. Just do what we planned. You knew this day would come. We got it. You're okay. Go out the back door and into the woods. Go to the creek, cross it and I'll be waiting for you."

"Hurry." She hung up and turned to her two perfectly created beautiful daughters. It amazed her that she'd been so blessed.

"Okay, girls, we have to play the quiet game or that angry man will come storming in here. I need you to grab your backpacks, and I'll grab mine. We're going on the adventure that we've been practicing for. But we have to be silent or we'll scare the animals away and then we won't have any fun."

Both girls looked at each other. Some sort of silent communication happened before they nodded and ran off to their bedrooms. Tyana hustled her little group out the back door, making sure that it didn't make any sound. The door hinges had been almost a daily task of being oiled, for she'd known this day would come but had hoped and prayed it never would. They had been practicing this event almost since the day they could walk.

They ran as fast as their little legs would carry them. Tyana's head swiveled around like the mama owl that often sat perched high in the tree in the front yard. As they approached the creek, Tyana realized that the spring melt and heavy rains they'd had recently, which had kept them housebound, had also raised the creek level by at least two or three feet. The girls were not going to be able to hop from rock to rock in the fast-running water. Frantic, she looked up and down the streambed, hoping to find a better place. To their left, there was a tree that had fallen across the rushing water. It would at least give them something to hang on to.

"They're not here."

"Find them."

Tyana's heart leapt into her throat. The two men had gone into and were now coming out the back of the house. They'd already discovered they were gone.

"Come on, girls, we have to hurry." She hustled them upstream. The sound of heavy footsteps through the trees made her shiver but also realize she didn't have time to use the rope in her backpack to tie the girls to her. "Grab my belt loops. Hold on to me like you do Marty and Mandy, your teddy bears. Do not let go."

She quickly ducked under the tree and stepped into the frigid water. Goosebumps immediately covered her body. The girls yelped when the water hit them. Seeing that the strength of water was way too much, she grabbed Tarin and hoisted her up on her back.

"Hold tight around my neck, sweetheart."

Next, she lifted Tijan and held her in front. She reached out, grabbing a branch on the fallen tree. Lifting her foot, she wobbled as the rushing water drove against her one ankle, almost buckling it. She shoved harder, finally able to push it through the water and put it back down.

"Eeek!"

She wasn't sure which one cried out or if it had been both of them, but she paused for a moment. "Hold tight, my babies. Please don't let go for anything. We'll make it. I promise." *I hope.* She snuggled Tijan a little tighter to her chest, making sure her arms were tight around her neck. Then she let go for a brief second to reach back and lift Tarin up so her tiny hands were clasped tight around her throat. "Squeeze tight with your legs, Ta."

There was hardly any pressure. The girls were struggling to hold on and were terrified as she was. She quickly took another step, shivering as the cold water burned her legs. Whether someone had found where they were or not, she didn't know because she couldn't hear anything over the sound of the running water and the echo of her heart pounding in her ears.

She only had to make it about another six steps. Holding onto her girls with one hand, switching from one to the other, while clinging to the log to remain upright, she took another tentative step. She lifted her cold, soaked, jean-clad leg and thrust it through the rushing water. Before she could put her foot down, though, the force immediately jerked her sideways. Her one knee buckled as she was pitched sideways into the tree.

"Mommy!" Tarin screamed as her tiny arms lost their tight grip and she slid off her mom's back.

"God, no!" She frantically grabbed for Tarin, but the water was pulling her away, tumbling her under the big log and sweeping her downstream.

Trying to keep her eyes on her daughter, who was being swept away, she held tight to her other one as she pushed through the cold water. Finally reaching the other side as fast as she could, Tyana set Tijan down under a tree. "Stay here, honey. Don't move."

Tripping and falling on the wet, soggy ground, she shoved her way through the thigh-high brush that hugged the bank.

"Tarin! Tarin!" Her eyes darted back and forth over the muddy water. There was no sign of her baby. She jumped into the rushing torrent, only to have her feet swept out. She went under. Coughing and choking, her arms swung and paddled like crazy as she tried to find footing and get her head above water. Finally, she managed to burst upwards, gasping for breath. As soon as she did though, she felt an intense pain, and a sudden lethargy invaded her body. That was the last thing she knew as she sank down into the murky depths.

CHAPTER 2

"WHY DO YOU HAVE to do this?"

"It's just a holiday, Trent."

"Yes, but I don't see you inviting me."

Tijan took a deep breath, regretting that she'd let him in five minutes before. It had seemed easier than listening to him whine. "That's because we're no longer seeing each other, Trent. We broke up."

"No, you ended it. I didn't want to."

He was never going to go away. "Okay. I'm going away for a few days. When I get back, we'll get together and see what we can work out, okay?"

He threw himself at her, wrapping his arms around her. "I knew you'd come around. Mom said you were the best thing that has ever happened to me."

That woman had been one of the reasons Tijan was no longer seeing Trent. She ran his life, right down to still buying his underwear and making his dental appointments. It had been too much for Tijan. The two of them had only been out on two dates—the second one had been more of a pity date. That hadn't stopped him and his mom from having the two of them married. They also had the house picked out and the number of grandkids ordered.

Tijan eased back. "I have to get this done." She waved at her clothes laid out on her bed. "If I'm going to go, I need to get back to this."

What she didn't tell him was that she hadn't made plans for her trip yet. All she was doing was going through clothes, seeing what she might take and what she should give away.

When he tried to kiss her, she ducked out of the way. He stepped back, acting all cool, like he was back in control. "Got it. See you in a week, babe."

She made gagging motions as soon as he turned his back. Once she heard the front door close, she scooped up the clothes on her bed and set them on her chair. The guy was a bit dense and had no clue that she had no intention of ever seeing him again, or he might not have left. A part of her was terrified to be leaving her little sanctuary, but a part of her knew this was long overdue. She had no idea where her new adventure was going to take her, but she had someone to find. Her sister. Thankfully, her mom wasn't too savvy on the Internet. The picture she'd come across hadn't shown much, but it sure made her believe it was her identical twin. Tijan had almost given up ever believing she was alive. But now she had a lead. Not a good one, but it was all she had. Her mom had told her that her sister had drowned. It had always felt to Tijan, though, that couldn't be true. She had no evidence, no facts, just a sense that it couldn't be true. For a long time, it had torn Tijan apart watching her mom say one thing but pray for another. Tijan had never been sure if she believed her sister was alive because she'd wanted it so badly for her mom or if there had been a connection. There was a part of her that knew something was missing, but not dead. After seeing the photo on the Internet, her gut had told her it was her twin. She was connected to that person. Her sister's body had never been found. So just maybe...

It was so crazy. Maybe the many hours out riding, and the one or two throws from her horse, had done more damage to her hard head than she'd thought.

Now she just had to find the person, who may or may not be her sister. All she had to go on was the city news-paper that took the photo and where it had been taken. It reminded her of searching for a calf in the brush in the mountains. It could take minutes, hours, days, weeks, or months. And sometimes it just didn't happen. That thought settled with a whomp in her stomach. If it were possible, she planned on finding her sister and bringing her home... soon. That was if she could find her. If she was alive. If what she'd seen even belonged to her sister. If she wasn't just making stuff up.

Maybe it was time she got a life.

It was all a long shot but was the best gift she could come up with to get her mom for her fiftieth birthday. Tijan pressed her hand to her chest, hating the overwhelming emotion because right behind that thought was, what if she couldn't? What if it hadn't been her sister? She hadn't seen her face, just her hand. How crazy was that? But for her, it had been enough. She couldn't explain it. Not even to herself.

Telling her mom she was leaving would not be easy, especially since she'd have to lie. One thing that she loved about her relationship with her mom was that they were honest with each other. Or at least they had been.

Pushing away her thoughts, she had to find her mom. It was time to break the news to her, or at least a small part of it. Stepping out of her small house, she made her way around the clump of trees and headed to the main house.

"Mom. Mom? Where are you?" Tijan wandered through the big sprawling ranch house. As a kid the house had never been big enough for her. She had loved to run through the house and ride her small bike. Now, though, it seemed way too big. She cut through the dining room, going around the large table that still had weekly gatherings of eight or so people. Her mom was always inviting the ranch hands and their families to dinner. And since she was such an excellent cook, rarely did anyone decline.

"Mom?" She peeked into the room she liked to call the library room, as it was full of books. It was the TV room, but for her it was a room filled with adventure. She loved to grab a novel, hop on her horse and go to her favorite place near a creek in the foothills.

"Are we playing hide and seek?" Tijan moved through the living room. The dark leather sofa always looked so inviting to plop down and sprawl on.

"I'm in the back of the greenhouse."

Heading down the hallway, Tijan made the first left, going through a small room, out into her mom's plant room.

"Hi honey. I thought you were taking Tango for a ride today?"

Tijan bent down to give her mom a hug. Her mom wrapped her arms around her but kept her dirty hands away from Tijan's clothes. Her mom shifted her wheelchair so that she could keep working but face Tijan as well.

"I was but changed my mind. You look like you're having fun."

"I am. I'm transplanting my spring flowers and vegetables, so they'll be ready for the outdoors in a few weeks."

Tijan sat down on a bench, allowing the warmth of the sun that was shining down on the glass room to warm her.

"So? I know you didn't come to help me. The last time I think I managed to get you to put your hands in the dirt, you were five. And even then, you were good at vanishing."

Tijan laughed. "Yeah, plants and I don't get along. Well, I like to look at them and maybe eat them, but that's as far as my interest goes."

"I think you were three when Cal finally persuaded me to let you ride a horse. From that day on, that has been the only thing you've wanted to do."

It was true. Tijan had tried a few times to bring her horse into the house, but that hadn't gone over well, so she'd spent many a night sleeping with her horse in the barn. Her stepdad, Cal, had often covered her with a blanket or carried her into the house on chilly nights.

"What's up, Tijan?"

She took a deep breath. One thing she loved to do was talk to her mom. They had some amazing conversations, and her mom always helped her to see a different side of things. Normally, she didn't have a problem with asking her mom questions, but this was different. There were two things they never talked about. One was her mom's past, and the other... well, Tijan knew she wouldn't be able to bring that subject up yet.

"Uh, I was thinking I might go on a holiday."

Her mom spun her wheelchair and rolled up to her so fast, she jerked back.

"You've been distant and preoccupied lately. What's going on? Please tell me you didn't fall off your horse and hit your head and decide that Trent was the one for you?"

Tijan threw her head back, clapping her hands over her heart. "Oh, Mom, you wound me. The love of my life, and you're dismissing him. I'm so offended."

"Well, shoot me in the foot, but that dude is never going to be my son-in-law. I'll send you to the funny farm myself."

Tijan couldn't hold it in any longer; she burst out laughing. Her mom soon followed. This was what she loved about their relationship. They could talk and laugh about anything.

"So, now what is this really about?"

Tijan rubbed her hands together but wasn't aware of doing it until her mom wrapped her hands around them.

"I'm thinking of going on a trip—"

"A vacation?"

At any other time, her mom's shock would have amused her, but it reminded her of the story she was about to tell.

"Yeah. A friend, Carol, from high school, has invited me to come for a visit."

"I knew you were close in high school, but I wasn't aware you kept in touch over the last ten years."

"It's more of a recent thing. Anyway, she got me thinking that I should visit her."

"I think it's a great idea. You've never gone anywhere for very long. Where does she live?"

"Toronto."

Her mom was pale by nature, but Tijan saw her go completely white. "Mom, are you okay?"

"It's time you told her, Meigan."

Tijan looked up. Her stepfather was standing in the doorway. She went to him and gave him a hug. "Dad, what's going on?"

CHAPTER 3

AUGUST CLIMBED ONTO THE dolly and rolled under the gigantic machine. It needed a lot of work, which was one reason he'd been hired by Caspian Winery. The previous mechanic had been fired. He'd been more interested in ordering parts for a '63 Mustang he'd been rebuilding. Perry, the apprentice, had tried to keep up with all the work. He'd finally gotten fed up and had mentioned that Dean wasn't doing anything.

Even though he hadn't asked for it, August was glad. He loved doing this work but hadn't been on the tools much in a long time. He'd run a successful mechanic shop but hadn't had much time to do very much work, although he'd always tried to keep his skills up. In the last year and a half, his life had changed so much. He was still pretty surprised that he'd agreed to work for Caspian Winery.

He wiped his hands on a rag tucked in his front pocket. He was enjoying figuring out the massive machine that was used for harvesting. The only thing he could compare it to, similar to something he'd worked on, would have been a combine.

He pushed himself out and stood up, walking through to the office. His eyes were immediately drawn towards the main building, less than a hundred feet away. It was a classy building that was a mix of glass, wood, and metal. They'd done a good job of making it look warm and inviting and at the top of the game. They were so successful that they could have hired anyone. It still seemed odd to him that he was working there. But they'd recruited him.

In fact, they'd flown to Winnipeg to find him. The question was why? He still didn't feel as if he knew the answer. His mind slid back to how he'd been hired.

****

"Are you August Renner?"

He turned, not liking that someone had managed to catch him off guard. Normally, it never bothered him, but the way the man said his name had him looking for the nearest exit. Hunching his shoulders, he sucked air between his teeth. Nothing annoyed people more than that awful sound. Something about the way they'd shown up left him feeling uneasy. They might not be people he wanted to have a conversation with.

"And you are?"

"I'm Graham and this is Tarin."

He studied the two people, sure they were a couple. The silent communication between them was something only those connected could master. Taking the rag from his pocket, he wiped the grease off his hands in a slow, methodical manner.

"And you're trying to find this guy, because?"

Tarin looked at her partner, obviously trying to tell him something. Graham nodded imperceptibly before turning back to him. "Look, August, is there somewhere we can talk?"

He didn't even bother to pretend they knew it was him. How, he wasn't sure.

"I get off at 5:00. So, about 45 minutes? Meet me at Sal's Pub down the street." His answer didn't sit well with either of them. They'd have to twiddle their thumbs. Or do whatever people did when dressed in stylish clothes, for a few hours. Although if he were to guess, the man looked like he would have preferred to be in jeans or grubbies. He did not appear too comfortable in the dress pants and shirt. Every now and then, he had that body twitch when someone had underwear riding up their butt. The woman looked very comfortable in her sky-blue skirt suit and heels. The two, though, looked very out of place in the dark, grease-covered, tool-cluttered, smelly garage.

"Sure. We'll meet you later at Sal's."

August watched until they climbed into a beast of a vehicle, a huge Hummer, something that was a little out of place in this small country town in rural Manitoba.

Taking a sip of his lukewarm coffee that he'd been ignoring, he stared down the street at Sal's Pub. He could just see the corner of the building. The two people waiting for him were still inside, but how had they found him? He cocked his head as he started to think about that. He'd used his bank card and credit card. For someone to have that information, they'd have to have quite some security clearance. He stepped away from the window.

Who the hell wants to find me?

Leaving seemed to be the smartest thing to do, but they'd tracked him down for some reason. His stomach churned as though he had drunk a pot of espresso coffee on an empty stomach. It wasn't until he headed out the door that he decided he wasn't about to start running. It made him wince when it dawned on him that what he'd been doing the last few months had been just that. After losing his mom the year before, he'd needed something different, some place where he didn't have to think or be responsible or feel.

He walked across the road, glancing down the street as he took a chance that the one car an hour had already passed by. Entering the dingy bar with its fuzzy ceiling that looked like dryer lint, he waited until his eyes adjusted. The usual ten people who seemed to think this was their home were either perched on a barstool or at their own table. The one thing about drunks was they liked to think they owned something, even if it was a bit of space in a sleazy pub. It wasn't hard to spot the two strangers. They stood out like two swans in the desert. They watched him. It made August feel a little better to know that they weren't comfortable. But he had to give it to them; they'd stuck it out for an hour past when he said he'd meet them, even though he hadn't shown.

Time to find out what made him so popular. He stood by their table, sizing them up. The barmaid, Danna, brought him a beer, the brand he always drank, and set it down on the table. Nothing could have told him more succinctly that he'd been spending way too much time there.

Without sitting down, he asked, "So, what brings you here?"

The couple looked at one another and then back at him before the woman answered, "Your mom sent us."

The conversation had been nothing like what he'd expected. After an hour of talking with them and coming to an agreement, the two strangers left.

As soon as they'd pulled away, he went back to the mechanic shop. He strode up the flight of stairs to the second floor. Without knocking, he walked into the boss' office.

"Don't tell me you're leaving?"

August chuckled. "Jim. We'd agreed I'd be here to help for a few weeks. It's been over four months. Definitely time for me to go."

"Yes, don't let the grass grow under your feet. And don't let the door hit you on the ass on the way out."

"Hey. I saved your bacon, man. Remember the combine that Mr. Jones needed work on? I got it running in record time. He said he'd hire me and pay me a monthly salary to keep that old beast working."

Jim laughed. August was glad. He hated the thought of leaving, but it was time. He'd never planned on staying long at all. And this invitation to be a mechanic for Caspian Winery had told him he needed to do it, if only to understand what his mom had planned for him.

****

The sound of the main door slamming jolted him. He was pretty sure it was Perry, a third-year apprentice mechanic. It would be several minutes before Perry was ready to work. The first thing he always did was to make a pot of coffee, or black tar, as August called it. He walked back into the shop, his mind still mulling over what he'd been thinking about. Their hiring had been very unconventional, especially on his mom's say-so. Well, they hadn't just hired him because she'd written and told them he needed a good job. They'd done their homework on him and interviewed him and called ten references. It hadn't been easy to get the position. The reason they'd sought him out, though bothered him. Who looked up a guy because a dying mom told them they should hire him?

It had intrigued him enough to accept.

He hadn't been searching for work, but it sure had made him curious. He'd found it difficult to decline the offer they'd made him—lead mechanic at Caspian Winery.

The company was not just a solid business but internationally known and respected. They'd had a few scandals over the last few years. A granddaughter kidnapped at birth was found thirty years later, and the year before, someone had tried to sabotage their business by swapping out the wine with vinegar. Despite this, they had an excellent reputation and were well liked.

What he didn't get was why they had wanted him. They had, of course, known pretty much everything about him, including the mechanic business he'd owned for eight years and had sold for a hefty sum. The worst though was that they'd known his mom had died of cancer.

His mom had been his only parent for most of his life. She'd been such a strong woman and had been the reason he'd started his business in the first place. She'd even worked for free in the early days to help him get it off the ground. He'd never been so thrilled as the day he was able to hand her a paycheque for the work she'd been doing.

When she'd gotten sick at first, the prognosis and her odds of beating cancer had been good. But then they'd discovered that she not only had breast cancer but her body had been filled with the deadly disease. As soon as he'd known his time with her was limited, he'd sold his business. His mom had been devastated that he'd done that; she'd never understood how well he'd been doing. It had been the excuse he'd needed to get out. He hadn't liked the pressure and the long hours. At least not anymore. Besides, he'd had a man who'd been bugging him to sell. The timing had been right.

"Damn, you like to come in early. I suppose you got in before the roosters at the farm next door started crowing."

August chuckled at Perry's headshake and eye roll.

"Actually, they start cock-a-doodling at 5:45 a.m. So, yes."

Perry groaned. He drank half his mug of coffee before setting it on the counter and plopping his six-foot frame down on the other dolly. "So what are we up to today, boss?"

August's cell phone rang. He pulled it out of his pocket, already knowing who was calling by the ringtone.

"August, good morning. Hey, Graham and I are going ATVing tonight. Want to join us?"

"Sure. Sounds great." After getting all the details, August hung up. He hadn't known a soul when he'd moved out to Ontario, but Guy and Graham had made him feel welcome. They'd included him for meals, to help him clean out a few sheds at Caspian, go ATVing, but there seemed to be another side to it. He felt as though they were testing him. Either it was the most in-depth probation anyone had ever been put through or they were testing him. But for what?

CHAPTER 4

TIJAN HADN'T FLOWN MUCH and wasn't looking forward to the experience. Sitting in her seat by the window, she thought about what she was doing.

She didn't even know where the woman she was searching for lived—or her name. All she had to go on was the little bit that she'd found in the media. The incident that had photographed the woman she was sure was her sister had happened in a hotel in Toronto. A daughter of a wealthy family had been getting married, and there had been a shooting at the wedding. The media said that a deranged, mentally ill man had broken in and had tried to take hostages. He'd been killed by police, but no one else had been harmed.

The photo hadn't had much, but when Tijan had accidentally come across it on the internet, it had stopped her cold. The hand that was visible in the corner of the picture had grabbed her attention. It had been enough to give Tijan hope and very curious. She and her sister were born with almost identical birthmarks. Both were in the shape of a C. Hers was backward facing on her foot, and her sister's, according to her mom, was forward facing on her hand. Tijan had flashes of memory of her mom teasing them about the similar marks, and how they'd make a circle if they were put together. For some reason, that had stuck in Tijan's mind, but she wasn't sure if it was a true memory. Over the years, her mom would often stare at and touch her birthmark and tell her about the one her sister had on her hand.

Tijan had always known she'd had a twin sister, but she'd been gone a long time. The loss still haunted her mom and kept her up some nights. All Tijan had been told was that her twin had drowned in a creek, but the rest of the details had been sketchy.

She thought back to her conversation with her mom.

****

"I was born in Ontario."

Tijan pressed her fingers to her forehead. "You've never mentioned that before."

Her mom looked at Cal, who sat down beside her on the bench and took her hand. Tijan stood tall, towering over them. It didn't feel right, so she sat on the floor.

"My parents disowned me. I wasn't a dutiful daughter and definitely not up to their standards. Anyway, I haven't been back there in a very long time. You caught me off guard."

Tijan couldn't look at her mom, but she wasn't sure if it was because her mom had withheld information or because Tijan was withholding information now. There was so much more to that story, but now wasn't the time, though the time would have to come someday.

"I've lived here all my life, though, right?"

"Yes. Well, not here at the ranch, but we didn't live far away."

"Is that how you two met?" Tijan had heard the story before but felt there was something her mom wasn't telling her.

"Cal came into the diner where I was waitressing, and that was the start of his courting me."

Although they looked at one another with love, Tijan noted something was different. It was almost as if her dad was trying to get her mom to say more.

"So, where were we living before this?"

****

Tijan didn't know what to believe. When she'd seen that picture, though, she'd understood that odd, kind of broken, lost feeling she'd always had. She'd always felt like something, some piece of her, had been missing. It wasn't something she could have explained. It just was. Seeing that picture had made it clear that she was missing part of herself—her twin. Although it was a long shot, she had to find out if that person was connected to her. Or maybe she was just going crazy. She didn't know. Her mom had said she had no relatives. She'd been an only child, and her deceased dad had also been an only child. That was all she knew about the man who was her biological father. Oh, and that he was evil. Tijan didn't even know his name. Her stepfather, Cal, had been such a wonderful dad. She'd never felt the need to find out who her real one was or had been even curious about him. Cal had treated her like his daughter. He'd taught her so much that she would never have hurt him by trying to learn about her real father.

Her sister, though, was a different thing. After doing some research into the wedding, Tijan discovered Caspian Winery and Knight's Associates. Both businesses were in or near Toronto.

Her fingers trembled as she thought about the trip she was now on to Toronto, Ontario. A province she'd never been to and a city she'd never wanted to go to. It had too many people, too many buildings and not enough wide-open spaces. It wasn't a place she wanted to go, but she didn't have a choice. There was only one thing her mom had ever wanted, and that was to be reunited with her other daughter—not that she'd ever told Tijan, but she had heard her and Cal talking many times about the regrets she had.

It probably was a wild-goose chase. But it felt right. She was never spontaneous or impulsive, but something was driving her. er mom deserved total happiness, and for some reason, she felt this was a gift she needed to give her—if there was anything to it.

What if I'm an idiot and I am chasing a ghost?
The thought that it might not lead anywhere, almost had her changing her mind. She looked out the window, glad that she'd been able to tamp it down until then.

To late to stop now.

Determination squared her shoulders and kept her focused on seeing it through. It hadn't been her belief that this was just any relative but that it might be her sister. Her twin. Her mind conjured up all kinds of possibilities as to how that might happen. She was trying to stay open to the idea but her doubt remained high.

It all seemed so far-fetched and so far from her simple country life. It made her wonder if she just didn't need an adventure. Things had been routine for a very long time. Trent's pushiness to deepen their relationship, had been a factor in making up her mind to get away, to look for something new and different. He was supposedly one of the best local catches. That made her shudder. Maybe it was her biological clock ticking, or a desire for what her mom and Cal had, but Trent was not it.

She hoped this was one of those times she jumped and it didn't end well. Like the time she'd dropped her horse, Tango's reigns, knowing she'd stand still. Tijan had gone up to the hayloft and jumped hoping to land on her horse's back. It had seemed like a cook trick but in hindsight, not a smart move nor a nice one for her horse, but she'd been ten. It had failed badly. Her step cousin had come roaring in on his motorbike. The horse had reared and bolted. Tijan's saving grace had been that when she'd leapt, she'd been able to grab the rope, that she'd convinced Cal to hang so she could play Spiderman.

She'd never told anyone about that crazy stunt. Nor a few of the others that hadn't gone well either. She'd been lucky many times.

Would she be this time?

This new adventure felt like she'd taken that kind of leap. Whether there was anything for her to grab onto was up for question.

What if it isn't her? What if it isn't my sister?
As much as she tried to push that thought away, it was like a swarm of bees that kept buzzing around her head.

Chapter 5

THE COUGHING WOULDN'T STOP. James reached for a glass of water and took several sips. He then grabbed a lozenge and popped it into his mouth.

His phone beeped. Mary, his receptionist, wanted to talk to him. He picked up.

"Carter and Associates are waiting for you in the boardroom."

"I know that."

"The meeting was to have started fifteen minutes ago. If you want, I can reschedule?"

"Tell them I'll be there in a minute. And that I'm busy running a hotel chain." He felt a bit guilty for yelling at Mary, but she'd heard worse from him and she'd stayed.

"I told them you were busy due to a call with potential investors."

Another coughing attack caught him off guard. He drank some more water. Finally, the hack-attack ceased, but it left him feeling weak, beat up and run down. If he hadn't thought his doctor would tell him he had to take time off, he might have gone and seen the man.

Being late was a demonstration of poor management skills. It was something James prided himself on—always being on time. Unfortunately, there was nothing he could do about it. As the owner of C-Lite hotels, he could do as he wanted, and he had done that most of his life. That's why he'd gotten as far as he had. He did not bend to anyone's will or demands. He set the rules, and his team of lawyers, who he paid well, would just have to wait.

After popping a couple of pills intended to help with a cold, he grabbed his phone and stood up. The room seemed to go a little fuzzy. Holding onto his desk, he took a moment until he didn't feel so dizzy. Once he felt he could walk and wouldn't collapse, he headed to his meeting. He might not feel well, but that wasn't something he was going to show anyone. Squaring his shoulders, he straightened to his 6'2" height as he entered the room.

"So, where are we with acquiring Caspian Winery?" he asked the moment he stepped through the door. He didn't apologize. Nor did he acknowledge the dirty looks he was getting from the junior members of his legal team.

"We've made several offers over the last year. The latest was no different. It was turned down. Not with a 'no' but 'never, so go away and stop asking.'"

James looked around the table at the three lawyers that he'd hired. They were to look after all his legal, above-board dealings. He'd hired Eleanor ten years before, and she'd handpicked her team, which had changed a few times. It seemed some people just didn't enjoy working with him.

He smiled inwardly. His hotel chain, C-Lite Hotels, was doing so well he needed not one but a group of legal eagles to look after his company. It did, however, surprise him that he was paying them such exorbitant fees and yet they still couldn't get the job done. Maybe he hadn't expected that they would. But he'd hoped.

"What price did you offer?"

"Eighty-five million, which is at least twice the value."

"That may be true, Ron, but I made it clear to all of you that I want that property. And I want it sooner, not later. Go back to the drawing board and figure out how you're going to entice Dorothea Lindell to sell to me. Her health isn't good. She has a new person in charge. Find out what you can about her—"

"She used to run a brothel."

"What?"

Eleanor, the senior lawyer in the group, spoke up. "She's the new CEO. And she didn't run a brothel, but she did run an escort service. Her business was aboveboard, but nonetheless..."

"So, how do we use that to embarrass the old lady to sell?"

"Dorothea Lindell doesn't embarrass, nor is she easily intimidated. We need a different approach with her. The woman who is running the company, LJ Brown, has been in place for a little under a year. She's done an excellent job of running the winery and expanding its reach. She's pretty savvy, and the newspapers can't praise her enough. There was an article about a year ago delving into her past, so everything has been out in the open for the public. Dorothea was, in fact, the one who broke the story. Smart woman. She jumped ahead of the media, who would have turned it into a circus. Since then, she's made sure the media hears about all the new CEO's accomplishments."

James stared at Eleanor for a few moments. She wasn't like her two junior lawyers, who couldn't look him in the eye. She stared him down, not blinking. He allowed the slightest of curl to edge up the corners of his lips, not that it was discernible to anyone. But he knew. He liked that she challenged him. He also liked the dark purple suit she was wearing. It was definitely flattering to her and her figure. That was one thing he liked about her, her sense of style and class; she knew how to dress to impress and be taken seriously.

"Can we buy the woman?"

"Don't think so. Rumor has it that Molson Brewery offered LJ an unprecedented five million to sign with them. No mention of what her salary would have been. She turned them down immediately, as she was not interested. She used to cater to some pretty well-known and powerful men, not that she has ever divulged who they are. But again, rumor has it that she is not to be harassed, nor is there to be any negative media printed about her. No idea how much truth there is to that, but I'm betting there's a lot. So the woman, LJ, has a lot of backing. And I'm quite sure that the men she catered to are men you don't want to tangle with."

"You don't want the winery for the winery, so what are you thinking you'd do with it? We could use that angle to appeal to them. I mean, if you're upfront and open about it, then I'm quite sure you'd get further." Martin, the youngest and newest of the three lawyers, spoke up.

James glared at him. "I pay you to do work for me. I don't answer your questions. Do you understand me?"

The young man's face flushed as he leaned back in his chair.

"He has a point, James. We need to come at this from a different angle. I don't care why you want it but the truth is that it isn't for sale. So, give us another way to approach it."

James looked hard at Eleanor but didn't say anything. She had a point, but it annoyed him that she defended her overeager newbie lawyer.

Ripping down that winery was of no concern to James. He wanted to own it, if he could hand it over to his daughter, Tarin, to run and make it her business. Maybe then he'd be able to bring her back under his wing. Her son was his heir and was one day going to take over his grandfather's dynasty. Tarin, though, was fighting him at every turn. She wouldn't send her son to the school he wanted. She kept saying he was too young. But three was the right age to start shaping him. James knew he could always take the boy, but he didn't want to do that. He wasn't interested in raising him, just in making sure that he learned from the best. And of course, that he knew how to run a successful hotel chain. One day it would be his. But first, he had to get his daughter to come back into his life. She'd done everything she could to stay away from him. She wasn't interested in running his hotels but maybe if he built a resort... or an apartment complex... something for those who had money and wanted to live outside the city... get fresh, country air... He stared off into space as the ideas came to him.

She'd wanted to run one of his hotels in her younger days, but he'd been too bent on making her climb her way up the ladder. He hadn't wanted her to get special treatment. Only she'd shown him instead, by quitting and having nothing to do with him. It hadn't bothered him for years that she'd been estranged. He'd always known she had something to prove to him. But now she'd just cut him out of her life. It wasn't sitting well with him. He didn't want to admit it but age seemed to be making him look more at who he had in his life, and she was his only heir. She had to come back. Who else did he have to share his dynasty with?

"Alright. I guess the meeting is done?"

James looked distractedly at Martin for a second before turning his attention to the table in front of him.

"Here's what I want you to do. I'm creating a new company, and we're going to go in a new direction." He explained his plan.

Someone knocked on the door, which he ignored as he continued to talk about what he wanted.

"Are you all clear about what I need you to do?"

The door opened. Chris Simmons, or JT as he liked to be called, his financial manager, stuck his head in. "Sorry to interrupt, but we have a problem with three trucks that have broken down and your limo isn't fixed yet."

"I told you to hire a new mechanic. Get me a list. I'll do it myself." JT had hired a mechanic, well actually two, but James had fired them within a few days. Neither had known who he was when he'd called down to ask about his limo.

Martin spoke up. "I know of a good mechanic—"

"Do you mind? It's none of your business. Do what I tell you to do and nothing else."

Eleanor stood up, looking at the two men who'd come with her. "I'll see you two downstairs," she said dismissively. Ron and Martin left.

Eleanor gathered her paperwork, but as soon as the door closed, she looked at James. "Someday, your attitude is going to bite you, James."

He smiled at her and shrugged. "I doubt it. Besides, you like that side of me." A few years younger than him, he liked that Eleanor always dressed professionally and conducted herself that way. But he also enjoyed knowing that he had seen the other side of her. Her hair had been down, and she had been naked and sitting on him.

"Stop undressing me. This isn't the time or place." Her face scrunched up in annoyance.

"I know. However, knowing what you look like under that very proper suit brightens my day."

"We agreed on no bedroom talk while at work. In fact, I'm sure that was your request."

James nodded. When they'd started seeing each other two years before, he'd been adamant no one knew and that they remain detached. To him, it hadn't been more than a physical thing. Lately, though, he'd been finding himself wanting to see more of the soft side of her. He wondered if he told her he wasn't feeling well, what she'd say, what she'd do. Realizing he was sicker than he thought, he changed the subject. "Your guy needs to be kept in line."

"Martin? He's harmless. And he's good. In fact, he reminds me of you in your younger days, when you were a shark in tame waters. He has ambition."

"And you sound like you're enthralled with him."

"I know talent. And I like talent."

"Keep him away from me. I don't like him."

Eleanor rolled her eyes. "He's a good lawyer."

"I'll see you later." He stood up from his huge boardroom table, glad he had placed his hand on it as he needed it to steady himself. Eleanor frowned. He moved over to the window and stared out over the city, where it had all started for him. Toronto. It was here that he'd taken flight with his hotel chain. He was doing very well, but the astronomical price that he was going to have to pay to get

Caspian Winery could be a challenge. But he always got what he wanted, one way or another.

"Sorry, I'm busy tonight." The slight click of the door let him know that she'd left.

Which was just as well, as the pressure building in his chest felt like an elephant was thinking of sitting on it. But he would have liked someone to take care of him.

If his damn daughter would come around, he wouldn't have to play this stupid game. Would she appreciate all that he was trying to do for her? That he was trying to get that place for her? The place held a soft spot in her heart, so if she owned it, maybe he'd bring her around to his way of thinking.

He pulled out his cell phone and made a call.

"I have a problem. Dorothea Lindell won't sell Caspian Winery."

"What do you want us to do?"

"Go out there. Snoop. Find her weakness. Find out how we can exploit her or her place."

"Alright. Any injuries?"

"No. Not this time. Get me some information. I'm not getting what I want from legitimate channels, so see what you can find out. For now, no strong-arming. Just be curious tourists. A happily married couple. Got it?"

CHAPTER 6

TIJAN KEPT HER HEAD bowed but peeked through her long strands of hair. She smiled. She could hear her step-grandmother say, 'Get your hair out of your face. You should never hide, Child'. And yet here she was doing just that, keeping herself hidden. Her focus was on the building across from her. She doubted anyone would even notice her, but she couldn't take the chance of being recognized. If she'd thought it through, she'd have done better at disguising herself, something she'd have to do the next time.

The area was quite busy with steady traffic, cars on the road, and people on the sidewalks. Each doing their own thing, but everyone seemed to be in their own world, oblivious to others. Across the street at the building she was interested in, it was no different. People seemed to be moving at their own pace, heading for some unknown destination. She should know she'd been watching for almost an hour. A few people came and went from Knights Associates' computer business. It was where she was focusing her attention. It was on the ground floor. For all those in and around the two-story building, there was never a familiar face. No one that looked like her.

Sighing, she rolled her head around on her neck, trying to work out a few kinks. She shifted a few times, her feet already feeling the hard cement of the city streets. She wore what she always wore, jeans, t-shirt and cowboy boots. She was going to have to dig out her runners, though. She'd never thought of herself as a tenderfoot.

The fast-paced, cement-lined city of Toronto, though, was making her rethink that. The occasional woman who passed by in high heels made her cringe. She couldn't imagine anything more painful. Not even that of being kicked by a calf she was wrestling.

Tired of waiting for something she wasn't even sure she could identify; she crossed the street. If she could get a closer look at the place, she might find some answers. At the far end of the block, she waited for the lights to change and the little white sign that said she could cross. It was one reason she hated the city. In the country, she could take a shortcut or a long cut and not have to worry whether she was taking her life in her hands if she chose not to follow the rules. Standing on the other side, she felt the tension creep in. The noise, the hustle and bustle and the thick, smelling air settled into her neck and shoulders like talons clutching deep. She shrugged her shoulders a few times to ease the pain.

The first few steps down the sidewalk seemed to break through the chaos and echo in her head. It sounded like she was walking in a steel tunnel with her cowboy boots. The sound was deafening. The closer she got to the one place that might give her a sign if her sister was alive made her stop. Thoughts that she'd tried to keep at bay bombarded her.

What if she's a city slicker?
What if it wasn't her?
The odds were pretty high on that one.
What if she doesn't care that she has a sister?
What if she doesn't want to meet Mom?
What if we don't like each other?
What if she's a bitch?
What the hell am I doing?
The one thought that she couldn't shake was that her sister had been at a small wedding where someone had been shot. What kind of people did she hang out with?

Someone bumped into her. It brought her back to where she was and the fact that she was standing in the middle of the sidewalk, blocking it. She stepped closer to the building and moved toward the one she was curious about. She reached the end of the wall she was hugging and stopped. Across the alley was Knights Computers. A few people entered. A few people left. Some carried their computers in and left empty-handed. Others came out with computers in their hands. Her research had shown her some of what they did. They fixed computers, doing pretty much what needed to be done. The reviews she'd found online had been quite positive. They had a good reputation. If the number of people leaving or entering was any indication, they were definitely busy.

Finding the place and a lead to her sister had been much easier than she'd thought. She'd arrived in Toronto Pearson Airport the day before. She'd wanted to search immediately, but the trip and the muggy heat had drained her. In truth, she'd been terrified to leave her hotel room. She'd been to Edmonton and Calgary, two large cities in Alberta. But they didn't come close to the scope of Greater Toronto, which seemed to go on forever. Going to any city was something she avoided whenever she could. And now she knew why. It was hot, muggy, full of traffic and people. Watching others fascinated her, but already she was feeling overwhelmed.

He was busy fumbling with something in his pocket, but the moment he looked up, everything changed. He stared at her with such intensity and confusion that it made her feel uncomfortable. When he started moving toward her, Tijan stepped back. But he kept coming, determined. She wanted to turn and run, but there was something that kept her standing there. He didn't seem to be a threat, but there was no question he was aiming for her. He didn't look homeless, at least not in the messy, kind of grungy way she expected, but maybe she should give him money. Whatever it was, something made her curious enough to stand there.

"Why are you dressed like that? What are you doing? Graham won't like it."

Tijan gasped. She got the implication of what he was saying, which got her so excited that she wanted to do a jig—not something she'd ever done before. It also meant it was her cue to get out of there. Now was not the time to pursue finding her sister, but it was definitely the place. She shrugged before turning and walking away. For an old guy who'd been shuffling his feet, he seemed to move pretty darn fast. He reached for her. Without waiting for the walk light, she ran across the street amidst car honks and screeching tires. As she ran, she glanced back across the road. The old guy was watching her every move, and he seemed to be tracking where she was going. She was glad to see he'd stopped chasing her. Ducking her head, she kept moving, thankful to reach the end of the block and turn down it. She hopped into her SUV. It had been foolish to show up. If her sister were alive, it would be obvious to anyone who saw her, who she was. It would at least cause some confusion. Although she'd wanted to believe her twin was alive, she hadn't truly bought into it. Her fleeting memories hadn't been much, but at times it had felt like half of herself was missing—until now.

Did she barge in? Or do more searching?

Her stomach was rolling and flopping like she was on a ship on the high seas during a storm with rogue waves. She pressed her hand over her belly and closed her eyes. Her sister was alive. Who was she? Why hadn't she ever contacted her? Or found her? Tijan wanted to charge in there and demand that her sister give her answers. But then she didn't know if her sister was there. And she needed to know more about her before she met her. It seemed ironic that she'd flown out to Toronto on a whim of finding her twin and now she was scared.

What if her sister didn't want to meet her?

The whole thing had come about because of a wedding her sister had attended. Caspian Winery had hosted it, and now it was time to go there and check it out. Feeling a bit like she was walking on quicksand, she so wanted to meet her sister but needed to make sure this was right.

And now it was time for a disguise.

CHAPTER 7

AUGUST FELT AWKWARD IN the office. He'd been in there a few times, but usually it had been first thing in the day or at least after he'd had a chance to clean off. Unfortunately, his coveralls hadn't protected him from the oil that had leaked while he was under the tractor repairing it. He was definitely going to leave a change of clothes at the shop.

The elegant, huge office with two desks was spotless and sparkling clean. It reminded him of the fact that he hadn't changed. He stood inside the doorway, avoiding touching anything.

They had done everything to welcome him to the job of being head mechanic at Caspian Winery, but he was rather curious when Guy and Graham had requested to meet with him.

"Okay, we have a problem," Guy said as he strolled in through a side door.

August realized it was an adjoining office. The two men had their business in downtown Toronto and also offices at Caspian Winery. They looked after the computers and security system.

"And what would that be, young man?" Graham said in a very stodgy but inadequate English accent.

"I thought Tarin broke you of your poor impressions."

Graham slapped his hand to his chest while tossing back his head. "You wound me, my good man."

Guy rolled his eyes, but there was a smile on his face. "Anyway, it appears that Mr. Madsen isn't done with trying to make trouble."

"Do you guys want me here for this? I can come back." August stepped away as though to leave. When he'd first arrived, Graham and Tarin had been busy talking in low, hushed tones but they hadn't wanted him to leave. Then Tarin had left, and he hadn't seen her since. But this was feeling awkward.

"No, you're good."

That's all Graham had said to him when he'd first met Tarin, but after she'd left, he'd started to talk.

"What an ass! What's he doing now? I know Tarin said to butt out, but her father is something else. For a while there, it seemed that she'd gotten through to him. We didn't hear from him for almost six months. Of course, I didn't think much of it but then he was on her case again. He wanted her home, but she refused. He wanted to hire a nanny to look after his grandson, whom he never asked to see. When she refused, it appeared he hired a bodyguard to follow her. Somehow, she got him to get rid of that guy, but it took three months.

"Her father is relentless. I haven't told her, but there might be another tail keeping an eye on her. I swear I'm getting paranoid." Graham turned his head and looked over his shoulder with such flair that August couldn't help but laugh.

Guy chuckled too. "Oh, so that's why you moved to that old neighborhood. Figure there won't be anyone new moving in?"

"Yeah. I was starting to feel like our neighbors were watching us. I even got suspicious of the mail carrier. I was getting paranoid, so I can't imagine what that was doing to Tarin. She and Chance finally have some freedom, but her father is slowly taking that away. So, what's he doing now?" Graham swore.

"He's trying to buy up Caspian Wineries. And it appears he's doing some heavy snooping into us."

August looked from one to the other. "Who is this guy?"

Graham sat up straight. "Tarin's father. What makes you say that?"

"LJ got a hold of me. Their lawyer contacted them to say an offer had been received. She didn't want to tell Dorothea. She might be in her eighties and the owner, but she does not want to give up control. I'm not sure how LJ does it. Man, we finally got that woman to slow down to a three-day workweek. If she hears about this, she'll be back to full-time. At eighty-four, it's time she got a break and enjoyed life. And no, I'm not brave enough to tell her that."

Graham laughed. "Love that woman, but you do not mess with her. So, keep it from her at all costs. And keep it from Tarin. Crap. That's just great. My soon-to-be-father-in-law is already making me lie to my future wife. Gotta love that guy. And the other part he's doing?"

"Guys, why am I here? I don't think this is stuff I should be hearing."

"He got a hold of Downey," he said, ignoring August, "our contact in the government that we do a lot of security detail for, and he asked for a reference. I asked Downey how he had figured out that we used him. He didn't know, but he played it cool, saying he'd never heard of us. Madsen has too much money and is good at paying people off and snooping. It appears things go his way... or they go his way."

"Yes, he's a bastard, but unfortunately there isn't anything I can do about that," Tarin said as she stepped through the doorway. Obviously, catching the tail end of Graham's comment.

August had felt uncomfortable listening to the conversation, but to walk in on it like Tarin had done made him feel even more like he needed to get out of there. The guys had included him in a lot of things. They'd welcomed him and been a friend to him, but this was not something he should hear. Especially since his first thought was to wrap his arms around Tarin and give her a hug.

Graham closed his eyes as his head dropped back for a second before snapping to attention. He walked over to Tarin, standing by the door. Her arms were wrapped around her waist. Graham took her in his arms and pulled her close. It made August envious. Not just because she was a gorgeous woman, but they had what he'd always wanted—love, friendship, understanding and the ability to work together.

"I'm sorry."

She sighed and laid her head against his chest. "I don't know how to get him out of my life. Now that Chance is three, my father is seeing in him the son that I never was. The jackass hasn't even asked to meet him, although he's known about him for over a year. Who does that? And now he wants me to come home and bring my son. He says it's time to raise him in true Madsen fashion."

Graham took her by the shoulders and stepped back, looking down into her blue eyes. "When did he do this?"

Tarin sighed before pulling away. "A few weeks ago."

"Tarin?"

"Alright, for a few months now. Just before we moved. Sylvia, the new neighbor who had moved in just before we left the area, was the new bodyguard he'd hired. She has quite an impressive background. She's military trained, an ultimate fighter, weapons trained, a black belt in karate and jujitsu. And who knows what else. What am I going to do? I thought that once Geo... Geof... Geoff... God, I can't even say his name." She shuddered violently.

August was already turning to leave when Guy nodded at him. He followed him into the side office.

"Mind telling me why I'm here?" August stared at Guy, who had moved over to the desk and now sat on the edge of it.

Guy faced him, a hint of uncertainty on his face, which only lasted a moment before he was all business. "How have you liked working at Caspian Winery?"

"It's a good job. I love working with the machinery. Perry's a pretty good apprentice. I get paid very well. I couldn't ask for much more."

Guy pushed away from the desk and moved past August. Unsure what to do, he followed.

"Tarin, I know he's your father—"

She leaned against Graham as she turned to face Guy. "Please. That bastard may have sired me and raised me, but he's no father. If I were more like him, I'd have him taken out."

Graham chuckled. "My wife, the tough lady. She catches flies in the house and sets them free outside. Her father is just the opposite. It's time to do some real digging into that man. And that's where you come in."

"Why am I hearing all this?" August knew even if he'd been blind, he would have felt the intensity of the three pairs of eyes that turned on him. He was still standing in the doorway but felt the need to turn and bolt.

"We know you've only been with us a few months, but we have a favor to ask, and it's okay to say no. We wouldn't include you but..."

"My mom said I was good."

There was a moment of awkward silence before Graham burst out laughing. He was laughing so hard that the others couldn't help but join him. He had one of those laughs that grabbed the others and pulled them in. August was glad that he'd lightened the mood, if only for a few moments.

Guy shook his head as soon as he could catch his breath. "Well that. And we do our homework. We know that you know how to run a business. We also know that your mom was right; you are a damn good mechanic. You've done some amazing things here. We know that you helped the police in breaking up a car theft ring. And we know that you're searching for your father."

"Mom." August had a feeling these guys were good, but the shock of what they were saying about him had him taking a step back. The moment he cleared the doorway;

his first thought was to keep walking. He didn't owe them anything. And as far as he'd been told, there was no record of him helping the police in their sting. The police had thought he'd been in on the carjackings, which was why he'd agreed to help them. High-end vehicles that had come into his shop had been stolen afterward. It had taken six months, but he'd discovered the leak in his business. Even with all the evidence, he still believed the guy was innocent, but he'd liked to brag a little too much to his new girlfriend, and she had been one of the masterminds. His employee had been an easy target for her to use without him suspecting anything. She'd been a pro, as had her team. Thankfully, they had been taken down. It had all happened when his mom was ill. It had been a good time to get out of the business.

"How much do you know about me?"

Guy cleared his throat. "We do a background check on everyone."

August nodded. "I'm sure you do. Obviously, you know a lot, including stuff that isn't supposed to be accessible. My mom didn't know about my role in solving the carjackings. So although she bragged about me, she couldn't have told you everything. You guys are good. I'm guessing you do a lot of stuff off the books. Your computer store and cybersecurity business are a small part of it?"

"You're right. We're private investigators with some big contracts with the government and their distant arms. No one knows that." He looked pointedly at him.August understood the implications of what he was telling him. "We do a lot of cybersecurity, but not for the basic computer owner, as our business suggests. We do it for those who are at risk of national and international security."

August whistled. He'd had a feeling they were a lot more than he'd seen.

Graham nodded. "Look, we need your help. We're a bit unconventional, but we know an honest guy when we meet one. You're a worthy guy. We've probably scared the

crap out of you, although I am told I could have been
Victorian—"

August couldn't help but chuckle. Unconventional
didn't even begin to describe Graham. His attempt at
British accents, though, was terrible. "So, this is the test
you've been putting me through? To see if I'd make a good
spy?"

Guy and Graham looked at each other. Tarin appeared
sick.

"Tarin's father needs a mechanic, and we need a spy
inside his business. We've been asked to do some digging
into the man. We've tried to hack his computers, but he
has guys who are almost as good as us. At this point in time,
they are one step ahead."

"Graham, maybe this is a bad idea. We already know
he's doing a lot of illegal stuff. We know he's a bad guy.
We—maybe I should just go to work for him. Find that
information myself. Be the dutiful daughter—"

"No!"

August was glad that Graham had yelled that because
he'd felt the same urge to tell Tarin no. He couldn't take
his eyes off her. Getting involved more in her life, though,
probably wasn't a good idea.

Guy's cell phone rang. "What...? When...? What's the
name again...?"

Tarin had pulled away and was looking out the window
by the time Guy hung up. Graham leaned against his desk.
August watched it all, feeling a bit like Alice in Wonderland, although that didn't make him feel any better.

"We have another problem." Guy mouthed to Graham.

Graham nodded, glancing over his shoulder at Tarin.
"Sweetheart, why don't you go home and spend time with
Chance? We've got this. If anything exciting happens, I'll
call you. Okay?"

Tarin turned, giving him a loving but sad smile before
facing Guy. "What's my father doing now?"

"Well—"

Graham shrugged.

"I don't think it's your father. But it appears someone else is trying to buy up Caspian Winery. This time, it's to tear it down and build some type of country living resort. It's a company called Wejo or something like that."

"It's We-Two. Damn him." Tarin had turned a pasty color.

"I've never heard of this company. Since you know it, I'm assuming you're damning your father?"

She nodded. "He took something that was precious to me and turned it into something ugly. We-two was something I used to say as a child. I don't know why, but I'd go around singing it all the time. It annoyed the hell out of him. My guess is that this is something new he's into. I haven't heard of this company before, but it's him, and he wants me to know it. But why?"

In that moment, August knew he was going undercover... again.

CHAPTER 8

TIJAN SAT UP IN bed and pressed her hands to her head. The dream she'd had was so real.

***

She was searching for a house with but a vague idea of where it was located—somewhere near the creek, five miles cross-country or about twenty miles by road.

Not wanting to make anyone suspicious, she'd ridden to her normal spot, which was a sort of in that direction but still a few miles away. She led Tango alongside the winding stream. At one point, she finally realized that the house must be on the other side of the creek because she'd been all along her side of it. Finding a safe area with a low bank where the water was shallow, she crossed over.

Her mom's voice immediately came to her: *'Never cross the creek. It's not safe.'*

Was there more to that warning?

After an hour of walking, the brush was getting too thick beside the stream, but she couldn't find a good place to cut back across the water. It was either turn around or move away from the creek. Maybe she could find a road.

It wasn't easy going, but much easier than what she'd been trying to fight her way through. Finally, breaking free of the trees and brush, she stepped into an open area. Following a rough path, that might have been a road at one time but was now overgrown with tall grass. The ground was uneven, making it imperative that she be careful about where she was stepping and where she was leading Tango. Her horse, though, was loving it, snipping bites of the grass as they walked. She slowed, letting him eat.

The sun was warm and had her turning her face up to the sky. It felt wonderful, but it also relaxed her. That moment of letting her guard down, let the questions flood her mind.

If her sister were alive, why didn't Tijan know it? Where had she been all this time? Why was she so compelled to go on such a crazy chase? What if it ended in nothing?

She'd never done anything impulsive like this, and definitely not something that involved going to the city. It was not her favorite place.

Looking around at the wild space she called home, maybe because the age of thirty was looming, she was feeling antsy. That might explain why she'd gone out with Trent. It had been a bad decision, which she hoped this new idea of finding her sister wasn't.

The road curved a bit; she urged Tango to start moving again. They'd barely gone fifty feet when the sight before her brought her to an immediate stop. It was real. There was a house about two hundred feet in front of her. It was a big, old, and beaten down one that would have been fun to explore as a kid. Taking a few steps toward it, snapshots started coming to her like flashes. She couldn't quite grab the images but could distinctly hear the laughter of little kids giggling. Tensing, she glanced around.

There was no one there, but there was a lone tree in front of the house. It was like it was pulling her to it. The high branches were filled with fresh green leaves.

She felt the urge to climb it. There was something familiar about it. But why? She didn't ever remember being there.

Walking past it, she stopped at the foot of the house but wasn't as compelled to check it out. She walked around the side of it as though she were being led. Her feet didn't stop when she reached the backyard, now wild and overgrown, but kept on walking. There was the soft gurgling of the creek. It wasn't far behind the house.

The sound became louder. More angry. *A roar..., her mom crying, begging for help... Tijan hiding, crying and shivering... Her mom screaming.*

Tijan pressed her hands to her cheeks, wishing she hadn't gone there. This is where she'd lost her sister. She'd never been told where it had happened, but this was it. The horror of that day didn't become clear, but the sense of loss did. Everything had changed after that.

Her feet kept moving, almost as if unaware of her inner turmoil. Stopping at the edge of the stream, she stared at the calm gentleness. But that was deceiving. She'd seen it at its worst. There had been many spring floods that had ripped out trees and decimated the landscape. The last one was about eight or ten years earlier. If it had been like that the day her sister disappeared, she understood why.

Dropping down onto the bank, she wanted to get some insight as to whether her sister had been swept away by the creek or if she really could be alive. Anguish crept through her, sending shivers of anxiety through her, but she could not get a sense of life or death. She just got a feeling of panic... of fear...

Something nudged her shoulder. She screamed and rolled to the side. Jumping to her feet, a little wild-eyed but ready to fight or flee, she looked into the soulful brown eyes of her horse. Her shoulders sagged with relief. Tango butted her again with her nose.

Tijan snorted. This was her best friend, and he knew when she was struggling. Throwing her arms around Tango's neck, she took a moment to calm herself. "There is nothing here telling me she is alive. I don't feel her here now, but I know she was at one time. Am I crazy, Tango? I saw a hand in a picture and want to believe it's hers. How crazy is that? I think I'm losing my mind, but I can't shake the feeling that I have to go. I have to see for myself. My gut, my instinct, my insanity is telling me I don't have a choice."

Tango whinnied softly.

"You're the closest thing I have to a sibling. But I might still have a sister. I can't explain it, but I have to go. Maybe... maybe... I don't know. Maybe I just need to spread my wings, and this is my excuse. I wish I could bring you with me. I'm scared of what I might find—or not find."

****

Only it hadn't been a dream. It had been what had convinced her she'd had to find her sister. Could she really have found her? Bounding out of bed, she showered and donned the disguise she'd bought the day before. She was pretty sure her own mother wouldn't know her.

CHAPTER 9

AUGUST PULLED INTO THE winery parking lot. He had a meeting in a few hours but thought he'd use some of his day off to look around. He'd snooped into Caspian Winery again. Anything that had been printed, he'd read it. Newspapers and the wine world spoke highly of it. It seemed to be well known and had existed for a long time—seventy plus years.

He loved working there. It had only been a few months, but he was well-treated, and he liked the young guy, Perry, he was working with. He had a bit of an attitude, but nothing that August hadn't seen before.

The meeting the day before had made him uneasy. They wanted him to be a spy, and he hadn't been able to decline. In fact, he quite liked the idea of going undercover and seeing what he could discover. The zing of excitement it had given him when they'd told him was like a reality check. It gave him a clue as to how deflated and depressed he'd been. Nothing had touched him since his mom had died, and if that was the only reason he was interested, that would be okay. But he couldn't ignore that there was something so beautiful and alluring about Tarin. Not that he'd ever act on it but she had definitely turned his head.

Realizing that was a bad path to go down, his plan had been to show up at the winery and wander like a tourist. He wanted to see it from the other side and to see what else he could learn. When he was hired, he'd been given the back-end tour and shown all the equipment he was to work on—everything from lawn mowers to harvesting machines. But he wanted to learn more about it. When he'd owned his garage, he'd made a point of being on the front line often so he could interact with customers and hear firsthand how they liked the service they were getting.

And he needed to distract himself. The meeting with Dorothea in a few hours was a little unsettling. LJ wanted to meet with him to do a three-month review and see how things were going, but Dorothea was also going to be there. He felt a bit intimidated by that and, to some extent, it was because he felt like he was there under false pretenses.

His brain had been on rapid fire since the meeting the day before, and knowing he had the upcoming meeting was making him feel like he was being underhanded.

Getting out of his car, he walked to the public entrance. The facade was modern and classy, and it looked like it had been recently remodeled. The fifty years since it had been built didn't show in front, but they had fixed the much larger section of building attached to the back and side to a lesser degree. He looked around, noting the other buildings in the back and some of the vineyards. A few people were wandering, suggesting they were tourists. Standing indecisively, a group of people exited a side door not far from him. The others immediately joined. The woman leading the group smiled at him.

"Hi. Are you here for the wine tasting or the wine tour?"

August was about to say neither but thought he might learn more by being a part of this group. He could slip away when he needed to. His presence was risky because, although he'd met some staff but not all, he'd felt the pressure to learn all he could about the machines he needed to fix.

"Wine Tour."

She motioned for the group of ten to follow. He fell in at the back. The tour guide took them toward the vineyard as she explained about planting, the types of grapes and their care, and how they would be harvested. August listened with half an ear. He didn't know exactly what he was looking for, but he'd heard rumors about the place, and many weren't good. There had been attempts to sabotage the place a time or two, and even though they had been dispelled, he didn't want to be caught off guard, and Guy and Graham had reassured him there wasn't any weird stuff going on.

"This vineyard was started by the Caspians in 1935, but it wasn't until just after World War II ended, that it saw any stability. It was small, but it made a good name for itself locally. It wasn't until Dorothea Caspian Lindell took it over that it flourished. She built it into the internationally known and respected winery it is today."

August scanned the area. The tourists were following the guide down the rows of grapes, and since he wasn't all that interested, he stopped. As he was about to turn, he noticed that one of the women who had been with the group was glancing around before hustling away to sneak into one of the buildings. Curious, he followed suit. Her behavior was very odd and raised his suspicions.

When he entered the dimly lit building, he couldn't see much but knew this was where they stored all the farm equipment—a few grape harvesters, a mechanical leaf remover—neither of which he'd known anything about. Perry was teaching him all he knew, and the Internet had become a good resource as well. In fact, before he'd started there, he'd thought that wineries still picked grapes by hand. That had made him chuckle, especially when he'd seen the size of the harvesters. He could see why they were used; they sped up the harvesting exponentially. The draw of the machines was magnetic.

"Do you work here or just like snooping?"

August had been bending over to look underneath the machine snapped up so fast, he whacked his head on part of it. "Dammit."

It would have made him laugh that he'd been so easily distracted by checking out the machinery and forgetting about the woman he'd been following if his head didn't smart. He rubbed the sore spot as he turned to see the woman who had sneaked in before him.

"Seems I'm not the only one; only I work here. But I've never seen you before."

The woman recoiled at his answer. She didn't respond, though she appeared to stare at him, but he couldn't be certain because he couldn't see her eyes behind the ridiculously big glasses she had on. She didn't belong there. He'd read that Caspian Winery had its share of problems—people stealing from them or trying to sabotage their wine—and he wondered what this woman was up to. Her fidgety, side-to-side head-turning attitude told him she was clearly doing something she shouldn't be.

"What are you doing here?"

"I came for the tour."

"And thought you'd leave before it even got started? Sorry but you'll have to come with me." He wasn't sure where he was going to take her but was certain he could find someone who'd be interested to know she'd been snooping in unauthorized places. If she had every right to be there, then it wouldn't be great for him as a new employee. On the other hand, they might appreciate being told of his concern. He hoped.

He took a step toward the redheaded woman, but she bolted. He followed her as she raced out of the building. She moved quickly back to the fairly sizeable crowd on the wine tour that was making their way around the first outback building to those behind it where the older equipment and supplies were kept. She shoved her way through. He followed but soon lost track of her as the people grew annoyed at being pushed aside a second time. Apologizing as he made his way through, he didn't stop. When he got to the far side of the group, he looked around but didn't see any sign of her. Frustrated, especially since he was quite sure she was up to something, he went beyond the farthest building. There was no sign of her, and he didn't have the time to snoop through buildings. He pulled out his phone to see how much time he had and realized that his meeting with the head of Caspian Winery was in twenty minutes. Taking one last look around, he made his way back to the main building to get directions to Dorothea Lindell's office, which is where his meeting was supposed to take place.

It was then that he saw her peeking around the corner of a building where the grapes were brought. He beelined it toward her, glad that she wasn't looking at him. Something held her attention, but it was in the other direction.

Was this a test to see if he had what it took to go undercover for Tarin's father—although no one knew he would show up early, did they?

CHAPTER 10

TIJAN TOOK A DEEP breath and peeked out from the back of what she guessed were the work buildings. The man who had been chasing her was headed in a different direction. She had no idea who he was, but she couldn't help but admire the way he filled out his blue jeans as he walked away from her. There was just something about a fit guy wearing blue jeans and a t-shirt, perhaps because it was her own favorite attire. Watching until he was gone from sight, she stepped away from her hiding place and looked around. She still wasn't sure what she'd been hoping for but she'd been curious. How had the woman, who she was feeling more inclined to believe was her sister, become connected to this wealthy family?

Tijan had never been one to take the roundabout way. If something needed doing, she did it. If something needed saying, she'd say it. But this was so far beyond her knowledge zone, she didn't know what to do—or to think. The only connections she had to her sister were Knight's Associates and Caspian Winery.

It was hard not to be in awe. The place was huge, well built, and classy. Everything she hadn't known a winery could be. The main building was glass and wood but had a very welcoming look. The place was clean—there was no garbage on the ground; the grass was trimmed, the trees pruned, and even the graveled road behind the main building seemed to be in alignment, like someone had swept it. Beautiful spring flowers were in bloom everywhere.

Not that Tijan had ever been overly impressed with money, but she had known the value of it and had never had to worry. Running a ranch was expensive and time intensive, if she was ever going to run her own one day, she would need money.

Owning her own ranch had always been an unwavering thought, but in the time she'd been away she'd enjoyed not being on call around the clock. Having to always be on the lookout for what the cattle needed—feeding them, checking every few hours during calving season, making sure they hadn't gone missing—was exhausting work. Though she'd always loved it, now she was questioning it. Pushing away her thoughts, she attributed them to the fact that she'd never taken a real vacation. As soon as she returned home, things would be back to normal. However, a little niggling thought that once she found her sister, nothing would be the same stayed with her.

As she was about to move away from her vantage point, a man and a woman dressed in casual clothes came around the corner behind her. Unsure why she felt the need to hide, she nonetheless hugged the side of the building behind some crates. They stopped not too far away. They talked in low undertones, but she could still make out what they were saying.

"That tour was a bust."

"Yeah. The place is well run, clean, and there's not too much that could be used against the old lady. I think we should go back to him and tell him the place is doing well. It's won several awards. People love a scandal, but it appears this place has weathered a few. A year or two ago, someone tried to sabotage the business by switching out its wine with vinegar. Pretty ingenious, really. But I think their reputation is pretty grounded when it comes to the quality of their wine and their service. The people I talked to love it here."

"Yeah. I think we dig up dirt on the whole family and the employees. There has to be something that will fall from the tree. Something that could be used for extortion.

I mean, the granddaughter got kidnapped and didn't return for almost thirty years. I think there is a lot more to that story than some crazy woman who took a baby from the hospital."

"And don't forget there's a prostitute now running Caspian Winery."

Tijan's eyes opened wide.

"I thought it was just a high-end escort service."

"Come on. Anyone who is in that business is into screwing on the side for the rich folks. I bet we could find some juicy stuff about her. Maybe kick-start some sort of past lover coming forward to cause some issues."

"Yeah, but what?"

A hand landed gently on Tijan's shoulder, but it might as well have slapped her. Tijan gasped and spun around, her fist coming up ready to swing, but she lost her balance and stumbled sideways, falling against the building. The loud bang echoed. Her eyes snapped open wide, and with barely a glance at the guy she thought she'd ditched, she dodged past him. Running through the first open door she found, she looked for a hiding spot.

"Wait, a minute." A hand grabbed her arm again. She drove her hand up and out to punch him in the arm, but her fist was blocked. It was the voices nearby that kept her from retaliating.

"Did you see where they went?"

"No, but we need to find out if they heard us."

The voices of the man and woman were enough to get her moving.

Since the man who held her wouldn't let go of her, she pulled him with her. "I'll explain," she whispered. He must have understood the seriousness of the situation when he followed her without objection. Tijan, with the guy glued to her, crept to what she hoped would be a good hiding spot behind some trailers. Crouching down, she yanked her unwanted follower with her. The door was pushed open wide, and a shaft of light penetrated the dimly lit area. Since she couldn't see them, she prayed they couldn't see her or her uninvited guest. After what seemed like forever, it sounded like they were moving off.

"What was that all about?"

Tijan stared at the guy, wishing there was more light so she could see his face clearly.

"Uh. Not sure. I couldn't hear all they were talking about—"

"Really? Because I clearly heard them say the woman running this place was a hooker and they want to cause some problems for her."

"Yeah, well, there might have been that." Tijan wasn't sure how much to trust this man, especially since he had just seemed to show up out of nowhere. "Do you know who they are?"

"No, do you?"

"How would I know? This is my first time here!"

"Yet you seem to know your way around."

Tijan stood up slowly, making sure there was no one else in the area.

"Wait. Now where are you off to? And again, what are you doing snooping around here? Are you with that couple?" August stood up beside her.

"Right, I'm the bad guy here. Get real. I was going to find someone in charge and tell them what I heard. And you?"

"Oh. Alright. I'll come too."

Moving quickly, hoping that she could lose him somehow, she was a bit dismayed that he kept pace with her. She walked a little faster, getting several steps ahead of him. As she came around the office building, stepped off the grass and onto the sidewalk, cutting August off, she came face to face with three people. She had no idea who two of them were and wouldn't have known if she'd seen them again, but the third person definitely grabbed her attention. The woman was stylish, wearing a beige skirt and jacket suit that looked cute on her, along with a matching pair of high heels. It wasn't something that Tijan could have pulled off or have even wanted to. The woman's blonde hair was cut quite short and had a flipped, messy look that made her appear all the more stunning. She was gorgeous.

The best and worst of it was it was like looking in a mirror, although Tijan had to admit, she'd never looked that good. A part of her wanted to laugh and say, 'Ah, you could but you won't'.

Tijan stood there, unable to move, to think, to do anything. Some part of her was waiting for the same reaction from the woman, but there was none. Eventually, it clicked in her fogged brain that her sister wouldn't know her or recognize her. Tijan was dressed like a redheaded country girl on vacation.

The three people barely glanced at Tijan or stopped their conversation, although they did nod in perfunctory greeting as they entered the building. It was a very brief encounter, lasting mere seconds, but it left an indelible impression on Tijan. She pressed her hands to her lips as her body almost vibrated with something just shy of the shakes. It was very unsettling.

Her sister was alive, and not just her sister but her twin. Her other half. But where had she been? Why hadn't she ever contacted her? Wanting to demand answers, Tijan knew she couldn't. At least not yet. This wasn't the time or place, and she was a bit of a wreck. She wasn't sure if she wanted to laugh, cry, or scream. Nothing made sense. She felt like the ground beneath was no longer solid and flat but was now like standing on a ship in a stormy ocean. Her queasy stomach was very much a testament to that.

"Hey guys."

Tijan was jolted back to the present. Her companion came barreling around the corner as he tried to get the attention of the three who had just entered the building. Thankfully, they didn't hear him or realize he was talking to them.

"Come on." He took her arm with the intent of propelling her forward, but Tijan used it to her advantage.

"Will you get your hands off me and keep them off me. I can't stand being manhandled." She purposefully spoke loudly and very snootily.

"Excuse me, is there a problem here?"

"Yes, thank you, security guard. This guy feels like he can grab me whenever he wants to. And I'm tired of it. I just met him." Tijan pulled her glasses down to the brim of her nose and screwed up her face like she was going to cry.

"Oh, come on. You've got to be kidding. That's the best bull—"

The security guard stepped forward. Tijan used that to her advantage and moved back several steps behind him. August glared at her. She shrugged. She'd never done anything like this, but inside she was freaking out and didn't know how to handle any of what she'd seen or heard, and she most certainly didn't have time to be detained or questioned.

"It's okay. I just need to get going. Thank you, sir." Tijan smiled winningly at him as she calmly walked away. She was under the impression August had tried to follow, but the security guard had stepped in his way.

"My name's August. I'm the new mechanic. I have a meeting I was just heading to but I was curious about why that woman was snooping around here."

Tijan didn't turn to look but hustled around the corner before sprinting for her car. It didn't take long to forget her encounter with the guy, her mind busy firing with thoughts of her sister. She'd found her. But why was she alive? And where the hell had she been all her life?

CHAPTER 11

"HELLO JAMES."

"Uh, Mr. Tesimmon. I didn't know we were going to meet today."

The well-dressed gentleman in his three-piece suit already had one of his bodyguards heading over to the hidden bar. He was in the process of opening it and pouring the man two fingers of James' expensive scotch. Mr. T sat down in the leather padded chair that he'd been sure had been purchased for him.

"Oh, it feels good to sit. It's muggy out today. It's a bit draining, isn't it?"

James had trouble with these benign, anal conversations that Mr. Tesimmon always started his 'visits' with. Even though it only happened once or twice a year, they weren't something he could ever forget. All they did was spark a thread of fear that slithered up his spine and perched in his throat, ready to strike. This was one person he hadn't been able to control.

"It is." He knew better than to try to steer the conversation or even start one. Mr. T always chose where it went and got annoyed way too fast. Two things he'd learned when this man was in his presence—never look him in the eye but never take his eye off him and never presume to know what he wanted. Oh, and one more thing he'd learned. Never interrupt silence, no matter how uncomfortable it was.

These were all things that James wasn't good at. As the owner of one of the largest hotel chains in Canada, he hadn't gotten there by being polite or silent, but he'd learned to be different with this man. He sat there, his fingers curled tightly on his desk chair, while he kept his gaze on the man who could make him disappear in an instant. A man he thought at one time he could control. James had been so set on taking his father down he hadn't thought about the consequences of his actions. He'd needed money and hadn't cared how he got it. His first choice had turned him down flat. If the Johansens had come through, he would never have been in this predicament. Their reaction when he'd presented their granddaughter hadn't been what he'd expected. Or wanted. And they hadn't been about to fork over several million dollars so he could grow his hotel empire.

It still didn't seem wrong to him. His goal had been to give them the granddaughter they didn't know existed from a daughter they'd disowned for money. Unfortunately, they hadn't wanted either of them, and most definitely not for money.

He'd done what he'd needed to do, and now he was reliant on this man. Although he'd tried many times to get him out of his life, James realized that was never going to happen. Unfortunately, this loan shark hadn't been the only one James had needed to borrow money from in the beginning. He'd played a dangerous game of getting money from one to pay off another while trying to build his legacy, a chain of hotels. He was going to have to do something drastic if he was ever going to get these lowlifes out of his life for good.

"You're trying to buy Caspian Winery."

James was too schooled to show any reaction, but he thought he'd kept that pretty quiet. Was it someone on his end? If so, it meant it had to be one of four people. Or had it been someone on the Caspian Winery's end? Who and how many were on this guy's payroll? The thought that he was being betrayed was unforgivable. But betrayed to this man? Dangerous.

"I've thought about it. It's like any business. If they are doing well, then they are worth looking into buying."

"Yes, and a winery, a very successful one, gives you a bit of that snot-nosed attitude that makes the rich think you're God. I like that about you, James. See, we think alike. I invested in you so that I would look legit. And you're investing in other snooty businesses, so you look legit. It works." He smiled, and the diamond on his front tooth sparkled as though mocking James.

"I just like to keep my options open. And a winery does work well with a large hotel. We serve a lot of wine. If I get the right one, it saves us money, and we'd be able to make more by selling the wine to customers." It took all of James' willpower not to tell the man to get the hell out of his office and out of his business.

"But you've already bought three wineries," he was saying, "and it appears that business isn't all that great at any of them. In fact, you shut one down. So why would you need that big, successful winery? Hmmm. I think this is a perfect time to expand my horizons. And you owe me."

"I paid you back the loan you gave me with interest."

"Yes, and without me, you wouldn't have been able to build this dynasty of hotels. Without me, you'd be nothing. You'd still be trying to take your father down. I helped you succeed with that. You're actually one of the few I've loaned money to that paid me back everything. But see, that's the problem. I decided that wasn't good for business. And since your business is doing so well, I thought I'd add in an 'I saved your ass' tax. The government does teach a person a lot about how to run a business, if one pays attention. Whenever the government needs money, it adds a tax." He shrugged. "I'm doing the same." He sat back and sipped his whiskey as though he had all the time in the world.

James felt sick. That didn't happen very often. In fact, the last time had probably been the first time he'd borrowed money from this creep. James had been young, impulsive, and pissed. His anger was aimed mostly at his father. He'd been willing to sign on with the devil to hurt his father where he could the most—in business. And it would now appear he had given his soul to the devil. James didn't know where this was going, but the more the man talked about it, the more it wasn't going to bode well for him.

"I want in on that deal."

"Mr. Tesimmon. You've been a great help to me in the past, but we concluded our business. I paid you back all I owed you, plus a hefty amount of interest." Like ten times the amount, but he wasn't going to say that to this guy.

"Here's the thing. I need to create a sense of legitimacy. And you were my ticket last time, so why go looking for someone new? You've done well, which wouldn't have happened without my money."

James kept silent. He was not including this man in any of his deals, no matter what he needed. This hotel was James'. He'd worked hard to make it the five-star chain that it was.

"I understand your daughter is an unwed mother."

He was sure the man also knew where she was living and with whom, but he wasn't about to ask that. But he wondered where he was going with his statement.

"Yes. She is."

"That's perfect."

James knew he shouldn't feel a sense of relief that the man wasn't going on about the business but he was. Mr. T had asked about his daughter off and on over the years but there had never been any interest in her, but something had changed in the way he asked this time. Biting his tongue to keep himself from blurting something out that wouldn't be good for him, James waited, curious about where this was going. Would the man use his daughter against him or his business? An uncomfortable feeling climbed up his throat, giving him a restricted feeling and making swallowing difficult.

Mr. T sipped the scotch that had been poured for him. "Hmmm. Not your best stuff, James. Trying to get cheap on me?"

James tried to swallow, but that would not be possible. The bile in his throat would probably choke him. "I'm sorry, Mr. Tesimmon. It's the same brand I always buy, but I'll look into it. I do have a new bottle of 40-year-old scotch, if you'd like—"

He waved him off before standing and setting his glass on the polished top of the desk. "No but don't make that mistake again."

James nodded, feeling too weak in the knees to be able to stand, although he would have to soon. He wasn't intimidated by many, but he was smart enough to be wary of this man. He was only a few inches shorter than James' own 6'2" frame, but the evil that thrived within him made him seem all that much larger.

"I want your daughter to meet my son."

"What?"

"I would like to see my son married and it would be a great merging of our two businesses. She seems smart, and she's gorgeous. And hopefully understands better than you, what this could mean to our businesses. My son has done well for himself. Got himself a respectable, highfa-lutin job." The man grinned as he stared at James and then burst out laughing like it was best joke ever.

James had never been one to squirm or shy away from controversy but Mr. T made him feel like the devil had just landed in his life and was going to dance around him until he was six feet under. It felt as though all the wrongs he'd ever done were coming back for payment and the payment was his business, which for him was his soul.

"I'll get a hold of you and let you know when."

James pushed himself to his feet and nodded as Mr. Tesimmon turned to leave. "By the way, that lawyer of yours is quite the shark."

"Oh?" James wasn't sure where this conversation was going but he knew that he'd never shared with this man the identity of his lawyer.

"Yes, Eleanor is superb at knowing the ins and outs of acquiring businesses, especially those that don't want to be acquired." With that, he had his two bodyguards, who'd come in with him, step into line close behind him. Two other bodyguards waiting for him outside the door took the lead. It made it pretty much impossible for anyone to get near the man or even take a shot at him. Something James had thought of many times over the years. Not that he would have done it personally, but he was sure he could have paid someone. The fear of failing had always kept him from even attempting it, though. He did not want to be on Mr. T's hit list. People didn't just die if they crossed him. They were tormented, tortured, beaten and then allowed to die in the most heinous, painful way possible.

That would not be him.

And it looked like his once-upon-a-time money savior was back in his life, whether or not he wanted him to be.

The conversation about his lawyer, Eleanor, left him feeling a bit unsettled. That she worked with Tesimmon bothered him a lot and surprised him she hadn't mentioned it to him. Not that they'd ever shared their professional business with each other, but he didn't enjoy knowing she was working with organized crime. He was sure that Eleanor hadn't had a choice. When Mr. T made a decision, you were going to help him, whether you wanted to or not. A fleeting thought that she would share details of his business with Tesimmon wouldn't go away. Eleanor was a professional and would never cross that line. He hoped. But if it wasn't her, how did Mr. Tesimmon know who he was using for legal advice? He'd have to ask Eleanor the next time he saw her.

Since that was a headache that he couldn't do much about at that point, he thought about what else Mr. T had said. It looked like he might have to sacrifice his daughter. Maybe he could use this to his advantage and finally turn the tables on this man, who felt he owned him. James just needed to know how badly and why Mr. T wanted his daughter for his son when he could have bought him any woman. It would not be easy to find information about the man or his connections. It was a tight-knit group of people who had no problems selling out anyone to stay on the man's good side.

He had to own Caspian Winery. Then he'd tear it down.

A cough caught him off guard. He reached for some more cold medicine he'd finally picked up that morning, sure that it would kick whatever bug he'd caught out of his system.

He needed to talk to JT, his Vice President of Sales, and not because JT knew anything about the potential deal with Caspian Winery since he hadn't been brought into those conversations, but rather to have him buy their wine for his hotels. He wanted to purchase a large amount of Caspian's wine and get it on their menus. Maybe he could get into their good graces. Dorothea had refused to meet with him, but if he was her biggest client? That might change things in his favor.

What he needed was to get his two 'helpers', as he liked to call them, out there and snoop around—they had done some snooping legitimately but now it might be time for some not so legal searching. The more he knew, the better the strategy he could put in place to make sure the winery was his.

Pushing himself to his feet, he was surprised that the world seemed to be moving. His hand slapped down on the desk to steady himself. One thing he'd learned early on was never to let anyone see your weakness. And this was definitely a weakness. He was going to do something he'd never done in his thirty-five-year career. He was going home to rest. But first he needed to talk to his daughter.

Could Tarin be the answer to him finally paying off his lifetime debt the man felt he owed him?

CHAPTER 12

TIJAN TUGGED ON THE wig. Being a redhead had never been something she aspired to be, but she had to admit she liked the auburn-colored hair. And it didn't look too bad on her. As long as she kept her hair down close to her face and kept on the large sunglasses that she thought looked ridiculous but was assured by the lady in the store they were the 'in' thing, she shouldn't be recognizable, especially if that was her twin or someone who looked like her. She'd read many stories and had seen many pictures of people showing a brother or cousin or even a parent that could easily have passed off as twins.

It could be just someone who looked like her. But it wasn't. It was her sister. Staying at Caspian hadn't been an option. She wasn't ready to talk to someone who hadn't been a part of her life and looked way out of her league. She tried to find information on her sister. No matter how much she searched on the Internet, she couldn't find a picture of someone who looked like her. And trying to find someone by their first name got her nowhere. Stopping at Knight's Computers was a last-minute idea. She'd called Caspian Winery but had been told that 'no Tarin works here'. Since the old guy had reacted so strongly to her a few days before, she had to assume that her sister spent time there. Other than almost running into her the day before the only other link she had was the computer place.

Parking in a new spot so she could approach the building from a different angle, she got out of her rental. This time, since she had on her wig, she crossed the street and walked by the computer store, Knight's Computers. A few people were entering and leaving the store. She lurked by the door, waiting to peek inside to see what was there. When the next customer came along, she waited until they'd entered and then casually grabbed the door as though she was going to enter. She dug in the massive shoulder bag she was carrying to make it look like she was searching for something, but her gaze was taking in everything. The inside was pretty much what she'd expected. It was nicely decorated, welcoming. There was a display area that had some computers there to look at but not for sale. There were some other displays that showed more about the inner workings of the computer with what looked like explanations for all the parts. That was something she'd never seen a computer store do before. A couple of customers were standing at the long counter, talking to a few clerks. And there were a few more in line, waiting. Beyond that, she couldn't see anything as the office area and the computer maintenance area were behind walls. It hadn't told her much.

Sighing, she released the door. The traffic was fairly heavy, as the afternoon rush hour was just getting started. Movement off to her right caught her attention.

"Hey, what are you doing there?"

She jerked back. The man's harsh tone startled her. It was the old guy she'd seen the day before, and who she was sure had recognized her was now glaring at her. He came out of nowhere. Again.

"Do you have an appointment?"

"Uh... no. Not today, but I just umm—wanted to know where the office was. You know, for when I do have to come here." It sounded so lame.

"Why? Who are you meeting with? When are you meeting with them? What's your meeting for?"

Clearing her throat, Tijan tried to get her scrambled brain cells to come up with something. "Uh—next week."

"What do you know about computers?"

"Very little."

"So, you're here about..."

She had the uncontrollable urge to scratch her scalp. The wig suddenly felt like it was made of little strands of wire. His intense look caught her attention. She'd missed what he'd said. "What?"

"Why are you here? Maybe I should call Graham. He might want to talk to you."

From her limited research, Tijan knew that Graham and Guy owned Knights Computers. "Look, I'm meeting them next week. I'm just finding my way around. Getting lost is something I'm good at and I don't want to be late when I do meet with them. Sorry if I've caused any trouble."

"Reconnaissance. Good." With that, he turned and ambled down the alley. Tijan was tempted to follow him just to see where he went and who he might be. He reminded her of someone who might live on the street, although now that she thought about that, she wasn't sure what that meant. His khaki clothes weren't maybe the cleanest, but he appeared to be fairly clean. He could have used a shower, but he wasn't as filthy as she'd thought from the day before. He just seemed to appear and disappear, like he was some sort of security. There were signs that he was definitely ex-military—the stance, the walk, the abruptness—all went with what she knew about that profession.

His disappearing around the corner was her cue to get out of there. She walked briskly to the other end of the block. A gust of wind suddenly whipped up, blowing her long red wig up into her face and spitting sand and dirt at her. It was like a mini whirlwind but lasted for only a few minutes. Hugging the side of the building, she ducked her head to protect her face. When it finally ended, she felt gritty and dirty. She took off her glasses and, with a quick glance around, pulled off the wig and stuffed it in her bag. The lights changed, so she made her way across the street, rubbing her head as she went. The fresh-brewed coffee scent from the coffee shop she'd noticed the last time wafted to her, begging her to come and get a good cup of coffee.

Holding the coffee creation that she was sure was loaded with sugar, she made her way back out and was headed around the corner when there was suddenly a commotion. A car slammed on its brakes and whipped around in the middle of the road. Car honks and other screeching tires soon followed. Tijan pressed her hand to her chest as she stared in horror at the idiot driver. Feeling stressed and having had enough of the city craziness, she rounded the corner and headed back to her vehicle half-way down the block. She'd almost reached it when suddenly there were more tires screeching. A car came to a full stop, blocking her way.

"He wants to see you."

CHAPTER 13

AUGUST STOPPED AT THE receptionist's desk. "Hi. I have an appointment with Dorothea Lindell. I'm August Renner. But I need to see her about something else. Right now."

Karen, the blond receptionist, eyed him for a moment. He'd met her in the first week but she'd been anything but friendly. He'd been so busy with getting the equipment up and running and figuring everything out, he hadn't had much time to get to know too many of the staff, something he was going to have to change, if he was staying.

"Have a seat and I'll let her know."

August wanted to remain standing at the desk, but it was obvious she would not do anything until he moved ten feet away. He sat down in one of the comfortable-looking chairs in the waiting room. Once he was seated, he could hear her whispering on the phone. A few minutes later, Guy and Graham came out to get him.

"Hi August. You're early. Sorry to call you in on your day off."

August knew he had crossed a line by insisting to see her immediately. Both men were standing in a way that let him know he'd have to go through them. August stood up, forcing each to take a step back.

"If we can go? I'll explain why."

"Alright." Graham led the way. And Guy fell in behind him, letting him know it had been done on purpose. They were very protective of the owner. He wondered if what he had to tell them was linked to why.

They entered a medium-sized room that looked small because it was swamped by a large boardroom table. Dorothea was seated at the end of the table while LJ was seated to her right. Even though they were both technically his boss, he'd dealt with Guy and Graham for the most part. August walked to the end of the table, quite aware that Guy and Graham were right behind him.

"Mrs. Lindell—"

"Thank you for your manners but it's Dorothea. And you're August."

He smiled as he took her hand, liking her directness. The one time he'd met her, she'd given him a brief run-down about Caspian and its high standards. He'd gotten the message. "Nice to see you, Dorothea." He then turned to the other woman.

"Good morning, August. I understand you have our roosters down the road beat."

August turned a bit red; it seemed to be a thing that he was an early bird. He much preferred working when it was quiet so he could get so much more done.

"Good morning, LJ."

"I also understand none of your additional hours are being reflected in your timesheet."

"We agreed on 40 hours a week—"

"Yes, but you're doing more like 60. I know your excuse is that you want to get things caught up and rather than ask for the time, you'll just do the work. I know that we've fallen way behind in fixing equipment around here. So I get it. But from here on out, you tell me when you are going to be putting in those long days. And they will be on your pay."

Graham laughed. "Damn, it's good to see someone else get hell—only you get it for doing something good. Jolly good chap."

August was never sure how to take Graham. He was a walking brain, but he also had quite a quirky sense of humor. At times like this, though, he appreciated it.

Dorothea looked pointedly at him. "You heard her. She's in charge."

"In title only. Second in command but please don't tell Dorothea I know that."

August smiled at the byplay. She had nothing but respect for the older woman. Dorothea had taken the reigns from her father and had turned the place from a small winery to a world-class one. They produced and shipped wine worldwide, which was not an easy thing to do. At least he'd surmised as much from the bit of snooping he'd done on the Internet about how wineries worked and the provincial and federal laws that regulated how and where they could sell them. LJ was truly a stunning woman, but there was no doubt that she had the same backbone as Dorothea. He could understand why she had been chosen, even if her previous business wasn't one that many would normally consider appropriate.

"Look. Sorry to barge in but I just ran into some characters on your property that I thought you should know about. I know this is supposed to be a review or a reporting of where we're at and where we need to be but I felt this was more important."

"Sit, please." Dorothea waved her hand. "Tea or coffee?"

"Coffee is fine. Thank you." August sat a few chairs away down the side of the table. Guy sat between him and Dorothea, while Graham and Tarin sat beside LJ, across the table from him. Waiting wasn't one of his strong suits. When he saw something that needed to be done, he did something about it. He started drumming his fingers on the table, not aware of it until Graham burst out laughing.

"Ole chap, I do believe you're one of us."

The others chuckled. Unsure what that meant, August smiled and shrugged.

Dorothea shook her head. "Impatient. You do fit right in. Okay, now tell us what this is about."

August leaned forward. "There was this couple and, well, this woman. But the two people, the man and woman, were talking about Caspian. I didn't hear everything they said, but they did mention that there was a hooker running—" August's eyes opened wide as they gravitated toward LJ, which is who he was sure they had been referring to. There was no secret that she had run a high-end escort service. That information was all over the internet. There weren't many details as to what that meant or looked like, though.

He hadn't thought through what he had been going to say. "I'm sorry. I'm just—"

"And?"

August turned to look at Dorothea, whose lips were stretched thin and whose pleasant demeanor had vanished. "And that they wanted to make some trouble for her."

"LJ, is something going on?"

"Thank you for your concern, Dorothea but nothing new, at least not that I'm aware of."

"Then why is someone targeting you? Do you think it's someone from your old business?"

"We can look into it if you don't mind us snooping a bit into your past?" Guy spoke up.

"Right, like you didn't do that before I was hired. I'm quite sure you know more about my past than I do."

"Uh. I don't think this is aimed at LJ personally. It's aimed at Caspian Winery. At least, that was the feeling I got. I didn't hear everything. That other woman I mentioned, I think she heard a lot more than I did." August interrupted their conversation.

"What woman?" Graham rested his arms on the table.

"Well, I'm not sure. I was trying to bring her in here when we met one of the security guards, that new guy, and she cried 'wolf'. I'm sure she left. She did not seem to want to meet with you. I don't know if she was with them, she just heard something she shouldn't have, or she was here to cause her own trouble. She seemed to be sneaking around when I caught up with her."

"Yeah?"

"Maybe that new camera we installed at the front of the building is angled enough that we can see what she was driving?" LJ suggested.

"It's not. We were more concerned about ensuring that no one could approach or leave the building without being seen. After those break-ins and the trouble last year with the wine and shipments being tampered with, we were more focused on the buildings." Guy sighed. "We might have to install more."

"We'll still be able to get her picture off the camera. August can confirm which woman it was."

"For sure." Suddenly, everyone went quiet. August realized that Guy, Graham and LJ were all on their phones, tapping madly. Dorothea, despite appearing amazing for someone in her 80s, suddenly looked very old and tired.

"Are you alright?" August asked. It was as if he'd set off the sprinkler system the way the other three jumped up and were soon hovering around Dorothea, encouraging her to lie down.

She looked around them at August and smiled. "Your meeting was not what it should have been. As my granddaughter would say, it's been a bit of a bust. Please excuse me. I do need to get some rest. Guy?"

He took her arm and escorted her from the room.

August felt guilty for laying that bit of news at her feet. The stress was obviously too much. "Hey, I'm sorry. I shouldn't have done that. It would have been better if I'd told you in a different way. I hope she's going to be okay."

Graham shrugged. "Honestly, some days I think she'll live forever and others, it scares me. She's such a driving force. And don't worry, you did the right thing. She would have been ticked if you hadn't included her."

LJ smiled. "Yes. And I would have been the one to tell her which would have been much worse. She knows she can't do the CEO role anymore, but she doesn't want to give it up. By the way, she's impressed, as am I, with the work you've been doing. I don't think we've had our machines up and running so far in advance of harvest time."

"I don't have them all—"

"No. But you have a few things fixed that have need-ed to be for a while, even the large garage door which wouldn't open all the way. That wasn't on your job list but you did it. That's what impresses us most. Thank you." LJ stood and offered her hand before turning to Graham. "We need to step up security."

She smiled at them both and left. August stood slowly, feeling like he'd stepped onto foreign soil and he wasn't clear on the language.

Graham laughed. "Don't worry. You'll get used to the quirky way people here work. Be straight with them and you'll never have a problem. Good job, mate. Only been here a few and already you've got several gold stars."

"Did you hear anything back about a job interview?" Tarin asked.

August had applied for the position as head mechanic at C-Lite Hotels, although he'd wondered if he'd known what he was getting into. "No. Nothing. I don't know if I'll even get an interview."

"Maybe I need to get a hold of my father and see if I can somehow bring up this position."

"I don't think it's a good idea to connect us in any way. If your dad is as savvy as you're telling me, it could alert him to my being a part of your life. So far, I understand that I'm not really on the books here, so if he checks, he won't find that out. I'll follow up and see if they are doing interviews yet." Shaking his head, he was more confused than ever about what he was getting into.

It reminded him, though, that he had originally had a plan for finding his father. After hearing so much about Tarin's, it made him wonder if he wanted to. His dad had abandoned him at age nine. That had to be a pretty cold man who would do that. It still baffled him why his mom had reached out to these people. People who swore they'd never met his mom and yet they'd hired him. Why? Had his mom just been taking care of him like she'd always felt she'd had to? Or was she leading him somewhere?

CHAPTER 14

STARTLED, THE CUP OF coffee went flying. Tijan wasn't sure which freaked her out more, the size of the guy in the suit or his macho stance.

"W-who?"

"Let's go."

"Uh, I think you have the wrong person. I am busy. Hey, let me go. Do you mind? Hel—" Her attempt at yelling was quickly squashed by the man who forcefully shoved her into the car, slamming the door in her face. The chht of the locks being engaged had her grabbing for the door but no matter how hard she pulled on the handle or slammed against the door, nothing happened.

"Really, Tarin. As if your behavior wasn't bad enough, what are you wearing?"

Tijan's head snapped around while her body jerked back to the relative safety of pressing hard against the door. Slipping her hand behind her back, she yanked on the door handle. Nothing happened. She stared at a middle-aged man, who had a light sprinkling of grey around his temples. He was dressed impeccably in a three-piece suit that didn't appear to have a single wrinkle in it. She stared at him with eyes wide.

"Who—?" She stopped talking. He'd called her Tarin. Although it was burning a hole in her head trying to figure out who he was, she figured it was best not to ask. He was talking to her in a way that suggested they were well acquainted.. Tijan remained quiet and stared. If she could find out something about her sister, then this might be worth it.

"If this is something new to annoy me, it's worked. Now you can stop. That's not why I wanted to talk to you."

"Abduct me, you mean."

"God Tarin, stop the melodrama. What's with you? I want to talk to you because I want to buy Caspian Winery. I need you to get me some information. What will make that old lady sell? I've offered her a good price, a great price well above market value, and she won't even contemplate negotiating with me. I had planned on calling you later, but when my driver saw you in that ridiculous get-up on the street, I figured now was as good a time as any."

Tijan glanced toward the front of the car, only to realize that a darkened glass partition effectively cut off the front from the back.

"W–w–." She wasn't sure what to say or how to figure out who he was. "Why do you want it?"

"For you, of course. It would be my present to you. You can run it. Tear it down. Show me you can run it, and you'll be the next CEO of the C-Lite Hotel chain. Until your son is old enough, anyway. I have to go."

The door behind her opened silently, almost causing her to tumble out backwards. Flailing her arms out, she was able to plant her hands on the interior and prevent herself from sprawling outwards onto her back. As soon as she felt stable, she didn't waste time but quickly turned and stepped out awkwardly as she grabbed the door to hold herself upright.

"I'll pick you up tomorrow, Tarin. And stop wearing those ridiculous clothes. You've made your point." He coughed. It was deep and throaty and sounded very painful.

"Hey, are you alright?"

"Leave it, Tarin. Now isn't the time for your concern."

She stared into the dark cavern, barely able to make out the man who was talking to her, the man who apparently felt he had some control over her. The door closed, forcing her to move her hand. The car pulled away and drove down the street.

The bizarreness of the situation wasn't even registering. In fact, she wasn't sure what made sense. She stared at the limo that soon vanished from sight around the next corner. Her brain felt like it had been stuffed with cotton, so she couldn't absorb anything she'd just heard. She drove back to her hotel, never quite sure how she had made it. The first thing she did was head to the liquor store across the street and grab a case of beer.

This was going to be a lot harder than she'd thought. The event revealed way too much that she wasn't sure she was ready to deal with.

All she'd wanted was to know if her sister was alive, and if things worked out, meet her and find out why she'd never reached out. But now she wasn't sure. Some middle-aged, wealthy man who seemed to know her well was ordering her around like she was his property.

Was her sister married to the old guy? Were they estranged?

That thought made her gag. If it were true, she and her sister were so very different. The man obviously had enough money to buy and sell anything he wanted. He was going to pay her to get dirt on someone. What kind of sister did she have? Was she an informant? Was he a high government official? He seemed too sleazy for that.

Was he Tarin's stepfather?

Tijan pressed her hands to her head. Who was she? She didn't even have her sister's last name.

Tijan flopped down on the bed in her room. She just wanted the thoughts to stop. They didn't make sense, and they just kept her head spinning around and around. Was she even going to like her sister if they ever met? She had a son?

Her mind would not stop. Jumping up, she opened a beer and downed half of it. The man said he wanted Caspian Winery for her. Was he trying to buy her?

Who the hell was he?

Chapter 15

"WHEN'S THE NEXT SHIPMENT?" Mr. T sat back on his plush leather sofa, drinking his scotch. There was a splash from the pool. He glanced up and couldn't help but smile. There was just something about scantily clad women frolicking in water. And they were so easy to find. Flash a little money and they came running. His four bodyguards, who were always stationed strategically around the veranda and pool, all seemed quite happy with their jobs, especially on days like this.

For Mr. T, it was a reminder that he'd made it. The scrappy kid from the streets, who'd had to use his smarts to eat and stay alive, had made it. He was now a very successful businessman. Even though most wouldn't see it that way, he was happy with the dynasty he'd created. However, it was time to expand it. He wasn't at the top. He was still seen as the scum of the streets, a street hustler. What he wanted was respect and the acknowledgement that the true mafia kings got. He deserved it and was going to get it. C-Lite Hotels was key to his plan. Even though he'd been using them for years to run drugs, it was time he stepped things up and showed them all who was boss.

"There's nothing booked."

The man swore. "There is always one happening. You've been stalling for weeks. I don't like that. I have things that need to be moved across the border. And now. So give me the date and time."

"I am telling you, there isn't one. I don't know what is happening or why, but there isn't anything, at least that I can find."

"Have they figured out what you're doing? Are you a problem?"

The woman gasped. "No. No, they haven't, and no, I'm not. I've done a lot for you over the years."

She was begging. He liked that. She knew what he was capable of. It had helped to keep her in line and helping him for a long time.

"Look, Mr. T. I've never let you down. I'll find out what's going on and why something hasn't been arranged. I think some of the problem might be that there have been complaints about the linens that we're getting. The last few batches were cheap, had some stains and smelled like coffee."

Mr. T. laughed. "The coffee is important, as it masks the smell of what we're shipping. It keeps those canine-sniffing animals from detecting my drugs. You get a date booked. You make sure that the hotel keeps using that company to buy its linens and supplies. Got it?"

"But I don't have—"

"You wouldn't want your son to be the next victim, would you?"

She gasped. Mr. T smiled as he clicked off. He knew that she'd understood the message—he didn't care what pull she did or didn't have. He expected her to come through. And if she didn't, he would.

CHAPTER 16

TIJAN CLIMBED OUT OF her rental, yanking off her wig and tossing it onto the passenger seat. Unpinning her hair, she rubbed her head as she did so. She hadn't realized that wearing a wig would be so hot and itchy. For some reason, she'd thought she needed it. But now that she was there, she decided against it. She just wanted to meet her sister. Enough of the games and the crazy running around. It was time to find out who this woman was.

The area was quiet, and the parking lot was empty. She casually looked around, briefly wondering if she'd lost her mind. Knight's Computers was the answer, which was the only reason she could figure out why parking at their office had seemed like a good idea. After seeing her at the winery, Tijan needed to be close to her. She wanted to meet her but didn't know where or how to make that happen. Coming in the early morning had seemed like a good idea and the best way she could accidentally meet her. And she needed to tell her about the crazy man who just might be stalking her. Since she didn't know how to walk up and demand to know why her sister hadn't been part of her life, she had the need to feel close to her, and this was the only place that seemed possible. She was feeling a bit like she'd been discarded.

It wasn't her sister's fault, but it hurt.

Leaning back against her SUV, she looked around at the deserted area. It was so far from what she knew and loved. There wasn't a stitch of grass or anything green other than the few dandelions that had found their way up through small cracks in the concrete. It was depressing and made her long for the wide-open ranges of Alberta.

A nice, sleek, black car pulled into the empty parking lot. Startled, she wasn't sure what to do. Since it was such a fancy vehicle, she had to assume it belonged to the owner. Could her sister be in it? She watched it for a moment, but when it pulled up at an angle, blocking most of the parking lot, she grew nervous. The man from the day before had said he'd pick her up. Although this was a different vehicle and not waiting to see if she was right, she yanked open the door and hopped in. Before she could close it, a large, beefy hand clamped down on the door, preventing her from closing it. Tijan leaned back and brought her feet up, ready to kick with all her might when she recognized him as the guy from the day before.

"Excuse me. I'm looking for—" *What the hell was she looking for?* "There's supposed to be a huge shopping mall around here. I think I'm a bit lost."

"Please come with us, Ms. Roth." The second man had gotten out of the car.

She looked from one to the other. "Who?"

"Please get out."

Her eyes darted around as she tried to determine her options. Both men, however, now stood in her line of vision, cutting off everything.

The guy holding the door indicated she should precede them.

"Look, I'm not Ms. Roth. I'm not sure who that is." Were they talking about her sister? She didn't know her sister's last name or if she still went by Tarin. Although the encounter the day before would suggest she did.

The two men were now crowding her. Though they hadn't touched her, she was feeling very uncomfortable with their closeness. One grabbed the SUV door, making it clear he was intent on closing it. She debated whether to drive away, but they were blocking not only her but her car. Straightening, she forced a smile she wasn't feeling and climbed out. It was either that or she was sure the other guy was going to grab her and haul her to their car. She started walking, hoping for some space, except they seemed glued to her back as they carefully steered her to the back door of the car. The door was open, but it was dark inside, like that of looking into a dark cavern. She tried to sidestep, only to find herself blocked. The only option was for her to climb in. People had vanished this way. Fear was doing a tango inside her. Her eyes darted everywhere as she looked for a mode of escape. She put her hand on the door, pasted on a winning smile and turned to face her two sour-faced abductors. She was about to scream 'fire', as she'd been told that would get people's attention where 'help' or 'rape' might not, but they didn't give her a chance to say anything.

"Your father says this can be done the easy way or the hard way. You decide."

She froze. Her father? The man she had asked about a few times but had been told he was a bad man but her mother was sure had died. The man who had never looked for her. Her father, the man she'd forgotten from a young age, as Cal had been more of a dad than she could have asked for. The man who had apparently felt it was okay to scare the crap out of her.

Her father... knowing this was probably the biggest mistake she could make, she freely climbed into the car. "Do you mind if we stop and get something to eat on the way? I'm kind of hungry. Is there anywhere around here where we could get a burger? One with good Alberta beef?" She almost laughed because she couldn't have eaten anything at that moment. It was funny that she'd chosen a burger for breakfast. Her nerves were getting the better of her.

The two men ignored her as they got in the front. The door locks clicked immediately, sending a shiver down her spine. Her mind was chaotic with questions. Who was her father? Why hadn't her mom ever told her about him? What did he want with her? Who was Ms. Roth? Her sister? Since her sister hadn't been named in the newspaper article, all she had to go on was Tarin, and there were a lot of them on the Internet. Finding one that looked like her was more difficult than one would think, and Tijan would rather ride her horse than be on the internet. Besides, it wouldn't tell her why she'd been ignored by her sister all these years. And it would appear it wouldn't tell her why she'd been ignored by her father as well.

What if these guys are going to kill me?

Feeling very freaked out but knowing there wasn't much she could do, she took some deep breaths. She sat back against the leather seat, appreciating the soft quality. It was expensive. The car was expensive. The two hench-men looked expensive. Did her father have money? Who was he, and if she was his daughter, why the kidnapping treatment?

She had no way of knowing who he was, although now that she was heading to see him, she remembered him mentioning something about a hotel chain. Or at least she'd thought that was something he'd said. A lot of the conversation was a blur, and she hadn't wanted to relive it. After four beers, she'd told herself it hadn't been as crazy as she'd thought.

Only it appeared it had been. Something was very off. She stared out the darkened window at the streets, cars and people whizzing by as she tried to get her bearings.

"Where are we going?"

As she expected, neither looked at her nor answered.

"Can we listen to some music? It's a little quiet in here."

Again, nothing. They drove for what seemed a very long time before they finally pulled into an underground parkade beneath a huge hotel. Unfortunately, she didn't know which one. They soon entered a large cubicle, but beyond that she couldn't see much. The windows of the car were dark, and there was only a faint glow of light coming from somewhere outside the car. The walls felt like they were moving in on her.

Weren't people killed in places like this?

She got an odd feeling that they were moving upwards. It was the smoothest ride she'd ever had, but it also left her feeling very unsettled. Her hands gripped the seat as her head snapped around.

"Hey! Where are we going?" Panic was setting in as she grabbed the door and yanked on it. As expected, it was locked, but that didn't stop her from diving across the seat to try the other door. No luck there either. Turning, she used her foot to kick the door.

Suddenly, the door opened and light spilled in. One of the henchmen stood there, frowning at her. She was stretched out on the seat with her feet pulled back ready to kick hard. He indicated that she should get out. Sitting up, she peered through the opening. She couldn't see much but slowly climbed out. They were in a wide-open cement enclosure, with only two other vehicles—a Mercedes and a sporty bright yellow Corvette. There wasn't anything else in the garage, though it could fit at least another thirty cars. She noted that the stairs and the passenger elevator were maybe fifty feet behind them and were side by side. They had gone in an elevator but she wasn't sure if they'd gone up or down.

Her bravado suddenly vanished. There was no guarantee that these men worked for her father, and even if they did, she wasn't sure she was prepared to meet him this way. She didn't even know his name.

Her two guides, who were dressed in nicely tailored and fitted suits, were slowly climbing out of the car, obviously not too concerned about her anymore. She'd never understood the need to be so dressed up. Even the Secret Service agents were always dressed as if they were going to a formal event. Didn't their parents ever tell them they just might ruin their suits dodging after some crazy woman trying to escape?

Thankful she'd worn her runners that day, Tijan didn't waste a minute as she headed for the exit. She could hear their pounding feet behind her. She reached the door, yanked it open and stopped dead. There was nowhere to go except through another door. The hardwood, elegant door made it very clear that it wasn't the opening to a stairwell as she'd hoped. Her two guards, huffing a bit, didn't say a word but crowded her through the door that one of them opened with a security code.

She'd been scared before. There was the time she'd been riding in the foothills, checking the cattle, when she'd come face to face with a bear. Her horse had become skittish and had bucked. It had taken all of Tijan's skill to stay on her back. The bear, feeling threatened, had stood on her hind legs and had taken a swipe at Tango, leaving scars across her chest. The horse had bolted with Tijan barely clinging to its back. Thankfully, she'd finally been able to get her horse under control, but not before they'd raced a few miles at breakneck speed through brush and over rough terrain. The panic and heart-pumping fear wasn't something she'd ever forget or want to repeat. She thought that nothing in her life would top that. But now it was clear she was wrong. The fear crawling through her body felt like an invader, wrapping her in its talons, choking off her air supply.

Had anyone ever been killed in a fancy office?

CHAPTER 17

"GOOD TO SEE YOU, Son."

"Father. Is there any reason we had to meet? I thought we agreed years ago, it's better that people don't know we're related. We should connect only through burner phones."

"Yes. There's a reason we had to meet. I felt it was important. Got it?"

His son stared defiantly at him but was smart enough to keep his mouth shut.

"I had my guys make sure you weren't followed. And although it burns your ass to follow my instructions, I'm glad to see you did. Switching vehicles three times makes it pretty hard for someone to tail you—especially with my men standing vigilant at each exchange. You're safe." Mr. T grabbed his son and hugged him. He'd wanted to be more a part of his son's life, but then his son probably wouldn't be alive. Some rival gang would have taken him out years ago to force Mr. T's hand in some dealing or another. No, he'd handled it right. He'd waited until the boy had been twelve and very impressionable. The kid had been dying to have a man in his life, and then to find out his father was the head of one of the most notorious organized crime syndicates, had solidified it. In fact, his son had been the one to come up with the plan of becoming educated and legit while secretly helping his father run an empire.

"What is so important that we have to meet suddenly ?"

The early days of his son patiently listening to him were obviously long gone. There were times he wondered if his son already had thoughts about taking over for him... sooner than later.

"Wait. Where's Will?"

"He's gone."

"What do you mean, gone? He's been with you for years."

"Yes, and been lying the whole time."

"He was stealing from you?"

"No. Worse. He was gay." Mr. T felt satisfaction at seeing the fear enter his son's eyes. But business was business. He couldn't have someone like that in his employ. It was not good for business at all. It was seen as a weakness, and he'd worked hard to have none. The fact that Will had been a devoted bodyguard and, to Mr. T's knowledge, had done nothing but his job for ten years hadn't mattered. That he'd accidentally caught Will in the act and just knowing what he was, it was too much. It would undermine him in a world where you had to be tough. Will had to go. His son looked ready to throw up.

"I understand C-Lite Hotels is trying to buy Caspian Winery."

"Yeah. I told you all about it."

"Don't get smart with me. I'm the one who paid your tuition, anonymously of course, made sure you had the best training and got you started at the hotel and then the cushy job you now have. If it weren't for me, you wouldn't have access to C-Lite Hotels and its business dealings." He stopped and looked at his son. Seeing him dressed in his suit and tie reminded Mr. T of the power he had.

His son shrugged but didn't say anymore.

"So, I don't know if that deal should go through. I met with James, and he was pretty shocked that I knew about it. Of course, I endorsed it and said it would be great for business. But he seems to forget who's in control. I'm the one who gave him money so he could start his hotel chain. I'm the one who backed him when no legitimate venue would. I'm the one who helped him surpass his father's hotels and become one of the top hotel chains in Canada." Mr. T walked a few steps to stare out over the city of Toronto. He'd chosen this spot because it was secluded but gave him a view of the city he loved. The city he controlled. He couldn't help but smile as he thought about the many police, the lawyers, city councilors and judges on his payroll. The thrill of that kind of power always got to him and fueled him to take more.

"I don't have all day. I need to get to work."

Mr. T's back stiffened and his shoulders snapped back. He turned slowly. "I'm going to forget you said that. Because I know you know, you're only a phone call away from jail and even closer to leaving this world. Do you understand me?"

Even though it was his son, seeing the fear in his eyes reminded him of the first man he'd killed. It had been an act of desperation, and he'd hated it, but it had given him status in the gang that he'd joined at twelve. From there, each kill had become easier. Then he'd gotten smart and realized he could make others do it for him. He'd never gained a taste for the actual job of taking another's life, but he loved the fear it instilled and the control it ensured stayed in his hands. If anyone was to understand it, it was going to be his flesh and blood. And although his men weren't within listening distance, he wanted there to be no mistake to his child or those who worked for him about who was really in control. There was no special treatment for family. Toe the line, or you'd be out. There was only one way.

"So, I have a better plan. I've found a woman to be your wife."

"You've got to be kidding me. There's no fu—"

The crack of his hand against his son's cheek was like gunfire as it echoed around them. The six men stationed a safe distance away came running with guns levelled. Mr. T put up his hand to halt them. His son glared for a brief second but was smart enough to drop his eyes downward.

"As I said, I've found you the perfect wife." He wasn't sure whether his son already knew the woman. "For now, we'll work on getting you properly introduced. You will stop sleeping around with every woman on two legs."

The blank, blinking look from his son was very satisfying. He didn't know all that his child was up to but he kept enough tabs to make sure he was aware that he was being watched.

"I have the perfect plan for that. First, I want you to stop the purchase of Caspian Winery, at least for now. I'll say when that deal goes through."

"I'm not sure how you want me to do that."

"I need to know you can follow orders and keep me on top of what is happening there."

"I get that, but what I'm saying is that it will be hard for me to stop that purchase. I'll throw what roadblocks I can."

Mr. T stared hard at him. His son had done well at planting the bug and reporting most of what he'd heard. Mr. T never left anything to chance. He had that place wired; the phones tapped, and was well aware of all Mr. Madsen's dealings. His son knew none of that. He also hadn't shared that he was expanding his empire. His son had been begging him for years to let him take over one small part of it. The kid still had a lot to prove to him, and first, that he was loyal and would do as told. If Mr. T's plans went well, he'd have C-Lite Hotels and Caspian Winery, and his reach would increase tenfold. He'd also be able to launder more money through his expanded operations. Only a handful knew about that part of his business.

"Find out what you can. Stall any paperwork if you can. Now go. Drive back the same way you came and do the vehicle exchange again. No mistakes. No detours. Leave the attitude next time." Mr. T turned and left, leaving his son standing there. It didn't concern him whether his son would follow through because he would or he'd be replaced. He wasn't the only one he had that could do the prestigious job at C-Lite Hotels. He just happened to be related, which actually made it all that much more difficult for Mr. T.

CHAPTER 18

"TARIN, WHAT THE HELL are you doing now? You look like a hillbilly. It's about time you let your hair grow, though. I didn't appreciate how messy it was yesterday, but I do like that it's long. More feminine. It will get you further with men. With finding a husband."

Tijan froze. The second encounter with her father was much like the first. It sent a cold, dark shiver down her spine. His voice was anything but what she'd thought a dad's voice should be. It was harsh and authoritative. She turned slightly, realizing that she hadn't even noticed him when she'd stumbled into the palatial room. All he needed to finish the look were drapes and veiled women. Everything in it dripped money. The office was bigger than her parents' house, and she'd always thought their five-bedroom rancher had been monstrously large. To her, it was ridiculous.

For the first time in thirty years, she was meeting the man she'd only been mildly curious about. Her stepfather Cal had been all that she'd needed as a father, and since her mom had told her that her real father was dead, she hadn't wasted much time thinking about him. The man who was supposed to be her father was evil. Her mom had never told her who he was or why she'd felt that way.

But he wasn't six feet under. He was sitting at a desk that she imagined was worth more than her SUV. Arrogance oozed out of him, wrapping him in a bubble. It let her know she wouldn't be getting close to him, physically or emotionally.

And he was desperately trying to save his youth. He obviously dyed his hair, and she wondered if he had hair plugs put in. Something about it didn't look natural. His face had too few wrinkles for a man his age, suggesting he was quite vain but not about to admit that to anyone. Or maybe it was the way he was sitting in his chair, staring at her, making her feel like he was a judge on his high bench about to hand down his sentencing. The only things they had in common were his nicely rounded forehead and the way his eyebrows arched. It was an odd similarity and told her that she favored their mother, and for that, she was grateful.

"Uh—"

"Is this another gimmick to piss me off? I'll have some clothes delivered from your favorite store so you can change out of those god-awful things you have on. Were you at a Halloween party? It's not even October. Or are you dressing like that to embarrass me?"

Tijan, feeling very stunned, looked down at her normal attire—blue jeans and a blue and red plaid shirt. They were clean and comfortable.

"Now that you're here, get over here and sit down."

Numbly, Tijan, who felt she might know how Alice in Wonderland felt after falling through the rabbit hole, made her way across the expansive floor. It seemed to take forever to reach the far corner, where there were two leather couches and two leather chairs, one of which her father was pointing at. As much as she wanted to look at the man responsible for her being in the world, she found she couldn't. All she had seen in his eyes had been disgust and a very clear message that she was lacking. Was this how her sister had been raised?

That thought stopped her cold. She'd done nothing but think about her sister ever since she'd seen that birthmark. Even though she hadn't been sure until recently that she truly did exist, she had wondered who her sister was and what kind of life she'd had. This man would have been very difficult to live with. If her sister weren't a cold bitch, Tijan would be surprised.

A middle-aged woman entered and set down a tray with a pitcher of water, a teapot and gold-embossed glasses and cups.

"Tarin. So nice to see you. I'm glad to see you've come to visit your father. You should visit more often."

"Thank you, Mary."

It sounded like his voice softened a bit, but regardless, Tijan felt like a kid who had just been chastised. She smiled weakly at the woman as she turned and walked out. Not sure what to do, Tijan turned her attention to the coffee table. It was incredible. It had to have been hand-crafted. Tijan reached out to touch the carved animals, only to realize that they weren't carved into the top but were the base instead.

"It is stunning, isn't it? I had it commissioned last year. The couple that made it took six months to craft it. If you look closely, you'll see the eagle, but within its wings you'll see a bear, an owl, three wolves and several other animals." Her father sat in one of the chairs opposite her.

Tijan kept her focus on the coffee table. She loved it. The craftsmanship was brilliant. They'd taken an old tree, carved several animals into it and then put a glass over top of them. It all looked so real. It was the only thing in the office that she could relate to.

Wouldn't her sister know all this?

"Alright. I know you're mad, but that's too bad. I needed to see you, and I'm tired of making requests."

"Oh?"

"Something is different about you, Tarin. I'm not sure I like it."

"You mean like growing my hair out?"

"Actually, that might work to your benefit. You kept it short only to annoy me. Glad to see you're coming around."

Tijan finally looked him in the eye, realizing she'd been avoiding it because she hadn't wanted him to discover that she wasn't who he thought she was. It didn't matter, however, as he wasn't really seeing her. He was looking at her but saw the child that he was hell-bent on controlling and bending to do his bidding. He had no clue that she wasn't the well-trained daughter he'd been expecting. This whole thing was making her itch with curiosity, but she had to play this game carefully. Her mom had always told her that her father was a dangerous man—though, admittedly, she'd also said he'd died. Tijan was pretty sure she understood why her mom had said that and had wanted nothing to do with him. He was cold and calculating in her estimation, and she'd known him for all of two minutes. But why had her mom left Tarin to grow up with him? And why didn't he know about her?

CHAPTER 19

TIJAN TRIED TO SIT patiently, but she'd had enough. She jumped to her feet, but that was enough for the two body-guards to puff out their chests and stand as though ready to tackle her. Smiling sickly, she sank back onto the chair. It was just as well. The office was beautiful and well-built, and as far as she could see, it only had two exits. And her father's friends were standing in front of each of them.

Her father, who had just up and left without an explanation, returned. The two men each exited the doors they'd been standing in front of, although Tijan was sure they hadn't gone far.

"What do you want, Dad?"

"Don't be smart with me. We agreed on Father. That will do. And of course, in public, I'm Mr. Madsen. I shouldn't have to remind you, Tarin. Your game of rebellion can stop now. You showed me how independent you could be. Marrying a rich playboy and having his child was one thing, but then to be a single mom... If that wasn't bad enough, then shacking up with a computer geek. I don't know where I went wrong with you. I sent you to the best schools. That boarding school should have straightened you out, but that was obviously money not well spent. And I know you're still upset about my not telling you about your half-sister, but I didn't think it was any of your business. And if your best friend Bobby had kept her mouth shut, you'd have never known."

What?

Tijan thought her head was going to explode. Not only did she have a twin she hadn't thought was alive, but she now had a niece or nephew and a half-sister? Were there more relatives she didn't know about?

"Yeah. You have to admit it's all pretty crazy. I mean, how do you hide a half-sister from me?"

"I don't have to explain myself to you. You so wanted Bobby to go away to boarding school with you, and the only way she could afford to go was if I paid. Her mom and I came to an agreement, but then I met Bobby's sister. She seduced me, wanting money. She got pregnant; her mom got the kid, and she died. There's really nothing to tell."

Tijan wasn't sure if the horror showed in her eyes, but she quickly looked away. She reached for the pitcher and poured herself a glass of water. She took a sip, trying to still her shaky nerves. Since she'd been brought to see her father, she'd been sure that she'd be safe, but now she wasn't so sure. She'd never heard anyone talk so crazy or so matter-of-factly about treating others so heinously.

Was it her half-sister who had died? Or her half-sister's mom?

"So you brought me here because?" Her question was met with silence. He didn't even give her the courtesy of looking at her or even acknowledge she'd said something. If he was thinking she'd already have answers about the winery, he had more faith in her than she did.

Her mind filled with all kinds of questions, but none that she could ask. Her father cleared his throat. When she looked at him, he was staring pointedly at her and then at the coffee table. He was expecting her to pour him a glass of water. Since she'd already filled hers, her first instinct was to toss it onto his very expensive silk suit.

"Sure. I'd love to be your maid." Curiosity was all that was keeping her sitting there. Well, that and the two men she was sure weren't far beyond the closed door.

"Really, Tarin, do you have to turn everything into a fight? I thought that since your ordeal with that rich gentleman, who I heard through the grapevine and not from my own daughter, might have curbed your sharp tongue. I guess being taken from that wedding, then almost getting yourself and your son killed, didn't help with that. I was rather surprised that you were invited to Dorothea Lindell's granddaughter's wedding and didn't tell me."

Your son, not my grandson.

Tijan knew that Dorothea Lindell was the owner of Caspian Winery and a very wealthy woman. Yet her father was offended that Tarin attended and didn't tell him, but not that she or her son had been taken and almost killed? Who was this self-centered, maniacal man? Tijan had dealt with a lot of ornery, miserable guys, but no one even came close to this man, whom she was supposed to call Dad. Or rather, father.

It was all very puzzling to Tijan. Her mind kept going to her sister, and what living with this person must have been like. She couldn't even imagine it. She just prayed her sister wasn't anything like him, though the odds of that probably weren't very good. Her hopes of having a normal sibling that she could be close to were slowly being flushed down the toilet. She didn't want to dislike her sister before even meeting her, but it wasn't looking good.

But then there was the bright side. She was an aunt. She'd always loved kids, even though she hadn't had much to do with any. But now she had her very own little relative she could spoil. She hoped.

She'd been so focused on all that she'd learned that she hadn't been paying attention to what she was doing. Water ran freely across the coffee table and dripped off the side. The glass she'd been pouring water into was overflowing. This time when she looked at her father, it was with trepidation. Without a word, his expression let her know that he was disgusted by her clumsiness and told her she'd done something idiotic. But that didn't stop him from also telling her.

His heavy sigh couldn't have been filled with more disappointment if he'd tried. "What have you done with all of those lessons you were taught? Can you please watch what you're doing?" He pulled out his cell and pressed a button. A few seconds later, the same woman entered and quickly and efficiently cleaned the mess. With only a cursory but very telling disbelief look at Tijan, she left.

The more Tijan experienced, the more she wondered if her sister might be a robot.

"Let's forget all the niceties. This is a waste of time. I'm sure you haven't found out much information for me about the winery. That's not what this is about. I still want you to look into that. I expect information, Tarin. You've done your rebelling. Now that you have a son who is my heir, it's time for you to start acting like that matters. I'd hate to claim that you're an unfit mother." He stared hard at her before saying, "I've found you a husband."

In a moment of defiance that she had no idea where it came from, she reached in her pocket and pulled out an elastic band she always carried and pulled her hair back into a tight bun at the back. His lips thinned as he stared at her, but then he got up and went to his desk. He sat down and turned his attention to his computer. She felt as though she'd been scolded and dismissed. Her two bodyguards appeared and escorted her to the car.

"Lower the window; it's not like I'm going anywhere." Tijan stuck her head out the window, needing the fresh air, even if smog filled, to wake her up. All that she'd just learned couldn't be true. That couldn't be her father. He could not be the man who sired her. It almost made her panic to think about what her sister must be like. She had to talk to her. She had to tell her that her father was nuts.

CHAPTER 20

AUGUST'S HEAD WHIPPED AROUND, and if a car hadn't honked, he might have driven right into another one. What was Tarin doing in the back of a limo, leaving C-Lite Hotels? And just before he was going there for an interview?

Everything about being hired at Caspian had been odd, but now his gut was telling him that something was off. Was he a pawn in some game they were playing?

Curious as to what he could find out, he headed to the top floor.

"I have an interview for head mechanic." He approached the glass-partitioned area behind which a receptionist sat. No one was getting through to the offices without some heavy artillery. The elegant lobby dripped money, but the large, heavily plated window was out of place. It gave him the feeling that not many people ever ventured up there.

The middle-aged woman behind the desk smiled at him. "August, right?"

"Yes."

She clicked a button and opened a door to the left of her desk. "Follow me." She took him down a short hallway and into a large boardroom. There was no one there.

"He'll be just a minute. There's water and glasses on the sideboard. Help yourself," she added as she left.

He sat at the far side of the table so he could see who came in. After a good five minutes, he was about to get up when a middle-aged man entered.

"You've been a mechanic for several years. You owned a business. Why did you sell?"

August felt like loosening the tie but refrained. He hadn't expected such a formal interview to be a mechanic, but Tarin had insisted he dress up. What surprised him, though, was that it was James Madsen himself who was interviewing him. The man hadn't even sat down and was already firing questions and insults at him.

"I sold because my mom became very ill. I wanted to spend as much time with her as possible."

"Did she die?" The man asked, as though he was wondering if the sun was shining.

"She did."

"And then you had nothing. That was a big mistake. You never let life get in the way of business. I hope you're a better mechanic than that."

August nodded, working hard to keep his face from twisting in disgust.

James stared at August for several moments before sitting at the opposite end of the table, leaving over twenty feet between them. It was so ridiculous that August was sure it was another intimidation tactic. The real question was where Tarin played in all this.

"I'm very good at business and as a mechanic. I also know how to supervise. So, let's cut the bull. What do you really want? There's no way this interview is just for a head mechanic. Or you wouldn't be interviewing me."

The guy never changed his blank facial expression. He just watched closely. It was one of those moments that August almost wished there had been an old clock on the wall that was ticking loudly, for it would have been preferable to the harsh silence. August stared back at him.

The man coughed a harsh, abrupt bark. August winced as it sounded painful. But other than pressing his fist against his chest for a moment, he seemed to ignore it.

"The position, for your information, is for Manager of my Transportation Department, not head mechanic. So, it would be me interviewing you. I make the decisions here as to who goes into any position of importance. You'd answer to me. I know that Dale Winters is thrilled with the business you sold him. He said you had built a well-respected and well-run business. The staff spoke highly of you as a boss and as a mechanic. I've talked with six references, and they all say the same. I'm always suspicious if someone doesn't have any dark horses in their pasture."

"I'm sure I have a few, but they are none of your business. Your job was posted as looking for a Head Mechanic. And that's what I applied for. I'm assuming this position would be overseeing all the transportation at all ten of your hotels, from mechanics to drivers to purchasing of vehicles. I haven't done all of that, but I do know how to run a good business, which you've already learned. It is interesting that you've already checked up on me. Doesn't that happen after you're sure you want to hire someone? Or am I the only sucker who applied?"

James' face had turned ashen, which left August feeling even worse. Had he said something he shouldn't have, or was the man unwell? Without a word, James got up, put his hand on his chair for a moment as though to steady himself and then left.

August sat there a bit stunned and feeling a bit guilty. Guy and Graham were counting on him as well as Tarin. But what had she been doing there? Everything about his life was off kilter and this was just adding to it. He had so many questions. Ones he needed to get some straight answers to. He'd had enough of this game.

Had Tarin been the one to tell her father all about him? Why would she have done that? A pressure settled in the middle of his chest.

He poured himself a glass of water while he loosened his tie. The view from the window caught his attention. Twenty stories up gave an amazing view of the city, but his mind was so busy with questions, he barely noticed. Knowing it was time to leave, he walked out the way he'd come in. When he reached the hallway, though, it was empty except for a closed door that he assumed led to offices. Curious and wanting to see if he could find something, he opened it. There was a long hallway with doors on either side. He walked a few feet but stopped when he heard loud voices.

"You told me you were making me CFO—Chief Financial Officer—and you were including Transportation under me."

"You couldn't even hire a competent mechanic to fix the vehicles here. And you think I'm going to let you be in charge of Transportation? I decide about what is best for the company. Right now, you're the manager of Finance. That isn't changing anytime soon. Get out."

August rushed back through the door he'd come through and stopped.

"Hi. Sorry. I got a bit lost."

"You don't want to go that way. This is the door to leave." The receptionist held the door for him to walk through, making it clear he needed to leave.

August smiled but hurried out. Rather than head back to Caspian, since Guy and Graham had arranged for him to have the day off, he planned on doing just that. His phone buzzed. It was Graham, but he wasn't ready to talk to him. He needed some space to figure out what he was going to do. Then he'd talk to Graham and Guy. Face to face. This time they were going to answer some questions, or he was done being the mechanic at Caspian and the pawn in whatever game they were playing.

CHAPTER 21

TIJAN LEANED BACK IN the luxurious car, deciding that this time she'd enjoy the ride. Although for a while there, she'd been sure that her father was going to lock her in a tower and throw away the key. It appeared, though she'd played the dutiful daughter well enough, that he'd let her go, but he'd made it very clear she was to be available when he needed her. He'd let her know when he had set up the meeting with the man, who she was pretty sure was double her age. Her father seemed to think she'd blindly date and marry the guy, if he wanted it.

The trip back to her car was much shorter than when they'd left. The parking lot was full. Her head was buzzing with questions. It felt like an ant farm had set up residence in her brain, and each one was a different question scurrying around trying to find answers.

Feeling claustrophobic, she just wanted to go home. She wanted to be back in the wide-open spaces of the foothills. She yearned to get on Tango and ride for hours... days... Just get away from everything and everyone. It had always been her favorite thing to do, especially when she was upset about something. And this ranked right up there with the toughest thing she'd ever had to deal with.

It was so tempting to just leave, but then her mom came to mind. She had fought every day to live a normal life and had always looked for the good in things. She had always been there for her with love and a smile. Tijan wasn't going anywhere until she had some answers.

She had to talk to her sister. What she would actually say was a mystery, but she needed to hear her version of things. Had she known she had a twin and perhaps she just hadn't wanted anything to do with her?

Tijan knew that what she was thinking was crazy, but she wasn't getting anywhere by trying to be sneaky. After her ordeal with the man who claimed to be her father, the first thing she had to do was warn her sister. The man was over the edge. She wanted to know if they could commit him. Was he really who he said he was? She could look him up on the internet but really didn't want that confirmation.

She'd finally been able to convince herself that since she'd come all this way, it was time to step up and see it through. She'd never backed down from a challenge, and she'd had many. Living on a ranch with mostly men had made it impossible for her to back down from taunts or challenges. It hadn't mattered that she was the boss's daughter. She had something to prove. Some things, though, hadn't worked in her favor, especially the time she'd tried steer riding.

She approached the front of the building but ducked her head as the door flew open. A man sailed past her. Hustling forward, she grabbed it and slipped inside. Yanking off her wig and glasses, which had only been so she could get by the old guy, she pulled the elastic out of her hair. Being inside was a bit of a shock. She thought she'd have to stand there for a while trying to figure out how to get to the offices upstairs.

Holding the banister as she wasn't sure her rubbery legs were going to hold her upright; she slowly climbed the stairs. Wrestling a calf with its mama about to charge her was less scary than this. The echo of her boots on the steps sounded like sonic booms. It bounced off the walls, almost mocking her. At the top, she stopped, noting there was a short hallway past the open door on her right. Peeking in, she saw that the room was empty, but the sounds were coming from a room beyond, telling her that someone was in there.

Now or never, girl.

It had taken her most of the day to get up the nerve; she wasn't about to stop now. She stepped through the door.

"Tarin, is that you? I was expecting you a while ago. I hope that means you waited for them to bake some new gooey cinnamon buns. You know, the ones you're trying to get me to stop eating."

Tijan mumbled a reply more from reflex than because she wanted to answer. Making her way toward the open doorway where the voice had come from, she dropped the wig and glasses on the empty desk as she passed. Stopping just outside the door, she shook her hair out. Taking a moment, she pulled her hair forward, needing the security it gave her, before she stepped forward. She wasn't sure what she was expecting, but the room was rather stark. The walls were off-white; a bed sat in the corner, and there was a desk against the windows with a man behind it. He was staring intently at his computer screen, not even glancing up when she entered. She took that moment to study him. He was kind of cute in a shaggy dog kind of way and definitely someone who fit the nerd look. A cute one, though.

"Tarin, what the hell? I love it." Graham chuckled.

"Uh—no—"

"Nice outfit. Not sure the boots are really you. How'd you get your hair that long? Is that a wig? Or that extension thing? I guess it couldn't be that. That takes a long time to do, right? The clothes are a fresh look, too." Graham stood up and walked toward her. A smile and a very warm greeting filled his eyes.

Tijan froze when he wrapped his arms around her and pulled her close. The soft smile he gave her definitely caught her off guard.

"I, uh... No, I'm not—"

"You look hot."

"Graham?"

He jerked back so fast, Tijan stumbled backwards.

"Tarin? Then who—"

Tijan could feel two sets of eyes boring into her. Slowly, she straightened her spine and turned, knowing that her life was about to change drastically. Her sister was standing in the outer doorway.

"Bee"

"Boo"

"Tee"

"Ta"

Tijan wasn't sure who moved first, but she was soon reunited with the one person who completed her. It wasn't something she could explain. They hugged and rocked and danced around, but their arms never loosened from each other. Tijan felt her heart swell, her whole body vibrating with emotion.

A long time later, they separated enough to cup each other's faces and stare as though looking into a mirror and each other's soul. It felt to Tijan like a rift within her had been sewn back together with an invisible thread. Everything was perfect in that moment. It was too much, even for tears.

"How—"

"Where—"

They smiled at each other. Tarin took her hand and pulled her along with her back into the inner office. Tijan followed willingly, clinging to her sister, scared she'd disappear if she didn't. The guy who had been about to kiss her had moved to the outer office as though to give them some privacy, but he pivoted to face them. The fact that he didn't get mad or blurt out something surprised Tijan. She wasn't used to men keeping their mouths shut when they'd had a shock, and this had to be a big one.

Tarin cupped her face and stared at her for a long time. "You're not a figment of my imagination."

Tijan smiled. She'd wondered that as well.

"Graham. I want you to meet my twin sister." Tarin hugged Tijan's arm as she introduced her. "I haven't seen her in a very long time."

Tijan wasn't sure if it was the catch in Tarin's voice or the reality of what she said that hit her, but she suddenly felt overcome with a myriad of emotions. Questions started flooding her mind. Why had they been separated? Who had kept them apart? Why had they been kept from each other all these years?

"I didn't think you existed."

Tijan could almost relate to that. She'd known she'd had a twin but had thought she'd died as a child.

"I'm Tijan, by the way. And I know your name is Tarin."

There was a stunned silence for a moment before Tarin squared her shoulders. Her pain and hurt were palpable.

"Tijan, I would like you to meet the love of my life, Graham."

Tijan was thankful that they looked lovingly at each other for a few seconds. It gave her time to tamp down her feelings and allow the happiness that had first welled inside her to come forth. She'd get answers later.

She gave Graham a huge grin. "I bet this is a little more of a shock than your computers give you."

He smiled, but Tijan noted the secret look that passed between the couple. "Yes, but this is a very positive one. Hey, we have to go out to Dorothea's soon. Why don't I call her and tell her there's one more?"

Tarin nodded vigorously. "I'd love that. Dorothea will too. Guy and Bailey are going to be there, right?"

Tijan stopped listening. It was so unreal that she didn't want anything to pull her from her fantasy. She wasn't sure she wanted to share her sister with so many, but the way Tarin was clinging to her arm let her know they'd have plenty of time to catch up. She was sure they both had quite a journey to talk about.

And at some point, she had to find a way to tell her sister that their father was crazy... and about to marry her off.

CHAPTER 22

"ELEANOR, WHERE ARE WE with purchasing Caspian Winery?" James stood in the boardroom, staring out the window. His talk with Tarin had left him feeling unsettled. She was acting even more bullheaded than normal. One part of him was okay with cutting her out of his life, but the other part wanted her son, the man he intended to take over for him one day.

He needed to know where things were at, but of course, he didn't want his daughter in on his business dealings. She'd made it clear she didn't like his methods.

"James, we've only had a few days. We do have other clients."

"Not ones that are paying you as much as I do. Although I do hear that you're taking up with organized crime now."

There was a full minute of silence. "He's not exactly someone you say no to, is he? It's your fault he found me."

"I never gave him your name."

"As if you'd have to. The man has connections that could get him access to national secrets and probably wipe out anyone he wanted to. To be honest, he's turned out to be one of my best clients."

"What exactly do you do for him?"

"Really, do you want me to tell him about your business?"

"I want to know that you're not sharing my company information with him."

"Screw you, James. If you want to hire another lawyer, go ahead."

James didn't reply, but the whole conversation wasn't going as he thought it would—or should.

"Look, I told you that acquiring Caspian Winery will take some time. Is there a reason why you're making it urgent? As far as I know, there are no other offers on the table. There have been a few in the past, but nothing recently."

"Who and when?" James wanted to know who his competition was. And he wanted to know if Tesimmon was playing him or if he'd tried to buy the place before.

"I don't have the file in front of me. I had Martin do some research on it. I'll get the information and get back to you. Why does it matter? There are currently no offers. You're the only one who has made a substantial offer in quite a while."

"Yes, but the more I know about who's in the game, the better I'll do. Also, find out some background information on who these companies are, the owners, the CEOs, and anyone else that might be important. I want to know everything."

"That'll take time."

"Which you don't have. I want that information now."

"I'll have to pull a lawyer off other duties to do this solely."

"Do it."

"Let's be clear that you will be billed for him full time."

"Just make sure it's not that little snot, Martin. Put Ron on it. And get me that damn winery!" He swore.

"You know, James, if you'd tell me what's really going on, I might be able to make this work."

"I have told you, Eleanor. You know all you need to."

"Got it. Put me in my place again. You know how to pull punches, don't you?"

"Does that mean I'll see you tonight?"

"Right, because I still have nothing to do but be at your beck and call when you need a release. We've been doing the nasty, as my mother would say, for what, two years? My mother always wanted me to get married; instead, I find a man married to his work."

"So, am I going to see you tonight?"

"I don't think so. I've got a headache."

"Look, I'm sorry. Let me make it up to you. I'll take you out on my yacht. We'll have a private catered dinner, and wine. What could be better than that?"

He heard her heavy sigh. "Alright."

"I'll meet you in the parking lot at 8:00."

James listened to the click that disconnected them. Eleanor seemed to be changing the relationship that he'd been quite comfortable with. They got together once or twice a week for mutual release, but she'd turned him down twice now. It made him wonder what else was going to change. Hopefully, he could put that back on track later. Sighing heavily, he buzzed Mary to come to his office.

"Hello, Mr. Madsen. How are you feeling today? I'll make you some tea."

"I'm fine, Mary."

"You've been coughing pretty badly. I don't remember you ever being sick in ten years. You should see the doctor. I can make the appointment for you."

"And I'm not now, so don't be sharing any of that gossip around. It's too bad you never had kids; then you'd have them to mother and not me." He put down her blanched face to his harsh words. He'd been hard on her. Normally she was the one person who didn't see his anger. But he couldn't have her thinking he had any weaknesses.

"I'm sorry. You're right, Mr. Madsen. I would never share anything about you with anyone. I was just concerned, but I'll keep that to myself in the future."

The quiver was ever so faint, but he heard it.

"Look, I appreciate your concern, but I'm fine. I don't need mothering. Maybe you need to get a dog to mother. Or smother." His lips arched slightly. It was the best he could do to appease her.

She smiled fully at him. He'd always wondered why she'd stayed but was grateful she had. She was the best personal assistant he'd ever employed. At times, he'd gotten the feeling she'd been interested in him, but other than being efficient and making sure everything was exactly as he wanted it, he hadn't seen much of that.

"Can you do some research for me on lawyers that handle big business, along with all their dealings?"

"I sure can, Mr. Madsen. When would you like that information?"

Mary sounded a bit too happy to be doing this job.

"A couple of days is fine. The sooner the better, though."

"Do you need me to write up something to Carter and Associates?"

"Not yet. Thank you, Mary."

James frowned as he watched her leave. She was very cheerful and left with a bounce in her step. Unsure of what had caused the change, but if he yelled at her too much, she might just leave.

Chapter 23

August grabbed one of the rags he'd left handy so he could quickly wipe the grease off his hands. He eased himself out from under the harvester. It was an older machine, but LJ, his boss, had said she wanted it fixed. He'd tried to take the day off, but he couldn't shut down his mind after meeting with James. He'd blown it. Guy and Graham and Tarin had been depending on him. Since they were the only people he knew, work was the only thing he could think of that would keep him busy and not thinking.

He cleaned up his area, putting away his tools and ensuring the parts for the harvester were sitting in a plastic bin, which he put the cover on just so no one would move them or accidentally spill them. Or take them. He had ordered a few parts, but they wouldn't be in for at least a day or so.

The other mechanic, Perry, walked into the big shop.

"Perry, how did you make out?"

Perry dropped the toolbox he was carrying. It made a loud bang. "Fine. Got it fixed."

August winced at the noise and the lack of respect for the tools. "What were you working on?" August had been hired not only as a mechanic but as the supervisor/manager of all the equipment.

"Look. I've been here for four years. I don't need you to watch over my shoulder. I know this equipment better than you. I don't need a babysitter." With that, he wiped his hand on a rag, tossed it on the ground, and walked out.

August sighed. This was one of the things he hadn't missed about supervising staff. Although he had picked the staff that worked for him and had built a good relationship with most, there were still a few over the years who felt they'd been cheated. When the last head mechanic had been fired, Perry, although only in his early twenties, seemed to think he should have been put in charge, despite the fact that he wasn't a journeyman mechanic. August was glad that management had seen that Perry did not have the skills or attitude to oversee the department.

Grabbing the rag off the floor that the kid had deliberately dropped, he looked around at the mess. Two large tool chests had drawers hanging open, tools scattered in no particular order. Three counters that should have been clear were cluttered with both old and new parts. It appeared as much as he cleaned, Perry dirtied. And they truly had been crazy busy. His first priority had been to get things fixed. Too much had not been well taken care of.

Setting about reorganizing the toolboxes, he started with one and took everything out and laid it on the floor. After a day of work and he'd already dived in and found that he loved being back on the tools. He'd been so busy he hadn't had much time to think. But now, in doing this, it gave his mind plenty of time to wander. He had to talk to Graham and Guy. He'd been dodging their phone calls. A few days before, they'd invited him to Dorothea's for supper that night.

And now he was struggling to make up his mind whether to go.

Finishing emptying one box, he started on the other while his mind immediately flipped through everything he'd been trying to avoid all day. Everything had been weird since Graham and Tarin had tracked him down in Winnipeg. It didn't surprise him that his mom had found him a job. She'd been quite concerned when he'd sold his business, but he'd wanted the time to spend with her because they'd known her time was short. Six months at best was what they'd been told. He'd only gotten three with her. He pressed his hand to his heart. It still choked him up. She'd been the world to him, mother and father most of his life. And she'd worked hard to make sure that he hadn't hated his father, even though he'd just abandoned them one day. August had been about nine.

The hurt had never gone away, and his mom's explanation that he'd been a war vet who just couldn't cope had done nothing to soothe the injured pride of a nine-year-old. He'd hated him for a very long time. His mom's tearful plea that he forgive the man and that he find him was the only thing that made him relent and put him on this crazy path.

He hadn't done much of anything to find him. He'd performed an Internet search but had found no known address for William Renner. He'd done what his mom had told him to and obviously, she'd known him too well. She'd known he wouldn't make finding his father a priority. She'd sent some private investigators to find him.

But the job offer was odd. Shouldn't they have just told him if they'd found his father, instead of pulling him into this game of being a snoop for them?

And then there was Tarin. From the moment he'd met her, he'd known he was in trouble. There was something so incredibly beautiful about her, warm and welcoming. She'd been way out of his league, though. Never mind that she and Graham were engaged.

August walked through the big open garage door and stood there. He'd never imagined he would like being back on the tools full time but he was loving it.

Unfortunately, his mind wouldn't shut down.

August believed that his mom had asked them to hire him, as she'd been very concerned about his future. She'd had no money to leave him. In fact, he'd supported her for years, which was probably why she'd assumed he was broke. When he'd given her the first pay cheque for the work she was doing around his shop—cleaning, answering phones, filing—she'd immediately torn it up and told him to put the money to good use. They'd finally agreed that he could give her some cash so she could pay her expenses. And he'd opened another bank account in her name so he could deposit the rest of what he'd owed her. It had taken a while, but she'd finally used it to buy herself a new car—well, really an old one that he'd rebuilt for her.

They'd had so many disagreements over the years, but his mom had challenged him at every turn. At the time, it had driven him crazy, but now... He stared upward at the blue sky as pressure built behind his eyes. A single tear trickled down his cheek. He pressed his hand to his chest to try to hold the memory in place so it would fill the void she had left.

"I love you, Mom," he whispered.

He blew out his breath and felt more lost than he had in a long time. Leaving his business had been easy. Losing his mom had been devastating. She'd hated that he'd been alone. She'd wanted him to have a wife and kids. So had he, but there just hadn't been time—or the right woman.

Had his mom sent these guys to find him a job? Find his father? Or was it a wife?

The mad rush of people who had finished their shift caught his attention. His watch told him that he'd better close up and get moving if he was going to make it to supper at Dorothea Lindell's. She'd been the one to invite him. Actually, she'd insisted he come. Guy and Graham had told him she knew nothing about what they'd asked him to do. She had taken a liking to him, and since he'd immediately told them of a potential threat, she'd wanted him to come for supper. It was her way of saying thanks.

It didn't matter though, because he did plan on making sure he found out what was really going on.

CHAPTER 24

"JAMES, I NEED TO speak with you." JT stood in the doorway.

James looked up, his eyes narrowing as he stared at his manager of finance. "You know I don't like surprise meetings. Book time through Mary." He didn't wait for him to comply before he dropped his gaze back to his computer monitor. He was looking at the latest sales results for Caspian Winery. His men had done much better than he'd anticipated. All he'd been hoping for was information about those who worked there. But they had incredible sales with steady growth every year over the last five, bolstering his resolve to own the company.

"I did. And according to Mary, you're free for the next hour."

James didn't acknowledge what JT was saying, but he did check his schedule. At the end of every month, he gave Mary access to some of what was on his calendar. One of the things he always did was give her a few hours a week that he was available to meet with staff. The time was meant to be booked in advance. He hadn't needed to look. If Mary said he was free to meet with staff, then he was. She was always correct and very protective of his time, knowing how busy he was. And he rarely forgot his schedule. It didn't make him happy to know that the stress in his life was increasing and his control was decreasing.

"That may be true, but I also know that Mary would have checked with me before sending you in. So what did you bribe her with this time?"

JT shrugged as he strode across the room. "You know, the usual—chocolates and flowers. Come on, she's a woman. It's pretty easy."

James didn't say a word but glared, allowing his annoyance to show. He didn't buy a word of that. Mary had taken a real liking to JT and seemed to feel that he needed mothering or spoiling. James wasn't sure which. It didn't sit well with him that JT could easily manipulate his personal staff. Mary would never cross boundaries or purposefully do anything to annoy James, but he didn't like her preferential treatment of JT.

He dropped his eyes back to the work on his computer. He'd finish what he was doing, then give JT his time. The guy needed to learn that barging in whenever he wanted wasn't the way to get James' attention. JT had taken a seat on his leather couch and was scrolling through his phone as if it didn't matter to him. Heat was climbing up his face. He suspected it had more to do with anger than with his illness. Finishing what he'd been reading, he closed it, came to his feet and made his way to the other couch across from JT.

"What was so important you had to burst in here?"

JT didn't look up from his phone for a few more seconds, obviously scrolling through something. If the guy hadn't been so good at his job and reminded James a lot of himself, James would have fired him long ago. Staring into space, he gave JT payback for making him wait. There was something about the kid he liked. He called a thirty-year-old man a kid made him smile. But the guy was always riding his bike, going rock climbing, doing something very physical and active. Nothing seemed to get him down, and he was always so energized, wired. He also had aspirations of moving up in the company, and he was getting crafty about it. It was almost as if JT thought if he said it enough and told enough people, he would become chief financial officer. James didn't see that ever happening, but he liked the kid's 'go-get-'em' attitude. He got things done. It reminded James a lot of himself in his younger days.

"Okay. I put in a huge order to Caspian Winery, but they've cut that down to about a quarter. They didn't give me any explanation. My thought is we find another local winery that is a big name or one that makes great wine. We order a huge amount through them and then we cancel our order with Caspian Winery. Maybe if we start putting out some subtle rumors about them, we can impact their sales. And we can help to make a name for another winery. Your thoughts?"

James knew he had to play this carefully, or he'd give too much away. He had not shared his plans for that particular winery. "Let me think about that. For now, take the order that they've agreed to. We might be able to use that later on. They're well known and could bring us more business."

"Got it. Do you think this is a ploy to see if we're legit? I think, if I'm not mistaken, Caspian Winery had approached us on a few occasions going back ten to twenty years? My predecessor left some notes suggesting they had wanted us to sell their wine at our hotels, but we'd turned them down."

"Hmmm. I'm not sure whether I was aware of that or not. I don't recall their approaching us. Maybe that's why they're reluctant to sell to us. A fence we'll have to mend." James allowed a puzzled expression to cross his face. There wasn't an offer or a sale that he wasn't aware of in the thirty years he'd been in business. When they'd been approached by Caspian to share their wine at their hotels, initially James hadn't wanted to take on a no-name—which, twenty years before, is what they essentially had been. They had been on the rise, but James had been focused on taking out his father, who ran a competitive hotel chain, so James had made the decision to go with a few well-known wineries. Caspian, though, had been persistent and had approached them a few more times. The last time was about five years earlier. They definitely hadn't approached his company since Tarin had gotten involved with that computer geek who just happened to work with Caspian Winery's owner, Dorothea Lindell's grandson-in-law.

"My guess is if they approached us before and we turned them down, they may be wondering why now?"

And the fact that James was trying to buy the place probably made them rather suspicious. It was a lot more complicated than JT knew.

"Since you're so good at schmoozing, see what you can find out about the company and what we can do to make amends. I'd like to stick with them. They already have a good name and would be good for business."

"Okay. Budget? Methods?"

James bit back a smile. The more people he had looking into this company meant someone had to come up with a good plan that would work. "Run everything by me first. Get the information and then let me know what you plan to do."

"Will do." JT got to his feet and made his way to the door but stopped and turned.

James' eyes narrowed. He was pretty sure of what was coming. He started to cough. JT hurried across the room, filled a glass with water and handed it to him. When he could finally catch his breath, he waved at JT, essentially shooing him out.

"You should have that checked. You've had that nasty cough for a while."

"I can look after myself," James managed to squeak out. If his face hadn't been hot and red from the coughing, it would have been from his anger. He hated showing any weakness to anyone, but in front of staff, it was unforgivable. JT knew he'd been unwell for a while. That bothered him even more.

"You have a lot going on and aren't feeling the greatest, but have you decided anything about your vacant vice president position? I am very interested and would be a good candidate. I could start there and show you I'd make a good CFO."

"Figure out how to mend things with Caspian and we'll see."

JT pursed his lips before smiling. "Got it."

James watched as JT left, closing the door behind him. He probably would be a good candidate but not one James would ever consider. It had all been taken care of already. There was a contingency plan in place should James need someone to take over for him. Until then, he had no plans to fill the CFO or the vacant VP position. He was saving a ton of money on positions he wasn't convinced he needed.

Feeling exhausted, he made his way to his office door and locked it. He buzzed Mary to let her know not to disturb him for the next two hours. That was in itself nothing new, but then he did something he'd never done in his life. He lay down on the sofa in his office and went to sleep.

CHAPTER 25

IT WAS LIKE DRIVING up to the White House, or at least that was what Tijan thought. The place was a monstrosity, but in a good way. The massive three-story pillars made her feel like a fairy princess being taken to the castle. She thought she had a pretty good idea of what Cinderella had felt like. Feeling awkward in her blue jeans and blouse, Tijan climbed out of the Hummer behind Tarin, who had only let go of her hand so she could change clothes at her hotel. Tarin had wanted Tijan to stay with her and Graham, but it was too soon. Tijan had a lot of questions; one she couldn't shake was why Tarin hadn't looked for her. Since Tarin had insisted that Graham come with them, there wasn't a moment for them to talk privately. But Tijan was okay with that and was sure that Tarin had done it on purpose. What needed to be said between them was too raw and was like bubbling lava just below the surface.

She had so much to tell Tarin, especially about her father, but she just couldn't find the words. Not yet. Once she went down that path, things would change. For now, she just wanted to enjoy the wholeness and warmth she was feeling from just being with her twin.

Gazing around at the beautifully ornate mansion and the sculpted and manicured lawn made Tijan feel as if she'd stepped into another world. It put her in awe. They'd driven around an enormous fountain to park in front of marble steps leading to towering pillars. It had her jaw dropping at the scale and beauty of everything.

"I think everyone reacts that way the first time," Graham laughed.

Tijan wasn't so sure, as Tarin and Graham seemed so comfortable in these surroundings.

An elderly woman accompanied by a younger man and woman were walking down the marble steps toward them. Tijan knew she must have tensed because Tarin squeezed her arm and smiled at her.

"You're just as gorgeous as your sister. And your eyes reflect that you have a kind soul. I'm Dorothea."

Tijan took the offered hand. "Thank you. I'm Tijan." The woman, who had to be in her eighties, had such a presence about her that Tijan felt like she was meeting royalty. She had this beautifully refined but not snobbish air about her. She was someone who was clear on who she was, someone others automatically respected and someone who could easily stand up for herself. Tijan was sure that not much got by this woman. Her piercing brown eyes were a little unsettling, leaving Tijan feeling like the woman had just read through her diary and knew everything about her.

"I'm Dorothea's granddaughter, Bailey, and this is my husband, Guy."

"Nice to meet you." Tijan shook the offered hands. She couldn't help but glance at the beautifully elegant ring on Bailey's left hand. "Congratulations on your wedding. I know it was a while ago but I had read about that crazy man who broke in during your marriage ceremony and started shooting. That must have been scary."

There was a sudden stillness and silence that happens when something bad was about to occur. It reminded Tijan of the calm before the storm. Of the few tornadoes she remembered happening in Alberta, there had been a moment of eerie quiet, the clouds bubbling and moving fast before the winds had picked up and the storm had started. The situation felt very much like that.

"Yes, it was a bit of a shock." Bailey answered, but the look that passed between the five of them definitely let Tijan know she was on the outside and there was a lot more to that story that the newspaper hadn't printed. She acted like it was nothing and looked around at the wealth surrounding her, not surprised that someone like Dorothea could keep family news out of the news.

"Please come inside." Dorothea took her arm and with Tarin on her other one, Tijan allowed them to pull her forward.

"First, where's Bill?" Dorothea asked.

"I offered to pick him up, but he said he'd make his own way here."

Graham shrugged. "He told me the same thing. I'll call him."

"I do hope he comes. It would have been a good opportunity to meet... everyone." Dorothea looked pointedly at Guy.

"I know it would have been good. But he's not big on group events."

"I should have picked him up, but I didn't want to push it. If not this time, there'll be another one." Graham pulled out his phone and stepped away from the group.

"August is still coming, isn't he?"

Guy nodded and shrugged at the same time.

Tarin smiled at Tijan. "Bill is an older man, a friend of the family. He has been invaluable to me. Although I will admit, it took a bit to warm up to him. He is amazing. I just wish—" She turned and looked at Graham, who was just hanging up. He shook his head.

Tijan was curious as to what that was all about but didn't feel it was her place to ask. She allowed herself to be led into the house. She'd never wanted for anything. Her parents had money, but they weren't by any stretch in the same class as this. The massive marble entryway was unbelievable. The enormous chandelier hanging overhead was dripping with what she was sure were real crystals. She'd have started spinning if she wasn't being held so tight by the women on either side of her. She tried not to look like she'd never seen anything like this before or be the kid whose mouth hangs open and says, 'wow man'. But it wasn't easy.

They stopped in front of an elevator, but Tijan couldn't take her eyes off the ornate stairs with the incredible curved banister.

Bailey chuckled. "I felt that way too when I first saw them."

"They must have been awesome as a kid to slide down."

That look that she wasn't included in happened again. Five minutes in and she'd already stuck her foot in her mouth twice. But she had no clue as to why.

"Do you mind if I walk up them?" Tijan looked at the elderly lady, whose arm felt a whole lot frailer than she looked.

"Of course, my dear. I used to love walking them as well, but they're too much for these old bones." Dorothea patted her hand and released her arm.

"I'll come with you." Tarin was still holding tightly to her other arm.

Bailey immediately stepped forward and took her grandmother's arm. "Go. We'll see you at the top."

Graham gave Tarin a quick kiss before joining the other three in the elevator.

"Isn't this something?" Tarin let go of her arm and twirled.

Tijan laughed and joined her. "I wonder if everyone does this the first time they come in here?"

"I don't know. I just know I've always wanted to do it but never had the nerve in front of Dorothea."

"She's something."

"She's amazing. She ran Caspian Winery all by herself for something like fifty years. I think her family started it way back when—eighty-some-odd years ago. In fact, she just stepped down. Well, if you could call it that. She still works two or three days a week. What a dynamo!" Tarin chuckled.

"What's so funny?"

"Oh. Sorry. That's Graham's word for her. I just found it funny that it slipped out. I was raised never to be disrespectful of others and definitely not my elders. In fact, I wasn't ever to call them by their first names. My father was such—"

Staring at Tarin, Tijan saw her eyes open wide as she looked at her. That simple statement reminded them both that the rift between them was as big as the Grand Canyon, and they knew nothing about each other. Tijan wanted to say something, but the lump in her throat prevented her from talking. She couldn't do more than stare at the mirror image of herself. Tarin flew at her and wrapped her arms around her. They hugged, and the tears flowing. No words were spoken, but a lot was said.

"Excuse me. I know I'm late, but I—"

Tijan and Tarin broke apart enough to look at who was addressing them. The man's eyes darted back and forth between them.

"There are two of you."

Tijan and Tarin looked at each other and laughed. Soon they were wiping the tears from their faces. "Yes, there are."

"Come in, August. I don't imagine you've met my sister, Tijan?"

August looked back and forth between them before catching her eye and holding it. Cocking his head slightly, he didn't say a word as he extended his hand. She was confident that he couldn't recognize her from Caspian Winery because her hair had been different, but she got the distinct feeling he knew something.

"August is our new mechanic at the winery. He's been getting all the machinery up to speed. I hear you're already doing amazing work."

"Thank you."

"Let's go up. Everyone is waiting. Come on." Tarin led the way.

Tijan could feel August watching her and could almost hear the questions going through his mind. It made her shake her head and smile. He probably knew more about what was going on than she did.

She was glad to hear that he was an employee and had at least told her the truth about that. But she still got the feeling that he'd been sneaking around the day she'd found him at Caspian Winery. Why would he have needed to do that if he worked there?

CHAPTER 26

"Tijan, this is my son, Chance."

Tijan had taken a moment to slip away and had found herself standing on a huge marble balcony that had the most incredible view she'd ever seen. Beyond the precisely manicured lawns, gardens and trees, there were some gently rolling hills and very few houses. It almost made Tijan feel like she was at home. But unlike home, this was polished and perfect, unlike her world, which was natural, raw, tangled, imperfect and to her even more beautiful than this. It definitely made her feel like an outsider.

When her name was said, something inside her added another stitch to the healing of her soul, which she didn't even know she needed—or wanted. Hearing her sister say her name was so perfect. She turned slowly, excited and scared to be meeting her nephew.

His eyes widened as he looked at her from his mom's arms. He looked at her, then at his mom, then back at her. Tijan and Tarin laughed.

"He's not sure what to make of this."

"This is my twin sister, honey. She's your aunt Tijan."

"You look like Mom. Like the same, like Mom." His eyes darted back and forth between the two women.

And just like that, he reached out with his arms to Tijan. Awkwardly, she took him as his small arms wrapped around her neck. It was the most amazing feeling. Some of it must have shown on her face as Tarin hugged both of them, her eyes full of tears.

Tarin finally eased back. "It is the most wonderful gift ever. I'm guessing you don't have kids?"

Tijan shook her head. "Nor a boyfriend. Although there is this guy who wants to marry me. We had all of two dates, even if he says three. His mom has the house and picket fence already picked out."

Tarin laughed. "Wow, she sounds like my father. He's been picking out husbands for me for years. His taste in men sucks."

Chance had obviously had enough and was squirming. Tijan set him down. Reluctant to face her sister, she had to bring up her meeting with her father. She still couldn't quite think of him as hers.

"Tarin, your father—"

"It just dawned on me. He's your father too. We have a lot to talk about, don't we? My head has just been spinning since I saw you in the office. I can't tell you how excited I am to meet you. I feel like the rift inside of me has been sewn back together."

Tijan gasped, "Oh my God. That's exactly how I feel."

"I've always known something was missing from my life, but I didn't know it was you. I always thought you were part of my imagination. And of course, my father was sure I had conjured up an imaginary twin. I'm so confused and have so many questions for him. Where did you grow up, Tijan?"

"Tarin! Tarin!"

"I'm in here. What's up?"

Tijan felt a shiver of fear course down her spine. The voice sounded urgent.

Graham flew through the door; his gaze immediately focused on Tarin. "Honey. I don't know how to tell you this, but your father has been shot. He's at the hospital."

The color drained from Tarin's face as she hurried out the door after Graham. Tijan remained there unsure what to do but felt a blow like never before. Tarin hadn't forgotten about her deliberately but could tell that the news had hit her hard. It just wasn't going to click for her that the man shot was Tijan's father as well.

A few minutes later, an athletic woman scurried onto the balcony. "Have you seen Chance? I'm his sitter."

"He was just here. Do you need help to find him?"

"No, he'll go to his playroom. He loves it there. Thanks." She left.

With a jumble of confusing emotions, Tijan slowly made her way into the house and down the three flights of ornate marble stairs. There was no one in the vast lobby. She assumed most of them probably went to the hospital, so she opened the door intending to leave, only to stop. She'd ridden there with Tarin and Graham. Unsure what to do and feeling a bit shaky, she walked out and sat on the steps.

The sun was just setting. Colors exploded along the horizon. It was still quite warm out, but Tijan couldn't shake the shiver that had crept inside and was spreading like a rain-swollen river.

"Tijan. There you are. Tarin just called. She'd like you to come to the hospital. She apologizes for running out." August came around in front of her.

"Did he die?"

"I don't think so. She wants you to come, though."

"Okay. I just need to call a cab."

"I'll take you."

Without a word, Tijan followed him to his car and climbed in. "Oh, wait. I need to thank Mrs. Lindell for having me over."

"It's okay; she's lying down. Her granddaughter is with her. I'm sorry about your father."

"He's not MY father." She kept her eyes focused blindly on the road ahead of them. August gazing at her oddly, though, silently questioning what she was saying, which, of course, made little sense. She felt for Tarin but, for some reason, couldn't conjure up much for the man she'd spent less than a day with, in her life. At least that she was aware of. It didn't surprise her that someone wanted to shoot him. In her short meeting with him, she'd gotten the feeling that he'd bulldozed over a lot of people, regardless of who they were. What confused her was how someone had gotten close enough to him to point a gun at him, never mind pull the trigger? He'd had bodyguards all around him when she'd seen him. Had it been one of them?

CHAPTER 27

FINALLY, FINDING A PARKING spot at the hospital, August knew they were going to pay an exorbitant fee for it, but there was no other choice. He'd barely pulled in when Tijan jumped out and headed for the entrance. He followed a fast-moving Tijan but stayed back to give her some space. She'd just crossed the road in front of the hospital when a Rolls Royce pulled up and stopped. August was still across the road but saw Tijan turn to look at the car. It appeared she was talking to someone inside. He stopped and watched for a minute as he wondered who it was. When Tijan jerked back as though avoiding being slapped, August ran, but as he arrived, the back window slid up and the car pulled away.

He looked at Tijan. She was pale, but she had been before, so he wasn't sure if this encounter had added to it.

"Who was that?"

She looked at him briefly, saying, "Someone wanting directions," before she turned and headed into the hospital.

That had been a lie, but he wasn't sure why she had. It hadn't appeared as though anything clandestine had happened, so why lie to him? So much about her puzzled him. Her emphasis on the man in the hospital not being HER father had revealed an anger which he could understand. Her reaction to his shooting had been very different from her sister's. In fact, why hadn't she gone to the hospital with her sister? Something was very odd. Since he'd met her, there had been an air of dishonesty. Although he didn't feel she was a liar, she sure had a mystery hanging around her like a fog settling in.

Once inside, she stopped. "I need to use the bathroom. I'll be right back." She followed the signs across the lobby.

He watched her go, liking what he saw but knowing that wasn't a good idea. He sat down and waited, as he had no idea of the man's name they were going to see. If he asked for the room of the man who had been shot, he wondered how many they'd come back with. Unfortunately, shootings were a little too common. The front cover of a magazine with a picture of waterfalls grabbed his attention. Flipping through it, he got lost in the pictures and in some of the stories of people who had gone on some amazing hikes in the backcountry. He was getting quite comfortable when he glanced at the enormous clock on the wall and realized that Tijan had been gone a while. Scrambling to his feet, he followed the signs and headed in the direction she'd gone. As he rounded the corner, he saw her standing there.

"You okay?"

She avoided eye contact with him. "We need to find my father."

Now the man was her father, he thought, where on the trip over she had vehemently denied that. He wondered why she was so angry with him. Not that he was one to judge; he knew a lot about that whole 'pissed off at the father' thing.

Seeing that Tarin had a twin threw him. Had it been Tarin or Tijan he'd seen leaving C-Lite Hotels? Regardless, it still didn't tell him if he'd been betrayed.

One minute she was there beside him; the next she was halfway down the hallway. She could move fast. August chased after her and caught up with her at the front desk.

"Uh. A man was shot. A Mr. Mardsen... Madsen... Marsden... He's my father."

August frowned but shrugged when the receptionist looked at him with a questioning look. Who doesn't know their father's last name? "Sorry, she just heard he's been hurt and is a little rattled."

Tijan barely looked up. She was fidgeting with the bottom of her plaid shirt.

"Mr. Madsen is heading into surgery right now. You can wait in the waiting room, 284."

Using the directions she'd given them, August led Tijan to the elevators. He had a ton of questions for her but knew this wasn't the time to ask them. Something weird was going on. He just didn't know what it was. That Tijan and Tarin were identical twins was a given, but they were so different. Tarin was all class, gorgeous, friendly, a classy dresser and carried herself with style. Tijan, on the other hand, was kind of wild and natural, and even he couldn't deny, gorgeous. Where Tarin's blue eyes had been arresting and would draw any man in, Tijan's had a depth that he couldn't explain. There was something compelling, but it wasn't anything he wanted to explore. There were too many secrets and way too much drama for him.

When Graham had called, all he'd said was they were sure Tarin's dad would need surgery, but he didn't know anything more. August followed Tijan until they finally found their way to the waiting room. Tarin was pacing, and Graham, who was sitting, never took his eyes off her.

As they approached the room, Tijan suddenly stopped. Only by using fast reflexes did August avoid running into her. He stepped to the side and looked at her. Her eyes were wide and focused on her sister, her face a mask of uncertainty. If Tarin hadn't turned and seen her in that second, August was pretty sure she'd have left.

"Tijan. Thank God you came." Tarin rushed to her and gave her a big hug before stepping back. "He was shot in the leg but has lost a lot of blood. They think he'll be fine but... Oh my God, for all the times he drove me crazy, I still wouldn't wish this on him. I may not want anything to do with him, but I didn't want this. I'm sorry I left you."

Tijan took her sister's hand and returned with her to the waiting room. August followed behind, unsure what to do. Tarin was obviously angry at him, too. The man didn't sound like he was ever going to win 'Father of the Year', yet he had two beautiful daughters who were there for him.

August felt awkward, as if he were privy to family secrets. He'd just met them. He didn't know any of them well, although they had gone out of their way to welcome him. Seeing what they were going through with their father just reminded him of his own. He had no idea exactly where the man was, other than maybe in Toronto. Finding him had been his mother's wish. Her dying wish. If it hadn't been for that, August would have been fine leaving him to whatever life he'd chosen. His mom had been insistent, though, and although she hadn't shared much information, she had said there was a lot about him that August didn't know or didn't understand. She'd felt he needed to hear the explanations directly from his father. It was only because he'd promised his mom on her deathbed that he'd started the journey to find the man who had sired him. Knowing that Tarin and Tijan's father might die, made him realize he wanted to know why his father had abandoned him. At nine, it had been devastating to know that the man who had barely had time for him had chosen to disappear from his life. For a very long time, August had been sure it had been his fault, no matter what his mom had told him.

Next time he had some free time, he'd really put in the effort to find his father.

CHAPTER 28

"HE'S OUT OF SURGERY. He made it through okay, but he's pretty ill. We've got him heavily sedated..." The surgeon who had completed the operation had gone on to explain that the bullet had caused some major muscle damage but had missed the bone. With some rehabilitation, their father should be able to walk again but may have a limp and may need the use of a cane. He was stable, but for now it was wait and see.

Tarin had stayed optimistic and positive throughout the six hours of waiting but burst into tears at the news. Graham took her into his arms and rocked her back and forth.

Tijan felt very left out. She should feel something about the fact that her father was going to be okay, but all she could conjure was numbness. Seeing the love between Graham and her sister stirred up feelings that someday that was what she wanted. It was also what her mom had. Thinking of her mom made her wish that she were there so she could talk to her about all that had happened. But really, she just wanted her mom to take her in her arms and hold her. It had always made Tijan feel better. It had been her cure-all for everything. But if her mom had been there, Tijan would have been firing questions at her faster than a torrential rain. She'd always thought her mom had never lied to her, but this omission was a whopper. The answers were undoubtedly needed, but not something she was likely to get soon. In fact, she was a little too raw to even talk to her mom.

Why her dad hadn't been a part of her life bothered her a lot; despite knowing he wasn't a nice man, had made it a little easier to handle. But not having her sister? She wasn't sure she was going to be able to forgive her mom anytime soon. She didn't know her father, and Tarin didn't know their mother.

So much was wrong with all of it.

Tears leaked from the corners of her eyes. She turned only to find August there. He reached out and put his hand on her shoulder. It was that awkward moment where he could see her hurt but was unsure what to do with it. Compassion was written all over his face, but also the barrier of two strangers. She could tell he wanted to give her a hug but didn't step over that invisible line.

"Oh, Tijan. I'm so not used to sharing the pain of my father... our father. I'm sorry."

Tarin stepped between them and enveloped her in a hard hug. The tears that Tijan had been fighting spilled forth. She didn't even know what she was crying about. A wall of emotion was crashing down.

Everyone finally sat as they waited to hear if they could see him, though Tijan hadn't decided if she could. On one hand, she wanted to see him without his stoic armor on. On the other hand , she wasn't sure she wanted to see him. Feeling a bit aloof, she didn't, however, want to take away from Tarin seeing him.

The nurse finally announced that the two of them could visit him for a few minutes. Tarin jumped up, grabbing Tijan's hand.

"I don't think I should go. I'll see him tomorrow when he's a bit stronger. I think this is for you. Okay?" Tijan held her breath. She hoped she hadn't insulted her sister, but she just couldn't go in there. Not only were there all the lies and the lack of feeling for her father, but there was also the matter of the two thugs who had approached her. They'd slipped her mind, but now she recalled they had told her that because she'd be in charge, they'd each be in touch to discuss 'business'. She needed to have a talk with Tarin, but this wasn't the time.

Tarin smiled and hugged her before rushing off, Graham close on her heels.

It was almost 3:00 a.m. by the time they left the hospital. As they exited the building, the shrill sound of an ambulance siren greeted them.

"That's a jolly good way to wake someone up," Graham said in a stodgy English accent.

Everyone laughed. Tijan was glad for the humor, but something dawned on her. "Umm. Shouldn't the police have stopped by and asked questions?"

Under the streetlight, the look that passed between Graham and Tarin was obvious. "That was taken care of."

"Oh, they were here before we arrived?"

"Y-eah."

Tijan frowned but decided to let it go. It wasn't her business what was told to the police. "I know we're all tired, but there is something I need to tell you, Tarin. It's really important. I haven't had time to say anything, or I would have already. But this can't wait."

"Sure. Want to get together tomorrow? I guess I should say later today?"

"No. I think I need to tell you tonight. Is there someplace we can go where we won't be disturbed or overheard?"

"Sure. We can go to the office. You can hop in with us or follow us?"

"I'll drive her." August stepped forward.

Tijan was about to argue, but he had taken her arm and was propelling her across the parking lot. "We'll see you there."

They each went their separate ways to their vehicles.

"Umm, do you know where the office is?" Tijan turned to August as they approached his car.

"Yeah. I've been there."

Tijan barely paid attention as they drove. Her mind was busy with what and how she was going to tell her sister about everything. It wasn't until they stopped that Tijan became aware of her surroundings. They were parked by the building she'd first scouted upon her arrival in Toronto. It seemed like such a long time ago, but it hadn't even been a week.

Who knew so much could happen in a few short days.

Graham's vehicle was already in the parking lot, but he and Tarin were nowhere to be seen. Sighing, she climbed out and followed August around the building and to a door at the back. Just as he reached for it, a man stepped out of the alley.

"Ahh." Tijan jumped back.

"Shouldn't be sneaking around here." The man stepped out of the dark alleyway and stood between them and the door.

Tijan realized he was the guy from her first visit there, who had stared her down on the street. She was glad she was standing in the shadows as she didn't want him to recognize her—not that she thought he would, but she didn't want to take chances. She clapped her hands to her face as she snorted. Of course, he'd recognize her. She looked exactly like Tarin. A giggle was threatening to burst forth. It was a good indication of how exhausted and punchy she was.

August put his hands up as though telling the man he meant no harm. "It's okay. Graham and Tarin have invited us here."

"They don't work at this hour."

"I know they probably don't, but they've made an exception."

"They tell me when they're here."

"Maybe they forgot."

Tijan listened to the two men argue. The man was blocking their way and was not about to move. He was a little shorter than August, who she guessed was around six feet, but he wasn't someone that he should take on. There was a hard protectiveness about the guy, and he seemed on edge. His rigid, almost military-like stance and the way he was blocking the door was making it pretty clear they weren't getting past him without Graham and Tarin.

"Do you have one of their phone numbers?" His question made Tijan realize she didn't even know how to contact her sister. She pushed the added hurt away.

"I'll text him."

Tijan stepped away from the building, seeking quiet, although sirens could still be heard in the distance.

"Why is your hair long? You're not Tarin. She doesn't have a sister."

Tijan whipped around. The man glared at her as if in anger. He took a step toward her, but August stepped in front of him and placed his hands on the man's chest. The man's arm came down hard across August's before he spun him and slammed him against the outside wall and twisted his arm up behind his back.

The door burst open.

"Bill. It's okay. Let him go. I forgot to let you know we were here." Graham spoke softly as he approached him cautiously and slowly. "It won't happen again. It was an emergency. They're with us. You can trust them.

"This is on me, Bill. You can let him go." Graham kept talking softly but did not touch him. "Deep breath." Graham then proceeded to do just that a few times.

Bill released August abruptly. He stepped back, and although he didn't look at August, he said, "You need your hair cut. Men don't have long hair. Disrespect." He disappeared around the corner.

"Sorry about that, guys. Go on up. I'll be there in a minute." Graham followed the man around the side of the building.

Feeling a bit shaken, Tijan headed up the stairs, hearing the clump of August's steps behind her. They reached the top.

"Turn right."

Tijan stepped through the open door. The office was rather stark, but there was no one there.

"I'm in here."

Following the voice, Tijan walked through into the second office. It didn't have much more furniture or pictures than the first one, but the bed in the corner caught her eye. Suddenly realizing she was sleep-deprived, she was very tempted to crawl into it. Blinking a few times to stave off sleep, she looked around and realized her sister was sitting at one of the two desks and was busy on the computer.

"Just give me a minute. I'm finishing up something."

Tijan was too wired to sit down but too tired to do much more than find an empty wall and prop herself against it.

Tarin looked up and smiled at her. It touched Tijan in a way she hadn't been expecting. Subconsciously, she pressed her hand against her chest.

"It appears the hotel has been trying to reach me. They've sent me an email, stating that with my father unable to fulfil his duties, I'm expected to stand in." Tarin popped her fist onto the desk.

Tijan smiled. It was such a controlled, gentle punch. It was so unlike what she would have done.

"Whoa, girl. What has your father done now?" Graham asked as he entered the room. He turned to face Tijan and August, who were standing not far from her. "It's the only time I ever see her mad. Her father has a way about him. Sorry about Bill. He's truly harmless and a good guy." He looked pointedly at August.

"It's okay. I get it; he's protecting you guys. I don't hold any grudges, but please let him know I'm a good guy too."

"I already have. He knows you're with us."

"They met Bill?" Tarin looked wide-eyed at Graham and then at August.

"Yeah. He didn't like that I had long hair. Or that I showed up here at night wanting to meet with you guys." August shrugged like it was no big deal.

Tarin gasped. "I never thought to say anything when we got here. In fact, I thought he'd gone home and—"

"Hey. It's okay. He didn't hurt me. Or you, Tijan?" August gave her a look that she interpreted to mean, lie if you have to but don't tell her he scared or hurt you.

Tijan shook her head. She'd been listening to everything that was being said, but it was the unspoken messages between Tarin and Graham that piqued her interest. They seemed awfully protective of the old guy, and he seemed to be just as protective of them. Yet they kept looking at August. He didn't look like a fighter, although his clothes fit nice and she would guess he had a nice physique; she couldn't imagine him hurting an old man. But then, as with all of them, she didn't know him either.

"You were talking about your father." Tijan found she couldn't say anymore. He was her father too, yet she just couldn't bring herself to acknowledge it, even if it felt wrong to call him Tarin's father.

"He's put me in charge. I almost think he got shot on purpose."

Tijan's heart thumped in her chest. Her father might just be worse than she'd thought.

CHAPTER 29

"WHAT DID YOU LEARN?"

"That if we want to make this happen, we are going to have to do it ourselves. My father is making plans for me to marry the old guy's daughter. Not impressed."

"She's hot, though."

"Yeah, if you swing that way. Anyway, I'm not interested. And never will be. I'm almost tempted to tell my father the truth about me, that all the women he thinks I bed are for his benefit. I'm sure it would give him a heart attack. That would solve many of my problems. Our problems." He sipped his glass of Chardonnay. He didn't share with his partner that his father had just killed a long-time employee for being gay.

"I'm glad you're not straight. Otherwise, we wouldn't be together."

He smiled, glad that his new 'friend' thought they'd be lovers. This was going to work better than he thought.

To anyone in the small, dimly lit lounge, they were two businessmen in suits. To the one who'd set this up, they were acquaintances, with the one a pawn. The other one thought they were friends and soon to be lovers. Either way, it was something they could never share with the world. At least, not the one they existed in. It would ruin both of their careers. Never mind that it might just take their lives—although what they were planning might definitely change that, anyway.

"I don't think we should wait. We should strike now. Take things over. Then you'll be in a better place to deal with your father. And then you won't feel we have to wait to take our relationship to the next level."

"I couldn't care less about him. I want to create my own dynasty, not his. He's old school. Can you imagine with this hotel chain what we could do? The money we could launder through here. The drugs. We'd be so rich and powerful, we could easily take out my father."

"I love when you get so fired up about stuff." The two men stared intimately at each other. They'd deliberately chosen this restaurant and the large booth in the dimly lit corner so they could have these private moments.

"I think we should approach James and give him an ultimatum—"

"Why? There is no way the man is going to take on partners. We'd be dead before the words got out of our mouths. You know that, right?"

"No, he is."

"What? No, you can't be thinking of doing that."

"No. But if I scare him enough, he might just agree that partners are a good idea. I mean, we've already managed to funnel off two million, and he hasn't seemed to notice."

"True. But that's because we've been smart about it. Setting up that fake sale of the winery was brilliant. Well, the winery isn't fake, but he thinks he owns it."

"You know what's even better? If we make it look like he's the one scamming and laundering his own money."

"That's brilliant. Is there any way we can make ourselves partners? Have him sign something that we can doctor up to look like he was clear that he was giving us 51% controlling interest? We don't want to be too greedy. We want him to sit and watch from the sidelines while we take control of his business."

"Yes. Now, that's what we should do. I'll set up a meeting this week with him. I'm sure there is some project that I could get him to sign off on. The Caspian Wine deal is never going to happen, at least in my opinion, but we could tell him that we need him to sign a series of letters that will be sent off to Caspian, giving them deadlines or something like that. Can you draft that up?"

"Yes. And I can forge his signature. Better yet, I'll set up a digital file and send it to him. I'll get him to sign digitally. Then I'll take that and put his signature on some legal documents, giving us fifty-one percent control. I'll look into how to do it."

"God, I am so ready for this. Can I see you later? Oh, forget it. I just remembered I've been summoned to see my father. And I don't want to put you at risk. He'd kill you."

"Don't worry. Soon we won't have to hide or worry so much. Just imagine this, we'll take the second floor of the hotel and turn it into our place. We can make it two suites, so we can still keep our private life private, but we'll be together."

The two men stared at each other for a long time, both knowing that they were taking an enormous risk.

"You know what would be so much easier? Have him signed over the hotel to us and then kill him. Make it look like a break-in."

"Or better yet, make it look like it was my father who did it."

****

"He's in." He took her in his arms and kissed her deeply, pulling her hair out of its tight bun as he did so. His hands were busy peeling off her well-designed clothes. The difference in their age didn't mean a thing to him.

"Hey, be careful with that. It's expensive."

"Soon I'll be able to buy you what you want, and you won't ever have to worry about something being expensive. I'll just buy you a new one."

"So, if I wanted a new house?"

"I'll buy you one on every continent."

She laughed. He loved hearing that and was even more excited, as he knew from working with her that it was something rare.

His hands were roaming over her skin, but she danced back out of his reach, and her arms extended toward him in an attempt to ward him off. Her smile softened her actions.

"This is going to work, right?"

"Yes, I've got him drafting some paperwork to get James to sign, get his signature and then transpose it onto legal documents. I'll tell him it's too risky for him to do anything with that signature. He's too close. But he'll make a great fall guy. We'll alter the documents, and then you and I will own 51% of C-Lite Hotels. Just enough to drive James crazy."

She launched herself at him and was soon divesting him of his clothes as fast as he was divesting her of hers. With one pant leg still on, he picked her up and wrapped her legs around his waist. They barely made it to the kitchen counter.

CHAPTER 30

TIJAN GRABBED A CHAIR and pulled it around the desk so she could sit facing Tarin. She didn't want any barriers between them, and she was too tired to stand anymore.

She took her sister's hands in hers, noting that although they looked identical, some things were different. Tarin's hands were soft and unmarred, while hers were rough and calloused. She went to pull back, but Tarin held tight.

"There's so much I want to tell you, but I think most of it will have to wait. But know this, I came here to find you."

Tarin squeezed her hands as tears welled in her eyes. "If I'd known you weren't a figment of my imagination, I'd have looked for you."

Tijan felt her throat close and looked down for a second. "I don't know who is responsible for that. For keeping us apart. We'll figure that out later. For now, your father—well, I guess he's mine too. Anyway, on the first day I was here, he abducted me."

"What!"

"Well, I should say two of his henchmen—"

"He makes me so mad. What was he trying to bully you into?" Tarin shook her head. "Wait. Did he know who you were?"

Tijan considered that for a minute. He'd called her Tarin, but he had to know she, Tijan, existed. Didn't he?

"He seemed to think I was you. By the way, he likes your hair long. Or my hair. You know what I mean."

Tarin sat back, smiling. "Yes. It's why mine is short. According to him, it's a boy's haircut. It drives him crazy."

"Got it. It's cute, by the way. I don't think I could wear my hair like yours, though."

August chuckled. All three turned to look at him.

He shrugged. "Really? You're identical."

Tijan looked at Tarin as his comment sank in. They giggled, and when they realized they sounded alike, they laughed harder.

"I guess that's true. If I want to know how I'd look in something, I just have to look at you. God, I've missed you." Tijan hugged her sister hard.

"I don't want to break this up, but what you were saying about your father?" Graham leaned against the other side of the desk.

Tijan sat back. "Right. The second time—"

"What?"

"Umm. Well, the first time was just a chat in his car. The second time, his two bodyguards took me to his office—which is pretty swanky, by the way. He wasn't thrilled with my attire and offered to buy me some clothes. He felt I, meaning you, should stop rebelling."

Tijan looked at her sister in an effort to see how she was taking it. There was an awkward moment of uncertainty, but it didn't last long. They both grinned.

"Our father has been a bear to live with. All my life, he's been trying to build a little robot—"

"Which I'm glad to say he failed at," Graham chimed in.

"Some days I wonder. Anyway, was he trying to tell you that you should come to work for him?" Tarin's voice lowered. "'This is your family legacy. Time for you to start acting like it means something. I haven't worked this hard for you to throw it away. You're my daughter. If you'd been a son, you'd have listened better.'"

Everyone chuckled at her poor imitation of her deep-throated father.

"He did make that clear. But what concerns me—" She looked between Tarin and Graham, there was not only love but respect there. Did their father know? Or just not approve?

"What? He's found me a husband?"

Tijan gasped. "Well, yes."

"It's okay. Really, he's been finding me a husband since I was about fourteen. Of course, they were all older, wealthy men who would benefit him financially or in the power status arena. Don't worry about it. I quit worrying a long time ago."

"That's not all, though."

"Oh?"

"Yeah, the first time he abducted me—"

"I can't believe him. But I guess since I've been refusing to talk to him, he's now resorting to these extreme measures." Tarin turned to Graham. "He's got to be stopped, Graham. What can we do? I'm so tired of this."

"Let's wait until he's better, then we'll figure out how to take him down." Graham shook his head.

Tarin screwed up her face. "Aren't I a good daughter? I'd already forgotten he's in the hospital with a gunshot wound. The question is, which of his forty thousand enemies did it."

"I haven't been around the man long, but believe me, I was tempted to shoot him." Tijan clamped her hand to her mouth. "Oh. I shouldn't have said that. I'm sorry, Tarin."

Tarin smiled as she jumped to her feet with a silly smile on her face. "I think the two of us would have gotten into so much trouble growing up."

Tijan grinned back. "What I've been trying to tell you is he's trying to buy Caspian Winery. He wants me, well, you, to do some snooping as to how to get Mrs. Lindell to sell to him. And he wants to give it to you to do whatever you want—tear it down or run it. Then he'll train you in how to run his company. I don't think you'll ever get that opportunity, though. I mean, he seemed only interested in teaching you until your son is old enough to take over and run his empire."

"I hate him. Running my life is one thing, but to try to take Caspian Winery? Unforgivable. Deciding my son's future? A child he has never even met? I'll go live in the desert before I let him touch Chance."

"Oooh. I'd love that. I can see you in a silky, flowing dress, fanning the man in your life and feeding him grapes... Aaaah. The life." Graham's joke broke the tension. Everyone laughed.

"And you in your fig leaf—" Tarin's face turned beat red.

Graham roared as he grabbed her.

Tijan had the impression that her sister didn't joke much. "I forgot to mention the mafia guys who want me to make sure Father steps in line. I think I'm—well, you—are the prize."

CHAPTER 31

AUGUST'S EYELIDS KEPT DROPPING like they were weighted with stones. The dark roasted coffee he'd drunk an hour before was already wearing off. Arching his back to try to get the blood moving again, he'd been sitting in one position too long. He'd tried to stay unobtrusive, as he hadn't wanted to stop the flow of conversation. Since he was the outsider and had no idea what had brought all this on, he was definitely fascinated by what he was hearing. He still didn't understand how the two sisters couldn't have known about each other, though.

"Okay, what's this about the mafia?" Graham asked.

"Well, I don't know if they were mafia, but they look like what I imagine the ma—"

Tarin's phone rang.

"It's the hotel. Dad's office. I don't feel like talking business." She sighed. "Excuse me." She got up and went to the outer office.

Tijan, whose head had been dropping awkwardly to her shoulder, sat up straighter and blinked her eyes several times.

Graham had his elbows resting on his desk with his face resting heavily on his palms. "I think it's way past my bedtime."

"Yeah. I can't do these all-nighters anymore. Did them back in my school days, but I feel like an old man right now." August wanted to say that he was ready to leave, but he was supposed to be at work in a few hours. Asking for the day off might be a bit much, but he wasn't sure how he was going to make it through the day.

Tarin came back into the room, which seemed to have the effect of waking everyone up. They all looked at her expectantly.

"Well, it appears that my father has a contingency plan that should something happen to him, I'm to be in charge. Wasn't that nice of him to tell me? I was sure that one of his two top vice presidents would be put in charge. This will go over well with them."

Graham stood and went over to her, taking her in his arms. "Are you going?"

"No. But I'm sure they'll keep calling me. I was already asked to make four decisions immediately. I said that I wouldn't do that. Mary told me they'd hold off doing anything until I was ready to give them some direction. Damn him. He just keeps screwing with my life."

Tarin's phone rang again. She looked at Graham and sighed heavily. "I'm not answering."

"I think it's time we all got some sleep. I'm beat." Tijan stood up.

August was still wondering what he was going to do about work. He was in no shape to be there. He didn't need the job. He'd call LJ and tell her not to expect him, and if that was a problem, he'd just leave. Everything had been rather off since he'd met these people, anyway, and his initial goal of finding his father wasn't happening. All the stuff that Tarin and Tijan's father seemed to be doing made him wonder if he wanted to find his own. He was quite sure that he wasn't prepared to hear why his dad had abandoned him. Knowing that Tarin and Tijan's father not only was a jerk keeping them apart but was also so underhanded. August couldn't understand why a man would do that. But then he couldn't understand why his father would just up and leave a young boy of nine.

Tarin's phone rang again. She glanced at the screen and then raised her arm as though going to chuck it.

"Can I answer it? Can I? Can I? Can I?" Tijan jumped up and down like a kid. "I think I'm getting punchy or silly. But I'm serious, can I answer it?"

Tarin frowned but handed her the phone. It stopped ringing. Tijan giggled and held out her hand to give it back. It rang again. She looked questioningly at Tarin, who shrugged.

"Hello. May I ask why you continue to call me? I'm tired and not in the mood to deal with your—" There was a long silence as Tijan listened intently to what was being said.

August wished he could hear all that was being told to her. The expressions crossing her face were quite interesting—annoyance, frowning, puzzled, thoughtful.

"Who's that...?"

"I don't think—"

"Alright, give me until 4:00." Tijan disconnected the call and then looked wide-eyed at Tarin. "I think that power has already gone to my head. Oh Tarin. I just jumped in like it was my place to solve you—our father's problems. I love to figure stuff out. But I had no right. I can't believe I just did that."

"What exactly did you get me roped into?"

"The CSIS—which I think he said was the Canadian Security Intelligence Service—which I didn't know we had, wants to meet with me, well, you. The guy informed me that they are responsible for national security. Anyway, there have been some questionable dealings with some known drug dealers. Do you know anything about that?"

Tarin's face went pale. "Did they tell you any more than that?"

Tijan shook her head.

"This is so my father's world. Let's all blackmail each other."

August wasn't sure why, but Tijan looked at him. He wondered if she wanted his opinion or was looking for approval. He held her gaze as he tried to read her. She suddenly looked away, glancing at her sister.

"Do you remember the mafia dudes I mentioned? I'm assuming they might be behind this. They do look like drug dealers. Mary said, 'Show up today to meet with the CSIS or they'll get a court order to access all the books.' She's concerned they'll leak to the media that your dad's hotel chain is linked to nefarious characters—my word, not theirs."

"It can't be true. My father is many things, but I can't see him running drugs. I can't put Chance through this. What am I going to do, Graham?"

August decided it was time; they needed a bit of privacy. Catching Tijan's attention, he nodded toward the other office. He walked out; she followed.

"At the hospital, was that encounter you didn't want to mention with one of those thugs?" August leaned his hips against the desk, surprised when Tijan did the same beside him.

"I think so. The guy seemed to think I was a prize of some sort. I don't know what her—my—our father is into, but I don't think it's good." She looked at him earnestly. "How do I tell Tarin that it's worse than she thinks? And I'm not sure if it was her-my-our father who sent those people snooping out at Caspian or if it was the mafia. But I don't think the mafia would do it so nicely, would they? Or is there someone else?"

"What do you mean, snooping at Caspian?"

"The other day. Or was that yesterday? You know they chased us into that shed, and we hid."

August looked at her warily, but her head was hanging down and she was staring at her hands. "You were the redhead?"

"Yeah. It wasn't a good look for me, I don't think. What do I tell Tarin?"

Before he could answer, Tarin and Graham came out of the inner office. Tarin was very pale and was leaning on Graham, whose arm was wrapped around her.

Tijan looked stricken as she stared at her sister. "Before you say anything, I know this may be crazy, but I feel kind of responsible for putting you in the middle, Tarin."

"No. Our father did that."

"Well, I'd like to be you. Just for the meeting, I want to find out what they want, what they know. This might be a good time to figure out what Father has been up to and come up with a way to keep him from running your life."

The silence was like the stunned aftereffect of a disaster—here was that moment when there was complete silence and stillness, as though the air had been sucked out of the room. When everyone realized the impact of what had been said, the air became electrified. August knew his plan of leaving to get his own answers was going to be put on hold. If they seemed stunned at what Tijan had said, wait until they heard his request.

"You can't."

"Why not? Even Graham thought I was you."

Graham turned red and shrugged guiltily. It made August wonder what had happened as the flush on Tijan and August's faces suggested a whole lot more than a casual mistake.

"But you don't know anything."

Tijan laughed. "True. But—"

"I didn't mean you don't know anything. I meant, you don't know my father's business. Do you?"

"No. But then you have..." Tijan pulled out her phone and looked at it. "Seven hours to teach me something about the hotel business, minus about three for a nap."

August spoke up. "I'm going to need some time off."

Tarin looked stunned. "I'm sorry, August. We know this has been a bit unconventional, but please don't leave."

"Hey look, as soon as this is over—"

"You'll give me the answers I want." August realized at this point the answers didn't matter. For whatever reason, they seemed to trust him. Tijan was slouched on the desk beside him, her eyes half closed. Exhaustion seemed to have drained her body of any stamina to sit upright.

Tarin stood beside Graham, her hands clasped in front of her chest. Her eyes were black, and her face was white with tiredness. The two looked the same, yet were very different. He averted his eyes lest they know he was studying them. They were both strong, beautiful women. Tijan leaned her head against his shoulder, unable to hold herself upright anymore. It surprised him but also reminded him of all she'd been through in the last twenty-four hours.

"I'm going as well. You can make me the Head of Transportation or Tijan's bodyguard, but I'm going."

CHAPTER 32

"THIS IS CRAZY!" TIJAN shook her head as she wondered what had happened to the down-to-earth, logical country girl. What she knew about business in general could fit in a glass. Her knowledge about corporate business wouldn't even fill a shot glass—which is exactly what she'd need to get through this insanity—and preferably it would be filled with whiskey. She glanced at August, not wanting to take her eyes off the road as the traffic was heavy and she was unfamiliar with the area. Her phone map might have given her the directions as well as Tarin, but it was like being in the bush for the first time—everything looked the same. August was staring at his phone. She wondered how he felt about being roped into this.

"So, exactly why are you coming with me?"

"Because we don't know what we're dealing with. And the guy at the hospital seemed to think I was your boyfriend or bodyguard, which just might work in your favor. And I'm the new manager of Transportation. At least I can be your backup if needed. Graham is going to keep your sister and son safe, and they've hired some security for us."

"Oh my God, that sounds so espionage-like." Tijan laughed nervously. "What experience do you have with any of this?"

"Probably the same as you."

Tijan snorted. "Okay, well, that means zero. We ought to do well. Think we can convince the lawyers, the CSIS and potentially the mafia, that we have a clue about running a multi-million—wait, it is just multi-million and not billion-dollar company—we're talking about? Did Tarin tell me about that? Good God, I've forgotten everything she told me. Were you paying better attention?"

August laughed. "No. But I have run a successful business—"

"Oh? What?"

"I owned and operated a garage."

"You mean, like a mechanic shop? Or are we talking about something else?"

"I had eight mechanics and two office personnel. It was by no means in the same league as this hotel chain, but I have a basic understanding of business and the legal aspects."

Tijan was glad to have him with her. Big business to her was shark-infested waters.

"Great, so you'll know how to handle any business questions. What the hell are they fishing for anyway? What was my father into? This is so beyond crazy. I think I entered a loony bin. I did, didn't I?"

She drove to the secret entrance she'd been privy to, thanks to her abduction. Honestly, though, she'd never have found it again without Tarin explaining how to find it and giving her the passcode. Once inside the car elevator, the doors immediately closed behind them.

"I'd hate to get locked in here." Tijan quickly keyed in the code and then, with her hands curled around the edge of her seat, she waited as the elevator lifted them to the twentieth floor.

As soon as the doors opened, she drove out and parked.

August got out of the car first. "That was kind of cool, but I don't think I enjoy being locked in a solid steel box for the time it took us to get up here."

Tijan shook her head. "It was a good thing I couldn't see the first time, either. I think I was too freaked out to notice. I don't like it either."

"And we come out of a steel-enclosed box to one that is concrete."

"It's a really sterile, inhospitable environment, isn't it?" Tijan dialed a number so someone would escort her into the building. Tarin didn't want her to use the private entrance that only a few knew about. Five minutes after she'd phoned, an attractive, stylishly dressed, fifty-something-year-old woman strode out of a different door than Tijan had gone through before.

"Hi, Tarin. Nice to see you. I'm sorry it's not under better circumstances."

"Mary." Tijan nodded in greeting, thankful she'd remembered the woman's name.

"I tried to visit your father at the hospital, but they wouldn't let me in. Though I've worked for him for ten years and know him better than anyone, it didn't matter. I wasn't family. Please know I tried." Her voice broke.

Tijan touched her arm. "He's still in a coma, so visitation is restricted. Thank you for stopping by, though. That was thoughtful of you."

Mary looked incredibly sad for a few seconds, but then her face hardened, erasing any trace of the soft woman she'd just shown. Tijan had felt like giving her a hug, but the moment was gone, and she was all business again.

"Follow me. Here is your set of keys and here are the codes that you'll use while here. These will get you in this way to your father's office." Mary reminded Tijan of an elderly neighbor back home who had the same brusque attitude and belief that things were done a certain way. And she didn't like change.

As they walked through the door and down a long hallway, Mary kept providing information. Even after they'd arrived at her father's swanky office. She was obviously used to doing things on the run, as she seemed was constantly moving around the room, straightening something or opening the blinds and then closing them a bit. Tijan listened but barely had a clue what she was talking about.

At times, she felt like she was getting the full rendition of a business, top to bottom, in twenty minutes.

"You've got a few things that you'll need to sign right away. One is a legal form agreeing to take over your father's position temporarily. The papers are on your desk. Please review them and sign them. If you have questions, ask me. There are other forms that need to be looked at. And you have—"

Tijan tuned her out. It was all a lot of babble that reminded her of listening to Charlie Brown's teacher in the Peanuts series—nothing but noise.

"I've set you up on the system. You can use your father's computer to access it. You'll be able to access all the general business and company files. You won't, however, be able to access your father's files unless you have his passcode." Mary stopped and gave her a pointed look.

Tijan smiled. It was almost as though she was asking if she had it. A young, tall, well-dressed man walked in from the main office.

"JT." Mary's voice had a warning in it.

He smiled at her but turned to Tijan with an intense look of sorrow. "Tarin. I'm JT. I'm the Manager of Finance but soon to be CFO. I'm sorry to hear about your father. I don't know how it happened. We have the best security. Honestly. To think he got shot just outside our building... We've doubled the security, just so you know."

"Thank you." Tijan nodded at him but stepped around him, disconcerted when he stepped in front of her again. It seemed like quite a leap to go from manager to CFO. She'd have to ask Tarin if that was normal or if this guy was praying for something that wasn't likely to happen. Tempted to look over her shoulder for August, she refrained. She was sure that if she caught his eye, the panic that was setting in would be obvious, so she kept walking.

"JT, mind telling us exactly what happened? We've had the gray version from the police." August stepped in front of them.

They had just entered the lobby. A waterfall covered one wall, the water racing over an etched, rippled glass design. Lights at the bottom gave it a soft, rainbow hue. It was a scaled-down version to one in the hotel lobby. The sound of water flowing almost had Tijan believing that if she closed her eyes, she would feel like she was back in the country. Mary's large oak desk had a raised privacy panel and jutted prominently into the wide-open space, separated only by a heavy glass partition. It was the first thing Tijan had seen when she'd gotten off the elevator. Other than the waiting room to the left, the only access to the main offices was around Mary's desk to the right. She wasn't sure where the door on the left went. Had Tarin told her?

Tijan was quite sure that no one got past Mary without her permission.

"Please, let's go into the office. You can talk there." Mary hustled them through the door to her father's office.

Tijan moved to sit on the far sofa, only to find JT seating himself beside her. She looked at August, who sat on the other leather couch across from her. He held her gaze for a moment. She hoped he understood that she was way over her head. This stupid plan she'd come up with was slapping her in the face.

"Why are you here?"

"I'm the new manager of Transportation and I'm here at Tarin's request."

JT's face hardened as he glared at August. Tijan frowned as she sensed an undercurrent of anger between them.

"Gray version?"

Even though JT was essentially asking August what he meant, he looked at Tijan for an answer.

August replied, "The version where there are more questions than answers."

"All I know is your father was leaving work. He stopped in the parking lot out back and got out of his car.

That's when someone shot him." JT reached over and took Tijan's hand in his.

Her first reaction was to pull it back, but he was firmly holding on. It took too much effort to fight him. Curious where this was going, she left it.

"That's more or less the version we got. Thank you, JT."

"You're meeting is in thirty minutes, Tarin. JT, you have work to do."

Tijan had totally forgotten about Mary but was thankful for the distraction. Tijan removed her hand from JT as she stood. JT stood beside her, and she stepped back to put some space between them.

"I think I should be in that meeting with you."

"Thank you, JT, but I can handle it. And I have August here to help me."

JT turned to August. "When exactly did you get hired?"

"The same day that James told you that you weren't getting the job."

The furious look came and went quickly across JT's face, but it was unmistakable. Tijan's eyebrows rose as she looked at August questioningly.

They'd agreed that August would be the new Transportation Manager of the hotels' vehicles, overseeing maintenance, the drivers and purchasing, and Tarin had signed forms giving him that role. All the paperwork was in place, should anyone snoop. Tijan wasn't sure if August was goading JT or if there was something else going on. It wouldn't surprise her. She wasn't sure that anyone had been honest with her since she'd arrived.

August smiled. "If you don't mind, JT, we have work to do. As I'm sure you do."

The glare that JT gave August obviously wasn't for her to see. When he turned to face her, he had nothing but a sincere, concerned expression.

"If there's anything I can help with, call me. We should sit down and meet soon anyway. We have a lot to go over. I am the financial manager after all. Soon to be CFO."

He seemed to want her to get that he was moving up in the company. She wondered if any of it was true or if he was hoping she'd be an easy boss to convince to give him the promotion he wanted. "Right, JT. Thank you." She nodded, hoping he'd leave soon. She had the feeling he was going to reach for her hand again, so she casually slid her hands into her pockets.

"It's a good thing I know a lot of the inner workings here. You can come to me with any questions."

As soon as he left, Mary checked to see if they needed anything else. "Again, I'm sorry about your dad. He's a good man. I can't imagine this business without him."

After she'd closed the door on her way out, August immediately opened his phone and began playing music at a high volume.

Tijan flopped onto the sofa, dropping her head against the back and closing her eyes. The music reminded her to keep her voice low, as they had no idea who could be listening. "People say that business is like a hamster wheel. Things just go round and round. But this is like being on a carnival ride. I feel like I'm spinning and going up and down and sideways and have no idea where I'm going to stop. This is crazy, and the circus act hasn't even started."

She felt the couch dip beside her but refrained from opening her eyes.

"You did fine. We'll get through this."

Tijan rolled her head to the side and opened her eyes. She was surprised at how close August was sitting. His gaze was fixed on her face. There was a moment of awareness as she found herself pulled toward the gold flecks in his tawny eyes. It was when his pupils dilated that she shot to her feet and strode to her father's desk.

Her butt hit the seat of her father's chair and something deep down shifted. She was sitting where her father had sat. He'd been doing it for years. It wasn't something new she should just be finding out. She should have had a lifetime of knowing it.

Why had she been excluded from his life?

That beat her down more than anything she'd ever dealt with. It reminded her of calving season. There always seemed to be one calf that the mother would abandon. Not that Tijan minded, because she always got to be the surrogate mother—feeding and nurturing the baby calf to stand on its wobbly legs, take its first steps and to know that it was wanted. In this case, it wasn't the mother who had rejected her. In fact, her mom couldn't have been more loving, but just like that calf, her father was not part of her life—had never been part of her life, at least not that she remembered.

But why?

There was a knock on the door. Tijan lifted her head and stared at it for a minute. In one part of her brain, the sound registered, and there was some niggling feeling that she should do something, but she couldn't manage to do more than keep her eyes glued to it. She missed the odd look that August gave her, but she was aware of him opening the door slightly. After a brief conversation, he stepped back. Mary moved past him.

"Sorry to bother you but there are two men here to see you."

"Can we reschedule?"

"This isn't a meeting that can be rescheduled. I think you'd better meet with them."

Tijan looked at the woman as she wondered if she looked like she felt—the five-year-old sitting in her dad's chair, trying to pretend she belonged in his world. "Give me five minutes and show them in."

"If I may, Tarin? Do not give them anything that will have them snooping into your father's business. Your father is a good man. I know those two men are government officials of some sort. Your father deserves your loyalty."

Tijan wasn't sure how to react, so she didn't. Mary left, but Tijan felt like she'd just been scolded. She stood. August looked a bit stunned, as if wondering what had just happened. "I didn't even ask who they were. I mean, I know they are CSIS but—"

"You'll do fine. Not that I'm sure of all that Mary was telling you, but I agree. Don't give any actual answers."

Taking a deep breath and trying to get some solid footing under her, she moved away from the intimidating desk and over to the leather sofas. Not having a clue who she was meeting with, she at least hoped she'd feel a little more in charge in the more casual setting.

CHAPTER 33

"HELLO, MS. ROTH. AND you are?"

August squared his shoulders, and for a moment Tijan thought he was going to punch the guy. Not that she could blame him, his tone was very condescending. Their dark suits were too cliché—black, identical and not a wrinkle in them.

August thrust out his hand. "Mr. Renner. I'm the director of Transportation."

Tijan tensed immediately, as if she hadn't been tense enough. What had made August lie right away baffled her.

August strode toward them as if he owned the place. Tijan wasn't sure what he was doing but didn't want to take her eyes off the men who seemed quite focused on her. She brushed her hand down the beige suit she was wearing. At least she looked every bit a businesswoman. But with her hair down and draped over her shoulders and her big blue eyes blinking at them, she was determined to use whatever tricks she could to throw them off. Of course, Tarin had to show her how to dress and behave, but the two men seemed a little dumbfounded, so hopefully that meant it was working.

If it wouldn't have given too much away, she would have stood by August for moral support. As if queuing her, he cleared his throat.

Tijan blinked a few times as she soothed her frayed nerves. She pasted on a smile and walked toward the two men, who were standing a bit awkwardly by the leather couch. She thrust out her hand.

"I'm Tarin. And you are?"

"Ms. Roth—"

"Please, Tarin." She stretched her smile further.

"Tarin. We're with the CSIS."

"Yes, the Canadian Security Intelligence Service. Can I offer you a coffee? Tea? Whiskey?" Tijan gave the men a full-blown smile.

"No. But we need to meet privately, so if your friend will wait outside?"

"No, he stays. Have a seat, gentlemen." Although she hadn't appreciated being abducted by her father, she was thankful she had been in that office before. It gave her a tiny bit of familiarity.

Once everyone was seated on the leather sofas, Tijan sat on the edge with her hands resting on the couch by her hips, gripping the leather tightly. She didn't let her gaze waver, although she now understood how her horse felt when it got spooked and bolted. Tijan wished she had that option, and it made her consider her offer to step into Tarin's shoes. This was not her world.

"Do you mind turning off your music?"

August smiled and shook his head, much to the other man's annoyance.

"We have proof that your father, James Madsen, is involved with organized crime."

Tijan wasn't sure what her reaction was supposed to be. If she hadn't already had the pleasure of meeting her father, she would have been shocked.

"What proof do you have?" August sat forward, his elbows on his knees.

"I'm sorry, but we can't share that. Ms. Roth, what we're here to tell you is that we will pursue legal action against your father."

Tijan swallowed forcefully, wishing she'd gotten herself something to drink even though the others had declined. "And you're telling me this because?"

Suddenly, a thought struck her. "Why are you here today? My father is injured and in the hospital."

"We're aware of that."

"I'm sure you are. But you see, he only went in yesterday. So, was this meeting originally set up with him?" Tijan didn't give them time to answer. "No, you didn't. You came here hoping to get answers from whatever schmuck you figured my father had put in charge. Did you wait at least five minutes before deciding on this meeting before you made the call?"

"Look, Ms. Roth. We came here to inform you—"

"No. Let me tell you something. I'm not an idiot. And I don't appreciate you showing up mysteriously the day after my father is shot and put in the hospital. Did you guys shoot him?"

"What? No."

"Let me see your search warrant." Would they need such a thing? They hadn't asked to see anything, but she'd used whatever might throw them off.

The two men looked at each other.

"Ah. You don't have one. So, you are here fishing. Your fishing expedition is over. Please leave."

"You might want to work with us."

"Well, I don't. If you had enough evidence to show that my father was indeed involved with organized crime, you'd have charged him. And you'd have a court order for search and seizure. Now leave."

"I don't think—"

"She asked you to leave." August was standing by the office door, holding it open.

"And I trust that none of this ends up in the news. I'd hate to call one of the judges or government officials that I know that can make your life difficult."

The look on both their faces became hard. They looked like they wanted to punch someone but instead, stood up stiffly and moved toward the door. "You'll hear from us soon."

"I'm sure I will." She was sure they hadn't heard her as August, who had followed them, slammed the door as soon as they crossed the threshold.

August started clapping. She flipped out her right hand before dramatically bringing her right forearm to her waist and bowing.

Tijan burst out laughing. "Oh my God, that was fun. That's not supposed to be fun, is it? But wow. Those guys were so intense. I felt like telling them to chill; they acted like they had a pole up—" She pressed her hand to her mouth to prevent what she'd been about to say.

August chuckled. "Yeah. They were a little over the top with their intimidation stuff. What do you think about their allegation?"

Tijan walked over and opened the drawn blinds. Looking over the city, she imagined her father doing just that. For her, it was an interesting view. She could see a lot of Toronto from the twentieth floor, but to be honest, it made her dizzy. For her father, she was quite sure it had a different appeal. He'd struck her as power-hungry. She was sure this view was a metaphor to him, as if he was lording over everyone, that they were beneath him and had to look up to him.

She sensed rather than heard August come to stand beside her. "I'm not sure. I've only met the man a few times. He loves being in control. Would he use organized crime to do that? I have no idea. I wonder what Tarin knows? Or if she does? And what is she going to think when she hears that I threatened our national security? I don't even know if my father knows people in high places. I'm assuming so."

"That was just a bluff?"

Tijan shrugged. "Yeah."

August burst out laughing. "They seemed to back off right away when you said that. So obviously, they were bluffing as well."

"Tarin is going to be so pissed at me. I may have just created so many headaches for her."

Lowering her voice, she turned to face August. "How do I tell her that our father may be a criminal?"

CHAPTER 34

"WHAT HAPPENED WITH THE CSIS?"

Tijan took a deep breath and eased out the back door, ensuring that no one was in the area to see her leave. She'd never been claustrophobic but was feeling a strong case of it coming on.

"They had an interesting accusation but really were full of hot air. They left, but not happily. It appears that they're after Father. Do you know anything about his past dealings?" Tijan held the phone tight to her ear as she looked around to ensure her privacy.

Tarin sighed. "Not really. I know he has poured his life into the hotel. I can't imagine him being crooked, but then again, I can. He's always had this mentality of him against the world. Or maybe it was the world against him. He started his business to piss off Grandpa."

Tijan tried to muffle her indrawn hiss but knew she'd failed when she heard Tarin gasp.

"Oh, Tijan. Are we ever going to be able to straighten everything out? Someday I hope you can meet Grandpa. He's a wonderful man. I hadn't met him myself until just a few years ago. I'd been led to believe he was a bad man, worse than our father, but he's nothing like his son. He's big-hearted, and he helped me to keep Dad in line once before. But he's in his eighties, and I can't bring this to him. I don't want him to know. I think father has hurt him enough."

"Could he be behind any of this?"

"Grandpa? No, he wouldn't do anything underhanded. I think all that he did wrong was put in a lot of hours and hard work when our father was a kid, and so he wasn't there for him. At least, that's what I understand. I never met Grandma, but I think she had a lot of mental health issues. I don't think she was an easy person to live with. She's probably the one who soured Father on life. Anyway, it's all stuff we can talk about later. We need to get you out of there. Thank you for standing in for me but let's get you out before it gets too serious. We'll figure something out from this end."

"But you need access to the computers, right? And potentially, who might know what?"

"Yes. But we'll figure something else out. I don't want you in danger. August is now in a position that he can snoop for us, especially if the CSIS is investigating. I can't imagine that's a good thing. Did they mention the Mafia or organized crime? You know, those guys who had the nerve to approach you at the hospital?"

Tijan pursed her lips. "Sort of. They did ask—okay, let me rephrase that. They told me they knew your father was involved with organized crime."

"Damn him. It wouldn't surprise me. It hurts me like crazy, but it wouldn't surprise me. All the more reason to get you out."

"But that still leaves you vulnerable. Let me do a little more digging and see what I can find. As soon as it gets scary, don't worry, I'll be running for the hills."

Tarin chuckled.

It made Tijan feel good to know that she'd been able to make her sister laugh. Neither spoke for a few minutes, just enjoying the connection that was alive between them. Tijan had never felt so connected to anyone in her life. But this went beyond connected; it was part of herself. It wasn't something she could explain or understood but she just accepted it.

"I have to go. We'll talk soon. And I will be careful." Tijan hung up but continued to hold her phone tightly.

The late-day warm air seeped into her frayed nerves. This was why she'd needed to get outside—to breathe something real. Moving away from the concealed door, she didn't go far. Concerned she'd be abducted again, she walked around the end of the building, where there was a beautiful garden area and a small area of grass. She kicked off her shoes and stood there in her socks. It felt wonderful. The tension was starting to ease when she heard voices. There was no one in sight. They'd already ruined her five-second relaxation. She slipped on her shoes and went to investigate. A few big fir trees hugged the side of the building. She skirted them and saw three women leaning against the cement of the parkade.

"Hi." All three women looked startled as they glanced at her and then away.

"Umm, hi. We're just having our break. We know we aren't supposed to smoke here, Ms. Madsen. Umm—"

"It's okay. Don't you have a smoking area?"

The three women looked at each other as though wondering how to respond. Finally, the same middle-aged woman spoke up. "No. We're not supposed to smoke on hotel property. We aren't supposed to smoke at all while at work."

Tijan pressed her fist to her lips before taking a breath and smiling at them. "Okay, I'm not a big fan of smoking, but I know it's not an easy habit to break. And I'm pretty sure that the hotel can't dictate that to you. I'll get some of those safe cigarette disposal stands for you here. Just keep the area clean, okay? Oh, and is this the best place? I'm guessing few people come this way?"

All three nodded but then shook their heads.

"By the way, I'm Ti—Tarin. What are your names?"

"Sorry. Have to get back to work." They all spoke at once and soon disappeared, hurrying through a side door.

Tijan frowned. They seemed scared. Heading back inside, she returned to the office.

"Mary. Who do I talk to about staff breaks and—"

"You can talk to me. What do you want to know?" JT appeared out of nowhere.

Tijan looked at JT but turned back to Mary. "Who's in charge of a staff area? Do we have one?"

"There's a lunch area," Mary replied.

"And a smoking area outside?"

"There isn't one. No one is to smoke on hotel property."

Tijan turned to face JT. "Well, I'm sure that's illegal. Do I want them smoking? No. Do they have the right to smoke? Yes."

"Mary. Please make sure that two cigarette receptacles are ordered and installed by the parkade door along with a picnic table."

"I don't think we should spend—"

Tijan counted to three before turning to JT again. "I do. This is a good expense. You'll make sure it's in the budget, won't you?" She gave him a full, warm smile, even while gagging behind it.

Turning back to Mary. "I'd like to talk to the person in charge of benefits. I'd like to know what we offer the staff. Thank you."

Tijan headed to her office, but JT obviously wasn't going to be put off. He followed her in but stopped suddenly. August was there.

"Is there something you needed, JT?"

"No, it's just your father doesn't like smoking. He says it's a poor reflection on the company."

"Thank you for letting me know, JT. I appreciate your valuable input. But for now, I want those smoking receptacles installed along with a picnic table. Thanks. I can count on you to look after it? Great. Let me know when you have it done."

JT nodded. Appeased by her request for help and the fact that she was closing the door in his face, he left.

August raised his eyebrows. "What was that about?"

"I was trying to make things better for some staff. They aren't allowed to smoke during an eight-hour shift. How crazy is that? I mean, they're doing it anyway. I'd rather they do it safely and not toss cigarette butts all over." On the ranch, there had been a few men who had smoked, and she couldn't imagine telling them they couldn't. She had done everything from getting information on smoking cessation to buying hypnosis CDs. It had helped a few. Maybe they could do the same here. Once she talked with those in charge of benefits, she'd see what was available.

Was all this power going to her head?

Tijan smiled. She wasn't sure, but at least she felt like she was doing something a tiny bit normal.

CHAPTER 35

"WHAT DID YOU LEARN?"

"Not much. The recordings aren't too bad, but some idiot played music the whole time. It'll take a bit of work to wade through what is in the song and what is said by the background voices. I don't think much."

"We have little time. The daughter's in play now. She might get a little too curious, so we need to move fast. This could be an excellent opportunity because she hasn't been involved in her father's business for years. She won't have a clue what he's up to. Not that I'm sure he ever shared with her his meagre beginnings and how he went from that to a multi-billion-dollar hotel chain. He may brag about being rich, but he sure isn't going to tell people how he got there."

"I thought you had a good handle on what was going on there?"

"I do. Her being put into his role is a minor setback. I am seriously surprised and pissed that's who he put in place. It isn't who he led me to believe would take over if something happened to him. The point is, he has put her in charge, so let's use her. Because she knows nothing, I can feed her the information we want her to know. I still have the inside line and ear to what's really going on. I know so much more than James could ever imagine. It will bite him right where it hurts when he finds out."

"Things need to change soon. Use your position to do something about it."

****

Tijan eased open her door slowly, peeking down the hallway to make sure there was no one about. She felt like a child who was going to be reprimanded for being up too early, but 5:30 was normal for her. She thought about going outside and walking around to get an idea of the area, but she'd heard a number of sirens through the night that reminded her she was in the city. Give her the Alberta Rockies and she was fine, but she wasn't quite comfortable wandering around the city by herself.

Squashing the idea of leaving the hotel, she decided she would do more research into Mr. Madsen's business—calling him dad or father just didn't sit right with her. After a quick shower, she dressed and sneaked into the stairwell to climb two flights of stairs. She felt a little guilty when she passed August's room, but she didn't want to wake him. Besides, she was sure that she was fine going to the office alone.

Once she reached the 20th floor, she discovered the stairwell was locked, and she didn't have any keys. Heading back down a flight, she entered the elevator only to discover that no matter what she did, it wouldn't go up one floor. It too appeared locked. She was glad to see that they took security seriously. However, it annoyed her to no end that she couldn't get in. She'd talk to Mary when she arrived to find out how to lock up and unlock after hours. Mary had stayed the night before to ensure that everything had been closed up and set, and it hadn't even occurred to Tijan to ask how to do that—or undo it.

Heading back to her room, she tossed her keycard on the dresser and walked to the window. A brief glance at the destroyed bed reminded her of the restless night she'd had. Being chased by thugs in her dreams felt a little too much like there was a reality to it.

The sun was just peeking over the horizon and brightening the day. She loved sunrises. Sitting on her horse in the field all by herself always made her feel like it was magic. She missed that wide-open space and feeling.

There was a soft knock on her door. Her head whipped around, her eyes immediately owl-sized. Moving as quietly as she could, she made her way across the room and peeked out the spyhole. She sagged against the door when she saw August standing there with two coffees and a bag. She yanked open the door, motioning for him to come in.

"You scared the crap out of me." She checked the hallway to make sure no one was watching. Her mom would be thrilled that she'd become so cautious, but it was wearing on her nerves checking around every corner.

August made his way past her bed, and she noted the quick glance he gave it. His gaze never lingered or hesitated, but she found her attention shifting to the view of his backside. He set the tray and food on the table and turned before she had time to adjust her attention. Heat crawled up her face, but she squared her shoulders and strode toward him, grabbing one of the cups.

"Did you bring milk?"

As he dumped out the contents of the bag, two over-size muffins, cream and sugar tumbled out. Hunger pangs immediately attacked her insides, making her wonder when she had last eaten.

"Which one?"

"Take your pick—carrot-blueberry or raspberry oatmeal. I'll eat either."

Once they were eating at the small table, Tijan felt herself relaxing, though she kept her gaze down as she found she quite liked a clean, freshly showered August. His long hair, which, if someone had asked her a week ago, she'd have said she hated, was definitely gaining way too much appeal.

"Okay, so what's our plan for today?" Tijan bit into one of the muffins. "Hmm. This is good."

August smiled. "I have to meet with Guy and Graham later to discuss things. I'm not sure why face to face, but they want to keep important information off electronic devices, inside or outside the office. No idea. But the crash course on being a detective left me feeling like an idiot. I'd love to be that white knight that can save the damsel, but I have to tell you this is way outside the world I live in."

Tijan snorted. "Me too. I live in the foothills of Alberta, with wide open spaces and not many people. There are some bad people there too, but I've never come across anything like this. And thank you for wanting to be a knight, but I already know how to ride my own horse."

"Well, that put me in my place."

Tijan felt a twinge of guilt until she met August's smiling eyes. "White knights don't do it for me." Realizing she was staring at him a bit too long, she took a sip of her coffee. Her gaze drifted to the view outside.

"Well, that's good because I don't ride a horse."

"I feel like a spec of sand on the beach and can't believe someone would be interested in what I'm doing. I don't know how Tarin has lived like this."

"Do you mind my asking, what happened that you didn't grow up together?"

Her gaze swung back to August. She gazed at him for a moment, but she didn't see him as her mind mulled through her own questions about why that had happened. "I wish I knew. To be honest, that's my goal. I want to know why a man I never knew existed may die before I get to know him. And why he didn't want me."

When her voice broke, she stood up suddenly, but a buzzing sound caught her attention. She cocked her head to listen. "What's that?"

"A cell phone?"

"Can't be. I've got mine here." She pulled it out of her pocket to prove her point. "Yours?"

August shook his head and picked his up from the table.

Tijan instinctively hunched her shoulders and listened intently for the origin. Moving toward her bedside stand, she knelt. Lifting the blanket that had half fallen to the floor, she uncovered a cell phone.

She pressed her hand to her chest before she picked it up. "I forgot Tarin gave me another one that I'm to use for the office. Good gravy, I don't like dealing with one cell phone, and now I've got two."

She skimmed the text. "It appears Mary has arrived at work. Cripes, it's only seven thirty. She starts early, doesn't she? I don't know how far away she lives, but we didn't leave the office until what—eight o'clock? I got the feeling she didn't want to leave me alone with all that power. She's rather protective. Anyway, she wants me up there. I guess I have a busy day ahead."

August rose. "I'll head over and meet with Guy and Graham, find out what they need to tell me. Everything has been so rushed. They want to fill me in on some details. I'll be back in a couple of hours. Be careful."

Tijan nodded. "You too."

CHAPTER 36

MARY POKED HER HEAD in the door. "Eleanor is here to see you."

Tijan lifted her head and blinked a few times. It took a moment for her to shift from what she'd been reading about her father. Even though she was supposed to be looking for more connections and more information on his business dealings, she couldn't help but feel she needed to use this time to learn who he was. There were a lot of newspaper articles on the Internet. Some were flattering, some hinted or outright stated that he was a ruthless businessman, and there was even one that questioned if he had any connections to organized crime. She was a little dazed when she glanced up.

"What?"

"Eleanor is here. She didn't have an appointment, but she said she wanted to stop by and lend a hand if it was needed. It's okay to say no if you're busy? I wouldn't have bothered you, but she can be insistent."

"Uh—" The expression on Mary's face made it clear that she should know who this woman was. And that she clearly disliked her. "Just tell her I'll be five minutes. Okay?"

"She won't be happy." Mary smiled. "If I can give you some advice?"

Tijan looked at her, interested in what she had to say.

"Watch out for her. She's quite a head stomper—leaning she'll step on anyone who might get in her way. If she thinks you're a threat, she'll do what she can to get rid of you."

"Oh, why do you say that?"

"I've seen her use Mr. Madsen. She leads men on and gets what she can. I just thought you should know. She'll be looking for your weakness." Mary withdrew.

Tijan grabbed her phone to text Tarin and noted she'd missed twelve messages from her sister. She'd silenced her phone the night before and hadn't even thought about receiving calls or texts. Unfortunately, there wasn't time to read them. She needed to know who this Eleanor was. Asking Mary had crossed her mind, but the woman obviously had strong feelings about her. And besides, Tijan did not want to let on that she might not know someone she should.

'She's dad's lawyer—Carter Associates. Haven't heard from you. Everything okay?'

'Yeah, get back to you soon.'

Tijan buzzed Mary. "Bring Eleanor in." She debated whether to move to the couch, but the door opened almost immediately. When she saw the tall, striking woman, who looked every inch like a shark lawyer—dark eyes that felt like she'd peered into her soul—Tijan was glad she hadn't. Standing slowly, she nodded at the woman.

"She has a busy schedule. Do not stay long." Mary stepped out from behind Eleanor, whose lips curled with contempt. Turning to Tijan. "You have five minutes until your next meeting."

Looking pointedly at Eleanor, she continued, "Do not keep her a minute beyond that." Mary slipped out, closing the door behind her. Although Mary had remained professional, unlike Eleanor, she had definitely gotten her digs in.

A myriad of emotions crossed Eleanor's face. There was a softening that seemed to convey understanding and sympathy, but it was mingled with arrogance, as if she wanted to say, 'Who do you think you are to be sitting there?'

Tijan stood up straight, squaring her shoulders. Was she imagining this stuff, or more hypersensitive because of Mary?

"Tarin. I know it's been a while since we've seen each other. I'm so sorry that it's under these circumstances."

"El—" Tijan started to say Eleanor, but she had an image of her father giving her a dirty look. Tarin had told her to use proper names, but she had no idea what this woman's last name was.

Eleanor smiled. "It's okay. You can call me Eleanor. Your father isn't here to say otherwise."

Tijan allowed her lips to curve slightly, but she truly felt ill. This game of lies just never seemed to end. She sank slowly onto her chair. What she wanted to do was slouch.

Mary's words kept playing in her mind, which made her wonder if they had anything to do with the instant dislike she felt. Eleanor attempted to appear warm, but something rang false. The woman was exuding power—her actions, her stance, her look, all said, 'You're not good enough to be here.' Even her dark royal blue suit with its prim white lapel trim screamed, I'm a professional and you're not. Her shoes matched perfectly, as did the necklace, bracelet and stud earrings she wore—navy blue with a touch of white. She was polished and hard, causing Tijan to feel like she was a dowdy country girl, something she'd never minded being until then.

She'd dealt with men tougher than Eleanor, though. Pushing away her thoughts, she met Eleanor's direct gaze.

"What can I do for you, Eleanor?"

The woman walked to the desk but didn't follow suit and sit. Tijan got the feeling it was intentional. The woman already stood at least five-foot-eleven in her two-inch heels. Those few inches gave her an edge while Tijan was standing, but now she had an even greater advantage.

"Nothing. It's what I can do for you. I've worked with your father for years, so I'm quite familiar with his business dealings. In fact, I negotiated most of his contracts. There isn't much that he does I don't know about or haven't been involved with."

Tijan nodded, though she had no idea what the woman was trying to tell her.

"Since you've been out of this for a while, I mean, you have a three-year-old son now."

Her smirk made it clear she was not congratulating her on her son but intended to be condescending. Tijan wanted to spit at her. She couldn't imagine what Tarin would do if she'd heard her.

"I can look everything over and let you know what needs your immediate attention and what I can handle for you. I can set up remote access, so I don't even have to be in your way to look after this stuff. Your father and I have done that many times in the past."

Tijan leaned forward, locking her eyes with Eleanor and resting her forearms on her desk. "I appreciate that, but I am my father's daughter."

Eleanor nodded, but her face shifted ever so slightly, like she had something distasteful in her mouth. "Well, if you change your mind? I'll continue to work on the acquiring of Caspian Winery. Oh dear. I'm sorry. You do know about that, don't you?"

This woman was not only tough as the white teeth she liked to flash but was insincere as well.

Tijan smiled. "He's always trying to retain one company, or another, isn't he?" She felt like she was being studied under a microscope, but just as she thought her forced smile would remain frozen on her face, Eleanor turned away. She wanted to sag with relief, but she held herself together. At the door, Eleanor stopped and gave her one last, lengthy stare.

"We'll talk soon."

"Sounds good. For now, though, hold off on any acquisitions until I establish priorities. Caspian Winery will always be there. Thank you. Good day."

The woman's jaw clenched as she seemed to straighten to her full height. Although the words weren't spoken, the look she gave seemed to be telling her where to go. She obviously didn't take well to being given orders, at least not by a woman. Finally, she nodded, turned elegantly and efficiently, and walked out without another word.

After the door closed, Tijan counted to forty before picking up the phone and calling Mary. "I don't want to be bothered for the next hour."

"Okay, I'll make sure there are no interruptions. Especially Eleanor. Although now that she's shown her face unscheduled, you probably won't see her again. I try to keep her out, but sometimes it's easier just to meet with her and then send her on her way. I know it's not the time or my place, but you might want to discuss with your father about finding a new lawyer."

Tijan was taken aback at the hardness in Mary's tone. Was it just professional annoyance?

"Did you have a chance to sign those papers?"

Tijan looked at the desk. She'd made sure there was nothing on the desk when the CSIS was there and now she mentally retraced her actions to figure out where she'd put them.

"I'll get to them, Mary. Thanks for the reminder." She hung up before Mary could answer. The way she was managing things made her sick, but Tarin had told her that in business you don't ask, you tell—especially when you're the boss. Tijan was sure she'd never get used to this cold, calculating world. The signing of those papers would have to wait.

CHAPTER 37

AUGUST STOOD AT THE street corner, which wasn't a simple thing to do. The number of people constantly waiting and moving was like being in the middle of a spring salmon run. There was just a mass of bodies with each person going in their own direction, pushing and shoving to get there. While he tried to determine whether he was being followed or whether he should simply go, the choice was soon taken out of his hands. He'd managed for a couple of lights to sidestep and retain his place hugging the lamp-post, but that suddenly changed. At first, he was panicked, thinking the bad guys had found him, but the foot traffic had swelled; he was just being taken with it. Getting into sync with everyone, he let himself be carried to the other sidewalk and then he deliberately pushed his way through, heading for the coffee shop that was supposed to be a few blocks off the main drag. Making his way down the busy side street, being pushed and shoved, he understood a little, the miserable expressions on most faces. The movement and force of the crowd made him feel as if he'd had no say in where he was going. It was not a feeling he liked, especially the few seconds of near panic. The only other time he'd felt so helpless was when his mom squeezed his hand for the last time and he knew no matter what he did, he couldn't save her.

Stopping at the end of the block, he stood next to the building, so he was out of the flow of people. Casually glancing around, he almost burst out laughing. Guy and Graham had instructed him to make sure he wasn't being followed, spending a good forty minutes telling him what to do, what not to do and what to look for. It had all made sense as they had coached him, but now that he was supposed to be using those skills, he sucked at the whole spy game thing. All he saw was a mass of people hurrying to get somewhere. There were a crazy number of vehicles driving at different speeds, amid incessant honking, tires squealing and the occasional 'asshole'. He'd been in several cities, but he'd never seen anything quite like this ordered chaos.

If someone was following him, they deserved a medal for being able to track him in that bedlam. A few people looked at him, blankly. He wasn't sure they even saw him—unless he got in their way, and then he got a dirty look. Pushing away from the building, he just hoped that he had lost whatever tail he might have picked up.

He walked three more blocks and then another four as instructed. He even walked around the block just to see if he recognized anyone or saw anything suspicious. Would he see a familiar face or recognize something that was there that shouldn't have been? As he strode, trying to act like he didn't have anywhere to be, he let his gaze wander over every person he passed, as well as every building and car. With cars, he could note not only the model but could guess the year. There were some old Chevys, Fords, Chryslers, Saturns, Kias, Toyotas, Hondas, and a few fancy sports cars—Camaros, Jaguars, Mercedes, and one Lamborghini. Other than that, everything looked the same, yet different to him.

Realizing he'd reached his destination again, he shook his head as if to clear it as he took one last look around. He did not see a tail or anyone who seemed interested in him.

The dimly lit, raucous coffee shop was a noisy reflection of the street. His shoulders slumped a bit as he had been hoping to shut out the monotony of racket. The place was packed. There was a long line up to the counter, and there didn't seem to be an empty table. He didn't see the two guys, so he stood in line and bought a cafe macchiato.

Just as he picked up his coffee from the delivery area, someone bumped into him. He turned to say something, only to realize it was Guy. He shook his head as he grabbed a couple of creams before making his way to a back stairwell. August waited a few moments before he followed. Once up the stairs, there was just a small balcony with four tables. All of which were empty, except for one. Guy and Graham were sitting in a space against the back wall. August made his way to them and sat down.

Graham immediately placed a barrier along the stairs that stated the area was closed. August wondered who they knew to have this kind of preferential treatment.

"Well, I don't think anyone followed me." August leaned back, feeling rather proud of himself.

"Yeah, that's what Pam said, too," Guy smiled.

August leaned forward. "Pam?"

"The person we had watching out for you."

"Oh, good."

Graham started laughing. "You didn't see her, did you?"

August thought about bluffing and found himself waving his hands palm upwards. "Uh... well..." He snorted. "Didn't have a clue. I don't know how you do this. A guy could have passed me twenty times and I wouldn't have known."

A look passed between Guy and Graham before Guy spoke up. "Actually, we did have Pam do that to you. We just wanted to know what you observed."

"Well, that sucks. I failed abysmally. Every face blended. People are pushy. Man, when they have somewhere to go, get the hell out of the way or you're going too. It's a little unnerving. I could have been stabbed, ripped off, beaten up and I'm not sure anyone would have noticed."

"It is a little overwhelming. The majority of people are good, just not in good moods. You get used to it."

"No, thanks." August drank some of his coffee.

Graham smiled and patted him on the shoulder. "If it's any consolation, she's very good, and to be honest, I often can't find her, and I know her. Besides, she said you did well; you paid attention to what was around you. You stopped a few times. You didn't just put your head down with the goal of getting from A to B, which is what most people do."

Feeling a little mollified, August leaned forward, keeping his voice low. "What's going on? What do I need to know? To watch for? I found only one bug in the office, but I am sure there are more. I checked all the usual places you suggested—the lamps, under the edge of the desk, behind the edge of the furniture. That's where I found one, on the backside of the liquor cabinet."

"Good job. We're dealing with pros that do this for a living, so don't beat yourself up. We'll need to send someone in after hours to see what they can find." Guy kept a close eye on the door to the coffee shop.

August wished he knew how they would know if a bad guy came through the door. Someday, he wanted to learn more about the skills that these two gentlemen seemed to have.

Graham pulled out his phone and scrolled through a few things. "First, Tijan needs to get in touch with us so we can set up remote access to her dad's computer. That way, we can search all that's stored on there and keep an eye on everything. We also need a list of employees so we can do background checks. And who are the lawyers they're using? That should give us a good idea of who we're dealing with."

"Alright. I'll see what I can get."

"Be careful. These people don't fool around. Tell Tijan that whatever her dad was involved in, they may figure they can get it through her. They may try to kill her, too. Stick tight to her."

Graham jumped in. "That's why this was such a bad idea. I mean, if Tijan hadn't done this, then Tarin would have had to. And there's no way I wanted that to happen. This is serious. No holds barred, people could die."

August was a little startled by the intensity of what they were saying. The thought of someone killing them hadn't entered his mind. He'd only thought of them as keeping an eye on the place. "Maybe I shouldn't have come then. She's all by herself at the hotel."

"No, she's not, and neither are you, but you still need to be aware of who and what is going on around you." Graham put away his cell phone.

"Time to go. Head back the way you came. No detours."

"Pam will escort me?"

Graham smirked. "Don't enjoy being tailed by a woman you can't see?"

"It is a bit unsettling, man or woman." August stood up. "Thanks guys. I think."

He headed down the stairs, being sure to pull the barrier across. Looking around intently as he made his way out of the cafe, he saw some really interesting, some ordinary, and some rather different individuals, but he did not see anyone he recognized from when he'd arrived. Sighing heavily, he made his way out onto the street. Hoping that Pam was somewhere in the vicinity, he made his way back to the hotel, finding himself moving much faster. The talk with Guy and Graham had instilled in him the gravity of their situation. It was one of those things he'd known was serious, but it was so outside of his world that it didn't seem real. Now he was realizing just how dangerous it was.

By the time he reached the hotel an hour later; after taking every side street he could, he felt a bit like an owl searching for prey. His eyes were wide open, taking in every little detail, even if he didn't know what he was really looking for. His head felt like it had been on a swivel stick.

Just as he arrived at the hotel and went through the large glass revolving doors, he noticed a black sleek car pull to the curb. It looked suspiciously like the one that had stopped beside Tijan at the hospital. Glancing around, he tried to determine if the bodyguards Guy and Graham had hired were visible. But again, he had no clue. It could have been the doorman that greeted him, the runner that looked terribly out of shape or even the old guy pruning the plants as well as any one of the hundred others coming and going.

Shaking his head, he raced to the elevator to reach Tijan before she might have company.

CHAPTER 38

RUSHING TO THE DOOR, Tijan locked it before making her way back to her desk. Eleanor had said she had remotely accessed files, which was something Tijan was supposed to have arranged so Tarin, Graham and Guy could snoop through the computer. Checking her texts, Tijan had received several inquiries from Tarin regarding a time, as Tijan had to be at that computer when they set it up.

She dialed her sister, but it wasn't until Tarin answered she remembered she wasn't supposed to talk freely in the office. There might be too many ears listening.

"Hi, Betty. Can you just give me a minute? I forgot something in my car. I hope I don't lose you. If I do, I'll call back." Tijan made her way to the door that led to the parkade. The minute she stepped into that cement area, her sister's voice started cutting in and out. Going back into the office, she debated about using the bathroom but figured that would be the first place someone might place a bug.

"Betty, I'll call you right back." Where the name Betty came from, she had no idea. It just seemed like the right thing to do. The only Betty she'd ever known was the one on the cartoon, The Flintstones. She clicked off before Tarin could argue. Grabbing her keys on the way past her desk, she headed out of her office, only to stop dead as she almost collided with JT.

"Well, hello. Nice to see you're in a hurry to see me." He gave her his megawatt smile, that he obviously thought made him a good-looking guy. One who was a little too in love with his own looks to be hitting on her. He made her uncomfortable. This was not a complication she needed.

"JT? Right?"

His suave smile dimmed a bit.

"I'm in a hurry. Make an appointment with Mary and I can meet with you tomorrow." She closed her office door. Standing so he couldn't see, she tapped in her alarm code.

"Is there anything I can help you with? I do know this business. In fact, your father was about to announce that I was going to be the new VP."

"Really? I thought you told me CFO?"

His eyebrows drew together. "Well, James didn't want to put me directly into the CFO position because that might have caused problems for others. I'm becoming VP and then will be CFO by the end of the year."

"Hmm. How long have you worked here, JT?"

"A few years. Why?"

"And what's your background?"

"I have a bachelor's degree in marketing and a master's degree in communications. Along with my experience, I am well qualified." He moved a little closer. "I could be an asset for you."

"Thank you, but I'm good for now. I have to run. Bye." She sidestepped him and almost ran for the elevators. "I'm out, Mary. Thanks," she said to a startled receptionist as she raced by.

Trying to make sure no one followed her, she took the express elevator to the lobby, changed to another one and rode it to the second floor. Careful to lose anyone that might be following her, she exited the elevator and headed for the stairs.

"Ms. Madsen. Excuse me?"

Tijan kept walking, but when a hand touched her arm, she whipped around and stepped back with her arms up, ready to defend herself.

The woman in the housekeeper's uniform stepped back startled, her hands immediately coming up, palms forward, to show she was harmless.

"I'm sorry, Ms. Madsen. I didn't mean to scare you."

Tijan pressed her hand to her chest as she looked at the woman. She had to be in her forties and had dyed her hair flaming red. She looked familiar, but Tijan couldn't place her. "I'm sorry. I was lost in thought. Can I help you?"

"Yes, Ms. Madsen—"

"Ti-Tarin, please."

"Thank you for setting up a smoking area for staff. We all appreciate it. Not just to smoke but to be able to take our lunch outside on nice days. I just wanted you to know."

Tijan was a little taken aback that it had happened so fast. "Good. I hadn't heard it had been completed. Glad to hear it has been. Sorry, what's your name?"

"Jill."

"Jill. Can I put you in charge of it? Will you do up a set of rules, or do you think we need that?"

"I can. Uhm. I think that we should politely ask everyone to keep it clean."

"Great. Can you draft something, send it to me and I'll have a nice sign made. Do you have time at work to do this?"

Jill looked around nervously. "No. I can do it during my break. There are too many rooms to clean for me to take time for that."

"How about this? Instead of doing it at work, I'll pay you five hours for you to come up with something to post. Would you mind also being the voice of staff? Talk with other employees, not just about smoking but about what else they'd like to see here for staff benefits. Get some feedback and then send me what you have." Tijan dug in her pocket and pulled out a business card. As she looked at it, she stopped and ran her thumb over her father's name—James Madsen. She had a feeling he wasn't going to like what she was doing.

"Ma'am?"

Tijan looked up, her mind still fathoming that she had a father. "Sorry, here's my card. Do you have a pen? I'll write my name and contact information on it."

Tijan filled it out and handed it back. "Send me what you've got to this email, and you can call and leave me a message on this cell. Okay? Oh, and who is your supervisor? I'll send her a note so that you won't get in trouble."

Jill nodded and quickly returned to her cart sitting just outside of a room before she disappeared inside the nearby room. Soon she was back with a stack of linens. She tossed them into the cart before disappearing again. Tijan was fascinated by how quickly she moved.

At one point, Jill looked at her. Her eyes widened. "Is something wrong, Ms. Madsen?"

The quiver in her voice reminded Tijan just how much clout her position carried.

"Sorry, Jill. I was just admiring how efficient you are at your job. You're a hard worker."

Her face turned red, but she smiled shyly. "Thank you. I try."

"Is there anything that would make your job easier?"

The warm, friendly look disappeared. She glanced into her cart just for a second. "No ma'am. Everything is fine."

Tijan moved closer to her, making a point of looking inside the bag of laundry. "Is something wrong?"

Jill shook her head.

Tijan pulled out one sheet. "It appears to be rather thin. Do we need to buy some new ones?"

"These are new."

Tijan reached for the nicely folded ones on the cart. The material wasn't very soft or nice to the touch. She stepped back. "Thank you for your help, Jill. I'll look into this."

"I don't want to cause trouble."

"You're not. If something isn't working well or looking good, I want to know about it. Okay?"

Jill nodded but wouldn't look at her. Sensing she'd made the woman uncomfortable, Tijan headed for the stairs, already focusing on her next issue.

She needed to talk to her sister. And soon.

As she made her way up a few steps, climbing them was going to be an issue. The three-inch spike heels Tarin had loaned her were killing her feet. She kicked them off and carried them up seventeen flights.

CHAPTER 39

ARRIVING ON THE FLOOR, August was about to step off the elevator when he noticed JT sitting on the edge of Mary's desk, laughing and joking with her. JT was obviously laying on the charm. Mary had a big smile and laughed a few times. She seemed enthralled with the guy who was at least twenty-plus years her junior. Age didn't seem to matter to him, from what August had seen so far.

It dawned on August that the door was taking a long time to close and then realized it wouldn't until he either stepped off or used his key to choose another floor. He strode toward the two people, noting when they turned to look at him, there was a guilty look on both their faces. Mary immediately dropped her eyes to his chin, obviously uncomfortable. JT, though, pushed himself slowly to his feet and sauntered around the desk like he owned the place. August sidestepped him and headed for Tijan's office.

"She's not there."

August spun around in time to see the smug, know-it-all expression on JT's face. He seemed quite proud of his knowledge.

"Oh. Where is she?" August didn't like that she hadn't let him know she was going out of the office.

"She had to leave and said not to bother her. That was about half an hour ago."

"Thank you, Mary." August almost flipped JT the bird but realized he was not in a position to be scrappy. Besides, he hadn't reacted that way to anyone since he was about eighteen and still blamed the world. Not a good time to be reverting to old habits, he spun on his heel and walked back into the elevator that hadn't left. He inserted his card. This elevator only went to the lobby, but it would have to do. Once the doors opened, he exited, turning left and rounding the corner to the other elevators. There was a nicely dressed guy wearing a massive gold chain around his neck. It was ridiculous. An uncomfortable feeling crept up August's spine. The man went in the direction that August had just come from. He was going to the top floor—which meant he was there to meet with Tijan.

August pulled out his phone and called her. There was no answer. Going back, he hopped on the main elevator up to the eighteenth floor.

When the doors opened, he barged out, heading down the long hallway. The stairwell door flew open, and out staggered a sweaty, exhausted-looking Tijan. Her shirt had come untucked, and she was in her stocking feet, carrying her jacket and her shoes. She looked a little too sexy and much more human. Rushing to her, he stretched out his hands to help her, but she jerked back, startled.

"Oh God, it's you."

Unsure how to take that, he stepped to the side, giving her space to pass, but she grabbed his arm and leaned on him. Walking her to her room. Stopping at the door, she pulled out her key and fumbled with it, trying to insert the card into the reader.

It was tempting to jump in and do it for her, but he waited patiently for her to succeed. The moment the door swung inward, he escorted her in and sat her on the freshly made bed. "Want to tell me what's going on?"

"Water," she squeaked out.

Since it appeared she'd drunk the two complimentary bottles that came with the room, August filled a glass of tap water. Handing it to her, she downed it in a few seconds and handed it back for more.

"Give me a minute."

Moving to the window, he looked out, trying to see if the black limo was still there. The large overhang at the front door obscured his view. Tijan started talking, so he turned but soon realized she was on her phone.

"I know I have to be in the office, but people won't leave me alone. And I realized I can't say anything, so we need to come up with a code or something. I don't know what I'm doing. I shouldn't have said I'd do this. I think I'm causing more harm than good. People think I'm you. They expect you, a savvy, beautiful woman, who gets this world. I don't. I'm a country girl, and that's it. How in God's name do you wear those freakin' heels? My feet are killing me."

August was unsure what he should do or say, but since Tijan seemed to be on a tirade and her sister was listening, he sat on the bed and watched her pace. Her hair, which had been beautifully styled earlier that morning in a tight bun at the nape of her neck, was now sagging just above her suit collar, and tufts of her hair were sticking out. She looked like she had a lion's thin mane around her face. He much preferred the look of this woman to the one he'd left earlier. Definitely sexier. He had been attracted to Tarin the moment he'd seen her. It made him wonder if his attraction to Tijan was strictly because of his reaction to Tarin.

As he watched Tijan pace, she yanked the rest of the shirt out of her skirt. The entire outfit wasn't her style. Her sister might have grabbed his attention, but it was Tijan who was holding onto it.

"Dammit!"

It took him a minute to realize that she'd hung up and was speaking to him. Or at least he thought she was.

"Bad day at the office, honey?" He burst out laughing when she gave him the finger.

"Did you know that walking seventeen flights of stairs is good for your heart? I think mine was ready to explode. And I thought I was in shape."

"And the stairs seemed like a good idea because?"

"Because I needed to get off my floor and had to go to the lobby but didn't want those in the office to know that I'd gone to the lobby and then I wanted to come to my room, here on the eighteenth floor. But we don't want people to know we're staying here. That's why we aren't getting any room service and why I'm making my own bed."

"You realize that they can't see the main hotel elevators from the office."

Tijan looked at him with the dawning awareness of I'm-such-an-idiot. "Holy crap. That never even occurred to me. I just knew I had to get out of there, and I didn't want anyone to know where I was going. I feel like I have to hide every move I make. Everything I say is calculated. My brain is going to explode. How do people do this?"

"I don't know. I loved having my business, but it was never on this scale. And I can tell you I know that not every business is run like this. There's obviously a lot of mistrust here. I feel like someone would use you as the fall guy in a heartbeat. You realize, though, that this comes from the top down?"

When she gave him a hurt look, August felt like kicking himself. He got up and stood in front of her, looking her in the eye. "I'm sorry. I shouldn't have said that."

"No. But it's true. It is because of my father. I just had a woman stop me to tell me thank you for getting them cigarette ashtrays and a picnic table outside. She made it sound like I'd just given them a spot that was fine dining. It's just a place where they can hang out. It's nothing special, just a space surrounded by cement. How can you hire people and not treat them right?"

August shrugged.

"Yesterday I asked Mary and JT to make sure that cigarette receptacles were to be placed outside, along with picnic tables for the staff. They've already been installed. Now, do I carry that much weight? Or did we already have that stuff in stock? And if we did, why wasn't it put out before? Is my father that much of a jerk?"

"Let's assume that they'd been ordered with the intent of being put out and that just hadn't happened yet."

"I'd go along with that, but something doesn't ring true about it. Isn't it odd that it was done so fast? Are people trying to win points with me?"

"I think JT would kiss the ass of a mule if it would get him ahead. And I'm not saying that yours looks like a mule's."

Tijan burst out laughing. "Thank you for that compliment, I think. Tarin said that all the anxiety I'm feeling might not be mine alone. She said she's been pretty freaked out since I decided to see this through for a few days. Could I be feeling what she's feeling? She asked me the same question. I've heard of identical twins having that connection, but do we? I don't know. I don't know. Could we, even though we were raised apart?"

August didn't answer, as he was pretty sure that she didn't want him to. He had no idea but didn't see why their growing up apart would change whether they had a deep connection or not.

"Growing up, I always felt like a part of me was missing. When I met her, I felt whole for the first time. I felt like a part of me had been stitched back together. So maybe we are connected. Maybe she can feel what I feel. Maybe I can feel what she feels. It's definitely something I need to talk to her about."

"I think you should, and hopefully that opportunity will come soon. Unfortunately, we have a problem upstairs waiting for you. I think the mafia has come to see you. Let's figure out a strategy of how to handle this."

CHAPTER 40

"THIS PLACE IS CRAZY." Tijan sat on the side of the bed and turned to face August at the opposite end. "Eleanor, father's lawyer, showed up unannounced."

"If it weren't so early in the day, I'd grab you a beer. Since I think we may have multiple issues to handle, take a deep breath and tell me what's going on. And I'll share what I know."

"You first." Tijan needed a moment to calm down. Her nerves were stretched taut. This feeling was not one she was used to, nor was it one that she wanted to experience again.

"I met with Guy and Graham. And I've determined I suck at surveillance. They had a woman tailing me. I never saw her and couldn't even guess who it might have been. I don't remember a single person of the thousand I saw this morning, that I might have seen twice. Just giving you fair warning that I might not be the best help. Although I think the dude that parked under the overhang downstairs is driving the same car that stopped and chatted with you at the hospital."

Tijan's eyes widened. "Did they come in?"

"Yeah, and I'm pretty sure that you'll be getting a call to say they are waiting for you."

As if he'd commanded it, Tijan's phone beeped. She grabbed her jacket and pulled out the cell she was using for work. She'd missed four text messages and two phone calls. There were some people who were insisting she come to her office for a visit. Mary had put them in the conference room, as they weren't leaving without talking to her.

"Holy crap. Now these guys. Eleanor, the lawyer, tells me she could help me—dammit. I have to get a hold of Tarin. We're supposed to set up remote access on father's computer, so they can take a look at the data."

"Okay. We'll go up and meet this guy. Want to tell me who he is? And how did Eleanor remind you that you needed to do that remote thing?"

"She said she had accessed Father's laptop remotely. It seemed to be something I had to initiate from the laptop. But what if it isn't? What if she's spying on what I'm doing?" She stood abruptly. "I need my horse and some wide-open space. But first, I need to look presentable. Please text Mary back and tell her I'll be there in fifteen."

Heading into the bathroom, she grabbed a fresh blouse out of the closet on her way. Looking in the mirror, she was shocked at what she saw and only one and a half days in. It wasn't that she looked so wild. She was used to that, but usually her clothes fit her appearance. In dress clothes, she felt like she'd committed a mortal sin by looking so harried, whereas in her blue jeans and T-shirt it would have been fine. She really had a disconnect to this world, like a horse on the downtown streets of Toronto—spooked, wide-eyed and ready to bolt. What was she going to look like at the end of two weeks? She hadn't considered how long she was going to have to play this role.

When she finally looked presentable, she went back into the room. Picking up her jacket off the bed, she shrugged into it. August was standing at the window but turned to look at her. His hair was pulled back into a small tight bun at the base of his head. Looking at him from the front, he looked like he had short hair. It so matched the suit he was wearing. She held his gaze for a few minutes, liking what she saw—a good guy. It made her feel a bit more confident about having him with her through this.

"James, shall we go?"

"My name—"

"Sorry. I was trying to be funny. You know, James, as in the limo driver, 'home James'. Which was in poor taste as my father's name is James and—" She dropped her head back, looking at the ceiling. She was a bit startled when she felt August's hand on her arm.

"It's okay. This is super stressful. I just didn't get the reference. And although this is not home, let's go find out what some well-dressed thug wants. You can share with me on the way down and then back up—unless you'd like to climb two more flights of stairs."

Tijan smiled. "No. My legs are still a bit rubbery. I don't recommend taking the stairs again if we don't have to. At least not seventeen flights of them."

August laughed. "I'll keep that in mind."

When they arrived at the office, Tijan stopped just outside the door. "I wonder why he called his hotel chain C-Lite Hotels. It seems like an odd name, no?" Tijan turned to August, who was watching her closely. "Just another thing I don't know about the man. And may never get to ask."

She reached for the door, took a deep breath, pasted on a smile, and walked in, hoping that her odd limp wasn't too obvious. She was in good shape, but the excessive number of steps to get to that top floor, were letting her know she wasn't in great shape.

"Hi, Tarin. The man, a Mr. Tesimmon, is in the conference room. JT is in there with him."

"Oh, who gave him permission to do that?"

Mary sat up squaring her shoulders. "He's worked here for several years. Mr. Madsen trusted him."

"Thank you, Mary. I'll be sending JT out soon. Can you have him look into the linens? It appears there is a problem with the last shipment."

There was a clunk, like a lock had been released. It seemed to have come from the door to the left of Mary's desk. Hoping she wouldn't look like an idiot, Tijan reached for it. It opened easily, and as she stepped through, she was a few steps away from the conference room. She stopped suddenly, causing August to slam into her back. She stumbled forward, but he grabbed her, which is probably what kept her upright. Ignoring the two deadly stares from the two huge men standing as guards outside the conference room, she stepped away from August but motioned for him to follow her. Back-pedaling a few steps and moving through the closed door that led to her office, she walked through.

"We need to find out who this guy is. I'm guessing he might be the organized crime dude that the CSIS wants us to inform them about."

"I think you're right. Those guys look like they could punch through steel."

Tijan shivered slightly. What had her father gotten her into?

"Okay, let's go. I don't want to keep that man waiting. Mainly because I want him out of here as soon as possible. Then we contact Tarin and get them access to the computer and do some research on the staff here. Then we get out."

August led the way back to the meeting. Tijan stepped around him, moving between the two goons before they could say anything. She opened the door quickly. There were four men in the room, but it was the look that passed between JT and Mr. Tesimmon that grabbed Tijan's attention. The two men at the door immediately grabbed her and August.

"Really? You came to meet me. Call them off or I'll call the cops." Staring at the only man who was seated, Tijan guessed it was Mr. Tesimmon. Or she hoped it was.

After a bit of a stare-down, he gave the slightest nod. The two men released them. Tijan had been kicked by a calf before, but the pressure the man had exerted on her arm had felt like it had been compressed in a vice. Keeping her focus on Mr. Tesimmon, she walked the length of the table toward him. Hoping that August, who had just admitted he sucked at surveillance, was keeping an eye on the rest of the men, she stopped a few feet away.

"You must be Mr. Tesimmon. I see you and JT know each other."

The man dressed in the three-piece suit, who had been leaning back in the chair like he owned the place, sat up abruptly at her comment. His eyes narrowed as he stared at her. "No. We were just having a conversation."

Tijan couldn't take her eyes off the ridiculous inch-thick gold chain he wore around his neck in lieu of a tie. At the end of it was a huge hunk of gold. It wasn't attractive in any way, but when she looked into his eyes, there was a smug look of having accomplished what he had wanted. He liked it when others noted his gaudy jewellery.

She turned to look directly at JT, who was across the table from her, leaning against the windowsill that banked an entire wall. "Oh, my mistake. Thank you for keeping our guest entertained, JT. I've got it from here."

"I'm fine to stay."

"No, that's alright. August can help me with anything I need."

The annoyed look came and went quickly, but Tijan knew that even if she hadn't seen it, she'd have sensed it. She'd been around men too often not to get the vibe that he was pissed, although in her world, the men often just outright stated when they were mad. JT, though, was good at masks. He soon flashed her a bright smile, showing her all his expensive white teeth, especially the one that had a small diamond perched on it.

"Alright. Don't let me interfere with a beautiful woman who knows her job." He smiled at her but took his sweet time sauntering down the length of the twenty-foot table and out the door.

If there hadn't been an audience, she might have done the eye-rolling or gagging reflex. "So Mr. Tesimmon, what can I do for you? I'm assuming since you felt it important to stop me at the hospital to tell me you'd be by for answers, that's why you're here."

"You're quite bright, aren't you?"

Tijan smiled, but rather than sit as she got the impression he was waiting for her to do just that, she remained standing. "My mom always told me I was."

There was an odd look that came over his face. "I thought you grew up without a mama."

Tijan shrugged, feeling her muscles tense up. "It's a figure of speech. What would you like, Mr. Tesimmon?"

"It's Mr. T. Your father and I have some dealings. Did he ever talk to you about them?"

"What do you want to know?"

"Where we're at with acquiring Caspian Winery. I understand you're living in sin with the best friend of the step-grandson to the owner. And with your three-year-old son. Of whom he isn't the father."

Tijan now wished she'd been sitting. Her legs felt awfully wobbly.

"That sounds like a bit of a veiled threat, Mr. T. For the record, that part of my personal life is over, so you might want to catch up on your intel." She did not know where this stuff was coming from but couldn't blame it on too much TV. The few shows she'd watched had obviously stuck with her. She had to protect whomever she could. This man was real and dangerous. It was great that August had come to stand on the opposite side of the table and take the man's scrutiny off her. She wasn't handling what he was saying very well. He knew too much.

His intense glare turned to August. "And who are you exactly?"

"I'm a business adviser." August strolled down the other side of the table and leaned against it, crossing his legs at the ankle. "If it's any of your business."

The smug look disappeared from the man's face. "Oh, believe me, it is. See, her father and I are currently in negotiations. He's taking on a partner." Mr. T turned to Tijan. "And I don't want you screwing it up. Do you understand?"

If she hadn't felt like he was the scariest man she'd ever met, one of his two henchmen had joined them at that end of the room. Tijan felt like he was breathing down her neck.

It took all her willpower to paste on a smile. "What I know, Mr. Tesimmon, is that I won't be doing any dealings without my father's input. And since someone felt they should shoot him and put him in a coma, well, that could mean it might take a while. Do you understand?"

Thankfully, her bravado worked. Mr. T rose and made his way past her but stopped long enough to stare her in the eyes from less than a foot away. "Oh, I do. I'm not sure you do yet. But I know you'll come around. My plans aren't changing at this point. I am becoming his business partner. And soon. And I have plans for you."

He held her gaze for several moments before continuing past her and walking out the door. August closed the door behind them, leaning against it. At the soft click, Tijan sank into the nearest chair.

August clapped. "Whoa. Are you ever a badass! I'm not sure of a smart one but—"

"When you're around men all the time, the really tough outdoorsmen, you learn quickly to call their bluff or they'll stampede you. I'm not sure that was the right approach here." Tijan dropped her head onto the table for a moment.

Some music began to play. Tijan lifted her head and looked questioningly at August. He put his finger to his lips and then pointed around the room.

Tijan nodded; she understood the room could be bugged, but she whispered, "What the hell have we gotten ourselves into? What was my father doing?"

"Why did that man say he had plans for you?"

CHAPTER 41

"TARIN, HI. SORRY, IT'S taken me so long to get back to you. Is now a good time though to set up that remote thing?"

"Where are you, Tijan?"

"Not in the office, if that's what you're worried about."

"Yeah, but we need you at the computer to be able to set up that remote access."

"Don't worry, I'll do that. Is now a good time?"

"Yes. But with the office bugged, I'm not sure that it's—"

"It's okay. August and I brought the tower and the laptop to my bedroom. Did you know that Ja—your fa—my fa—? I don't even know what to call him. Anyway, he has two computers. Just found the laptop. And he has a back way that leads from his office to the parkade area. There's a car elevator, which is cool and creepy at the same time. I'm going to park my car in the main lot. I don't like feeling caged. And there are stairs and a human elevator that takes him to the lobby."

"I did. He used to enter the hotel that way sometimes when he wanted to check on the staff. He'd surprise them, make sure they were doing a good job. So you found his special key?"

"Yeah. That's actually how we found the laptop. He has a lot of hiding places in that office. Some are safes that we couldn't get into. Who knows how many others we didn't find? August and I spent four hours combing that office. We waited until everyone left at 5:30, although it was hard to convince a few to leave on time. Mary likes to hang out here a lot. She doesn't seem to trust leaving me on my own. I told them I'd deduct pay if they stuck around. Can I do that? I don't even know how payroll works. Mary, of course, didn't listen, but the rest did. Well, really, that would be just JT. There's no one else on this floor. Everyone else is one floor down. Or at least that's what I've figured out so far."

Tarin laughed. "Oh my God, you might be more of a business mogul than you thought."

"Oh no. Not doing this. My blood pressure has seen highs I never knew existed. Tarin," Tijan took a deep breath. "Father is into some scary stuff. Mr. Tesimmon stopped by. You guys need to look into him."

"Okay, but first tell me about your meeting. Did you hear any more from CSIS?"

Tijan looked at August, who was busy transforming the desk in the hotel room into a working space, hooking up the computer and laptop. What was she supposed to tell her sister?

"Not again. No, they think he's involved with organized crime. And after meeting Tesimmon, sorry, Mr. T, I have to say I'm inclined to agree. Sorry, Tarin." Her breath hitched, which made Tijan feel worse. "I'm sorry. Maybe I'm wrong."

"No, I'm quite sure you're not. I've always hoped that it wasn't true, but my father has always been about getting ahead, no matter who he had to step on or how he had to do it."

"That Mr. T knows a lot about you, Tarin. He knows you're living with Graham and that you have a three-year-old son. I felt like he was threatening all of you. He's scary."

"I've got Guy and Graham doing some research on him. They have some good contacts in the police force, so we'll see if they can find out anything. Don't worry about Graham, Chance and I. We've been taking precautions for quite a while, and Graham has stepped them up a lot since Dad was shot. Let's get this remote access set up, and then I think we should get you out of there. This is too dangerous."

"I'm with you. If we can find something on the man and get him charged and off the streets, I'm good with that. The sooner I'm out of here and back on the prairies riding my horse, the happier I'll be."

Her comment was met with complete silence. She couldn't even hear her sister breathe. That's when it hit her what she'd said. "Tarin. I didn't mean that the way it sounded. I'm a country kid though, and this city life, well, it isn't for me. We don't know each other well, but I want to get to know you and be a part of your life. I don't want to lose you now."

The voice that responded was a bit unsteady. "Me too. And I get it. I'm so sorry this is how we had to meet and that you've been pulled into this ugly world."

"That's okay. I'm glad I can help. But I do want to show you my world someday. Soon."

Again, there was complete silence. Tijan closed her eyes and let her head fall back. She was opening her mouth without thinking about what she was saying. Tarin probably had as many questions about their mom and why she hadn't been a part of Tarin's life.

"Okay, I've got this all hooked up."

Tijan blinked a few times, turning her back on August and the understanding expression on his face. "Look, Tarin—"

"It's okay, Tijan. Let's get this figured out and get you out of there. Then we'll sort out twenty-seven years of our lives. Okay?"

Tijan nodded, unable to find her voice. She handed the phone to August, who was a few feet behind her.

"Hi, Tarin. It's August. I have the computers set up. What do you need us to do on this end?"

Tijan walked to the window and stared out over the city. It truly was beautiful in its own busy, light-filled way. It just wasn't for her. But this was what her sister knew. Would they be able to be friends when all this was over?

"Got it. Okay. I'll get Tijan to log in and then you can walk her through the rest."

Tijan went to the computer and pulled up a chair. August set the phone beside her on speaker.

"I'm ready, Tarin."

"Let's do the computer tower first. Login and then I'm going to give you some URL addresses you'll need to type into the address bar."

If Tijan hadn't seen it herself, she wouldn't have believed it was possible. But not only was Tarin able to see all that was on the computer, but she had full control of it, including moving things around, starting up programs, shutting things off, and even turning on the webcam so they could see each other.

"Is this legal?"

"It all depends on how it is being used. There are companies out there that have this installed on their employees' computers without their knowledge. Most say it's to make sure they can track what the employees are doing and to ensure they aren't stealing secrets."

Tijan gasped. "Does anyone trust anyone in this world?"

"Not really. Sorry, I know you're getting a rather harsh look into my world, but I promise you not all is as sinister as this. And not all businesses are run like this."

CHAPTER 42

"WHY'D YOU SHOOT HIM?"

"I didn't."

"You told me it would solve all our problems."

"Yeah, but not until he'd signed the paperwork."

"What if we get caught? What if people think we're behind the shooting?"

"We're not, so stop acting like a freaked-out kid. We're fine. I've hidden our tracks so no one will be able to trace all the money we've laundered—or how we've done it. At least not without some exceptional skills. We're fine." He reached under the table. Taking his partner's hand, he squeezed it. "We're fine. You just keep doing your job and I'll do mine."

"This isn't good. I think we should flee the country."

"No. I think I can get his electronic signature from something else. He's been dealing with Eleanor for years. So if I hack her system, I should be able to get a hold of something he's signed and transfer it to the paperwork we want signed."

"If you're going to hack hers, why not just hack his?"

"See? That's why you're my partner. I can't do it, but it can't be hard to find some whiz kid who can, though we might have to do away with him after."

"I'll look after it. I knew I partnered up with you for a reason. Also, make sure the Caspian deal doesn't go through. It's the only way I can stop certain things from happening. It won't just piss off one boss but two."

"How?"

"They've had problems out there this past year. Give them some more."

"I'll make it happen. Can I see you tonight?"

"We can't be seen together too often. My father is savvy. He'll kill both of us if he even suspects that I'm gay. Don't worry, we'll have everything we ever wanted. Just keep playing it my way. I can't wait to be with you."

"Me too."

~~~~

"Okay, what do you have for me?"

"Hello, Mr. T."

"What do you have for me?"

"If you're referring to C-Lite Hotels' papers, you already know that James got shot before I could get him to sign anything."

"I know, but I also know you have access to much of his business, and the new boss isn't sharing anything with you."

"How do you know that?"

"That's why you should never lie to me. I know everything. Now I want his business. Even if I'm not legally part owner, doctor some papers that state I am his partner."

"I could be killed, fired, and/or arrested."

"True. But I'm paying you enough that you could live quite comfortably."

"But I wouldn't be of use to you or be able to make these ridiculous, illegal deals you want."

"So, what do you want now?"

"I think this is worth a lot more than you're paying me. You run close to twenty million dollars through your business annually. I want two million to do this latest deal. Half now and half when I deliver."

"Aren't you getting greedy? That might get you killed."

"It might, but I've gotten smart. Since you shot—"

"I didn't shoot him."

"Of course not. You don't do the dirty work yourself."

"I'd watch what you're saying. I have no problem getting rid of problems."

"And then you'd lose the best asset you have. I've been loyal and brought you a new way to smuggle across the borders. I—I can make your life just as miserable as you've made mine."

"We have a deal."

"Yes, we do. It's one that I agreed to a long time ago. It was the only way you'd let me stay in my son's life. But now I want more. And I deserve more. I've been very valuable to you. Two million up front."

"Not likely. You get paid when you deliver."

"Which I have, time and again. I've let you know when there's been a big shipment of linens coming across the border, and it's been an easy way for you to conceal and smuggle drugs in. I've given you many opportunities to grow your drug business. Have you ever been caught? No, because I've made sure of that. You owe me this one."

CHAPTER 43

"AUGUST. AUGUST."

He was having a great dream, and the web of sleep was not letting him go. He was aware that someone was trying to awaken but he couldn't quite seem to make it over the threshold.

"Look. I can't wake him. He's out. And snoring, I might add. Throw cold water on him? I guess that would work. It's a rather rude way to wake someone."

The voice was filtering through; the words reaching his brain, but the meaning was not quite registering. Since there was silence again, he stopped even trying to come out of it, but when he heard rushing water, that pulled him back to the brink. When he felt a few drops on his face, it catapulted him upright.

"Ahh. Geez. When you wake up, you don't do it in half measures, do you?"

August blinked a few times, looking wide-eyed at Ti-jan. Her hair was pulled into a ponytail, and her face looked fresh and wholesome and very tempting. He knew he was staring, but that was the price she'd have to pay for looking so damn good and for waking him from an incredible dream. The telltale red that was creeping up her face let him know she was uncomfortable with the look in his eye. Suddenly, she turned her back on him and sat at the laptop she had open.

"I can't get into this. I think this is my father's personal laptop. Can you take this to Graham this morning? He's going to see if he can bypass the password."

"Yeah, sure. Same scenario as last time?"

"I don't know. I said I'd have you call him as soon as you got up."

August scrubbed his hand down his face. He could just imagine what he looked like, definitely not fresh and bright like Tijan. A big yawn reminded him that sleep was not letting go of him easily.

"Okay. What time is it anyway?" He glanced toward the window, noticing it was getting light out.

"5:30."

"Did you get any sleep?"

Tijan shrugged. "A bit."

August looked at her and then at the bed. He vaguely remembered being sprawled across the bed. He hadn't given her much space. "Sorry about hogging your bed. I guess once I crashed, that was it. I remember thinking I should go back to my room but thought I'd just close my eyes for a moment."

Tijan turned sideways to face him, resting her arm on the back of the chair. "Don't worry. I got some sleep. By the way, Guy is sending over a friend today to do a sweep of the office. Since there always seems to be someone there during the day, he'll come over this morning and do a check of my office, the parkade, the back stairs and elevator from Father's office. That way, we won't have to be as secretive or paranoid. He'll come back tonight when the office staff has gone home and go through every office. Guy said the man could get in even without all the electronic codes, but it would make it a lot easier if I could get them. I guess that means schmoozing, Mary."

"Or JT. He seems to like you, and he seems to know a lot. Ambitious, I think."

"Oh, yay for me. He's always there, isn't he? He seems to be around every corner, always waiting, always ready to pounce. Did you see him with Tesimmon? I get the feeling they know each other."

"Which means Tesimmon has been coming around the office a lot? What makes you say they know each other?"

Tijan seemed lost in thought. August was relieved she didn't seem taken with JT, even though the guy poured on the charm when he was around her. He was definitely looking for his opportunity to move up the ladder.

"I don't know. There was a familiar look between them that raised red flags for me. I could have imagined it, but... I don't think so. Let's just say it's bugging me."

"Could JT and this Tesimmon have a deal going behind your dad's back?"

"I don't know, but I don't see JT as that smart. He obviously wants to get ahead, but to be part of taking someone down... damn, I don't know." Tijan clapped her hand over her mouth. "Oh my God. I haven't even asked how my father is. What the—I need to call Tarin. She must think I'm the worst human being ever. It just never occurred to me."

August knelt, so he was looking at her at eye level. He put his hand on her shoulder. She turned wide, distressed eyes toward him. "It's okay. I think anyone would have reacted that way. You don't know your father. You've barely spent any time with him and then suddenly you're in charge of a multi- million or even billion-dollar company. I think your sister understands."

"I don't want her to hate me."

The barely whispered words were so soul-wrenching that August stood, pulling her into his arms. He didn't say anything but only held her while she worked through a storm of emotions. The tears didn't flow, but he knew she was battling to keep them at bay. She laid her head on his chest and just stood silently, unmoving. Her pain radiated from her. He pulled her closer, trying to absorb the ache that came from deep within.

Time had ceased to matter. He quite enjoyed having her in his arms. His resistance was wearing down. He nuzzled his nose against her hair and took a deep breath.

That's when he knew he was in trouble. She froze. He closed his eyes, trying to rein in his wayward thoughts and actions. Adding to her distress was not something he wanted to do. Gently, he eased away from her, letting his arms fall. Before he could take a step back, though, she looked up at him with her big, beautiful, blue eyes.

He was pretty sure it wasn't he who moved first, but he did nothing to stop her from leaning into him and kissing him. His instinct was to wrap his arms around her and pull her in tight, but with how gently her lips touched his, she was exploring, testing the waters. He did with his lips what he wanted to do with his hands. He let her know he was very interested, and he gave back all that she did and a bit more. She arched as he leaned down.

She eased back but held his gaze for a long time. "Nice. You're not a complication I need right now, but—" She smiled before gently kissing him again.

It was over before he was ready for it to be, but he understood her reluctance to jump in. He was definitely having some second thoughts himself. He wasn't sure he was in a good place emotionally, mentally or life-wise for a relationship, partly because he knew with her there would be no half measure.

Tijan had moved close to the window. He stood with his back to her, taking deep breaths. He could hear her on the phone with Tarin asking about their father. From what he could hear of her end of the conversation, there was no change. He wasn't doing well, and although he was not in a coma; he wasn't far from it.

"Pneumonia. Really, so on top of being shot, he's as sick as a dog... You don't remember him ever being ill..."

August quit eavesdropping and crossed to the adjoining door that led to his room. He'd unlocked his side the night before, just in case. Now he wasn't so sure he shouldn't lock it behind him.

One thought, however, that raced through his mind was, 'I think Mom would have liked her'.

CHAPTER 44

THE GUY SHOWED UP at six o'clock. He buzzed from the private elevator to her father's office.

"Hi. It's Randal. I'm here to check your heating."

His Australian accent sounded as fake as his name, but Tijan was going to trust her sister and those her sister trusted.

Tijan gave the man the guest code so he could use the back elevator. The guest code was reset every twenty-four hours, according to Mary.

When he knocked, she went down the hallway to let him in.

"Who are you?"

"Sent by Graham and Guy. I hear you have a heating issue."

Tijan felt silly with the game they were playing, but she opened the door. He wasn't what she was expecting. The first thing she noted was that she dwarfed him. She stepped back to let him in, still wondering if he was the right guy or someone she could trust.

"Come in. I'm Ti—arin."

He nodded as he passed. "Randal."

She trailed behind him as he moved brusquely to her office. He didn't waste time on explanations. Standing there awkwardly, she watched as he pulled a gadget out of the satchel he had over one shoulder. After punching a few buttons on it, he started walking around the room, slowly moving it over the walls and all the furniture.

"Do you—"

He spun around and snapped his index finger to his lips. Startled, Tijan jerked back. Even though he was across the room from her, she felt like he was going to throw a ninja star at her. Why that came to mind she wasn't sure but she'd seen a movie once where the character, a repair guy, dressed like her guy, had gone into an office meeting, all casual and nice but then he'd pulled ninja stars out of his uniform and had started throwing them at the people.

He, though, seemed unaware of her thoughts, ignored her and went about his business. Returning to her desk, she discovered she'd forgotten to return the computer. It was going to look awfully strange not to have it if someone came in. She didn't want to get caught carrying the thing through the hotel. Nor was she about to leave her guest, even if he seemed to know what he was doing and was trusted vicariously by her sister.

The guy worked methodically and slowly. The thought entered her mind that she was trusting a lot of people she didn't know. It wasn't the first time. She'd always approached life that way. Whenever new hands arrived at the ranch, she always trusted them to do their job and be honest—at least until they showed her otherwise. She truly hoped that her trust wasn't being misplaced now.

The machine started chirping. Tijan looked up to see Randal peel the cover off the thermostat. As she joined him, he flipped it over so she could see what he'd found—a small flat disk. He carefully removed it and placed it into a lead vial he pulled from his satchel.

As he continued to search for more, Tijan realized at the pace he was going, he would be there a while. She pulled out her phone and moved down the back hallway. Knowing she couldn't go into the parkade, she stepped into the bathroom, praying it wasn't bugged.

She'd been about to text Tarin, but the image of herself in the mirror caught her attention. She had never been one to do that, but then this whole situation was showing her a side of herself that she never knew existed. Color had never been something she'd stopped to think about. If it was a t-shirt, plaid or jeans, then it was good. But she had to admit that her sister was showing her a new appreciation for clothes. She brushed her hand over the silky, pale-yellow blouse, enjoying its softness and admiring its lightness and breezy feel.

She snorted. The men on the ranch would have a field day with razzing her if they knew where her thoughts were going. Really, they'd have been shocked at her attire—and so would her mom.

Her eyes popped open wide. Her mom. She hadn't been in contact since arriving. Her phone suggested she'd missed several texts and phone calls. She quickly sent off a text.

'Doing fine. Busy. Will call soon. Sorry. Love you.'

Heading back to the desk, a noise from the outer office that caught her attention. She looked at Randal and then at the door. Hurrying over to it, she opened it slightly. JT had apparently just arrived. He gave her his full white-teeth-blinding smile and headed her way. She eased out and closed the door behind her, casually leaning against it. Pretending to scratch her head, she hit the button that would automatically lock her door.

"Good morning, Tarin. Don't you look stunning this morning?"

She gave him a half-smile. "What are you doing here so early, JT?" Glancing at the clock in the lobby, she noticed it was only seven fifteen.

"I need to get an early start."

"Oh? What's so pressing?"

"Some things your father wanted me to do. Don't worry about it. I've been doing this job a long time," he said evasively.

"Oh, how long is that?"

"I think I've been here five years. Paid. But I worked here as a practicum for about a year before that. I started out in the hotel, learning from the ground up, until I learned enough to move into this position." He smiled at her. "Why are you here so early?"

She saw August exit the elevator holding a big box. Relieved that he'd thought to hide the computer, she smiled at JT. "Because I run the business. Let's go to your office, and you can tell me what you're working on."

"Well, I—"

"It'll give you a chance to show me what you do. And thank you, by the way, for setting up the staff area so fast."

She managed to steer him down the hallway toward his office. She signaled to August behind her back, hoping he understood her cryptic message.

"You're welcome. We actually had that stuff in the back storage shed. I had purchased them a few years ago, but your father wouldn't hear of it. I had maintenance haul it out at the end of the day." JT stopped at his office, but before he punched in his code, he looked at her. "I didn't even grab my coffee yet."

"Why don't I grab us each one while you get settled? I'll be right back." Without waiting for an answer, she headed back the way she'd come. When she passed the lobby area, she was glad to see August hugging the wall so JT couldn't see him. She glanced over her shoulder in time to see JT disappear through his door. Stopping at her office, she punched in her code and shooed August inside.

Blowing out a heavy breath, she took a moment to gather herself. There were too many things she had to do and figuring out what JT was up to just wasn't that high on her list. When she returned to his office with coffee, his door was closed, so she quietly eased it open. When she heard him talking to someone on the phone, she hesitated.

"... you found someone..."

"... what do you need..."

"... if you can get into that comp..."

"... soon. He won't be..."

She pressed closer but couldn't quite make out what he was saying. She made a point of pushing open the door, and letting her heels click noisily against the ceramic floor.

He had his back to her but spun around quickly, eyeing her suspiciously before jerking his phone away from his ear and abruptly hanging up.

"Sorry if I interrupted anything."

JT immediately smiled, but it didn't touch his eyes. "No. Just talking to my mom."

"Here's your coffee, but now I see that you have your own Keurig machine. I'll catch up with you later, DC. Something's come up, but I do still want to talk to you." She softened her words with a smile and left.

Was she paranoid, or was he planning something? He seemed eager to move up in the company. Could he have shot her father?

CHAPTER 45

"HE'S GUILTY OF SOMETHING."

August looked around the office. Randal assured them that he'd found all three bugs, but he'd be back to do another full sweep of the office as well as all the others. August still wasn't comfortable discussing business there. Instead, he played some music on his phone. Tijan frowned at him as she returned to her desk before carefully she looking around. Miming to him, he got the gist that she was asking if there were more listening devices. He shrugged as if to say he really didn't know. She joined him on the sofa, kicking off her shoes to arch and curl her toes.

"Damn, these things are awful."

She was the first woman he'd met who was honest about the heels, but since it was an area, he knew better than to wade into, he didn't reply. Keeping his voice low, he asked, "I'm going to take a guess and say you mean JT?"

She nodded.

"I don't like the guy, but I'm sure it's for very different reasons than you. What makes you think he's guilty of something?"

"He's cagey. Always there. He was on the phone with someone when I walked into his office. He brushed it off as his mom, but I truly believe he was planning something. Could he be behind Dad's shooting? If so, why?"

August wondered if she realized what she'd said. She'd struggled with calling him Father, and now she casually threw out Dad. Her mind was definitely a little preoccupied.

"I don't know. Graham and Guy are doing a background check on everyone here. They haven't been able to get into your father's laptop yet. But then they've only had it a few hours. They said to see if we can find a password. Graham is going to catch up with Tarin and see if she knows."

"Alright. But I've been through everything, and I can't find anything. He doesn't keep a lot of paper. I mean, there are all the legal files, but almost everything else is done electronically—or at least, from what I can tell. I can't believe that just two weeks ago; I was riding Tango at full gallop across an open field and not worried about a soul. And now, I don't know who to trust, who I can even pretend to know."

There was a knock on the door. August looked at Tijan questioningly. She shrugged, slipped on her shoes and made her way to the door.

"Who is it?"

The door opened slightly. Mary poked her head in. "Hi. Sorry to bother you. Did you sign those forms? The ones I left on your desk the other day? The lawyers are asking for them."

"No, I haven't. I'll get them to you. Was there anything else? Wait. Mary, come and sit down. Since you probably know this place better than anyone else, I'd like to ask you some questions."

With her hands clasped tightly in front of her, she made her way to the couch, standing awkwardly beside it. August watched her with curiosity.

"Have a seat, Mary. Can I get you a water or coffee?"

Mary, who was the epitome of efficiency, stood woodenly with her hands clasped in front of her. Tijan had already gone to the side cabinet and was pouring a glass of water. She carried it back and handed it to Mary before sitting down. Mary remained standing.

Tijan stood up. "Is something wrong?"

"I've never sat on the furniture in here, and I'm not sure that I should."

Tijan blinked a few times, obviously taken aback. She gave her a full smile. "It's okay. Have a seat, I promise not to tell. Besides, I'm the boss right now." She waited until she perched awkwardly on the edge before continuing.

"Here's something to drink. I'll make you a coffee if you'd like one? Although, to be honest, you'd have to show me how to use the Keurig thing." Tijan set down the glass of water she was still holding.

Mary smiled wanly as she patted down her short, stylish, salt and pepper hair. It reminded August of something his mom would have done when nervous. It dawned on him that they would have been about the same age. That jolted him, but he pushed away those thoughts.

"Water's fine. What would you like to know?"

"How long have you been here?"

"Well, I've known you a long time."

August realized immediately Tijan's mistake, and he was pretty sure she was aware of it as well by the way she tensed up.

She cleared her throat. "I know that, but how long would you say it's been since you started here?"

"I think I started working for your father in... I'm not sure of the year but let's say twelve years or so."

"Has anyone been here longer than you?"

"Hmm. You might have to ask Personnel about that one. None in management have been, but I do think there are some staff that have been."

"Okay. I don't think I've met everyone though, right? I mean, in key positions?"

"You've met Chris—"

"I'm sorry, Chris?" August frowned. He did not remember meeting anyone named Chris.

"Oh, I mean JT. And then Arlene, she does payroll. Shannon is her assistant. You met them briefly the other day. Carl Jones, VP of Human Resources, is off because of a heart condition. He's been gone for about three months. No return date yet. And Don Melner is off on a month-long holiday. He doesn't even know what has happened. When he goes on vacation, he does not take his work phone. There's no way to get a hold of him."

"And Don does what?"

"Oh, sorry. He's Vice President of Customer Services. He's who should have stepped in to take over for your fa—" Mary put her fingers to her lips. "I'm sorry. I had no right to say that. It's just that's the norm. But your father never did things by any rulebook. He didn't trust anyone. I mean, doesn't. I—"

Tijan touched Mary's arm. "It's okay. I know my father does things his way or no way."

Mary smiled. "Yes, he does."

"How have you lasted so many years with him, Mary?"

"He's a good, kind man. I know not many see him that way, but he's always been good to me." Mary's smile faltered. "It's a good job. I like all the responsibility I have. There isn't much that happens here that doesn't go through me."

August hoped he'd kept his face neutral, but from everything he'd heard, none of those words had ever been used to describe James Madsen.

"What exactly is JT's position?" August realized he might have said that a little sharper than he needed to when both women snapped their heads toward him.

Mary smiled, a deep-seated, warm smile. "He's the Finance Manager and in line to be the VP of Operations, although he calls it CFO. He has such high aspirations. In fact, he and your father were in negotiations when your father was injured. How is he, Tarin?"

Tijan opened her mouth but hesitated before saying, "He's okay. It'll be a while before he's back to normal. But he's doing well."

"Do you know anyone who'd want to hurt him, Mary?"

Her body snapped upright as if she were physically and emotionally withdrawing. "Why would you ask me? I already talked with those men from the CSIS, and I told them I don't know anything. Your father didn't have a lot of friends, and many didn't like his business dealings, but

I don't know much about that. Your father is a good man. He doesn't have good taste in women but, umm—I have to get back to work. Sorry for taking up so much of your time. But I have a lot of work." Mary hastened to the door and left without turning back.

"Well, that was obviously a good question, August. She left like a scalded cat. So what does she know that she doesn't want us to know?"

CHAPTER 46

TIJAN ROUNDED THE CORNER of the hotel, having stepped outside to get a breath of fresh air. She'd never been indoors as long as she'd been with this job, and she'd only been doing it for a week. How had her life gotten so crazy?

Walking across the street, she strolled a few blocks before cutting across to a park. She needed grass and the outdoors. Leaning against a tree, she pulled out her phone and dialed her mom. She needed to talk to the one person who could always ground her.

"Tijan. Where are you? I've been worried sick. Are you okay?"

Tijan took a deep breath, feeling a lot of the stress and pressure ease. "Hi, Mom. I'm fine. I sure do miss you. The big city isn't like anything I've ever experienced before."

"You're still in Toronto, right?"

There was almost a sound of hope that she wasn't. If only her mom knew what was going on. Tijan tensed. "Uh, I'm kind of switching places. I mean exploring and I'm currently in Montreal." She winced as the lie rolled off her tongue. The last time she'd fibbed to her mom, she'd been thirteen and had wanted to wear a certain short dress to the school dance. Her mom had said no, so she'd snuck it out. That had been the last time she'd worn a dress. Kyle, her boy-crush, had laughed at her. It had all backfired.

She just hoped this wouldn't. This entire trip was a lie.

"Oh, tell me about some of the places you've been. Who have you met? Did you go to Niagara Falls? They're amazing. But it is a very touristy place. I bet it's crazy there."

Feeling deflated and not really chatty and having totally killed the good feeling she'd had from hearing her mom's voice, she looked around. What was she supposed to say?

'I met a man who's my father that you told me was dead. I found my sister, who you told me was dead, but I know you kept hope that she wasn't. But how did that come about? How come she wasn't in my life? What the hell, Mom.'

"Tijan?"

"Sorry, Mom. I just wanted to call and let you know I'm okay. I'll send an email soon. And tell you all about it. I've been putting in some long days. I'm exhausted."

"Oh, that's good to hear. I hope you've seen a lot and met a lot of people?"

"Yeah. I have. I have to go."

"Is there anything you want to tell me, Tijan? I get a sense that things aren't good."

Tijan closed her eyes. At any other time, that would have been a welcome thing to hear. In fact, in the past they'd have stayed up late talking. Her mom was her best friend. But right now, her best friend had a lot of questions to answer, and Tijan didn't know quite how to ask them.

"I'm good, Mom. We'll talk soon. I miss you. Love you."

"Love you too. Don't ever forget that."

Tijan hung up as tears pricked her eyes. She clutched her phone in her hand, wondering again how life had gotten so crazy.

Kicking off her shoes, she walked barefoot, loving the bright green grass under her feet. For a few minutes, she let herself enjoy the beauty. But it didn't take long for the noise and general hum of city racket to infiltrate her senses and destroy any peace she'd been feeling.

The entire purpose of the walk had been to get rid of stress, but that, too, had backfired.

Her phone rang. Glancing at the one in her hand, she frowned before remembering that she carried two phones. She pulled the one Tarin had given her out of her pocket.

"Hi, Tarin."

"Are you alright, Tijan? You sound down."

Tijan shrugged her shoulders a few times to ease the tension. "Yeah, just a bit overwhelmed."

"You don't have to stay. We can figure something else out."

"That would mean you'd have to come out of hiding, and that might put you and Chance at risk. I'll survive. I am making a serious mess of everything. And I don't know that I've done one single solitary thing for the business, but it has been an eye-opener."

"Yeah, sorry for the crash course in being a shark. Anyway, the reason I called, wait... do you have a minute?"

"Yeah. I'm at the park, so we should be fine. No ears to hear me." She looked around to make sure.

"Great. Okay, we looked at all the employees. There are a few who have had interesting pasts, including several who lied on their applications. But the most interesting thing is what we found out about Chris Simmons."

"JT?"

"Yeah. He was an orphan who was adopted at five. Interestingly, though, there are no records of who his parents are. Nothing."

"That's weird, right? How can there not be any record of that?"

"Someone obviously destroyed it. He does have papers mentioning his adoption, his name and a date of birth but no other information—at least not that we can find."

"Okay, this may sound odd. But are you guys any good?"

Tarin laughed. "Very. I'm quite good at hacking a lot of websites, but Guy and Graham not only surpass me, but they also have some crazy mad skills when it comes to the Internet and cybersecurity. They also have some good connections."

"So essentially, you hack for a living?" Tijan was sure that wasn't meant to be a good thing.

"I guess that's one way of putting it. We try to figure out what the bad hackers are doing so we can stop them. The focus of Knight's Associates is stopping cybercrime. Initially, it was finding the bad guys by following their digital footprint. Now the company has developed into a major contender in preventing hackers from accessing personal data in big companies and the government."

"Someday, we need to sit down and talk about that. I'm fascinated. For me, turning on the computer is an accomplishment. Hey, I'm getting a text. Hang on." Tijan looked at the message. "Well, it would appear that JT wants to meet with me. And Mary has texted me four times. I guess sneaking out on this job isn't a good thing."

"Be careful, Tijan."

"Oh yeah. Do you know a good lawyer?"

"What?"

The shriek in her sister's voice reminded her that she couldn't just jump topics, especially not when it involved legal stuff.

"Sorry. I need someone to look over some papers. Mary keeps at me to sign these papers that say I'm in charge. But shouldn't a lawyer be going through those with me? Eleanor, who is quite a delight, never mentioned them. I haven't looked at them, and I don't know legal jargon, but I'm not about to sign something I don't understand. And since I'm not you, I shouldn't be signing them anyway."

"Can you scan them and send them?"

"I don't recall seeing a printer in your dad's office. I'll take pictures and send them. It'll be faster. By the time I figure out how to scan and send, Chance will be graduating high school."

"There's a printer in the cabinet beneath the windows."

"Oh, beside the liquor cabinet. Which is really well stocked."

"Yeah, that's one thing he never scrimped on."

"By the way, I've been spending money on improving staff conditions. Just thought you should know I've signed your name a few times."

"As long as you aren't giving away millions and doing anything illegal, I'm sure I'm fine with it. Be careful though."

"I will. You too. Keep that cute nephew safe." Tijan hung up. The warm sun felt so good, she tilted her head back and just stood there for several minutes enjoying it. One of her phones buzzed, reminding her that there was no rest. Glancing at her phone, she saw it was from Mary. In fact, there were now five texts from her. Not bothering to read any of them, she slipped on her shoes and started walking back to the hotel. Distracted by all that she and Tarin had discussed, she wasn't paying attention to what was around her. The information about Chris or JT seemed to set off some alarm bells, but she wasn't sure what that meant.

There had been something about him that had bothered her from the beginning, but knowing he'd been an orphan didn't sit well with her. On the ranch, she'd hated it when a calf or a foal had been orphaned. Although she'd made sure they'd been raised with love and a lot of attention, humans that tended to be orphaned didn't always have that kind of upbringing. She felt for the guy. Was he just someone out to protect himself, since no one probably had, or was there something more sinister about him?

CHAPTER 47

A CAR CAME TO a screeching halt beside her, and Tijan's head whipped around. The doors flew open, and two men, whose faces looked carved in angry stone, rushed her.

"Get in."

Tijan tried to shrug off the man, but he had her upper arm in a vice grip. It was going to leave some deep marks. Fleetingly, she wondered if they could get fingerprints off her skin. "I'm fine."

She soon found herself tossed in the back seat, her head down and most of her crumpled up on the floor of the limo.

"Things don't have to be difficult." Mr. Tesimmon grabbed her hair, snapping her head back. "But I like things done my way. If you do that, there won't be any harm. If you don't, well..."

He released her hair with almost as much force as he'd grabbed it. "Now, sit up here so we can talk."

Rubbing her head, and feeling a weighted, sick feeling invade every pore of her being, she gingerly climbed onto the seat. Hugging the back corner, she put as much space as she could between her and the only other person in the back. The gold, heavy chain he wore flashed at her as they turned the corner.

"It appears that your father was smarter than I gave him credit for. All his electronic signatures have vanished. He had someone create an app for him. When he signed something with his signature online, it was only good on that one document and could not be copied or used elsewhere or it would disappear I don't like when people screw with me."

Tijan found she could barely swallow; her mouth had gone so dry. His look felt like it could singe her hair. She was almost tempted to put her hand up to check but didn't want to make any sudden movements in case he took them the wrong way. She almost went limp when he looked away, but she had to be aware of every move he made. Keeping him in her sights, she glanced around to see if there was anything she could grab if she needed to protect herself.

"I hear your father is awake."

Tijan froze.

"It's good that you've been visiting him."

The impact of that hit her like a sledgehammer to the gut. He'd been watching her father, which meant he knew that Tarin was going there. Did he know there were two of them? Struggling to swallow, she determined her best defense was to remain mute.

"Now that he's coming around, you're going to get his signature on these documents for me."

He handed her some papers, but she didn't reach for them. Grabbing her hand, his nails biting into her bones, he forced it open. He set the pages in her open palm. Curiosity got the better of her, and she glanced at the top sheet. It was an acquisition agreement. Reaching with her other hand, which she assumed he took as her acceptance of them, she flipped through the pages. The sick feeling that had invaded her body the moment she'd met this man suddenly felt like a geyser about to erupt.

"He'll never sign these." She didn't know her father at all but from what she'd discovered, a man who had given his life to his business and who'd pretty much given up family to do so would never sign it away—and certainly not fifty-one percent of it. It would mean he was giving up majority control.

"See, that's where you come in. Because I know that, you'll want your father around for a while. If I have to, I'll fake these papers. But see, I'm trying to turn over a new leaf. I'm going legit. So don't fuck with me."

The car slowed. Tijan hadn't paid attention to where they were going. Glancing out the almost black window, she could make out an extensive structure. Her stomach felt like it had dropped twenty stories. They were at the hospital.

"He may not be awake."

Mr. T smiled at her. At least that was what she was sure he'd call it but it was the most evil, venom-filled thing she'd ever seen. "Then I guess you'll wake him. I want these back." He glanced at his watch. "You have fifteen minutes."

The door opened behind her, and she was ruthlessly grabbed and yanked out. The pages in her hand went flying.

"Fourteen minutes."

Scrambling to pick them up, she scrunched the sheets in her hand and took off running. Entering the hospital, she went straight to the bathroom.

"Tarin! Tarin! He wants me to force Dad to sign forms that will give up Dad's company. I have only ten minutes. Tarin!"

"Tijan. It's okay. It's okay. He, meaning Tesimmon? You're at the hospital, right?"

"How'd you know?"

"Our security saw what happened but couldn't stop it. One of them followed you. We're on our way. We'll be there in five."

"He's here. He brought me here but he wants me to get Dad to sign these forms. I can't do that."

"It's okay. Tesimmon wants Dad to sign forms? I'm assuming it means he wants to take over the business."

"He knows too much. He knows I—you, have been coming here and that Dad's awake. Wait. You can't come here. He'll know there are two of us."

"So, why don't we use that? Where is he?"

"Illegally parked in the drop-off area."

"Good. I'll get Graham to drop me off a short distance away. Then he'll drive by that area. I'll come running, hop in and we'll take off. That should get them to follow us."

"Are you crazy? They'll kill you."

"Call those guys from the CSIS. You have their number?"

"I'll get it." After hanging up, she called August.

"Are you in the office?"

"No. The hotel room, why? Where did you go to?"

"I need you to go to the office and get me that card for the CSIS guys. Oh wait, it might be in my room."

"Just give me a second and I'll check. Good thing you didn't lock the door between our rooms."

She could hear him moving around, searching. She couldn't even tell him where to look.

"Here it is." August gave her the number. "Care to tell me what's going on?"

"Mr. T. kidnapped me and dropped me off at the hospital to get Dad to sign some papers. He wants him to give up the majority of his business. I have about five minutes to do so. Tarin and Graham are on their way. They're going to lead the guys away from the hospital. And then I don't know."

August was silent for a few seconds. Tijan didn't blame him. It was a lot to take in.

"I'll be there, in however long it takes to get partway across Toronto in a cab. Stay hidden. Get those CSIS guys to put security on your dad. Talk to the hospital as well. Stay hidden."

Tijan wasn't sure how she was supposed to stay in hiding and do all of that, but she proceeded to call the Canadian Security Agency.

"Is this Jim?"

"Just a minute."

She was immediately put on hold.

"This is Jim. Hello, Ms. Roth."

"How—" Tijan felt a little sick but decided to let it go. "Look. The organized crime dude you're after is here. At the hospital. He wants my father to sign some papers. I have about two minutes to do that. Then he's going to, well I don't know, but I'm quite sure it isn't good. I need some security for my father."

"We already have a plainclothes officer guarding your father."

Tijan placed her hand over her mouth, although about twenty questions started firing through her brain. She shoved them aside, deciding she'd ask them later. "Okay. But you may need more. Can't you do something to arrest that man?"

"Mr. T, you mean? He wants control of your business so he can run more drugs and do some money laundering, using the hotel as a front."

Tijan put her hand to her forehead, surprised to find it cool but damp. "Look. I have to go. Keep my father safe."

"Stay where you are. We'll pick you up and put you in protective custody."

"Keep my father safe." Tijan hung up and peeked out the bathroom door. Her phone rang. Startled, her hand automatically opened wide. She fumbled with her cell for a moment before clutching it in her hand and answering it.

"Tarin. Where are you?"

"We're now zipping through downtown Toronto with a tail."

"This is crazy."

"Guy is on his way to pick you up. Stay out of sight."

"August is on his way as well."

"I know. They should be there in about fifteen minutes . Go out the back and make your way to the parkade. That's where you'll meet them both. Be careful."

Releasing her hair from the tight bun she'd gotten in the habit of putting it in, she shook her hair so it draped forward and would better cover her face. She came out of the bathroom, turning left to head to the parkade. As she stepped into the open lobby trying to decide which direction to go, she looked to the front of the building.

Two men were standing just outside the door. She was sure she hadn't seen them, but it didn't take much to know who they worked for. They had that beefed-up, brawn look that said if they couldn't stop a Mac truck with their muscles, their fierce, I'll-kill-anything demeanor would have.

Unfortunately, one of the guys turned. Tarin suddenly felt zapped with adrenaline as she turned and fled out the back doors. If she'd been smart and just casually turned, she might not have attracted their attention. She glanced over her shoulder; they were charging through the lobby, heading in her direction.

She ran, barely noticing the signs giving her directions. Her head felt like it was on a swivel stick, snapping around to see if there were any others and how close they were to her. Heavy breathing and a lumbering sound had her looking behind her. The two gorillas were still chasing her. She'd never been so glad to have her runners on but wished at that point she had a horse.

Heading for the large parking structure, she was about to zoom inside when someone stepped out of the shadows. She jerked back, almost tripping over herself in an attempt to stop. She spun around and was about to sprint away when she heard her name in a familiar voice.

"Tijan."

She wasn't sure what kept her upright because her whole body seemed to have dissolved into jelly. August was soon by her side, wrapping his arm around her and steering her into the darkness of the underground car park. He held her close while they stood in the shadows. She was never so thankful that she didn't have to do this on her own. A beige SUV pulled into the parkade and stopped.

Tijan's breath caught in her throat as she clutched August's shirt, whispering. "They're right behind me."

The driver's window lowered as the vehicle slowly started rolling forward. Tijan dropped, yanking August with her so they were hidden behind a truck.

"August. Tijan."

Not that she knew Guy's voice well, having only heard it a few times, but she was never more thrilled than recognizing that friendly voice. Running awkwardly in a crouched position, she and August made their way to the vehicle.

"There she is." A gunshot rang out.

August yanked open the back door, and they both dove in. Guy stomped on the gas pedal. As they hit the street, an ambulance with lights flashing and sirens blaring roared past. Guy hugged its bumper as it soared through the heavy afternoon traffic.

CHAPTER 48

"WHERE ARE WE GOING? What about Tarin? Chance?"

"Chance is fine. He's with Grandma at Caspian. It's like a fortress. No one will get in. Geoff wouldn't even have been able to get in." Guy was maneuvering in and out of traffic like a race car driver.

Tijan was thankful he was getting them out of there despite being tossed around the back seat—although having August to cushion some of the blow wasn't hard to take.

"Geoff?"

Guy expertly moved them across four lanes of traffic and then shot through a light just as it turned red. "Long story. You'll get the edited version later."

"Is my father going to be okay?"

"He's been moved. As soon as we knew what was going on, we had him loaded into an ambulance and moved to another hospital."

"The ambulance you were following?"

"That was your father."

Tijan breathed a sigh of relief and would have closed her eyes, but Guy was careening around another corner. August's warm, calloused hand took hers. She curled her fingers around his as she looked at him. It was the first time she had felt like she were feeling something real—calluses. They came from hard physical labor. It was something she could relate to. Her hands, although they had been getting a break from her usual hard work, were still a lot rougher than most women's. Her mind seemed to wander to weird things, considering all that was going on.

"Thank you."

August leaned forward and gently kissed her. Guy zipped in and out of lanes, tossing them around in the back. They were both soon flopping sideways, unprepared for his driving. Tijan giggled. August kissed her again and then sat up, helping her to as well.

"Feel like a teenager trying to cop a feel in the back of your parents' car?"

August snorted with laughter.

Guy looked at them questioningly in the rearview mirror. Tijan smiled but shrugged. It felt good that August was holding her hand. It gave her something solid to hold on to.

"How did you get to the hospital so fast?"

"Taxi. $50 extra bucks was enough incentive for the guy to step on it. And man did he."

"Good." Tijan, though, was already distracted. Her mind retraced all that had happened. The men her father was dealing with weren't joking around. They weren't just angry men or even normal men; they were the ones who set their own rules and made everyone else play by them. Tijan knew people like that existed, but they didn't in her world, and it surprised her that they existed in Canada. She was probably naïve, but she'd liked the safe bubble she'd been living in, even if it had been delusional. In some ways, she definitely needed to leave the ranch more, but in others, she was more than happy with the safe life she led. Her mind tried to make sense of all that had happened. It felt like they drove forever, but it couldn't have been more than twenty minutes later when they arrived at an isolated area.

She found herself on a pockmarked road surrounded by trees that seemed more like the cowpaths she often traversed when going out into the field.

When the car stopped, she was hesitant to get out until she spotted Tarin coming around a clump of trees.

Running before her feet hit the ground, she collided with her sister, and they tumbled to the ground.

"You're alright?"

"You're alright?"

"Geez. I was so scared for you."

"I was so scared for you."

As they continued to talk, Tijan realized they were both saying the same thing at precisely the same time. She sat up without releasing her grip on her sister. They gazed at each other for a long time. Tijan felt conflicting waves of joy and sorrow swarm through her. She had an over-whelming sensation of being complete but yet she also wondered why she'd never been allowed to experience it before. Why she and her sister had been torn apart.

"Chance is okay?"

"He's with Grandma. He's been out there pretty much the whole time. Allison, his nanny, is amazing, and she'll protect him with her life."

"And since she's been trained as a bodyguard, no one is getting near our son." Graham sounded like a proud papa. He now stood with Guy and August a few feet away. All looked at the two of them.

Tijan gazed questioningly at her sister.

"We had some trouble a few years back. We thought it better to have someone who would keep Chance safe."

"Have these awful guys that Dad is dealing with been after you for a while, then?"

Tarin glanced at Graham and Guy. They gave her a slight node. "Come, let me show you this place, and I'll give you the Cole Notes version."

The five of them made their way back the way Tarin, and Graham had come. As they rounded the corner, Tijan was surprised to see a scorched area with burnt stubs of trees sticking out of the ground. And a brand-new house without siding sat in the midst of it, well hidden from the road.

Tijan had a ton of questions but wasn't sure if she should ask any.

"I don't even know where to start." Tarin obviously knew she was confused.

Guy stepped forward. "Let me. Bailey, my wife, who is also at Caspian with Chance, was kidnapped as a baby by her great-uncle. She never saw her family until I found her thirty years later. She was just getting reunited with them when her uncle again tried to kill her by blowing up the house that was here before this one."

Tijan's eyebrows shot skyward as her gaze swiveled from the destroyed house to Guy and then her sister.

Graham said, "We thought Geoff, the uncle, had been killed in this house, but it turns out he'd built himself an escape tunnel. He was way sicker than we thought. Anyway, it turns out, he is—"

Tarin squeezed his hand before standing on tiptoe to kiss him. She turned to face Tijan. "He's Chance's father. He had me drugged and impregnated. It still sounds awful."

"He what?" Tijan pressed her hand to her chest, sure she'd heard her wrong.

"I'll give you the long version another day. Anyway I didn't know who the father was. He decided when Chance turned two it was time to mold him into what he wanted him to be. He wanted to take Chance away from me and raise him. Thankfully, I had these two men." She nodded toward Guy and Graham. "To save me and my son. We set up a plan that almost backfired but, by some miracle, didn't. We got him."

Tijan remembered what she'd read when she'd first been sure she'd found her sister. She looked at Guy. "Your wedding. Was that what that was about?"

Guy nodded. "Yeah, it was a little more excitement than we wanted, but we knew we had to draw him out. We thought of everything except how devious he was. He won't be bothering anyone again."

Tijan felt like throwing up. What they all had gone through hadn't been easy. It was clearly written on their faces despite how they talked about it with such ease.

Tijan took her sister's hand. "You know, it was the picture from Guy and Bailey's wedding that led me to you."

Tarin pressed her fingers to her lips. "Really? But I wasn't in any. We made sure of that."

Tijan reached for her hand and rubbed her finger over the birthmark that adorned her hand in the webbing between her thumb and index finger. "This made me think I had found you. This forward 'C'."

Tijan slipped off her shoe and showed the birthmark on her foot. "Mine is a backward 'C'."

Tarin threw her arms around Tijan and started to cry. Tijan hugged her back, tears pricking her eyes. It truly felt like coming home.

CHAPTER 49

"SO, WHAT'S THE PLAN?" August looked pointedly at Guy and Graham. He'd learned quickly these two were prepared for anything.

Guy jerked his head sideways, indicating that he and Graham should follow him. "We don't have any proof that Mr. T shot their father. The police have a lot of speculation but nothing concrete. The Canadian Security Intelligence Service also has a lot of circumstantial evidence, but any witnesses soon disappear."

August looked over his shoulder at Tijan and Tarin sitting on the grass, just looking at each other. He couldn't imagine how it must feel to find a sibling who was a mirror-image.

"We need to set up another sting." Graham also turned to look at the two women. "I can't put either of them through that."

Guy nodded. "I know, but I don't know what else we can do."

"Why can't I be put in charge?" August wasn't sure where that came from, but watching Tijan definitely brought out his protective nature. It was interesting that he could look at the two identical women and know which one was Tijan. The hair did help, but he was quite sure he could tell them apart even with the same hairstyle and outfits.

Both men looked at him.

"I don't want to put either of them back into that situation. But couldn't you guys create an agreement that states I'm the one to take over for their father? We can say we kept it a secret."

A strange look passed between Graham and Guy. Guy spoke up, "Bill—"

August frowned. "Bill? The guy at Knights Computers? What's his story?"

Guy said thoughtfully, "There might be something to what you suggest. We could draw up some fake papers that say you're the one who has been given the authority over the company. We could say that you're actually Tarin's—well, Tijan's—husband. That would carry more clout. It's a man's world. They don't like to deal with women. Sad we're still in these times, but we are. But then what do we do so Mr. T doesn't shoot first and ask questions later?"

"It can't be that hard to find one of his goons. I'm sure if you checked with hotel security, a few of his men are camped out there, waiting for Tijan's return."

"Right, and we have to act fast. He's capable of storming in there and taking over whether he has legal papers—which reminds me Tijan had some legal papers when she climbed into the SUV. Do you know where they went, August?"

It took him a moment to realize that Guy was talking to him. He'd been fascinated with listening to the two go back and forth. He shrugged. "In the vehicle, I guess. I'll get them."

He came back quickly with some crumpled papers.

Graham took them and looked them over. "Ooh. This guy is good. This is quite a legal and thoroughly laid out document. I wonder who he used?"

"You can recreate those, right? And use Jason, our lawyer, to go through them." Guy nodded towards what Graham held in his hands.

"What are you guys talking about?" Tarin asked as she moved to stand by Graham

Graham smiled at Tarin. "We're just going over the legal papers that Mr. T wanted Tijan to get your father to sign. Well, you were meant to, but she was standing in for you, so she was going to do it. By George, I think we have a conundrum."

August snorted with laughter. Graham seemed to have a way of making light of things when it was needed. His English accent impersonation was terrible, but it did the trick.

"And what are you thinking we should do to take down this guy?" Tarin said. "And get that look off your faces, guys. I can't speak for Tijan, but I can tell you, you aren't going in without us. So start talking."

"Woman, you are going to make me old and grey before my time." Graham flipped back his head of shaggy blond hair as if it were long and flowing. Then he grabbed Tarin and kissed her hard.

"Okay. So, we thought we'd put August in charge—"

"Oh no, you're not. I'll go back as Tarin."

August thought about debating her suggestion, but he'd discovered Tijan wasn't about to back down just because it was difficult.

"So, how are we going to get a hold of Tesimmon?" Tijan held her hands palm up.

"It just dawned on me," Tarin said. "I have Dad's belongings, like his cell phone. There must be something on there that might help us. I'll need the password, though." Tarin walked up to Tijan. "I need to meet with him. I need some answers—or at least some passwords."

August could tell how hard it was for Tarin to say those words. She was essentially telling Tijan that she couldn't come. The timing wasn't right. There were identical looks of understanding intermixed with pain on each woman's face.

Tijan nodded but didn't reply. In fact, August noticed she remained quiet for the rest of the conversation.

"How could we possibly send you back with August? Tijan said Mr. T knows all about Tarin, Chance and I." Graham tapped his fist against his chin.

"Actually, I told him you and Tarin were finished and he needed to up his intel."

Graham roared with laughter. He grabbed Tarin in a bear hug and swung her around. "Damn, she's like you. So, how do we bring August into this so Tesimmon buys his being there?"

"I told him I was her business adviser." August had never had siblings or much of a family, but being with this group made him wish he did.

"Great. But we're going to need a tighter connection. This is a serious situation, and we can't underestimate him."

Tarin took Tijan's hands in hers. "We could say he's your husband or partner, and if anything happens to you, it's all left to him, including C-Lite Hotels."

"Is that a good idea, though? Our father said he'd found a husband for Tarin. He couldn't mean Tesimmon, could he?"

Tarin shook her head. "It doesn't matter. It won't happen. We'll make August your love interest, so if something happens to you, it reverts to him, and if something happens to him, it reverts to someone else."

August didn't move, but his eyes scanned the group to gauge their reaction. He didn't want to seem too eager, but the suggestion sat right with him. It was only to ensure that Tijan was safe; he told himself. The group was quiet for a time while he and Tijan conspicuously avoided looking at one another.

"What about the CSIS?" August looked at Guy and Graham.

Tarin spoke up. "We're going to leave them out of it for now. We'll stall them for a day. They'll just complicate things. And it will have to be done their way. Just say we need a bit of time to regroup. We'll give them what we find."

Everyone went silent, but no one contradicted her.

Finally, Tijan cleared her throat. "How do we make this work?"

Twenty minutes later, they had hashed out a rushed plan. Granted, it had too many variables, but they agreed they had to do something. They were going to contact Mr. T and say that Tarin was now in charge and the deal would go through her, not her father. They all hoped that Mr. T would buy into that. If they needed to, they'd tell him her father was unable to sign because he'd been declared mentally incompetent and Tarin had been appointed his trustee. August was sure that her father would sue them if he ever found out what they were planning.

They acknowledged the easiest way to give August more clout was to make him Tijan's fiancé. A husband was too easy to verify. Other than the pensive look on Tijan's face, she didn't argue and she wouldn't look at him. It wasn't how August would have preferred to get to know her but he honestly couldn't say he was against posing as her partner.

Even if only temporarily.

CHAPTER 50

"WHAT TIME IS HE supposed to be here?"

August watched Tijan pace. It wasn't something he'd seen her do before, and she hadn't seemed the type, but the situation they were in was anything but normal. In fact, she'd been acting rather oddly since he'd put that ring on her finger. Even though she'd been trying to hide it, she'd often posed her hand at different angles, staring at the beautiful diamond ring that was on loan to them. Guy and Graham had some interesting contacts. That much he'd give them.

He wasn't sure this was a smart plan, but they had to do something. They had discussed their idea with CSIS. They'd thought it was a good idea to use Tarin as bait to catch Mr. T. Tijan had been ticked at their eagerness to use her sister. Because they weren't sure what they were getting into, and Tijan was insistent that they do what they could to protect James, they'd agreed to tell CSIS they would meet with them in a couple of days to set up the sting. August was sure that Tijan was trying to do what she could to save face for Tarin. If possible, she wanted to keep their father's illegal activities from potentially becoming a headline in the media. Stuff like that always got leaked. Guy and Graham were sure they could handle it. All they needed to do was get Mr. T to have an incriminating conversation with Tijan, one that they'd catch on tape.

That was all they needed to do. August shook his head. There were too many unknowns. He would have been quite happy to have CSIS backup, but no, they'd given him the homeless-looking guy who had taken an instant dislike to him and his long hair. By the dirty looks he kept giving August, he was sure his opinion hadn't changed. Guy and Graham had sworn he had some amazing tactical moves and was incredibly alert. He might not be able to take on the bad guys, but he'd know when and how to get them out of there. There was no question he was ex-military—the way he walked, talked and did a security check of the area—showed he knew what he was doing. It still didn't sit right with August, but he had learned to trust Guy and Graham, and they insisted he was good.

Sitting on the sofa in the office, August watched Bill, who hadn't left his post by the window since they'd arrived an hour before. He was quite stoic and alert. He also knew how to be very still, although every now and then he'd do a subtle, controlled move of his body. It would only last a few seconds, but August found it rather amusing. Bailey and Tarin had taken him shopping for a new outfit, and they'd returned with one that was great for a golfer—navy blue pants and a white with green and blue stripe golf shirt.

As if on cue, Bill said, "Damn clothes. They itch."

August snorted but covered it with a cough when Bill glared at him. Bill hadn't been willing to give up his khaki ball cap or his sunglasses. He looked the part he was to play, that of an overindulgent, rich man, who wore and did what he wanted. Bill definitely had the aloof attitude down pat. They had brought him in as August's 'father', who was also going to be their adviser on this deal with Mr. T. He was the only way they knew they could get someone else in the room that would be acceptable to Mr. T.

"Bill, here's the folder with the papers that we will need in the meeting." August handed it over.

This whole situation was scary.

The desk phone buzzed. Tijan's head snapped around to look at it, but she didn't make a move toward it. August crossed to where she was standing by the back hallway as if she had been deciding on whether to stay or flee. He took her hand. Absently, she lifted ocean-blue eyes that drew him into their depths. It wasn't intentional that he held her gaze for a moment, but he didn't seem to be able to pull away.

The phone buzzed again, but this time Mary's voice came over the intercom. "Tarin? Tarin, are you there? Mr. Tesimmon is here to see you."

Tijan jerked back. August wanted to tell her that things were going to be okay, and he wanted to reach for her again. Instead, he remained quiet but kept his attention focused on Tijan. Her eyes were darting all over the place, as though she was looking for a way to bolt. He took an exaggerated deep breath and slowly blew it out. He repeated it a few times. It was something he had done with his mom many times through her chemo treatments when she was feeling pain or weakness or overwhelmed.

August wasn't sure if Tijan was aware of what he was doing, but she seemed to calm down. She squared her shoulders, took a deep breath and with a fleeting glance at August, she stepped around him to return to the desk.

"Mary? Show them into the conference room. We'll be right there. Offer them something to drink." Tijan looked at Bill and then August. "It appears we're about to do a deal with the scariest man I've ever met. God, I hope this works. It is crazy though, isn't it?"

August nodded but didn't say anything. He followed Tijan and Bill out of the office and down the hall to the meeting room. Tijan stopped outside the door, with her hand on the knob. August looked at her questioningly, but it only took her a moment to gather herself, take a deep breath and pin on a smile. She threw open the door.

"Mr. T. Nice of you to make it." She looked hard at the man, who looked like chewing on steel was a natural thing for him.

"No more games," Mr. T said. "I didn't like the one you played at the hospital. I have no problem killing you or anyone close to you."

"Bill, can I have those papers?" Tijan reached for the folder that had been given to Bill to hold while back in her office.

"Who are these people?"

"This is my fiancé and his father."

"You were with that computer guy. What happened to him?"

Tijan cleared her throat. "The father of my child came back into my life." She smiled warmly at August. "And I felt it was important that my son get to grow up with him. Not that it's any of your business."

"I had plans for you."

The two stared at each other while the tension in the room climbed to cement-cracking pressure.

"Should misfortune happen to any one of us, I have the Canadian Security Investigative Services on standby to arrest whoever attempts to step into the role of CEO. I have videos and documents implicating you."

"You bitch. I said no games."

"And I want to live. Sit down, and we'll get started with giving you forty-nine percent of the company."

"The deal is 51%."

"Yeah, but I don't like that arrangement. Why should I give you the majority when you'd also be making money on the back end, through money laundering, drugs...? So, you agree to forty-nine percent, and I get a cut of what you're shoveling through here."

The guns snapped up, pointed directly at Tijan. August had barely been able to contain himself to stand behind Tijan while the two were talking, but it had gone downhill fast. Before he could move, Bill grabbed her and shoved her to the floor, shielding her with the table and his body.

The weapons swung in August's direction. He lifted his hands as though he were under arrest. "Do you think killing the fiancé is a good idea? Did you not hear her? If anything happens to any of us, you're finished. We agreed to this arrangement only because we want to increase our capital, and you appear to be able to do that. We have plans to expand internationally. And just think what it would do for your business. Wouldn't that make it easier to get things across the border?"

August turned his hands palm up in front of him, as though he was harmless. His heart felt like it was going to jackhammer its way out of his chest, but he kept his focus on Mr. T, who hadn't blinked the whole time he was talking. There was a tense moment of silence. Even though he could hear Tijan whispering to Bill to let her up, he wasn't moving. August didn't want to take the chance of taking his eyes off the dangerous man he was facing down to ensure Tijan was safe. He was putting his faith in Bill.

"You want to expand, and you want me to pay for it?"

August swallowed. "Yes. With just the twelve hotels we have in Canada, you can move product across the line at several borders. But let's be honest, it's limited. If we go international—for starters, the US, UK and maybe Australia—then you'll be able to expand your operations into those countries. You'll use C-Lite Hotels as your cover."

Tijan finally popped up beside him, with Bill close beside her. Tijan's hair, which had been pulled into a neat bun, was now loose and had a frizzed look to it. Her suit jacket was wrinkled, and her blouse hung halfway out of her pants. She looked like anything but the CEO of a company.

"I like how you think. We'll do this deal, but there are going to be some guarantees." Mr. T sneered with a twist of vengeance.

"First, guarantee that nothing will happen to any of us or any of my family." Tijan looked almost as hard as the man she was staring at.

August was a bit shocked by Tijan's toughness, but he had to admit it made it much easier going into this crazy scheme.

"Give me the papers. No one gets hurt." Mr. T didn't break eye contact with Tijan as he spoke. He reached for the papers that Tijan held in her hands.

"This is a good deal for you as well, Mr. T. I understand you want respectability in your world and of course, to increase your capital. Well, I want the same. I don't do business like my father. I'm much more forward-thinking than he is, and I can see the bigger picture."

Mr. T inclined his head as he watched her. August could feel the sweat trickle down his neck and track down his spine. The seconds ticked by as if they were hours.

The guns finally lowered. August didn't see anything to indicate that Mr. T was a man of his word, but he wasn't about to challenge him at this point. He was sure that Mr. T made up rules as he went, and if they didn't benefit him, they got changed. And he was quite sure he was already figuring out how to make C-Lite Hotel the fall guy while he got away without a blemish. The man came across as trying to stay one step ahead.

Tijan kept the papers just out of reach until Mr. T looked at her. She held his gaze for a time before he finally nodded. August watched a tiny shift in the four men, who eased their full attention but were no less ready to shoot those 9mm Glocks. August had been ready for one of them to take out the first person who pissed off the man. As Tijan was handing the papers to Mr. T, August had the urge to dive across the table and stop the deal. Mr. T didn't even stop to read the document. He flipped to the last page and scribbled his signature.

The quickness with which he signed the deal wasn't lost on him, and he was pretty sure that, by the frown creasing Tijan's brow, she was concerned as well. They had expected he'd read it and make some additional demands. He hadn't. It left a cold feeling in August's belly.

They were in it now.

CHAPTER 51

TIJAN TOOK THE PAPERS and signed them as Tarin Roth. She'd been reassured by Tarin that although it was illegal to impersonate someone else, no one would ever find out. It felt incredibly wrong, but there wasn't much choice—not if they wanted to catch this guy.

"We're done doing business, Mr. T." She stood up and offered her hand.

The guns immediately snapped up. Mr. T looked at her with a sneer before getting to his feet.

"It's customary when two people sign a business deal that they shake hands." Tijan left her hand hanging in the air, not releasing his intense gaze. They were the blackest eyes she'd ever seen. It felt like she was about to fall down a dark, endless tunnel. Suddenly, he took her hand. She forced herself not to flinch at the excess pressure he applied. When he released her, she stepped back.

"I see you're a bit out of practice." Tijan pasted on a smile to take the sting out of her words.

August eyed her with a look of 'are you nuts' but she couldn't back down now. She almost felt lightheaded and wondered if the pull of power was literally going to her head.

"Since we're doing this all civilized," Mr. T laughed like it was the best joke he'd ever spoken, "I want my copy."

Tijan nodded. "It'll only take a minute." Walking out, she was aware not only of the weapons following her every move but the massive muscle that stepped in behind her. Tempted to look over her shoulder, she decided it was best for her shaky nerves if she didn't. It dawned on her as she made it to the lobby, she wasn't sure how to use the massive photocopier. "Mary, could you make me two copies of this?"

Mary rose from her desk and turned to face Tijan. She hesitated for a moment. The man behind Tijan didn't make her feel any better about her escort, but she wasn't about to tell the behemoth that he didn't need to follow her around.

"Sure." Mary hustled off down the hallway.

Not sure what to do, Tijan followed slowly behind her. She stood in the doorway, watching Mary. The room was small, with a row of cupboards along one wall, the photocopier in the middle. When Tijan looked the other way, she noted there was a closed door.

"Thank you, Mary."

Tijan took the papers and turned, only to find her bodyguard blocking her way. "Excuse me."

He stepped aside to let her pass, but she could feel his lumbering presence behind her.

Entering the conference room, she noted that Bill was still standing at attention but August was lounging back in a chair with his feet on the table.

"Comfy, are we?"

August grinned and winked at her. "I'm just seeing if I can get used to the pampered lifestyle. All I need is for you to get me a beer and we're set."

His subtle eye movements let her know this was a test. She grimaced. "Yeah. Don't count on that, honey."

August smacked her butt as she passed by. She whipped around but saw his warning look before he smiled at her. It took her a moment to remember what role she was supposed to be playing. She felt safe knowing he was there.

"You'll pay for that one. Just wait until I get you home."

She turned to see Mr. T watching them closely. "Here is your copy. If you don't mind, I do have a business to run. We'll meet tonight to hash out what that will look like. I don't want you to show your face during the day again. We want people to believe we're legitimate, don't we? Now more so than ever. I'll show you out."

"Don't forget who your partner is now."

"And don't forget who makes you look legit." Tijan walked as tall and straight as she ever had. Even though she never looked back, she was very conscious of her back and the fear that she just might feel a knife thrust in it at any moment. When she opened the door to the lobby, she walked through and held it. Snapping her knees back to keep them from wobbling, she kept her face neutral as Mr. T and his goons strolled past her.

It wasn't until she was back in her office that she remembered to breathe. Her hand was shaking so badly she couldn't even pull the curtains back to look outside. She was going to have to talk to Mary about leaving them open.

This moment ranked way above any of the craziest things she'd ever done.

August grinned at her. "Hey, way to go. That was impressive stuff. You put him in his place. I guess you took to heart what Graham and Guy said about standing your ground."

"I'm used to dealing with rough or ill-mannered men, but this guy has taken that to a whole new level. I have an idea. Just give me a second." Tijan made her way back to Mary's desk. "Mary, what is in that room just off the photocopy room?"

"Old files."

"And that room is locked?"

"Yes."

"Who has the code?"

"Mr. Madsen and me."

"I'd like the code."

"I can give you mine. I don't have your father's."

Tijan headed back to her office with Mary's access code. Bill was standing at attention outside her office door. "Come in, Bill."

"No. I can do better recon here."

Tijan nodded as she passed, noting he discreetly closed the door after she entered her office.

"August, there's a filing room off the photocopy room, and I have a hunch that we should look in there. I know it's a long shot, but what if we could find something on Mr. T? From the little the CSIS has told us, he and Father had been acquainted for many years. Would my father keep any of that information? Probably not, right? That would be stupid."

As August touched her arm, she looked up at him. His amber eyes looked like beacons of honesty and safety. She felt calm just knowing she wasn't alone.

She had no idea what he saw in her eyes, but she was thankful that he pulled her into his arms. It was one thing to be tough, but it was another to know that your life and all those around you were on the line.

August gave her a strong, warm hug, and then he leaned down and kissed her. It felt so right but all that kept going through her mind was that the timing was wrong. She pulled back, giving him a soft smile as she stepped away.

"I have to call Tarin" She took out her phone. "Tarin... hi... yes, it's done... no... we're okay. A bit shaky... do you know if Father kept meticulous files? I found a file room... oh, you know about it... anyway, Mr. T said he's what got Father started. Do you know anything about that... Okay. We'll leave in about ten minutes and meet you guys in Father's private parkade... Okay. Bye."

Tijan leaned against the edge of the desk. "Tarin says Father is meticulous, but something like that he wouldn't keep at the office. She thinks it might be at the house. She wants to take me there."

Something raw was churning inside her at the mere thought of going there. August moved to stand in front of her. He lifted her chin, so she was looking at him, although she was sure her vulnerability was glowing like the northern lights.

"It's okay. I'll be there with you. I'm going to get Bill. Tell Mary you're booked for the rest of the day."

Tijan felt like she was in a bit of a time warp as the three made their way out of the office. She was going to the house that she should have grown up in—or could have, if her father had wanted her.

CHAPTER 52

"MARY, I'M OUT FOR the rest of the day."

"You can't. Eleanor just called. She'll be here at four. She has some urgent legal information for you, and it has to be done today."

Tijan hung up, wondering what the lawyer had that was so critical. She'd deal with that later. Right now, they needed to meet with her sister, Guy, and Graham.

Tarin ran up to Tijan and grabbed her, staring at her intently. Nothing was said between them, but she understood everything in Tarin's expression. It reminded her that although this was the scariest thing she'd ever done, meeting her sister and finding this connection was more than she could have hoped for.

"Okay, who's got the recording?" Guy asked as soon as they joined them in the middle of her dad's private parkade.

Tijan frowned as she stepped back from her sister and looked at Guy. She remembered them talking about someone wearing a wire, but it hadn't been her. She'd forgotten all about it. Her focus had been on how to get this deal done and get the incriminating evidence against the man.

Bill stepped forward and opened his shirt. Gently, he removed the microphone taped to his chest that had captured all that had been said. Guy took it and handed it to Graham.

"We listened in from downstairs in your hotel room. We heard it all and have it recorded. Guy and I will go back to the office and analyze it right away. Then we'll hand it over to the CSIS." Graham held the microphone carefully in one hand.

"And the document?"

Tijan handed a copy to Guy, but he shook his head and pointed at Graham. He took it immediately and checked the last page.

"This is perfect. Good job, Tijan. We have his signature. We can use it."

"I know you had said you needed it but what are you going to do with it?"

"Create some incriminating stuff."

What they were going to do with his signature intrigued her, but she didn't allow herself to ask. In some ways, she felt she was better off not knowing.

"Did anyone else feel that he signed too fast?"

"Maybe, but we've got his signature, so we can use it against him. Tijan, you have done amazingly with this. My heart felt like a boxer was punching it from the inside the whole time you were in there. Guy said he'd come with us out to the house—just in case." Tarin pressed her hand to her chest.

"Mine too! I was sure Mr. T could see it. God, that was crazy." She bent over and placed her hands on her knees.

"Are you okay?"

She was a little startled when she felt August's hand on her back. She straightened up. "My legs have never been this shaky, even after chasing cattle in the mountains for a week."

Five pairs of eyes were fixed on her. Heat crawled up her cheeks. It was another reminder of how very different their worlds were.

"Tarin, I can't go to the house right now. I need to wrap up a few things. There are a few staffing issues I've been dealing with."

Tarin shrugged. "Maybe it's time we pulled you out. I can easily deal with that kind of stuff."

Tijan wanted to say, "God, yes," but the words wouldn't come out. Catching Mr. T seemed to be all she'd needed to do, and that was now finished—or would be soon. But something told her there was still something to find, something to solve. If she stepped down now, that put Tarin at risk, and the thought of that made her sick. Her sister had a son who depended on her. Tijan couldn't imagine how she would feel if something were to happen to her. "I—"

"—can't. Because you're worried about what might happen to me."

Tijan's head snapped up as she looked at her sister, who seemed almost as stunned as she was. Almost at the same time, they grinned.

Graham groaned. "Oh man, I can see that you two reading each other's minds and finishing each other's sentences could be a problem. For me."

His dramatic voice and slap to his chest made everyone smile. It also made Tijan appreciate him all the more. He was a good guy. She was thrilled for her sister.

"Yeah. I'm pretty happy too."

Graham snapped his head back and forth between the two of them. "See. See. It's already happening. I can't take anymore. I have to leave."

He walked to the Hummer but said over his shoulder, "We need to get this done."

"My cue." Tarin looked sternly at her sister. "Be careful. I think everything is okay, but we still don't know who shot Father. Mr. T is the likely candidate but—just be careful."

"Bill, you can come with us. We'll take you home. We're all done for today."

Bill shook his head but didn't say anything.

Tijan frowned but approached him slowly. She touched his arm tentatively. "Thank you for your help today and for protecting me. You were amazing... but I think I'm okay now."

"I'm staying."

Tarin waved as she climbed in the Hummer. "Okay. We'll see you all later."

Tijan nodded as she watched them leave. Tarin seemed so happy and content. This world of concrete and business dealings and back-stabbings didn't seem to faze her. A part of her was envious. Tijan realized she wanted to stay behind to see what she could learn about her father. Going to the house with Tarin seemed unfair. Unfair that she hadn't even known it existed. Unfair that she hadn't been a part of this life at all.

She headed back into the office. As Bill made a point of walking between her and August, she got the distinct impression he had wanted to stay to protect her from August.

CHAPTER 53

THERE WAS A SOFT click. Guy was standing by her desk. Tijan looked at him and then at the back door she'd just come through. She thought he'd left.

"August, I don't want to pull you away from this, but the parts you ordered are in. And I guess another machine is down. Can you call Perry and see if he can fix any of it? Or walk him through it?"

August looked at Guy for a moment as though he'd been caught skipping school. Tijan didn't blame him. That world was so far removed from what they'd been doing for the last week or so. And he'd been hired to be their mechanic. A dark red flush crept up his cheeks.

"Sure." He pulled out his phone and dialed. And waited. "Call me when you get this, Perry. It's urgent."

"No answer. It's probably better that I go out there and figure out what's going on." He looked at Tijan, holding her gaze for several moments. "I..."

"It's okay. That's what you were hired for, not to be my bodyguard. Besides, with that recording, they should charge Mr. T by the end of today?" Tijan looked questioningly at Guy.

"Within a few hours. We just want to make sure there's a copy of that recording. They've gone missing in the past when handed them over to the authorities. We've learned to keep our own copies."

"Things should be quiet here, right?" August looked at Tijan before turning to Guy.

Guy nodded. "Bill is here. And I'm staying too. I have some work to do but can do it from here. I don't want to be seen on this floor, though. I'm going down to the restaurant, find a quiet corner and make some calls. I'll have a good view of the front, so if anyone unexpected arrives, I'll know."

August smiled but looked at Guy. "Can I talk to you for a moment?"

Guy followed him to the far corner of the office. Tijan was listening with only half her attention, but she was sure that he was questioning leaving Bill as her bodyguard.

After a couple of minutes of whispers, August turned to face her. He gave her a long, searching look. "Be careful. This isn't over yet." He seemed reluctant to go as he walked slowly to the door, hesitating before opening it and walking into the parkade.

"I'll go down the back way as well."

Tijan felt a bit deflated and abandoned, even though Bill stood off to the side at full attention. He seemed to be the only one fully immersed in his role.

Sitting at her desk, she placed her hands on the gleaming surface. Other than her keyboard and monitor, her desk was empty. Opening one of the drawers, she examined its contents - pens and a pad of sticky notes. In going through each drawer, she was surprised to see them empty. In the bottom right drawer was where she found the papers she'd been asked to sign. She pulled them out and called her sister.

"Tarin, did you ever find out about those legal papers I was to sign?"

"I forgot about them. I'll contact Jason and see what he says. I'll get back to you right away."

Tijan booted her father's computer. Randomly opening files to see what he stored there, she didn't even know what she was looking at. There were spreadsheets with numbers that she couldn't even fathom. Finding it fascinating, she read through several such documents. It was quite a while later that she stopped what she was doing and looked up. Bill was still standing at attention just inside her office door.

"It's okay to sit down, Bill."

He glanced at her but didn't move. Her computer beeped, and she turned her attention back to the screen. An email announcement had appeared. She clicked on it, and when it opened, there were at least a thousand that hadn't been read.

Groaning, she started skimming them. Reading through, she noted there were several from managers of the other hotels in the C-Lite Hotel Chain.

At first, everything sort of blended as if it had been written in Russian. Finally, one word grabbed her attention. Linens. As she continued down the list, she saw there were several emails with that word in the subject line.

She had a spooky feeling she was being watched. Her immediate response was to look at Bill. He was standing at attention with his hands held behind his back, staring vacantly at the window. She glanced around the room as she considered the possibility of hidden cameras, despite the search for bugs. Her computer could be accessed remotely. She stared at the monitor and the webcam that sat on top.

Inching herself slowly sideways in her father's very comfy leather chair, she made sure she was out of eyesight before pulling out her phone. She was being a little paranoid, but the whole situation she'd been involved in was making her a little wary. She texted Tarin.

'Can someone remotely watch me through the webcam? Are you?'

'No. Why?'

'I get the feeling that someone is. I might just be reacting to everything, but I feel watched. Am I paranoid?'

'Don't worry, that computer is not being used for remote access. It has a lot of security, and no one would have had time to do that.'

Tijan kept glancing at her computer as though it were going to come to life and pounce on her. Feeling unsettled, she stood up and moved over to the couches. That didn't help at all. Even though the webcam wasn't facing her, she felt like it was tracking her every movement.

Tijan had a feeling she was going to have a weird quirk of being like an owl when all this was over. She would stare intensely at things while her head whipped from side to side. It might even spin all the way around by the time this was finished.

CHAPTER 54

TIJAN WAS ABOUT TO buzz Mary but felt she needed to thank her face to face. Exiting her office, she came upon Mary, who was intently reading a stack of papers.

"Mary?"

The woman's head snapped around, and the mulish look on her face stopped Tijan immediately.

"Are you all right?"

Mary turned away, setting the pages face down on her desk before turning back to talk to Tijan. She forced a smile, but it didn't eliminate the angry red splotches on her face, nor did it reach her eyes.

"Sorry. A family matter."

Tijan relaxed a bit. That she could understand. "I hope its nothing too serious."

Mary shrugged. "What did you need, Tarin?"

There was a hard edge to her voice that Tijan hadn't heard before. She'd been businesslike and direct, but she'd never had that tone. It gave Tijan the feeling that she was pissed off at her.

"Thank you for dropping everything earlier and running those papers off for me. I truly appreciate it. Sorry to have taken you away from your other work. I know you're very busy." Tijan smiled warmly at her.

"It's my job. That's what I do, drop things to run things off. I do what needs to be done around here. I keep this place running smoothly even while your father is away. I stopped again to see him at the hospital, but they wouldn't let me in. I understand he's awake. How is he?"

"He's getting better." Tijan felt guilty. Apparently, the hospital wasn't sharing that he'd been moved to a different location.

"I hear he had pneumonia. I tried to get him to go to the doctor, but he wouldn't. Your father is stubborn. I've tried to make sure he has taken care of himself over the years, but he rarely listens."

"Yes, he is stubborn. I just came to tell you I'll be busy the rest of the day. If you need me, I'll be on my cell."

"Have you been out to check on things at your father's house?"

Tijan's shoulders tensed up, feeling like she was on a spooked horse, ready to bolt.

"Actually, that's where I'm going right now."

"That's good. Usually, I go and ensure everything is fine. He's had me many times in the past look after his house. I didn't this time because he hadn't asked. But I know his staff is quite efficient, but everyone needs someone looking after them; that isn't just about a pay cheque."

"Okay. Thank you, Mary. I'll see you later. If you need anything, call."

"Tarin, wait! Remember, Eleanor has an appointment with you at 4:00. That was the latest I could put her off. Something about some legal documents. I hope she isn't trying to convince you to sell this place?"

Even though Mary's face had softened while they'd talked, the mention of Eleanor seemed to bring back the angry face. And there was something in the way she said, 'Sell this place'. Tijan wondered if she'd read the documents she'd photocopied. But there hadn't been time.

"Did you sign those forms that give you managing control over the business while your father is away?"

"I have them, but I took them home last night. I'll get them back to you soon."

"Nothing is legal until you do. And you know it's temporary. That means nothing you sign is legal until you officially sign that document, giving you control."

"Thank you for letting me know, Mary. Make an appointment with Eleanor for early next week."

"She won't be happy at the delay." Mary reached for her phone but stopped. "JT is up for VP of Operations. He'd be good at it—if you want my opinion."

"I'll keep that in mind. Thank you, Mary." Tijan turned and left, even though she was sure that Mary had a lot more to say. Their entire conversation didn't sit well with her, but she had no idea what it meant.

She closed the door, but before she could make her way across the room; she heard some loud muffled sounds. They appeared to be coming from the main part of the office. Turning on her heel, she retraced her steps. As soon as she opened the door, the raised voices hit her.

CHAPTER 55

"SOMEONE SABOTAGED THE EQUIPMENT." August felt an anger he hadn't felt since his mom died and he'd been helpless to stop her downward spiral. The harvesting machine parts he'd been waiting for had been pounded and sawed. It looked as if it should have been on a junk pile. The mainframe was still intact but looked like a terrible art design with jagged pieces of metal hanging off it.

Guy swore. "Any idea who?"

"I don't see Perry, but I can't imagine he'd do this. I just got here but wanted you to know immediately. Someone is pissed. Any ideas?"

There was silence for a moment. "The list is too long. Damn. We were just getting things running smoothly after that last attempt a year ago."

"What happened?"

"Someone tried to sabotage the winery by replacing our wine with vinegar and then sending it out on the market. It brought a lot of unwanted media attention and almost brought us down. We caught that person, but I can't help wondering if this is related."

August whistled. "What do you want me to do?"

"Can you close the doors and lock them up? Do not tell Dorothea or LJ. I'll tell them, but not quite yet. Let me get back to you."

August felt sick. Even though he'd only been there a few months, he was already feeling quite attached to the place. For someone to do that kind of destruction, they had to be furious. Rather than leave immediately, he checked the place once more to determine what kind of damage had been done. The shop had little space to begin with, but with all the debris, he had to be careful where he stepped. Circling the machine, it didn't look any better from any other angle. He noticed the older machine in the corner hadn't been touched. Curious, he stepped toward it.

It was tucked in the corner against the side and back walls. As he turned, he noticed the dirty floor had an odd pattern in it. In that unused corner, the floor was dusty, but there was one area near the front that looked different. Cautiously, August crept around the front. As he drew closer, he heard movement. He grabbed a jagged piece of metal that had been sawed off the harvester. He heard his mom's voice, loud and clear, saying, 'get out of there', which was his own gut reaction as well.

Despite his trepidation, he made his way to the corner and crouched. The sound was originating near the wall. Inching forward, he raised the metal piece in his hand. It was dark enough along the wall that all he could see were shadows. But something was moving. Unsure of what he was going to find, he considered seeking help but decided instead to turn on a light. As he turned away, there was a loud groan and more thrashing. Realizing it was a person, and they appeared injured, August quickly moved forward. When he got close, he saw Perry was tied up and his mouth was taped. He quickly untied him and helped him to sit up.

"Two guys attacked me and ripped this place apart. I was here late. I had wanted to get the new parts into Betsy." He looked past August to motion toward the big old machine he'd nicknamed.

"Are you injured?"

Perry moved tentatively. He groaned as he stirred. Perry touched the back of his head. "Got a bit of a melon back there but other than that I'm okay. Just pissed."

August took Perry's rough, oil-stained hand and pulled him to his feet.

"I need to call the police."

"My wife will be glad to know that I'm finally going to be famous. She always said my hard noggin would be good for something one day."

He liked that nothing seemed to faze the guy's sense of humor. He was a typical guy in his twenties who thought he might be invincible.

"Let's get you to the office." He held onto Perry, who was trying to be stoic but was acting a bit unsteady. Once he had him settled and gave him a bottle of water, August stepped out and called Guy.

"Need the police and an ambulance. Someone knocked Perry out and tied him up. He's okay, but he might have a concussion."

"Sit tight. I'll call them and LJ."

CHAPTER 56

No ONE LOOKED IN her direction. JT, Mary, and Jill were having a heated discussion.

"What's going on?"

Intense, angry silence followed, but no one looked at her.

"I need to see you, ma'am," Jill pleaded through the opening in the glass partition.

"She doesn't have an appointment."

"I can handle anything to do with staff. You don't need to worry about stuff like this." JT smiled at her with a poor imitation of charisma.

"I'll meet with Jill. Thank you both for your concern, but I've got this." Tijan opened the door.

"Jill, go into my office, please. It's the one with the open door. Close it behind you and have a seat on the sofa. I'll be right there." Tijan gave her a warm smile and waited for her to disappear before turning back to the other two. Both had a look of defiance.

Tijan's smile disappeared, pleased that her change in demeanor got both their attention.

"I'm sorry, but she—"

"It's not right for front-line staff just to walk in here. They have a manager for a re—"

Tijan put up her hand. "I don't want to hear it. I don't want to see that kind of behavior ever again. You're adults; act like it. If either of you ever raises your voice in this office again, you're fired. Now get back to work."

She returned to her office, closing the door behind her. It might have made her feel good to know that handling men and women on the ranch was no different from those dressed up and working in expensive offices, but that wasn't true. On the ranch, she could tell them to stop being petty and get over their issue, and they would, or they'd leave. She had a feeling JT and Mary had been smart enough to keep their mouths shut, but this was far from over. They left her with the impression that they were going to do something to make her life miserable.

"Jill, sorry about that. Can I get you something to drink? Some water? Coffee?"

"Water, thank you. I'm sorry to show up like this, but it's my day off, so I thought rather than send an email..." Jill sat tentatively on the edge of the couch, her hands held tightly in her lap.

"Is this about the smoking signs?"

"No ma'am. The other day when we talked, you were asking about the sheets." Jill took a deep breath. "I talked to some of the other staff. All of our supplies have gone down in quality, and we seem to be ordering more of the same. I've been here for twelve years. We used to get high-quality linens. I just thought you should know."

"Thank you for telling me, Jill."

"I know it's not my place, but things have changed over the last few years. Supplies we're expecting aren't very good or don't show up at all. It's hard to keep a five-star hotel even at a four-star level if we don't have the supplies."

Tijan sat beside Jill and waited until she looked at her. "It is your place. This hotel does not run itself, and although it's been around for a long time, there are always things that need improvement. I'm grateful you came to me. Next time, text me and we'll schedule a time so that type of incident won't happen again. And if anyone ever treats you like that again, please inform me immediately. Okay?"

"Thank you, ma'am. I won't keep you. I just thought you should know. You seem to care." She popped up and headed toward the door before Tijan could respond. Jill's eyes were glued to Bill, who was still standing at attention.

"It's okay. He's here to help me." Tijan put her hand on Jill's shoulder. "Let me walk you out."

Tijan went first, opening the door. As she headed to the front area, she was surprised that Mary wasn't there. She wasn't anywhere in sight. After putting Jill on the elevator, Tijan stood by Mary's desk. It seemed odd not to have her sitting there.

Almost laughing at her own silliness, she had the urge to check the locked file room. She slipped into the copy room and closed the door. She approached the file room, but didn't have a code to unlock it. Pulling her phone out of her jacket pocket—its only redeeming feature—she texted Tarin.

'Have you ever been in the file room?'

'No. Mary has a master list on her computer of what's in there. I think anyway. You can access it through your computer, though. It's saved on a cloud server. Or I should say, that's how it used to be. I doubt it has changed, though.'

'Thanks.'

Frustrated, she returned to the lobby just as the elevator doors were opening. Her first reaction was to duck, but she stopped herself, which turned out to be advantageous as Eleanor had seen her immediately.

Eleanor walked briskly to the partition. "I need to meet with you."

"Yes. And Mary was to arrange a meeting next week."

"No. You don't understand. It needs to happen now."

Tijan seriously wanted to tell her to get lost but, deciding it was easier to get this over with, she unlocked the door, allowing Eleanor entrance. Eleanor walked briskly to her office and sat on the couch. Tijan closed the door behind her.

Eleanor pulled some papers from her briefcase and set them on the coffee table. Tijan was tempted to tell her she doubted her father would appreciate her setting something on his coveted coffee table. Instead, Tijan observed her brisk, focused demeanor. It almost made her laugh when Eleanor looked up impatiently, only to jerk back when her gaze fell on Bill. He was still standing behind the door, unmoving but hyperaware. His eyes hadn't left Eleanor since she'd entered.

"He can leave."

Her dismissive attitude annoyed Tijan. "Actually, he can't. So what do you need, Eleanor?"

Her lips pursed into a pucker as though she'd chewed on something sour. "Your father left some papers for you to sign to say you were in charge."

Tijan sat on the opposite couch. "Why am I just getting them from you now, Eleanor?"

"I've been trying to make an appointment with you, but I keep getting put off."

A guilty flush crept up her cheeks. "Yes, but if they were that important, then you should have said so. And you could have emailed them."

"Fine. Nevertheless, you need to sign these." She set the papers on Tijan's side of the coffee table, with the package open to the last page for her to sign.

"You're going to go through these with me, aren't you?"

Her teeth clenched, and her mouth returned to that sour, pursed appearance. "They state you have signing and decision-making authority over all aspects of the business."

Tijan picked up the document, deliberately flipping to the front page. "You wrote these up?"

"Yes. I am your father's lawyer."

"And yet it has taken you a week to mention this to me. I wonder why." Tijan stared at her pointedly. "You didn't think to drop them off?"

The woman didn't flinch but held her gaze. "I wanted to make sure they were for your eyes only. And I needed to make sure that you weren't going to be flighty. You have run out on your father before, when he's needed you."

Alarm bells were going off in Tijan's head. So much of what this woman was saying didn't make sense.

"He's talked to you about me?"

Eleanor's normally pale complexion became dotted with a light pink flush. It was so faint that Tijan was almost convinced she'd imagined it as it faded as quickly as it had appeared.

"He did."

"Oh, what did he have to say?"

"It doesn't matter. You need to sign these papers so we can make this legal."

"You know what, Eleanor? You're right. I'll read through them and I'll get them back to you as soon as possible." Tijan got up, clutching the papers in her hand as she walked to the door.

"I need you to sign those right now."

"Thank you for coming, Eleanor. I appreciate your dropping these off. I'll make sure to mention to my father what an efficient job you did."

They locked eyes, and it was only when Bill stepped into Eleanor's line of sight that she looked away. Getting to her feet in a very controlled but efficient manner, Eleanor picked up her briefcase and walked briskly to the door. Tijan pulled it open for her. Without a word, she left. Slamming it behind her, Tijan leaned against it.

"We're quite a team, Bill. Thank you." She instinctively hugged him. The instant she touched him, she felt him stiffen. She pulled him in tight before she backed off. Too many of the men she worked on the ranch with were the same, but she truly believed a hug was good for people. In fact, Pete, one of the older men on the ranch, no longer turned beet red when she hugged him. And he'd stopped mumbling and running away immediately afterwards. It had taken a year, but he'd changed. There was hope for Bill. She smiled at him.

"I think it's time we got out of here. Enough of this game. I'm done. That woman is scary." She waved her hand, which reminded her of what she was holding. She looked at the papers. Opening them, she quickly skimmed through them. They looked identical to the ones that Mary had given her, although she hadn't read them. So how had Mary gotten a copy? And was it even the same?

Her insides twisted. Although the two women didn't seem to like each other, were they planning something?

CHAPTER 57

"JUST GIVE ME A minute, Bill."

Tijan opened her door and looked out, making sure that Eleanor had left. The lobby was still empty. Going to investigate, she stopped at Mary's desk. It was immaculate as always. No papers on it and nothing was out of place. Instinctively, she reached for a drawer and opened it. Mary's purse and office supplies, such as pens and paperclips, were all that was there. But it reminded Tijan that she had no right to snoop. She was not Tarin. Or had any legal right to be there. Grimacing, she glanced around, glad to see that no one was there to see what she had done. Standing completely still, the quietness of the floor enveloped her. With the two VPs away, there was only her, JT and Mary. There had to be more people responsible for running that empire but she didn't know the location of the accounting department.

Needing answers, she made her way down the hallway to JT's office. As she got closer, she could hear JT yelling. She gently opened the door. JT was standing toe to toe with Mary. Both were raising their voices, their faces red, as though a thousand capillaries had broken open.

"What the hell do you mean? You can't be."

"I am. That bastard took you away from me. You—" The anger in Mary's voice startled Tijan.

"Get away from me. I hate you."

Glancing around, she noticed a gun sitting on JT's desk. Her mouth dropped open, but she didn't stop to ask questions. Believing it was the same gun that had been used to shoot her father and thankful they were on the other side of the room, she made her way cautiously toward the desk. Before reaching it, both had turned toward her. She was no longer incognito.

She glanced at them and then at the weapon. It was evidence. She sprinted to the desk.

"Tarin."

JT's silky way of saying her name made her skin crawl. Holding a gun was nothing new to her, although she'd only ever shot a 22. A handgun had a different look and feel. The weight of it surprised her as she grabbed it. JT was suddenly between her and the door.

Having no idea if it was loaded, and although it made her want to heave, she raised the gun and pointed it at JT.

"You wouldn't."

"Do you really want to test me?"

Her words or her tone was enough to get him to move to the side every so slightly. She waved the gun at him to direct him to move further out of her way.

Mary, thankfully, had stayed where she was, her hands pressed against her face. "Tarin, you can't. Tarin, we found the gun. We were going to bring it to you."

Tijan eased her way to the door, turning so she faced JT as she moved. He stepped toward her, she jerked the gun so it was aimed at his face. He stopped, and Mary was soon by his side with her hand on his arm, restraining him.

"Just go."

He took a small step to the side at Mary's urging.

Tijan inched her way out and slammed the door. Spinning, she sprinted to her office, locking her and Bill in.

"Bill, we've got to go." She raced for the back door just as there was a pounding on hers.

"Where'd you get that gun?"

"I'll explain. I think this was used to shoot my father. We have to get out of here." She tucked the gun under her shirt, into the front waistband of her pants. She wasn't sure she could shoot it, even if it did have bullets. Reaching the parkade, she found her vehicle wasn't there. It was in the main one because she hadn't wanted to feel like she was caged in. Racing to the elevator, she punched the ground floor button. As they descended, she typed a text to August and to Tarin.

Racing out the doors, she had two choices - go through the door to the lobby or head out the exit to outside. It was a quick decision, but outdoors seemed to be the safer choice. Ensuring Bill was with her, she sprinted to the edge of the building. Once they'd made their way around back, she jogged across the open paved area, knowing from Bill's labored breathing that he was doing his best to keep up. They reached the courtyard, which contained a dining and relaxation area. They would either have to pass through a lush garden or head toward the outer edge. But it looked like there was a cement barrier at the end, preventing them from getting around the area.

"Bill, we need to go back. We might have to grab a taxi." She went back the way they'd come, moving quite quickly across the open lot. As she approached the road, she looked both ways, noting it was a quieter street that looked like it ended in a few short blocks.

A car careened around the corner, and Tijan instinctively ran, but the sound of a gunshot beside her was enough to make her stop. She spun around as the car came to a screeching halt. A gun was pointed at her from the front passenger seat.

The back window was lowered. She didn't have to see the face to know that voice.

"We're going to finish our deals. You're also going to get us Caspian Winery. Today."

Within seconds, her arms were grabbed and forced behind her as she was stuffed in the same black car she'd been in a few days before.

She fought for all she was worth, preventing them from closing the door. She dove out, but was yanked back into the car by her hair.

Her last vision was of Bill lumbering toward them, his hand clutching his chest.

"No!" The door slammed in her face, and they were soon speeding away. Spinning around to look out the back window, Bill collapsed on the ground. She had no idea if it was his heart or if he'd been shot.

"No. You'd better hope he's fine."

"It seems, Ms. Roth, that we have more to discuss."

Tijan turned to face the one man who once scared the crap out of her but now she was too mad to care anymore. "What do you want? You got part of the company."

"Yes, but it appears I've been duped. See my lawyer here—"

Tijan's gaze swung to the other side of the limo. Her hands trembled slightly when she recognized who sat there.

"Eleanor. This should surprise me, but it doesn't. Do you always sleep with lowlifes?"

Eleanor smiled condescendingly. "It appears so. I slept with your father."

Tijan wanted to throw up, but she watched the woman closely. This was a chess match, and in order to win, one had to study their opponent to figure out their next move. She hoped she caught on to this game fast.

"So, what's this about?"

"You didn't sign the agreement."

"You saw me sign it. Let me see your copy." Tijan held out her hand.

"No, that's fine. See, I had my lawyer draft a new version. One that suits me better."

Eleanor held out some papers to Tijan. Even though she held Eleanor's gaze, her mind was bombarding her with ideas of how to escape. The doors were locked. She'd heard them clunk down the minute the door had closed behind her, and she was quite sure there wasn't a way for her to unlock them. There had to be a button on her door to lower the window, but how she be able to do that in a short period of time, she wasn't sure. Even if she got the window open, she'd have to dive out and pray that she didn't get run over. Feeling panic threatening to settle in, she surreptitiously looked around inside the darkened car for something she could use. It appeared they were prepared for her.

"You need to sign these. Now."

Eleanor's voice was hard and cold, causing her to wonder whether she would live much longer after she'd complied with their demands. As she leaned forward for the paper, the gun's cold metal pressed against her skin. She placed her hand on her stomach as though she weren't feeling well, which was the truth. Taking the papers, she set them in her lap, barely glancing at them.

"So you came to my office with those other papers, because?" It didn't make sense to Tijan.

Eleanor thrust a pen at her. "Because if you'd signed like you should have, I would have used your signature and attached it to this agreement. Which ultimately gives over the hotel chain to Mr. T. But don't worry, that's not what it says in the document. You're signing over the company to Donte Ltd."

"Yes. You gave me the idea of creating my own legitimate business. You are going to sell C-Lite Hotels to my new company. On paper, it looks like you'll be paid $450 million, but don't worry, that won't happen. But I will own that company. Eleanor is going to run it for me." Tesimmon's smile couldn't have been more smug or condescending. "So sign the papers. And you won't send anything to CSIS because we can get to your son. Keeping him out at Dorothea Lindell's won't protect him forever."

Tijan shivered. They knew too much. "I need something hard to write on or my signature will not be legible."

Mr. T nodded at Eleanor. As Eleanor reached into her briefcase, Tijan yanked out the gun.

"Stop the car. Now."

Mr. T's face contorted into a mask of hardened stone that looked ready to crack. Eleanor appeared stunned, like she was someone who wasn't easily surprised.

Tijan waved the gun so they'd know she was serious.

"You can't kill both of us." Eleanor sounded confident as she leaned forward.

"Not at once, but I can kill one of you. So, do you want to choose which one of you it is?"

Eleanor sat back in the far corner. Tijan hoped that meant she was staying out of it. Tijan swung the gun at Mr. T.

"You're dead." He glared at her with a ferocity that felt like it could have stripped her skin off. He stared her down, but Tijan tightened her grip.

He pressed a button. A few seconds later; the car slowed.

"Unlock the door. Now." As soon as she heard the electronic lock disengage, Tijan reached for the door handle behind her. Before they had pulled to a complete stop, she yanked open the door and dove out. Thankful there wasn't oncoming traffic, she hustled to her feet to run back the way they'd come. The heavy traffic on the two-lane highway kept the vehicle from immediately turning around. Tucking the gun in the back of her pants and pulling her shirt down over it, she was tempted to stop one of the passing cars but couldn't take the chance. As soon as she saw an opening, she raced across the highway and into a wooded area. She crouched down, waiting for the squeal of tires. When there were none, she rose and moved as fast as she could in heels through the brush.

CHAPTER 58

"BILL JUST CALLED. THEY'VE got Tijan." Tarin's voice was hysterical as she told Guy what was going on. "Tijan texted me. She has the gun she thinks was used to shoot Dad. JT had it."

"Dammit. Have we heard from them? Are they making any demands? Is Bill okay?"

August held the phone tight to his ear as he maneuvered through traffic. He was glad that Graham had included him in the call.

Tarin explained what had happened. "Nothing from them. I think Mr. T didn't like the original deal. Bill said Tijan had found a gun, and they had to leave the office. Mr. T abducted her in the parking lot. Bill feels as if he has failed. He was having chest pains and collapsed. I called an ambulance. I'm following it now, and I'll stay at the hospital until we know he's okay," Tarin explained.

"Dammit. Where the hell would he have taken her? He's going to kill her, isn't he?" August punched the steering wheel. "Look. I'm on my way. Perry's been sent to the hospital. I left it in LJ's hands. I'll be there as soon as I can. Meet at the hotel."

"No wait. I think they're on their way out there. Bill said something about Mr. T mentioning Caspian Winery," Tarin said. "I've got to go. Call me later."

August tuned out as she and Graham said their goodbyes. He couldn't stop his mind from going to the darkest place. Mr. T didn't play by any rules, and murder appeared to be something that came easily to him. It was the torture he might do beforehand that played heavily on August's mind. How was he going to find him? Was there any way they could save Tijan now?

His cell rang. "Hang on, it's Guy."

"Graham's on the other line," August said as he connected the three of them.

Graham started talking immediately. "Bill is on his way to the hospital with Tarin. Possibly his heart."

"Where's our guys?"

"They called just before Tarin. One of our security guys is following Tarin, and the other is trying to find Tesimmon's car."

"I thought you had the best security?" August thumped his hand on the steering wheel.

"We thought CSIS would have taken him down by now, so we backed off. Dammit! Look, August, I'm sorry. This is on me," Guy swore.

"Let's keep focused on what we need to do. We can get mad later. Tarin had started doing some research on landowners. She didn't get far, but I've been tinkering with it for the last ten minutes. I found something interesting. Eleanor Carter owns land. Guess where?" Graham said. "Yup, you got it. Right near Caspian."

"What made you look into her?" August asked.

Guy replied, "Bill mentioned something about a classy woman in the car that took Tijan, so I took a chance. This has to have something to do with Caspian Winery."

August listened to the conversation but wasn't quite making the connection. Then it hit him. "Isn't Eleanor James Madsen's lawyer? Why would she have land out there? Is that a coincidence, or are you guys thinking she's in bed with the mafia?"

"Probably. So, if she owns a huge chunk of land in the middle of wine country, why? I'm still at the hotel. I'm going to go to James' office and see what I can find."

"Good question. I hate to ask it, but did Geoff and Mr. T have business dealings? Or Geoff and Eleanor? I think that Geoff has come back from the grave to make our lives miserable." Guy's voice had a hard edge to it. "I'm on my way out there, August. Tell the security guards to get everyone into the main building and lock it down. I have the police on their way."

"Geoff?" August remembered hearing his name but not who he was.

"Sorry. Geoff was Dorothea's brother. He caused nothing but problems. For all of us. He's the one who tried to kill Guy's wife, Bailey, and through a sick set of circumstances is the father of Tarin's son, and he tried to destroy Caspian Winery. That's just the short list of his wrongdoings."

August remembered some of the story they had told them a few days before. The man had done a lot of destruction before he'd died. August shook his head and suddenly realized he was still traveling away from Caspian. He pulled into a driveway and stopped. "Was that the story you were telling us about the other day at that old house? He faked his death and blew it up?"

"Yeah, that's the guy."

Graham spoke up. "I don't know if the two knew each other, but I'm quite sure they did. I don't think Geoff ever ran drugs. Money laundering was definitely his thing—and hookers. Human trafficking? Probably. They definitely ran in the same circles, I'm sure."

They were all silent for a moment as they listened to Graham click away on his computer.

"Interesting. There is some land purchased by Chris Simmons. The land is near Lake Ontario. What a great way to run drugs across the US and Canada border. When did that deal go through?"

"Sixteen months ago."

"That's way too close to Geoff's demise to be a coincidence. That bastard Geoff would do anything to make his sister's life miserable. So, let's say, he also put in play for the man to take over Caspian Winery. Would he do it himself or would he get someone like C-Lite Hotels to do it for him?"

"Geoff was always about making things appear legit. Wouldn't that be interesting if he was teaching the mob guy how to appear more lawful."

"How do we find Tijan?" While they'd been talking, August was feeling increasingly frustrated. He was sitting on the side of the road, feeling like he needed to be doing something.

"Does Mr. T own any other land?" Guy asked.

"Not that I could find. Just that owned by Eleanor and by Chris Simmons. Also out in that area."

"Who's that?"

"Just give me a minute." The sound of Graham's keyboard was loud. "Chris Simmons, aka, JT."

August swore. "Is there any way you can hack his computer or his cell phone? Find that little creep. I swear if Tijan is hurt, I'll mangle that pretty boy face myself."

"Guy, can you get into his office? You're still at the hotel, right?"

"I'm in James' office, actually. I thought there might be something we could find. I'll head to JT's." There was a loud bang and then a harsh snap as Guy kicked in the door.

"Both Mary and JT are gone. You might want to keep an eye on the airports, trains, and buses. You know the drill, Graham. Okay, give me a few to get into his laptop."

August swore. He'd never felt more useless in his life.

Guy piped up. "There's a copy of the contract that Tijan signed with Mr. T. How did he get a copy?"

Graham whistled.

"So, we know JT has a connection to Mr. T. Was he going to double-cross him? Or was he the reason that Tijan got picked up?"

August's phone rang, and he pulled it away from his ear to see who it was. He immediately answered it.

"Tijan. Where are you? Are you okay?"

CHAPTER 59

TIJAN HAD NO IDEA where she was. But it was finally getting dark, and she hoped that Mr. T and his goons, who she was sure had been looking for her, had finally given up. After hiking for a ways, she found a good hiding place in the brush. Staying in a cramped, uncomfortable position under the trees had seemed like the safest thing to do. But now it was time to move. She didn't want to stay there though, knowing that at some point they'd probably be back if they'd ever left the area. Knowing how to track lost calves in the foothills had taught her how to stay out of sight. Avoiding the road, she now moved as quickly as she could in her awkward high heels. Taking them off hadn't been an option in the rough terrain.

Her heel caught on something and pitched her sideways. Her hands barely stopped her head from cracking against a tree. Crouching down in a dense area, she took a minute to catch her breath. Her head was pounding as she pressed her thumbs into her temples, trying to ease the pressure.

She shifted, feeling the gun rub against her back and her cell phone dig into her thigh. She pulled it out, almost crying with relief. Since she never carried anything like that when in the mountains, it hadn't even dawned on her to think about her phone. And she actually had two of them—hers and the one Tarin had given her.

She used hers. "August, I don't know where I am. I'm hiding in some woods and there may be a lake near me. Can you track my GPS?"

"Are you okay? Do you think you could be out by Lake Ontario?"

"Wait—I'll use Google Maps. Just a minute. It isn't locating me. Do you think they can they trace my cell phone? Or the one Tarin gave me?"

"Just a minute, I'll ask Graham."

The sound of a vehicle passing slowing by had her scrambling deeper into the bush. Her cell jostled out of her hands. She felt around, but couldn't find it. She scrambled onto a trail alongside a fence, hidden from the road by trees.

Stopping for a moment to catch her breath, she pulled out the phone Tarin had given her and turned it on. Closing her eyes for a few seconds, she prayed that the bad guys wouldn't be able to find her but the good guys would. She first opened the maps app on her phone. If it was right, she was somewhere near Lake Ontario.

A shiver went down her spine. August had asked her that. How had he known? Who was the good guy and who was the bad guy? Feeling very freaked out, she put away the phone and continued to move.

She skirted several houses before arriving at an open field. Though it was dusk, she was sure that someone crossing an open field would still be easily seen. Some cows were grazing in the pasture. Not always a good idea to enter an area with cows and calves, she continued along the fence line.

It seemed to take forever to get anywhere, and in truth, she felt like she was going nowhere. She was so lost and exhausted. Every time she heard a noise, she'd crouch down. Too many times, the barbed wire fence snagged her clothes or her skin. Feeling every ache and pain and scratch and cut and swollen feet, she felt almost like a zombie trudging along.

When the fence line finally came out of the trees to meet the road, Tijan knew she was finished. She couldn't go any further. She found a place just far enough back that she wouldn't be seen but could watch the traffic and catch her breath. Leaning against a tree, she eased her shoes off. They were like suction cups glued to her feet. Grabbing the back of the shoe with both hands, she rocked her foot back and forth until she managed to ease it off. She groaned in agony as her foot immediately ballooned up. Doing the same with her other foot, she soon had her feet free. Even wiggling her toes felt like too much work.

The sounds of the night penetrated her thoughts. Frogs croaking, cows mooing, every now and then, birds chirping, other sounds she was too tired to distinguish and the distant sounds of traffic all felt rather soothing to her. It almost reminded her of home.

She pulled out her other cellphone and turned it on. She needed to hear the sound of her mom's voice.

"Hello?"

"Oh, Mom." Tijan had rarely allowed herself to cry, but hearing her mom started the waterworks.

"Tijan? Honey, are you okay? Whose phone are you using?"

It took her several moments to pull herself under control. "Mom, I found Tarin. That's why I left home. And I found my father. You didn't tell me."

Tijan felt like she was mumbling and not making any sense, but when she heard her mom sobbing, she pressed her hand to her chest.

"Oh, Mom. I'm sorry. I didn't mean to bring this up like that. I've wanted to tell you, but we haven't had a chance to talk. But both of us are confused. How could you keep us apart?"

"Tijan?" a male voice said.

Tijan let her head drop back against the tree. Tears leaked out and found their way into her hair. "Dad." It was more difficult for her to say than she had thought it would be. He'd been her dad. That she didn't question, but she now knew her biological father, and she felt cheated at not having a choice in whether he was a part of her life.

"We're coming out there. Where are you?"

"In the middle of nowhere." A sob caught in her throat. "I don't know. Somewhere outside of Toronto."

"Where are you staying?"

"C-Lite Hotels. I'm in charge. Well, Tarin's in charge, but I'm pretending to be her. I hate this craziness. I miss you guys."

"Tijan, are you okay?"

"I don't know, Mom. I'd rather be chasing chickens about now."

"You're not making much sense. You hate working with chickens. We'll be on the next flight. We love you."

"If you want to talk to her, here's her phone number... she has questions, too."

Tijan's arm felt weighted, and she didn't have the strength to hold it up anymore. Her hand slid down her body and fell onto her lap. There was still sound coming from her phone, but she couldn't do anything about it. Her eyes closed. She couldn't remember when she'd last eaten or drunk anything... or slept. She had hit the ground hard when she'd jumped out of the car. Her body slumped sideways.

CHAPTER 60

AUGUST DROVE LIKE A new daddy who was late for the birth of his first child. It had been ten minutes since Tijan had called, and though Graham had said he could find her from the GPS, it was now getting dark. He couldn't see much beyond his headlights.

"Okay. You're in the right area. It's showing that her cell phone is there somewhere."

August slammed on the brakes, fishtailing sideways, realizing he hadn't been listening or comprehending Graham's voice telling him to slow down. It was only when he yelled, 'She's there,' that he pulled onto the side of the road and jumped out.

"I'll look around and see if I can find her. Stay on the line. My GPS is on, so you should be able to find me if we get cut off."

"Tijan, Tijan." He started calling her name but didn't want to be too loud in case Mr. T was still around. Saying she was in that area was a bit vague. To his left were a few hills and housing. To his right were a stretch of trees and an open field. At least that's what it looked like when he flashed his flashlight in that direction. He chose the trees and fence, carefully making his way through the woods until he found himself at a fence. There was no sign of her in the field, nor could he see anything near the fence.

"Tijan. Tijan!" He started yelling louder. When he stopped, all he could hear were the moos of a few cows and the distant sound of traffic. Taking a deep breath to calm his frayed nerves, he headed back to the road and crossed it. Climbing the slight embankment, he'd barely crested the top when he was startled. A dog raced toward him, growling, barking and lunging at the chain-link fence. August stumbled backwards, tumbling down the incline he'd just made his way up.

Getting to his feet, he went back to the car.

"Any sign?"

The muffled sound he'd heard was his cell. "Nothing yet."

"Tijan. Tijan."

He climbed into the car and kept driving.

"You're going away from her."

August turned around at Graham's information. He drove slowly, keeping his beams on high even when a car came around the curve and flashed him several times, trying to get him to dim them. Other than being honked at as the person passed, nothing untoward happened. He kept creeping along.

"She should be right around there."

August had a sick feeling. That was where he'd stopped before. There had been no sign of her. He kept driving and yelling out his window. When he came to the curve in the road, Graham again said, "You're going away from the cell phone."

August drove a ways before stopping to walk along the bush. He was pretty sure Tijan wouldn't be on the other side of the road with barking dogs to give away her location. He made his way back through the trees to the narrow path that hugged the fence.

"Tijan. Tijan, are you okay? Dammit, will you answer me!"

"Wh-"

His head whipped to the left, and he stomped into the clump of trees. Although he wasn't sure it was a voice he'd heard, he hoped it was. Shoving back branches, he saw her feet. Gently moving aside more bush, he knelt down beside her.

"Tijan, are you okay? Is anything broken?" He gently inspected all her limbs, torso, and head. When he didn't feel anything serious, he said, "I'm going to pick you up. Let me know if I hurt you."

She groaned slightly as he lifted her. It took agonizing minutes as he made his way through the brush and to the car. Using his arm and knee propped against the car, he opened the passenger door and eased her in. Having the interior light on her revealed how pale she was and how many scratches and bruises marred her skin.

"Hey big eyes, you okay? Open up. Let me see your baby blues." He whispered as he urged her to come to. His fingers brushed her cheek and pulled a few twigs from her hair.

Finally, her eyes fluttered open. "Thirsty."

He always kept a couple of bottles of water in his trunk and snacks. He quickly retrieved both and gave them to her. She drank the water slowly but steadily. Her eyelids drooped.

"Just eat something, okay? Here's a granola bar. I'm going to take us someplace safe." He eased out and pulled out his phone. "I've found her. She's okay. Tired and scratched but okay. I need to take her out of here. Any ideas?"

"The house we showed you the other day. Take her there. We've put in a gate with a security code. I don't think anyone will find you. We'll be out—"

"No. Is there food? A bed or two?"

"Got it. Yes, it's well stocked. You won't have to worry. Take good care of her."

As August climbed in the driver's side, her head rolled against the seat toward him. Her eyes looked brighter and more alert.

"How'd you know I was near Lake Ontario?"

"Graham pinged the GPS on your phone."

A look of relief came over her. "Tarin gave me that phone for work. Thank God."

August nodded. "I'm taking you to the house they took us to yesterday. Graham said it's safe."

"Thank you. I just had to know you were one of the good guys."

She looked at him with such a look of relief that he took it as an invitation and leaned over to kiss her. She met his lips eagerly. His fingers brushed some dirt off her cheek as he eased back.

"Let me get you out of here, and we'll feed you and clean you up."

Tijan laughed. "Are you saying I stink?"

"Well, there is this kind of 'eau de cow' aroma."

She gently punched him on the arm. "For the record, I love that smell. It's earthy, real, and it's me. But in this case, it just happens to be coming from the big field I was beside. There are a lot of cows in there."

"Sure. Sure. We'll go with that. Drink some more water. You are okay, though, right?" August squeezed her hand.

"Yes. But I promise you that I won't ever wear heels again. They are not made for anything other than to stand for short periods of time, to show off your sexy legs or to sit. They are not made for walking—and definitely not in the back forty. Even if I wanted, which I don't, I don't think I can even squeeze my feet into them. Ouch."

August chuckled, glad that was all that was hurt.

CHAPTER 61

"IT'S A GOOD THING he gave you directions because I'd have no idea how to get there, would you?"

August shook his head.

Tijan snapped on her seat belt but lowered the seat back some. Her body ached, and exhaustion was still dragging her down. The whole week of events was taking its toll on her, but her escape and run from Tesimmon was at the top of that list. As they curved around the next bend, a speeding oncoming car hogged the road down the middle line. August pulled to the shoulder, but as it continued speeding toward them, he was forced into the soft grass alongside the road. As it got near, Tijan snapped upright.

"It's them. Step on it."

The car roared past, but a second later, the brake lights came on. August hit the gas. The car fishtailed as they took off. Tijan put her seat up and held on as August was flying down the road and careening around corners. She turned to look out the back window.

"I don't see any lights. I don't know if we should continue to that house."

"We need to lose them."

August flicked a glance at her. "Call Graham. Here." He pulled out his cell and handed it to her.

"Graham. We need help. Tesimmon is after us. I think we lost—" Just then a flash of lights flipping through the interior caught her attention. She spun around again. Headlights were quickly gaining on them.

"It's got to be them." Tijan screamed. "Graham, we need help. Now."

"I can't lose them. Their car has way more power than we do."

"You have to lose them, August. Graham!"

"I'm on it. Let me see where you are."

It took him only a moment to find them.

"Okay, you need to—"

"Hang on." August's arm flew across her chest, pinning her to her seat.

The other car rammed them. The impact slammed her back and then threw her forward. August's hands were both back on the wheel, frantically working to control the car and straighten it out.

"Get ready."

Even though she knew it was coming, the second hit jolted her bruised body hard. The seat belt cut into her neck and shoulder, and the phone flew from her hand and landed on the floorboard.

"Turn left, next turn."

She could still hear Graham's voice from the phone on the floor, and Tijan wasn't about to try to retrieve it now. She grabbed the overhead handle with one hand, clutched her seat with the other and held on as August hurtled around the next corner. It was too much for the big Rolls Royce that flew past them, but the brake lights soon came on.

"Go. Go. Go. We have a slight edge. Graham, where can we hide?" She yelled, hoping he'd hear her.

"There's a barn coming up on your left. Maybe you can hide behind it. Not sure; there aren't too many options. It's about a kilometer ahead," Graham said.

Tijan twisted around in the seat. "August, you watch our hiding spot and I'll watch for them."

August cut off their headlights. At the speed they were going in the dark, she hoped that Graham was accurate. The odds of seeing a barn and getting to it without detection were slim.

"I don't see them."

"Hold on. There's the barn Graham was talking about." Though August slowed, they still took the corner quickly, slamming Tijan against her door. "Ugh."

"Sorry." A few seconds later, they were behind a dilapidated, obviously abandoned building.

Almost as though they'd agreed, they sat in silence, their breaths soft and quiet. August took her hand and squeezed it gently. Tijan smiled despite the tension, finding comfort in the silence and the quiet message passing between them.

It was a while before Tijan finally broke the silence. "I feel like something isn't right. You?"

August turned to face her. "I don't think they cracked up. I don't think the car died. Didn't it look like they'd stopped?"

"Yeah." Tijan sighed heavily. "So, what are they up to?"

"Graham? Graham? Are you still there?" She fished around on the floor, finally finding the phone under her seat.

"Dammit. They have Tarin."

"What? No! How did they get her?"

"We knew they'd been watching her when she visited her father. We had eyes on them. Since we moved your father, she'd stopped. But then she went to the hospital to visit Bill. They were still watching, thinking James Madsen was still there. But obviously, Mr. T's goons didn't know that Mr. T thought they already had Tarin. So when they saw her, they grabbed her. They left the city, heading northeast. They must have thrown her phone out. We don't know where they went."

Tijan's head pounded as pressure built around her eyes. Her heart thumped hard in her chest. Tarin, whom she hadn't had a chance to get to know? Tarin, who seemed to have a gentle soul even though she'd been raised by a cold-hearted man. Tarin, who was the other half of her.

It made her sick with fear to think she could lose her. She'd only been that scared once before, when she'd been searching for a calf in the bush and she'd encountered a bear. She'd managed to get out of that situation, and she was going to get her sister out of this one.

"What's out there? Where would they take her?" August asked.

"Caspian. But what would they achieve by going there?" Graham couldn't hide the panic in his voice.

"Wait. They might be." Tijan pressed her hand to her heart. "They told me they were going to settle it once and for all about Caspian. They wanted me to sign the papers to take over from my father. What are they going to do, use her for blackmail?" It hit Tijan; that's exactly what they were going to do. That's why they had wanted her. Mr. T was expanding his empire, whether anyone wanted him to or not.

But not at the expense of her sister.

"We have to go there, August. Now." Tijan was shaking so much, she was tempted to open the door and run to the winery.

CHAPTER 62

As they approached Caspian Winery, August slowed down and pulled into a copse of trees, a ways from the entrance to the winery.

"We have to walk from here."

"Damn."

Tijan climbed out and wobbled a bit, grabbing the car's roof.

"I'd tell you to stay here, but I don't think you'd listen." August kissed her gently. "Listen to me. We don't know what we're headed into. The police, as well as Guy and Graham, are on their way. Maybe we should just wait."

"Like that's going to happen." Tijan started limping down the side of the road.

August jogged after her and swept her off her feet. "If you're going to be so determined, I can at least save your feet a bit."

"Ahh. My knight. Just need a steed and we're set." It was hard to break from her intent of saving her sister, but August was trying to make things easier for her. She couldn't fault him for that.

"I hate to break it to you, but I don't ride."

"I'm wounded. Now hustle up. We've got to save Tarin."

When they got to Caspian's driveway, they had the proof they needed. The long limo was left at an angle in the middle of the parking lot like a black menace under the winery's yard lights.

"Put me down," Tijan whispered in his ear. As soon as her feet touched the ground, she darted behind a tree, waving to August to do the same. "How are we going to get past those two idiots, they've stationed by the car? I already had my fight with them today. They don't play nice."

"Stay here. I'll distract them." August jogged down the road in the dark.

Tijan soon lost track of him, but a moment later, she heard pinging as though something was hitting the car. The two men drew their guns and moved toward the road. Tijan took the opportunity to hug the treeline and make her way to the building. The rocks and twigs that dug into her soles brought feeling back into her swollen feet.

Hoping August knew what he was doing and having limited knowledge of the place, she went around the side of the building to the back entrance, the one she'd seen Guy, Graham and Tarin enter. She made it to the back door and slipped inside. It took only a second for her to realize she'd been expected.

"Hello. Two of you. Isn't that quaint." Mr. T grinned. "Do you know that I killed two men because I thought they were incompetent? They told me they were shooting at you at the hospital when I was chasing you through Toronto. Their deaths are on you."

Tijan's heart thumped loudly, echoing in her ears.

"Now it's time for business. James had more secrets than I gave him credit for. Now that I have his two prized possessions here, we're going to do the deal up right. You're going to sign over C-Lite Hotels. I'll own a large hotel chain. And I'm going to inherit Caspian Winery. The two of you are my ticket."

Tijan wished she had some cow manure to throw at Mr. T. His white suit and gold shoes mocked her, and if she was going to be fed bullshit, she'd rather it look like it.

"I haven't been this excited about anything in a long time." Mr. T. smiled.

Tijan felt like throwing up. "Where's my sister?"

"Oh, that's so nice. You're worried about her. Well, since there are two of you, we'll see which one of you is going to follow my orders and do as I say, while the other will stay with me."

Tijan shuddered, horrified at his sinister leer.

"A threesome with twins isn't something I've tried before, but I'm game."

"And you won't ever get that opportunity. Not if you want to keep that undersized, limp thing between your legs."

Tijan was ready for him. He growled and took a step in her direction as she pulled out her gun and sidestepped so he was between her and his bodyguard. She stopped just out of reach.

"Tijan!"

Her sister's voice jolted her, but she'd expected he'd play dirty. Out of the corner of her eye, she saw one of the goons drag her sister in with her arm twisted high behind her back.

"Let her go, or I shoot you."

Mr. T looked bored. "Not going to happen. Now you have the count of three—"

Tijan shifted to her right and fired toward his feet, hoping if it ricocheted, it would not hit her sister.

"You bitch!"

He lunged for her, and she danced to the side as the gun tumbled out of her hands. She ran past the reception-ist's desk, ducking behind it only to pop back up a moment later, throwing whatever she could get her hands on.

"Let her go," she yelled as she fired the stapler, tape dispenser, pens, pen holder and keyboard as she peeked over the desk. She could no longer see her sister, but the goon had retreated behind a large column.

Mr. T pulled out his gun, and Tijan dove through the doorway, quickly scurrying down the hallway.

"Tijan. This way."

She almost collapsed with relief at the sound of her sister's whisper. She dashed down the short hallway toward her twin, who was holding open a door. Tijan shot through as Tarin slammed and locked it. Tijan grabbed her outstretched hand.

"Are you okay? How'd you get away?" Tijan hurried after her.

"I'm good. The idiot loosened his hold when you started throwing things. Let's go."

They were in a room with massive steel containers. The smell of yeast hit her. She wrinkled her nose.

"It takes a bit to get used to. Come on."

They wound around the large vats. A loud banging on the door jolted them, and Tarin pushed her back against one of the steel tanks.

"How are we going to get out of here? August has his hands full outside with two thugs."

"He knows the area well if he can manage to outrun them."

Tijan grimaced at her sister's familiarity.

"Oh my God, you like him."

Tarin hugged her hard, but Tijan found it difficult to reciprocate.

Tarin eased back. "What's going on?"

There was another loud sound. Then it repeated. It sounded as if someone was shooting at the door.

"Okay, we're going out through the front entrance."

Staying low, Tijan followed her twin in the opposite direction of the noise.

"Find them now!" The words were bellowed just as the door flew open and banged against the wall.

Tijan hurried after her fast-moving sister. Reaching the door, Tarin hurriedly keyed in a code. As it opened, the two raced through, quickly locking it behind them.

"Look what I caught."

Tijan turned slowly, putting herself between Tarin and the voice of the man she thought they'd eluded. "What do you want? The company my father built?"

"Your father couldn't have built that huge chain without me. Where do you think he got the money to start it?

Money that put clothes on your back, gave you bobbles and a fancy education. Now it's my turn."

Tijan's eyes flicked toward the door in an attempt to determine if she could sprint through it. She noted that Tarin was standing beside her.

"Pull another stunt and I'll shoot."

Tijan's stomach did a flip as she looked at the ominous black gun he was pointing at her. A movement through the large glass window caught her eye. The yard was fairly well lit, but whoever was moving was sticking to the shadows. Something told her it wasn't Mr. T's men.

"Fine. So, you want his business. I guess since you think your slimy money built it into what it is today, it should be yours. Do you realize you could have given him all the money in the world, but without his hard work, it wouldn't have been successful? You think you're the first person to be pissed at him? Well, you're not. There's a long line that would probably wrap around Tor—"

Tarin seemed to catch on to what she was doing. "It's true. He's not a nice man. He's caused a lot of problems. And let me tell you, being his daughter hasn't been easy either."

"Shut up."

"No, that's true. It's been difficult. Have you ever had a parent reject you?"

"Or smother you?"

"Shut up!" He waved the gun in their direction before pulling out his cell.

"Now," Tijan said softly to her sister, instinctively knowing she'd understand. They were to tackle him from different directions. She ran to her left, knowing Tarin was going to the right.

"Where the hell are you? Get in here!"

Tijan dove low, hitting his knees with her full body momentum as he fired the gun. She quickly climbed up his body and flipped the stunned Mr. T onto his belly. She kneeled on him, relieved to see the gun had gone flying when he'd landed. Grabbing both of his wrists, she pulled them hard up into the middle of his back.

He grunted and started bucking like a mad bull. Tijan held on with all her might as Tarin arrived at her side with some rope.

"Get off me, you bitch. I'll kill you and your sister—and your father."

"Shut up. You already tried to kill my father." She tied the rope into a noose.

"I didn't, but I will now."

"I'm tired of listening to your hot air. You launder money, kill, steal, sell drugs and you want respect?"

"Damn right. I didn't kill off my competition and any judge or cop I couldn't buy just to have a little snot of a girl take me down."

Tarin slipped the noose she'd made over one of his hands just as a commotion caught her attention. As she turned her head, she was sent sprawling sideways.

CHAPTER 63

"ALRIGHT, THAT'S ENOUGH, TARIN. Wait, there are two of you."

Tijan looked up from her position, slouched on the ground beside Mr. T, who was struggling to sit up. Her jaw couldn't have dropped any further. So much for thinking it was help that had been outside.

"Mary. What are you doing?" Tarin sounded as shocked as she felt.

"I'm here to get what's mine. Get away from him. The two of you over against that wall." Mary waved the gun she was holding at them. "Get up, Don."

Tijan looked at Tarin, but she was watching Mary closely. "So, the two of you thought you'd team up and take down my father?"

"Give me the gun, Mary." Mr. T slowly got to his feet and brushed off his white suit.

Tijan shivered as much from the situation as from the cold cement floor. "Which one of you shot our father? Mr. T, you'd be my guess. Tarin, who do you think?"

"I think Mary tired of waiting for my father to fall in love with her."

"I was good to him. I did everything he asked. I looked after him like a damn wife, and he couldn't give me the time of day. And he wouldn't give my son—"

"Your son?" Tarin was quick to ask.

"Shut up, Tarin. Miss goody girl. Your father doted on you, and what do you do but embarrass him?" Mary waved the gun as if she were waving a wand.

The door opened. JT strolled in as if on cue.

It hit Tijan the moment he stepped into the light. "JT, or should I say, Chris Simmons, is your son."

"And he's going to get the recognition and position he deserves."

Tarin gasped. "Mary, I know my father is not always a nice man, but you don't—"

Mary snorted.

"I'm sorry about JT. It can't have been easy knowing he was adopted."

"Shut up! JT, tie these two up," Mary snapped.

JT moved to do his mother's bidding.

Tijan's mind had been blank, watching the whole thing unfold.

"You're going to forgive a mom who gave you up?"

Tijan caught on to what Tarin was doing. "Yeah, you didn't want anything to do with her at the office, once you knew who she was."

"Shut UP!" Mary screamed. "JT, if you want that VP position, move."

The door flew open again.

"Isn't this a quaint family reunion?" Eleanor waltzed in as though she belonged there. Her gun was pointed at Mary. "Mary, put the gun down or JT will get it first. Good girl. JT, tie up your father. Then, those two."

Tijan's head was muddled with all she was learning. Tarin's expression of shock mirrored her own. JT was doing as she asked.

"You bitch! You and JT?" Mary screeched.

"You double-crossed me with him?" Mr. T swiped his hand across his face as blood trickled from his nose.

Tijan felt some satisfaction that she'd done some harm. Everyone of them was crooked. They were people she didn't like, but she'd never have guessed this.

Eleanor, who looked as cool and collected and stylishly dressed as though holding a board meeting, shrugged nonchalantly. "Yes, he's a good lay. Almost as good as you, Mr. T. But the truth is JT is self-serving. He hooked up with my lawyer, Martin, to defraud C-Lite Hotels. He only played me to find out what you were doing and what James was up to. You'd be happy to know your son, JT, is as crafty as you."

There was a collective gasp. Tijan was sure she wasn't the only one shocked.

"You and he?" Tarin asked of Mary as she nodded toward Mr. T.

"He raped me and then took my baby away from me. He let someone else raise him. I had no choice." But rather than tears, there was fury spitting from her eyes.

Tijan felt like she'd been dropped into a dangerous family reunion.

"The joke is on all of you. I'm walking out of here with all your money and assets. Each of you will sign them over to me. See, I'm not just a smart lawyer. I'm a smart person who knows opportunity when she sees it. I've been funneling not only information but money from each of you for a while now. All except for you, Mary. You turned out to be a complication I hadn't counted on. James will never love you. He's incapable."

Mary moved fast for her age. A gun fired. Tijan grabbed her sister and dove behind the wine tasting counter amid more shots. They shuffled on hands and knees as fast as they could. Tijan scooted to the far end, sure that Tarin would know her way around and get them out of there. Just as she was about to make a run for it, the front door flew open and several armed men entered.

"Police. Hands in the air."

Tijan looked at Tarin, who nodded. Tarin inched past, indicating she was going to scoot through a side room and that Tijan should follow. Tijan couldn't help peeking around the end of the bar. The police had Mary, who was bleeding, and JT on the ground. Eleanor had also been shot. But there was no sign of Mr. T.

Suddenly, Tijan was grabbed from behind and jerked to her feet. "I'm leaving. Get out of my way or I'll kill her."

Her hands grasped the arm lodged around her throat. She was startled that she'd underestimated the slimy guy. He shoved her upright and pushed her toward the door.

"Open it," he barked.

"Can't breathe," she squeaked out and let her body sag a bit.

He shoved her forward, face first into the door. Her hands rose out of reflex. The door opened. Several police officers had their guns drawn and pointed at them. Tijan wanted to beg them not to shoot. They'd barely cleared the door when someone tackled Mr. T and she was cat-apulted forward. The sudden jolt loosened his arm, and she scrambled on hands and knees away from him. She'd barely made it a few feet before someone grabbed her arm. She spun around, swinging. There wasn't time to stop her punch, but she was glad the policeman had quicker reflexes and was able to block it.

"Sorry."

He moved her away from the area. She gladly followed but, ever curious, she glanced over her shoulder. August was punching the crap out of Mr. T. She jerked away and ran back.

"August, stop. I'm okay. I'm okay." She grabbed his arm to stop him.

He looked up at her and then down at the man, who had his arms covering his face. The police grabbed August and held his arms until he got to his feet and stepped to the side. Tijan leaped at him. His arms snapped around her, holding her tight.

Police swarmed the area. Mr. T, his men and JT, who was pleading he was a victim, were put into the police cars. Mary and Eleanor were loaded into an ambulance. It was very chaotic, and Tijan was glad she was safely able to watch it unfold.

"You don't listen very well. I told you to stay." August set her down gently as he leaned back and looked at her sternly.

She looked up at him. He looked so good. Even with his hair mussed and sticking in all directions and dirt smudging his face, she liked what she saw. She reached up and removed the elastic from his hair.

"Time to let your hair down." She finger-combed it to fall gently onto his shoulders.

He chuckled. "It still doesn't change that you didn't listen."

"Well, my sister was in danger. I had to do something."

"I can vouch that she doesn't listen well. I told her not to keep playing me, but she wouldn't stop," Tarin smiled at her sister from beyond August's shoulder.

"You're okay," Tijan smiled at Tarin.

August held her as her legs were rather wobbly, while she took the few steps to fall into her sister's arms. "Well, this is a hell of a way to get to know each other."

"That it is. But we are so kick-ass together."

Tijan stared into her sister's eyes, so identical to hers, yet full of so many different memories. However, when they'd needed to work together, they'd known what the other person was thinking. Somehow, they knew each other. Tijan had never felt so whole in her life.

CHAPTER 64

"WELL, THAT'S THE CRAZIEST thing I've ever been through. And you guys have been through this more than once? No thanks." August took a drink of his beer.

"Yeah, a bit convoluted. JT was Mr. T and Mary's son. It appeared Mr. T played her for years on that. He took her son away at a young age and put him in the adoption system. Felt he could better control her. He got her the job with James at C-Lite and forced her to give him important information for smuggling across the border. Then she got JT the job there." He sighed. "I think the plan was that JT would be the CFO, but it turns out he had other plans. He was stealing money.""What a family," Guy muttered."JT learned who his father was, but didn't like not being in charge, so he persuaded Eleanor to team up with him. He didn't know she was also sleeping with James and Mr. T. JT thought he had all his bases covered. I think he wanted to impress his father, to show him that he could create a larger dynasty. JT was also seeing Martin, one of Eleanor's lawyers. Martin thought it was serious, so he was doing what he could to help JT. Poor guy was in love with JT and all that he'd promised him. JT had big plans for taking down his father, Mr. T and James, and was going to use whoever he could, even pretending to be gay. JT, stands for Junior Tesimmon. Cute, hey? Tesimmon nicknamed him that at twelve. Meanwhile, Eleanor was just playing all of them." Graham arched his eyebrows. "Lovely, aren't they?"

"So, who shot my father?" Tijan asked quietly.

August squeezed her hand.

Tarin shook her head as she leaned against Graham. "Mary. I was right. She was jealous of him and Eleanor. When he kept putting off giving her son, JT, the position she felt he deserved, it was too much. It was one thing that he wouldn't return her unrequited love, but to dismiss her son like that? So, she shot him. It appears it was in a moment of anger, but she has no regrets about doing it. Although she still professes her love for him."

"I don't know what to say. All the people you're supposed to be able to trust ripping each other apart and all for what? Power? Money?" Tijan appeared stunned.

Tarin smiled at her sister. "Please don't measure all of us because of our father. He has a bit of a good side. It just doesn't show up all that often. He was so bent on power and money that he surrounded himself with people just like him."

August couldn't fathom any of it. It appeared that James had attracted like-minded people into his world, only they had wanted to take him down as badly as he'd wanted to be the most powerful. And he hadn't seen any of it coming.

August didn't want to get sucked into that world. To him, it was done and over with, and he didn't want to go back there. He watched Tarin and Tijan together. It was Tarin who had first caught his attention, but there was no denying it was Tijan who kept it. She looked amazing now that she'd showered and changed into blue jeans and a silk blouse. Her long blonde hair cascaded over her shoulders, begging him to lose his hands in it. But he couldn't shake the feeling that there was a sadness about her. He wasn't sure whether it was because the excitement was over or because she was going home. She didn't know it yet, but he planned on following her. He wasn't going to let her slip away from him.

"Tijan. Tarin. Someone is here to see you. I've had them shown to the drawing room. I'll take you down." Dorothea walked onto the balcony, beckoning both women to come to her. She took both their hands and squeezed before walking slowly with them inside.

August knew there was a strong connection between them when Tijan turned and looked at him before leaving. He was tempted to go along, even though he hadn't been invited.

"Uh, there's something we have to tell you, August."

He turned to look at the two men with whom he'd become good friends, but their guilty expressions had him wondering what was coming. Since they were constantly ribbing each other and didn't take the world too seriously, he wasn't sure how to take their somber expressions. "Okay."

"It's about why we hired you." Guy gave a sideways glance to Graham.

"Uh. Yeah. We uh..."

"You hired me because my mom told you I was a wonderful mechanic? You searched me out, found out who I was. But then got the great idea to use me as bait and a date for Tijan and now you're feeling guilty?"

The two looked at each other before giving him a sickly smile.

It appeared there was more to it. Now he was getting uncomfortable. "Who's Tijan meeting with?" It would be just his luck that she disappeared... for good. He stood and looked out over the expansive view from the Caspian mansion.

"Hey. No man. This has nothing to do with her. It's their parents."

"What?" August spun around.

"Tijan and Tarin's mom and stepdad are here. Alright, look. We hired you because—well, we think we know who your father is."

August turned away, pressing his knuckles hard against the marble edge. He'd been looking for a long time and had come to the conclusion that the man must be dead. Or maybe that's just what he'd hoped. It would save him a

MAGGIE THOM

lot of heartache as to why a man had left a nine-year-old boy.

"We know we should have told you in the beginning, but we didn't want to have him hurt. He's been through a lot, and we wanted to protect him. And your... uh... mom..."

August turned quickly. "My mom, what?"

They exchanged guilty looks again. Guy cleared his throat. "She kind of asked us to find him and to make sure that, if possible, the two of you met."

He was glad he was leaning against the balustrade or he was sure his legs would have given out. His mom hadn't said a word to him. In fact, they had rarely talked about his father, other than his mom saying his dad had good reasons for leaving and he was a good man.

"Look. We'd like you to meet him. Well, properly, that is."

August tried to talk but found his throat had dried up and closed up. He cleared his throat a few times before finally giving up and nodding instead.

Finding his father had been on his mind for so long, he was almost sure this had to be a joke. He followed them wordlessly, leaving them to talk and look at each other awkwardly as he followed them down the stairs. August wasn't sure what to expect. Feeling a little less like he was being put on the spot, he walked slowly down the winding staircase. At the bottom, they looked at him and then walked out the front door. Not having a clue what was going on, he strode out behind them.

"Hello, son."

It was like having that dream fulfilled when you least expected it and weren't ready to believe it—no matter how much you had wanted it. August stared at the older man standing in the shade beside the building. He wanted to be angry, but he wasn't. His mom had always said he was a good man, but he'd been deeply wounded and scarred thanks to the war. August took a step towards him.

"Bill—Dad?"

Bill walked towards him and stood at attention. "I'm sorry, son. I couldn't be the man I wanted to be and felt you were better off without me."

August didn't even try to speak. He pulled the man he'd been searching for most of his life into his arms and held on with a nine-year-old's desperate urge to know he wasn't at fault.

"Maybe I can even get used to your long hair."

August's heart swelled. "And maybe I can get used to your brush cut."

CHAPTER 65

"TARIN, THIS IS—"

"Oh, my baby. I thought you were dead. I saw you tumble through the water. You just disappeared. I prayed you weren't."

Tijan stood back as Tarin ran to their mom and wrapped her arms around her. Tijan didn't try to stop the tears that flowed freely down her face. Her stepfather appeared at her side, hugging her close. It was a long time before anyone moved or talked.

"He paid me to get pregnant."

Tijan heard her mom, but it didn't make sense—not for the woman. Taking a deep breath to calm her nerves. She had a feeling that this would not be easy to get through. Meeting her mom and dad at the hotel the night before had been amazing, but their getting to meet Tarin had been the best present Tijan had ever given them.

"I grew up wealthy. My parents, your grandparents, are still alive. I haven't spoken to them in about thirty years. They disowned me. And though I did what I could, when they cut me off, I had no way to make money. I started dating men for money." She looked at Cal for a moment. "I was a paid escort but no sex. When James said he'd like me to have his child, I—" Their mom turned away to look at the ornate gold-trimmed mantel over the fireplace.

The twins looked at each other at the same time. Tijan didn't have to read Tarin's mind to know that she was as steamrolled as she was. Tijan was debating about pinching herself when her sister did just that. Confused, she looked at the mirror image of herself.

Tarin gave her a half-smile. "I don't know why I did that. It just felt like I needed to."

Tijan smiled and moved to one side of her mom, while Tarin moved to the other. Tijan knelt down beside her wheelchair. Her mom looked at her with pain-filled eyes.

"I loved you from the moment you were born." She caressed Tijan's face and then turned to do the same with her other hand on Tarin's face. Looking back and forth between them, she continued, "You both were perfect. So beautiful. So happy. I just couldn't turn you over to that bitter man. He was ruthless and controlling. He told me what I could eat, when I could eat and what exercise I was to do. I was young and had just left that kind of tyrannical lifestyle. I wasn't about to stick around to endure it again. And I sure didn't want my baby to grow up in that. I only knew about one of you. I didn't trust doctors, and I was able to convince the one that James had me go to not to do any ultrasounds or anything like that. And of course, he couldn't tell James. It wasn't easy to convince him, but he was a nice older man. He hated a woman's tears."

Tijan felt as though she had stepped into the world of Oz. It was like her mom was telling them a bedtime story. Only not one that should be told to children.

"Anyway, I ran away. When I gave birth to twins a few weeks early, it eased my mind. I've never been so happy as on the day you arrived—4:03 and 4:45 a.m. I still remember the exact times."

Tijan felt like she was in a vacuum where words were going in but nothing made sense.

"I rented a big, old farmhouse in rural Alberta. We lived in the foothills. Actually, not too far from where we now live."

Tijan couldn't tell her that she'd already gone there to see it.

"For two years, we had so much fun. It was beautiful. The two of you were best friends, always checking on this owl and her babies—"

"In a tree in the front yard." Tijan and Tarin said it at the same time and then grinned at each other over their mom's head.

"Yes. You were so concerned about them. One sadly didn't make it, which made you two even more determined to make sure the other one did. Then... then came the day your father found us. He didn't know there were two of you. I thought I was prepared. We snuck out, and I tried to cross the swollen creek with both of you. The water knocked me over, and Tarin, your tiny arms couldn't hold on. I tried to find you. I tried!" Sobbing uncontrollably now, she clutched at Tarin, who held on tight.

Tijan's hand pressed hard against her chest as she tried to choke back the tears and pain. Giving in she hugged them as best she could, leaning over her mom's wheelchair. They stayed like that for a long time.

"I put Tijan on the far bank and went after you, but your little body was being swept down the creek. I couldn't grab you." Their mom pressed her hand to her chest. "They shot me, and I went under. Cal saved me, but I didn't come to for days after."

Tijan jerked back. "That's why you're in a wheelchair—because our father shot you?"

Tarin couldn't have looked any more stunned. Tijan clapped her hand over her mouth. "I'm sorry. I shouldn't have said that."

"Is it true?" Tarin asked tentatively.

Their mom took Tarin's hands. "I—it is. Your father just wanted you so badly. He—"

"No, what he wanted was a robot. He took so much from me. He almost killed you. God, I hate him."

"No honey. Don't do that. Don't hate. Then you will be like him, and he will have won. I know it hurts. It kills me to know that you were alive and out there and I never knew.

I thought you had died. The rescue workers couldn't find you. Your father rescued you. He saved your life."

Tijan rushed to her sister's side and pulled her into a bear hug. "Please don't change. I love you the way you are. We didn't get to grow up together, but we can be together now. He's not worth it."

"What am I doing here? I need to go back to the office."

Tijan's head snapped around at the voice she heard. Tarin was much faster though and was already across the floor and slapping the face of the man who had raised her.

"How dare you? How dare you keep me from my mom and my sister? We are finished."

He looked stunned. It was almost comical as he looked from Tarin to Tijan. "There are two of you. Tyana?"

Tijan frowned as she turned to look at her mom, who was now locked in an eye duel with James.

"Who's Tyana? Your Meigan."

Her mom pressed her hand to her mouth and took a deep breath before replying. "My original name was Tyana. I changed it to Meigan so that James wouldn't find me."

"You shot her." Tarin was back in his face, not ready to let him off the hook. "We brought you here to look after you so you could heal. But you're an awful man."

Her father, who had looked almost robust and healthy, now seemed to have aged ten years in front of her eyes. The gray at his temples, which had looked distinguished, now appeared dull and was almost like a fungus was spreading. Wrinkles he'd been keeping at bay with Botox seemed instantly to reappear. His face looked pale and stark, like he might pass out.

Since Tarin wasn't in any mood to help him, Tijan walked over and took his arm, steering him to a chair.

"I want answers." Tarin was back in his face.

Tijan thought about telling her to give him a break, but she could understand her anger. Tijan was angry too, but she'd grown up in a loving home. Tarin, she was sure, had not.

"I wanted a child to teach my business to. To leave my business to. She was from good stock."

"Jesus, she's a woman, not a breeding horse," Tijan snapped.

He shrugged. "I needed a child. And she agreed. I paid her good money."

"You unfeeling bastard. Know this: you will never get near my son. He is not taking over your dynasty, although as we speak, it is going into receivership. Yes, I made that happen. I have also hired Cooper Hotels to take over management. You shouldn't have left me in charge, Father."

"You can't take all the credit, Tarin, I helped."

They grinned at each other. They had done what they could to right so many wrongs.

"It's my company."

"Not anymore. Remember all those forms you signed at the hospital—the ones you couldn't take time to read? I tried to tell you what was in them, but you weren't interested. All you heard was I was protecting your business. Which I did."

"I'll sue you."

Tijan shivered, never having met someone like her father, who was so single-minded.

Meigan wheeled forward. "No, actually you won't, James. If you go after one of our girls, I will charge you with attempted murder and kidnapping."

It seemed that their raised voices had grabbed attention—Graham, Guy, Bailey, August, Bill, and Dorothea soon joined them—along with an elderly man who was holding Dorothea's arm.

"What are you doing here?" James snapped. "Come to gloat?"

The elderly man, Calib, patted Dorothea's arm before letting her go and sitting in a chair across from James. "No, son. I came to put this crazy vendetta you've had against me to rest. You hated me so much that you got into bed with organized crime? That saddens me but I will no longer let you bully anyone. If you want a job with C-Lite

Hotels, we'll talk. But I won't give you back your hotels. When CSIS is done investigating, you're probably facing jail time. Time to grow up, James."

Tijan felt like she'd just heard a child being scolded. Age didn't matter. If a parent thought you'd done wrong, they'd let you know. Already she was warming up to the gentleman that she was going to guess she and Tarin got their blue eyes from.

"Grandpa, I'd like you to meet my sister, Tijan."

CHAPTER 66

"HAVE YOU EVER EXPERIENCED anything so crazy?" Tijan brushed her hand down the silk shirt Tarin had loaned her.

August smiled as he took her hand, his thumb caressing her palm. "No. I've had some odd moments in my life, but this beats them all. I met my father. You met yours."

"Yeah, but I think you got the better deal."

"My dad is a war vet. It sounds like he has been suffering from PTSD for many years. I guess that was why he left. Guy and Graham have done a lot for him. They got him some help, gave him a place to live, and gave him a security job. I've been angry with him for so long."

"I didn't know my dad existed. I thought he was dead, which is just as well because I would have hated the man. I still get angry that he took my sister away from me and disabled my mother. But I need to remember the good that has come out of this. I have a cool grandpa. And I found my sister. And I have the cutest nephew." Tijan looked around, wishing there was more of a view but loving the beautiful area surrounded by trees. She leaned forward in the deck chair. Her sister and Graham, and whoever else they'd let in on this, had gone to a lot of trouble to make this romantic. When she and August mentioned they were going for a walk, her sister gave them directions to the old house across the field from Dorothea's mansion.

August turned away for a moment before handing her a glass of wine. "They seemed to have thought of everything. A toast to new beginnings."

Tijan raised her glass and clinked it with his, letting him hold her gaze. She took a sip. "Hmm. Good wine. I guess that might be why Caspian Winery has won awards."

August nodded.

"I hope you don't feel like—well, I mean I know that we don't know—"

August got out of his chair and kneeled in front of Tijan. He leaned forward and kissed her. "I like you too."

Tijan wrapped her arms around his neck as she laid her forehead against his. "Good thing, because I was going to ask if you have some vacation coming. I'd like to take you to Alberta and show you the foothills and the Rockies."

"I don't know if I'm even still employed. So, yes. It might be too soon, but I think I'm falling for you."

"Don't get too caught up in the excitement and drama that we just went through. It's really far from my life and who I am."

"Good. I couldn't handle much more of that. And it's really far from my life too. I'd love to come to Alberta."

"So, I'll get you on a horse?"

THANK YOU

Thank you for reading Split Seconds, the final book in the Caspian Wine Series.

Keep reading to read an excerpt from
Concealed Inheritance

Book 1, The Family Heir Looms Series

As she settles into her new role, she is forced to confront a chilling reality... someone is sabotaging her quest for the truth.

CONCEALED INHERITANCE

Book One
The Family Heir Looms Suspense Thriller Series
by
Maggie Thom

———◆○◆———

Excerpt

The moment she pulled up in front of Rina's house, Rina ripped off the seatbelt and bolted from the Jeep. She vanished inside. Skylar could have easily caught up to her but knew that it wasn't the time to push her.

Pulling around to the front of the main house, Skylar parked and went inside. She hustled up to her father's office and logged onto his laptop. She did another thorough search, just in case. Nothing. The thought of what might be on those files kept her searching.

Someone didn't want her to know what her father had been up to. *Why?* That question seemed to come up almost every other minute.

Was it him?

She couldn't shake that thought.

Her father had taken a long time to embrace using a computer and not having everything on paper. Getting up, she wandered around her father's office, looking for any hidden safes. If he had any in there, she was unaware of them. In a 12,000-foot house, there were a lot of places a safe could be. He'd never shown her one, though.

The clock said 3:35 p.m. She closed up and headed into town for her meeting. Pulling up in front of the lawyer's office, how nervous she was. This could be it.

Squaring her shoulders, she made her way inside. The receptionist, Mrs. Ashburn, greeted her and told her to take a seat. Skylar was alone in the waiting room. The tiny clock on the receptionist's counter said 3:50 p.m. When it said 4:05 and Mrs. Ashburn hadn't come back, Skylar approached the desk.

"Hello," she said loudly. "My appointment was for 4:00."

Mrs. Ashburn came out of a room down the hall and went behind the counter to her desk. "He's running a bit behind. Have a seat."

Not happy at the delay, Skylar returned to the waiting room. Before she could really work herself into a nervous ball of energy or take in the art adorning the walls, Mrs. Ashburn was standing in the doorway.

"He has to cancel. Something came up."

A door clicked. Skylar rushed past her and ran down the hall to the back door. Which was the one she was sure she'd just heard close. She thrust it open. Mr. Ashburn was driving away in his Jaguar.

"I'm sorry but you'll have to leave."

Skylar closed the door and turned. "I want all the contracts I asked for."

Mrs. Ashburn marched down the hallway to the front, disappearing behind her counter. "Mr. Ashburn wants to go through everything with you."

Skylar followed her. "What about my father's will?"

"I'm sorry."

"Look. It has been a few weeks since my father—" She couldn't say the words as emotion choked her up. Forcing that back, she continued. "I should have gotten a copy of his will. In fact, there used to be one at the house. It's missing. Weird stuff is going on. I need to know why. And who's behind it. I need those documents."

A hint of conflict was visible on the woman's face before she ducked her head and leaned down as though checking her computer.

"Your next appointment is Thursday."

"That's days away. Can you get me that information sooner? Please? I really think that my father might have been murdered and someone is getting away with it." Skylar wasn't sure who was more shocked by her words, her or the receptionist.

"I'll try to get you copies by tomorrow. I'll call you."

Skylar left, tired of fighting and knowing she was going to get nowhere. Hopefully, the woman would follow through.

She headed to Linc's garage. She parked and walked in. Music was blaring but no one was in sight.

"Hello?" She practically yelled.

"I'll be just a minute."

She wandered over to the sofa. Feeling parched, she helped herself to a glass of water. Linc joined her.

"Hi. I wasn't expecting you. Is something wrong with the Jeep?"

She nodded. "My dad's SUV. Could it have been deliberate?" It wasn't what she had planned on talking to him about, but it was what came out. She wasn't even actually sure why she'd gone there but one look at his concern and his not giving her a look of 'are you nuts?' confirmed why.

"I don't know. I haven't really had a chance to look at it."

"Can we do that now?"

"I don't have the key. My dad does."

Skylar closed her eyes and took a deep breath. "I think my father was killed..."

Continue reading in **Concealed Inheritance**

She's a week too late...

ACKNOWLEDGMENTS

TO EVERYONE WHO LOVES to read, you are what fuels writers. You are why I continue to write suspense/thrillers.

To family, friends, and those who have inspired and continue to inspire me, thank you.

I absolutely love this journey I am on and couldn't do it without any one of you. Thank you.

About the Author

Whether her thrillers are set in a real town, city, countryside, or one pulled straight from her imagination, **Best-Selling and Award-Winning Author Maggie Thom** writes engaging suspense that dives deep into a family's lies, ties, and deceit. Her stories are rollercoasters, featuring strong women who know what's right but must navigate a maze of twists, turns, and dangerous secrets to get there.

Maggie believes in happily-ever-after, but she'll take you on one unforgettable adventure before you reach it.

Buckle up, you're in for quite a ride.

Growing up in a house full of books, Maggie made weekly trips to the library and often disappeared into stories when the weather was too cold to play outside. She started experimenting with writing at a young age, letting her imagination carry her away on countless adventures. As an adult, she's had just as many real ones: white-water rafting, sky diving, travelling, mountain hiking, kayaking (lakes, rivers, and ocean) and more.

Now, she writes so *you* can go on thrilling adventures too.

Become a member of Maggie's Readers' Group and get a free suspense thriller.

Her motto: *Read to escape... Escape to read.*
Take the adventure and enjoy the rollercoaster ride.

"Maggie Thom ... proves her strength as a master of words, plots and finely chiseled characters ... she weaves a brilliant cloth of the many colors of deceit." Dii – Tome Tender

Maggie

www.maggiethom.com

Connect with Maggie: Facebook / Goodreads / Book-bub / Pinterest / Amazon

Email: maggie@maggiethom.com

Books by Maggie Thom

The Caspian Wine Series

Captured Lies | Deceitful Truths | Split Seconds

The Twisted Deception Series *(read in order)*

Fostered Identity | Shadowed Footsteps | Exploited Innocence | Lost Tears | Last Betrayal

The Prairie Crime Thriller Series

Poisoned Promises | Toxic Attention | Collision Course | Breaking Free (TBA) | Shattered Dreams (TBA)

The Family Heir Looms Series

Concealed Inheritance | Saving Her | Unwavering Greed | Defying Death (TBA)

The Overton Files

Tainted Waters | Broken Trust (TBA) | Buried Sins (TBA)

Standalone Thrillers

Deadly Ties | Fractured Lines | Blurred Lines *(free at maggiethom.com)*

Join Maggie Thom's Readers Group

Receive a **free exclusive suspense-thriller eBook** and a bonus full-length thriller.
Visit: **maggiethom.com**

Connect with Maggie

Facebook | Goodreads | BookBub | Pinterest | Amazon

maggiethom.com

www.ingramcontent.com/pod-product-compliance
Lightning Source LLC
Chambersburg PA
CBHW030658120726
47905CB00001B/260